Angel's Gaiden:
Birth

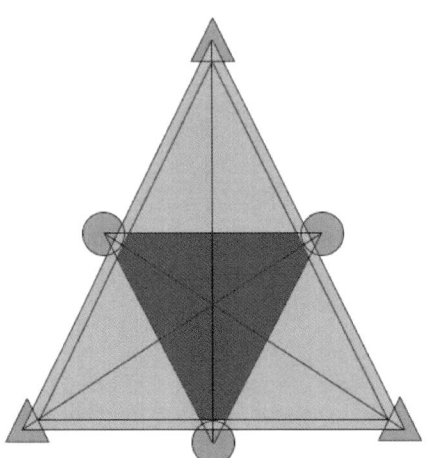

Angel's Gaiden:
Birth

Tyler Kelso

Tyler Kelso
2015

Copyright © 2015 by Tyler Kelso

All rights reserved. This book or any portion thereof may not be reproduced or used in any manner whatsoever without the express written permission of the publisher except for the use of brief quotations in a book review or scholarly journal.

Any characters or events in this book are fictitious or used fictitiously, and any likeness is entirely coincidental. Any locations used are purely for realism and any opinions against them are not true. Any bands or products mentioned are only used for realism and to represent characters' interests. No mention of a band or product is an endorsement of any kind.

First Printing: 2015

ISBN 978-1-329-61833-6

Tyler Kelso
P. O. Box 612
Cornelius, Oregon 97113

Dedication

To my editor, friends, and family

Without all of you and your support, I don't think I would have ever finished this book. Thank you.

I also dedicate this book to James Briggs. Though I may not have known him well, he was my stepfather's cousin, and best friend. In this I know he was a good man. For during the whole time I have known them, not once did they fight. Not once did they turn their back on each other. Not once did they ever give up on one another. They were brothers. They loved one another dearly and stuck by each other's sides through Heaven and Hell. He was a good man, a good father, a good husband, a good son, and a good brother. And wherever his soul may be, I know he is blissfully watching over everyone he loves.

Contents

Acknowledgements ix
Preface x
The Birth 1
Assignment 13
Experiment 32
Reunion 53
Wolfstorm 70
Blood Thirst 95
The King Reborn 108
Fallen City 122
Fortunate Son 130
Summer of Monsters 148
Vengeance 171
Old Acquaintance 186
Honor 199
Double-Edged Sword 224
An Ally Discovered 234
No Rest for the Weary 257
Nightmare 281
Hell Rises 301

Hell's Bells	315
Eight Legged Bastards	355
Glossary	381

Acknowledgements

I want to thank everyone that helped me push through to the end, to see this book finished: My family, my friends, and my editor. You guys helped make this book happen by helping me when I was stuck and encouraging me to complete it. Thank you.

Aside from them, there is one more person I would like to acknowledge. I find this man to be a brilliant writer, and his works astounding. His own writing had inspired me to start writing my own stories, to write this book, and I hope to one day be able to write as well as he had. You may know him as Robert Jordan, author of the Wheel of Time series. A series I have loved since I picked up the first book. Not only is the story itself in-depth and remarkable, but the writing in those books is simply beautiful, and it immerses you into the story as if you're actually there. That kind of writing, that kind of author, is what I look forward to becoming. Thank you, Robert Jordan. Wherever you are, thank you.

Preface

What inspired me to specifically write this book, would probably be the fan-fiction this was originally meant to be. No, not that kind of fan-fiction, get your head out of the gutter. It was filled with action, story, love, and even a little bit of drama, just as this book series is. But the problem was that it didn't feel original; I had characters from video games, movies, and anime all thrown into the story. I didn't feel like it was mine. So I took some of the things that were original like Cloukora, Wolfstorm, Darkstar, as well as a few other characters and bits of storyline, and built up my own, original story. A story I have built up even past this book, and a story I am proud to consider my own. I hope you all can sit back and enjoy the tale of Cloukora Skyrell.

I would like to note I created something special for you, the reader, at the end: A bonus chapter. This chapter is non-canon, meaning it has no effect or relation to the actual, main story. So what happens in that chapter, stays in that chapter. This is meant to be a special chapter that I felt would be really cool for Cloukora to go through, but it just didn't fit in with the main storyline. So I decided to still write it up, but make it a treat for you all.

Angel's Gaiden

The Birth

June 15, 2010
Forest Grove, Oregon

    A teenage boy walked through the bright halls of the large high school. This was a normal boy, who lived a normal life, went to a normal school, and did normal things just as any other teenager would. Minus the partying and booze. The only thing that made him stick out from a crowd were his deep-set brown eyes that made him look as if he were angry all the time. And with his chin-length brown hair, lack of muscle, and his tall height, he unintentionally frightened people whenever they would so much as glance at him. It was something he always hated. He wondered how people could judge so quickly, because if they actually got a chance to know him, they'd see the kindness and the heart he had. But that is not the only thing he had inside him, there was a part of him that *wasn't* normal. A part he didn't know he had. A part of him that would change his life forever. A part that would forever make him a beloved hero.

    He wore his favorite Dio t-shirt that was all black with the band's name in bright red font. On his legs he had on his usual dark blue jeans, and on his feet his grey skate shoes with some black and green to make them less dull. "Hey, Cloukora!" Another teenage boy jogged up to him. He was never sure why his parents chose that name; he always assumed it was a random name they came up with. He once searched the name on the Internet, but found nothing; it wasn't even part of any foreign language.

    "'Sup, Jake." Cloukora replied. Jake Levner had been his friend since freshman year, the term "friend" being used loosely. During the

school years they hung out a lot and went to a few parties, but whenever summer hit, they wouldn't say a single word to each other. Jake stood a couple inches shorter than Cloukora, but had a lot more muscle on him, which he used to his advantage on the school's wrestling team. He had short, blonde hair, blue eyes, and was overall an ass sometimes. He was essentially the opposite of Cloukora.

"You did your Algebra final yesterday, right?"

"Yeah, it was easy." Cloukora said as if algebra should be something everyone knew how to do.

"Man, that shit was hard. I just don't get how to find 'X'."

"Really? *That's* the trouble you have with it?"

"Hey, not everyone has the same amount of intelligence."

"I suppose that's true."

"Can you believe it though? Next year we're gonna be seniors! All the women will be all over us, and we'll finally get laid!" He looked at Cloukora. "Well, at least I will. I don't know about you."

"Probably not. I don't even care for sex anyway, it's not really *that* important to me."

"Bullshit. Every guy wants it, you just won't admit it."

Cloukora laughed. "Seriously though, I got more important things to worry about, like what college I'm going to, and what I'll major in."

"Mr. Skyrell." A teacher they walked past was just locking his classroom door, before turning to face them.

Cloukora stopped mid-walk and turned his attention towards the man. "What's up Mr. Faw?"

"I just wanted to say again that your report on eukaryotes and the difference between mitosis and meiosis was just perfect. Quite a few students had been getting them mixed up, and I think the way you explained it made them understand it a little bit more. In fact, I may use part of your speech for my future lectures." The man chuckled. "I mean, if that's alright with you."

"Um, yeah sure. I don't mind." He shrugged his shoulders. "At least it can get put to some use." It was Cloukora's turn to chuckle.

"Alright, well, I'll leave you two be now. Have a great summer, kids." Mr. Faw walked off down the hallway towards the doors at the end.

Jake continued on as if nothing had just happened. "Dude, you're not even a senior yet. Chill out, those things will come to you eventually. Oh hey, speaking of chill, there's a party tonight at Amanda's house, you comin?"

"Nah, I got my mom's wedding."

"Ah shit that's right." They both walked out the school doors into the hot and sunny outside. It's where they always went for lunch. Though, Cloukora never understood why there was even lunch that day when it was only half a day of school. "I feel sorry for your step-dad."

"Jake, not every marriage is as bad as some people make it sound."

"Sure, whatever you tell yourself." Cloukora only shook his head. They sat down on a bench and bullshitted for awhile until the bell rang, then they headed towards their next classes. Cloukora's being on the other side of the school, and if he didn't hurry, he'd be late for it. As Jake split off towards his class, Cloukora began to feel a slight dizziness and lightheaded, and started to walk in a trance, unaware of where he was going or how slow he was moving. It wasn't until the hallways were empty he snapped out of it and realized he was even further from his class. Suddenly he felt something lump in his throat, causing him to rush to the nearest bathroom to open up a stall and put his head over the toilet. But instead of vomit, he coughed up blood. His body felt like it was on fire, and he could feel the sweat dampening his clothes. After a couple of breaths, he was calm again and the dizziness went away. But as he looked up into the chrome flush handle, he saw a bright green color in place of his originally brown eyes. He quickly backed out of the stall and paced out of the bathroom. "I-I'm hallucinating. It's stress coming from tonight. It has to be."

Someone walked past him into the bathroom and let out an "Aw sick, someone got blood all over the toilet seat!" but Cloukora ignored it and kept walking towards his class, the last one of the day. After that,

he'd be in his cozy home, getting ready for tonight. "I'm going to be fine." He assured himself one more time. "I'm going to be fine..."

Portland, Oregon

Cloukora was bent over next to a hallway wall, trying to keep his breathing normal and relaxed. It wasn't completely working, he was way too nervous. He was getting worried sweat might start to soak through his black tux. "Hey, Cloukora, are you ready? We're about to go up there." said his band mate as he walked up to him. "You alright?"

"Yeah, I'm fine. Just uh, last minute jitters is all." Cloukora replied as earlier swarmed into his mind. The blood. His eyes. What was happening to him?

"Ah, well just relax; you'll do fine." he replied. "You won't mess this up."

"It's their wedding, Paul, and what if I forget the lyrics? What- what if I-"

"Don't worry, you'll be fine." He assured Cloukora. "We've rehearsed this a hundred times, you got this. Trust me."

"You're right. I should calm down and take a deep breath. There's nothing to be afraid of." He took a deep breath and stood up. "Alright, I'll go introduce us." Cloukora patted his friend on his shoulder, came out of the hallway and got up on the little stage where all the instruments were set up, including a grand piano. The instruments were for the actual wedding band that had been playing that night. Cloukora and Paul were only using the piano for their one song.

The church's main hall was brightly lit, as bright as a church could get that is. The usual pews were replaced by white-clothed tables with vases of flowers in the center, and people sitting around those tables. The men were dressed in black tuxedos, some without bows tied around their necks, and the women wore a variety of dresses that differed in color, tightness, design, and material. The wearers made sure that the dress was fancy enough for the occasion, but not too fancy

that it would look better than the bride's dress. Everyone now had their eyes on him.

He struggled with the words a little before speaking. "Alright, I uh, have a special surprise for the bride and groom, also known, as my mom and step-dad. But first, I'd like to say a few words. I know you all think it's tough with my parents being divorced, but honestly, it really doesn't bother me that much. I do love my biological father, I always will; he helped give life to me. But you know, what happens happens, and you can't change that. Jack is a good man, and a good father, and I wouldn't want any other step-father than him. So, anyways, to help me out, here's my good friend, Paul!" Paul joined him on the stage and sat behind the piano placed there. "Mom, when you and Jack got together, I knew you two were perfect for each other. I knew you would last and eventually get married. And when I heard you finally were, I really wanted to do something for you guys, and so, I decided to sing a song. A song you should know, since it's 'your' song. I just hope I can do it justice. Paul, hit it." Paul started playing a few keys on the piano, and then Cloukora began to sing.

> *As I dream the night away*
> *I lie in the darkness*
> *And wish I could relive today*
> *Seeing you in that red dress*
> *We had met at that dance*
> *And when I saw your face*
> *I knew I had to take the chance*
> *You didn't even put up a chase*
> *We ditched the losers*
> *And headed to the field*
> *To lie on the hood of my cruiser*
> *I told you I'd be your shield*
> *We kissed under the moonlight*
> *And we held each other*
> *All through the night*
> *Until you had to leave to your mother*

All I want is for you to be mine
All the way until the end of time
I swear I am losing my mind
Because I wish you were mine

We might be called crazy
And sick in the head
But our love is far from hazy
And I wish you were in this bed
We have connected Hearts
And our love is bleeding
We are two parts
That are now meeting
We just want happiness
And to be together
You in that red dress
And me in this jacket of leather
I won't ever leave your side
And you can squeeze my hand
Because I know life is a rollercoaster ride
High above the land

All I want is for you to be mine
All the way until the end of time
I swear I am losing my mind
Because I wish you were mine
Because I wish you were mine

After the last few notes were finished everyone began clapping. He swept a bow and walked off the stage toward the table where his mom, stepdad, and the rest of his family had been sitting. "So, what'd you think?"

"It was terrible." Jack replied jokingly and got a nudge from Cloukora's mom. "Just messin with ya, it was awesome. Thank you."

Jack, his stepfather, was about an inch taller than Cloukora, and was way more fit too. He had dark brown eyes and on his face was a five o'clock shadow that met with his short, black hair.

"I thought it was sweet and thoughtful. Thank you." his mom said. His mother Laurel was a short, but still slim woman besides the large bulge in her dress from the baby she carried inside her. Her eyes were brown, as was her long hair flowing down to her white strapless wedding dress, and she wore a smile that could light up an entire room.

"I didn't even know you could sing!" His oldest younger sister Alyssa remarked. She was tall for a would-be high school freshman, and she had dirty blonde hair and dark brown eyes.

"Yeah, that was amazing! But Jerry Star is still better." His other younger sister said. That comment was expected of Hayley, since she was, after all, going into her second year of middle school. Her hair was dark brown, and she had green eyes that she inherited from some aunt a couple generations ago. Both girls were wearing identical dresses: silk, spaghetti-strapped dress with a peach tint.

"Are you gonna be famous?" asked his seven year old brother, Skyler. Skyler would always ask silly questions like that, because he knew it'd always get a smile or laugh out of people. Cloukora always thought of him as a shorter version of himself, which was probably true, because Skyler had always looked up to him, and wanted to be just like Cloukora. He was a bit on the short side, had light brown hair, and brown eyes. Just like every other male in the room, he wore a black tux that had been tailored to fit his size.

Cloukora laughed. "Nah, nah. That was only a one-time thing, I'll probably never sing again. Plus I don't think my voice was that good anyway; I just can't get my pitch to change like I should." He said, gesturing to his throat.

"Aww."

"Hey you two, congratulations on the wedding and the baby!" a family friend said to the newlyweds as they passed by.

"Thank you." his parents said at the same time.

"Hey, Cloukora." The voice came from his uncle walking up to the table, and Cloukora turned to face him. "I was going to go outside

for a quick smoke, but your grandfather doesn't feel like going out there. And I like to talk while I'm smoking, so I was wondering if you'd wanna step out with me for a bit?" His uncle was tall, just as he was, and he had short, jet black hair, a clean shaven face, and dark brown eyes.

"Yeah, sure. I'll be back in a minute." He said as he glanced over his shoulder to his family. They both walked out the door of the warm and brightly lit room, and out into the cool night and leaned against the wall of the church. Cars passed by on the lively city streets as quick as they could go, which wasn't very fast since they were in the city and all. Cloukora figured most of them were probably going to party with their friends around the city. Friends. Something he wished he had. Sure he had Paul and Jake, and a few other people, but none of them wanted to hang out during after-school hours. Paul was only there tonight because he was getting paid for it. Those were thoughts he tried not to dwell on long though, it wouldn't be healthy to make himself be depressed.

"There's something…I need to tell you." his uncle finally said, snapping Cloukora out of his trance.

"Like what?" he was unsure what his uncle was going to say. *Oh no, am I adopted? Am I being sent off somewhere? Ah shit, he's not dying is he?*

"You see, your family…there's more to it than you know. We're a bit different from everyone else."

"What do you mean?"

"I can't explain just yet, I don't think you're ready. I'm not actually supposed to mention anything right now, but I just thought I'd warn you that strange things are about to happen, mostly to you. You may think you're going crazy, or even insane, maybe even question your own reality, but I assure you, it's all real."

"I don't…I don't understand?"

"I know you don't, and I wish I could tell you more, but I can't. Not just yet. However, I do have something for you." He pulled out a silver chain with a pendant shaped like three triangles forming a bigger triangle that had a small circle on each of the three sides, and a

small triangle on each point. "This should help you." But before he could hand it to him, Cloukora took notice of a burning smell in the air.

"Wait...is that-? Smoke!" He turned to look around to see a building on fire down the street a few blocks down, and immediately felt compelled to run off to help.

"Wait! Cloukora, wait!" But it was too late, he was already out of earshot.

The old, brick building was engulfed in flames, and wooden planks could be seen falling through the roof and ceilings inside.

"My little girl's in there!" shouted a woman nearby.

"Typical. There's always someone trapped." Before even thinking it over, he ran inside and tried looking for the child as quickly as he could. Inside the building some of the flames burned brightly, so bright that they made Cloukora have to cover his eyes. The heat began to make him sweat and the smoke started to fill his lungs and cause him to cough and his eyes to water. He needed to hurry and find the kid before this place killed him. Dodging the falling debris and wood, he moved swiftly, checking each room on the first floor. One room he almost ran in to, but then somehow, he knew the roof would collapse due to the burning rate of the flames, the strength of the wood, and the estimated weight on the next floor. All the calculations went through his head in an instant. How, he didn't know. It just happened. Not pondering the reason any longer, he turned as the ceiling in the room fell, and ran as carefully as he could up the stairs until he got to the fourth floor and heard a scream. "Don't worry, I'll help you! Stay where you are!" He yelled back.

Running down the hall, he searched every room until he found one with a little girl huddled in the corner. But as he tried to go through the doorway, some of the roof caved in front of him. The debris was too hot to try and dig through. This was it. There was no other way for him to get through. That girl in there would die, and then him not too long if he didn't make it out in time. If he did make it, he'd have to face her parents and look them in the eye to tell them that he couldn't save their daughter. *Why wasn't I quick enough? Why couldn't I save her?* His

fists clenched, his heart beat faster, and he began to feel hotter. Not by the heat of the flames, but from his adrenaline beginning to pump rapidly through his veins. He felt like he could break down a wall, or run a mile without breaking a single sweat. Then he felt his hand get hot, and when he looked down at his palm, he couldn't believe what the source was: he was holding in his hands a scimitar surrounded in flames. An etching of a flame was melded just above the hand guard, on the steel of the blade. Both ends of the hand guard were fashioned into a hollowed flame that closely resembled candlelight. An actual flame emitted from the bottom of the circular pommel. *Where the hell did this come from?* He shook his head. "I'll worry about it later. I should just be thankful right now." Gripping the blade in his hand he swung it at the pile of debris, slicing everything in half as if they were butter, clearing a way in. He ran in and the sword disappeared as he picked the girl up in his arms. "I'm gonna get you out of here." He assured the girl as he ran back towards the door. But as he passed the used-to-be-bathroom, he saw something in the mirror and stopped. His eyes, they changed: They were the bright green color, just as he saw earlier. *What is going on with me?* Continuing out the door and towards the stairs he halted in mid-run as the staircase collapsed. Their only way out was now gone. *Unless...* Spinning around he dashed into the nearest room and looked out a window to see emergency vehicles lined up around the building. He backed up a couple steps from the window. "Hold on." The girl's arms grew tighter around his neck as he ran towards the window, turning his back to it right before impact, and flung himself out and into a free fall. The building window seemed to drift further and further away and he felt his stomach lurching, his hair flowing upwards, his heart racing, and his mind hoping they land on the target. Then he felt a sharp pain in his back, and heard a loud boom from a cop car's glass and metal colliding against each other. Then everything went black.

There was a steady beeping when he started to wake. He opened his eyes and saw the square-tiled ceiling above him. "Where-Where am I?"

"At the hospital, you took a pretty nasty fall from what I heard. Nearly broke your back and damaged your head. But you had quite a resistance to the fall it seems, just a few fractures that will heal in a couple weeks and a concussion. Man, you are one lucky kid." A doctor said, checking his machines to make sure they were in working condition.

"The girl, is she ok?" Cloukora asked.

"Yes, she's fine, not a scratch on her. Watch, you're gonna be in the newspaper for your bravery."

"Heh, it was nothing." *Did I really just say that? No person in their right mind would do what I did.*

"Well, think whatever you'd like. I think you were a hero. Oh, you have family waiting to see you. Should I let them in?"

"Yeah, go ahead. I'm fine now." Rubbing the sand out of his eyes, he sat up in the hospital bed. Slowly of course; his body was still somewhat in pain from the night before.

The doctor walked out and a few seconds later, his mom, step dad, dad, uncle and grandfather walked in. His grandfather, Aaron, was a tall man, just as Cloukora was, and despite his wrinkles and balding, grey hair, he stood with strength. Not even age would make him weak.

"Hey sweetie, you ok?" his mom asked?

"Yeah, I'm fine." Cloukora replied

"Heard you took quite a bit of a fall." His step dad put in.

"We decided to get you a few things as a reward. Since you were brave and everything." His dad said, and handed him two gifts: one was a thin square, and the other was a cylinder shape.

Cloukora opened the thin one to find that it was a Dr. Feelgood album by Mötley Crüe. "Awesome. Thank you, you guys. I couldn't have asked for a better gift." He then opened the second one: It was a can of No Fear: Motherload energy drink. "Well, I guess I *could*. This should get me on my feet in no time." He said with a grin.

"Your grandfather and uncle want to talk with you." Said his mom.

"I actually would like to speak with them as well, alone, if that's okay." He sat his gifts to the side of him on his bed so they wouldn't be a distraction.

"Alright, we'll come back later to check in on you." His mom said as she, his dad, and her new husband stepped out of the room.

"Ok, what the hell happened? Last thing I remember is Uncle Daniel talking about how our family isn't what it seems, and then I jumped into a flaming building, somehow knowing how and when everything would fall. Then…Then I had a flaming sword in my hand that vanished into thin air! What the *hell* is going on?" He demanded.

His uncle and grandfather sighed before looking at each other. "I guess you *are* ready then. But it's best if we just…show you. I'll make the preparations, you just rest up. Everything will be clear within a couple of weeks." His grandfather replied.

"This would have helped, but you ran off before I could give it to you." His uncle said as he took out the necklace from last night and tossed it to him. They both started out the door.

"So, what am I supposed to do?" Cloukora asked.

"Accept your destiny." His uncle said as he shut the door behind him, but not before saying "Good luck with deciding a name."

"I think I got a name." he said to himself as he looked at the Mötley Crüe album. Then shook his head. "Nah, that wouldn't be original."

Angel's Gaiden

Assignment

June 21, 2010
Tillamook, Oregon

    The man ran. He ran through the apple orchard as hard and as fast as he could. The fear of what was behind him drove him forward. But with the cool, dark, starry night adding to that fear, the decline in vision made it difficult for him to see, causing him to trip over an unseen root sticking out of the ground, and sending him toppling down to the dirt floor. The growling behind him got louder and more ferocious. Scrambling to his feet, he got back up and continued running in the direction his friends had went: into the thick forest just a few feet from the orchard's edge. He knew they were probably far away by now; he was the slow one of the group. He needed to find a place to hide and lose whatever it was that was chasing him. Quickly, he ducked into a thick bush next to a tree and inhaled before holding his breath as much as he could. Then there was no more growling, just silence. Suddenly something grabbed him as a long claw slit across his throat, causing a great amount of blood to start pouring out. Pulling out the pistol he had in his pocket, he tried to fire a few shots at whatever had a hold of him until he had grown too weak from losing too much blood through the wound in his neck, and the gun fell from his limp hand as he was dragged away through the silent night. He heard shouts for 'Zack' in the distance, but he couldn't answer back, and in seconds, his eyelids shut, and everything went black.

Forest Grove, Oregon

Cloukora sat up in his bed, rubbing his eyes to wake himself up. His room was like any other teenage boy's bedroom: the walls were pastel white except for where an assortment of band posters were hung up, a closet with a wooden sliding door and a dresser inside, a television set resting on top of a television stand that stood against the wall across from his bed and his nightstand, and a computer desk with a swivel chair in front of the only window that had been installed in the room. Other than those features, his room wasn't much different, except for perhaps the cleanliness part; he always made sure to keep his room nice and tidy.

He had finally recovered from the incident that had happened only a week before. The incident he could find no explanation for: The sword, those calculations, and most of all, his eyes. It all felt like a dream to him. They couldn't have been hallucinations, at least the first two, because they actually happened. Otherwise he wouldn't have been able to save the girl from the fire. Tossing his blankets aside, he noticed a small brown package sitting on top of his desk. He climbed out of bed and slowly stepped over to it to see that it had no name or address written on it; it came from an unknown sender. He leaned his ear on the box and listened for any kind of ticking. There was none. Despite the silence in the box, he still opened it carefully, and inside was a white envelope resting on top of Styrofoam. He opened the envelope and found a letter that read:

Cloukora, we have been keeping an eye on you for a while now. Do not panic, for we do not wish you any harm. Rather we would like to help you. We will not reveal our identity yet; we want to find out if you are worthy enough first. To prove yourself, you will be sent on a mission with one of our operatives, and they will test both you and your ability. Your mission will be to go to Tillamook and investigate the recent disappearance of a missing local. You will meet with your contact at the Starbucks there. We'll be seeing you soon.
Good luck,
WS

"A mission? And I have to meet at a *Starbucks*?! Really?" he noticed something else in the box: there was a piece of cardboard under the Styrofoam and it was lifted up just a hair. He pulled it out to find two things underneath. One of them was a standard FBI badge with his photo plastered on it, but with the name Tyler Jordan in place of his. The other object was a black Jericho 941 F 9mm handgun and he just about dropped it as soon as he picked it up. "A fucking *gun*? What the hell am I supposed to do with *this*?!" He heard someone walking towards his room and he quickly tossed the gun beneath his blanket to hide it before whoever it was walked in.

It was his mother. "Everything ok? I heard you freaking out." She asked, poking her head through the door, before opening it all the way.

"Oh, no, I'm fine, it was just a stupid spider. It's gone now."

"Ok then, let me know if you need anything." She gave him an odd look.

"Actually, I need to uh, borrow the car." He asked hesitantly and prepared himself for the backlash he was about to receive.

"You don't even have a license *or* a permit. So no." her laughter showed she meant it. "You're insane if you think I'll let you borrow the car."

"Mom, please? Just this once."

She crossed her arms and for her own amusement asked: "Where do you want to go?"

"Tillamook."

"That far? Yeah, you *are* insane." His mother couldn't believe the distance he wanted to go. "Why do you want to go there in the first place?"

He shrugged his shoulders. "To see a friend. He moved down there recently."

"Ah, I see. Fine, I'll take you."

"C'mon mom. You know how good I am at driving." He protested.

"I said no, I'm taking you, and that's final."

"Well I don't know how long I'm going to be down there. Maybe a couple days tops."

"Then I'll pick you up when you're ready."

"Alright, fine, I'll pack my bags." He said with a sigh. There was no use arguing anymore.

"Oh, and by the way, being able to back out of the driveway isn't 'good driving'." She ridiculed before leaving his room.

"You push the gas to go, the brakes to stop, and the steering wheel to turn. I don't understand how that's even difficult to learn!" He remarked back.

The two-hour drive to Tillamook was mostly boring for Cloukora, besides the view of the forest they had to drive through. Whenever his family took a trip to the beach he would always look out the car window to take in the beauty of the landscape. And sometimes in hopes of seeing a wild animal roaming through the trees, but of course he never did; the animals were smart enough to stay away from the road. He had a couple short conversations with his mom, but none of them were worth continuing. Besides, he'd rather keep to his thoughts and try to piece everything together.

"Where are you meeting him at again?" his mom asked as they entered the town of Tillamook.

"Starbucks." She raised an eyebrow. She knew he wasn't big on coffee places, or even coffee for that matter. "I didn't choose it, he did."

They pulled into a white-lined parking space in front of the café. "Do you see him?"

"Not yet." All he could see was a tall woman with wavy blonde hair who was leaned up against the wall of the café, crossing her arms. She seemed to be looking for something. Or someone. *Could that be my contact?* She wore a charcoal black blazer over a white blouse with several buttons undone, enough to be casual but still professional,

silver-rimmed aviator sunglasses, black skirt, and a pair of black open-toed heels.

"Cloukora, listen to me. I'm not sure where you're really going, or what you're doing, and I know I'd never find out, but whatever it is, just be careful. Okay?"

"Don't worry, I always am." He assured her as he got out of the car and grabbed his backpack. "Because I'll be at my *friend's*."

"Cloukora, just promise me."

"Yes, mom. I promise. You don't have to worry." He shut the car door. He let out a deep breath. "Alright, I'll see you when I'm done." He waved as she pulled out of the parking space, and drove off.

He was on his own now. He had never been on his own like this; he was somewhat sheltered and would always be around someone he could depend on. Never being independent. That would all have to change now as he watched the SUV drive down the road, out of sight. A voice came from behind him. "There you are. We got work to do, come on." It was the woman that he had noticed when they pulled in.

"Hold on, before I even go anywhere with you, who the hell *are* you?" he asked as she started off, expecting him to follow.

"The name's Brev. Now come on. We don't have a whole lot of time."

The walk to the nearest motel wasn't that long, maybe about a block down from the Starbucks. When they checked in at the counter, the rugged clerk looked at them oddly but gave them the key to their room anyway. He wanted to say something to the guy, but decided it best to leave it be. The room was a little rundown and old, as if no one had taken care of it in years, but it would have to do.

"Here, put on this suit." She tossed him a suit that looked like one an FBI agent would wear.

"An FBI suit? Is this legal? I mean, are you even FBI?"

"Yes, no, and no I am not."

"Great, I'm hanging around with someone who is posing as an FBI agent. Why did I even come down here in the first place?" He said regretfully.

"Curiosity. Trying to find answers."

Birth

"Yeah, and curiosity killed the cat."

"But satisfaction brought him back. Believe it or not, curiosity can be a good thing. It can lead to great things, and great inventions. Sometimes even great people..." A frown formed on her face as she stared blankly at the dull, brown shag carpet. After a moment she snapped back out of it and shook her head. "Now, go put the suit on." Cloukora could tell she was starting to get a bit irritated with him. Why, he wasn't sure. Of course he was asking a lot of questions and not showing much enthusiasm or submissiveness, but that should be expected of someone who wasn't even sure of what they were doing there in the first place.

Cloukora went into the bathroom and slipped on the trousers, shirt, jacket, and tie. The bathroom was even worse than the room: the tiles were falling off, mold covered the walls, writing was on the mirror and the toilet looked unusable. "Gross. How did this place even pass inspections?" He shuddered as he walked back into the room to see Brev putting her cellphone away in her pocket.

"Ready?" She said as she put her sunglasses back on. But before she did, Cloukora was able to get a glance at her bright blue eyes. He also saw that she now had a holster hanging from her shoulder with a gun resting in it.

He gave a sigh of reluctance then said "Sure. Hey, do I get a pair?" He asked jokingly, pointing to her sunglasses.

"Nope." She said and tossed him an extra clip. That reminded him to dig the gun from out of his backpack and put it in between his waistband, and then dropped the extra clip into his pocket. "Our person was last seen at the bar with a few of his friends. We'll start there." She started out the door, leaving Cloukora to have to hurry and rush out of the motel room, almost forgetting to shut the door behind him.

The bar wasn't anything fancy, in fact all it had was a single pool table, an old dart board, and a jukebox that looked it had broken down years ago. There wasn't a whole lot of room either: there weren't many tables and only five stools were placed in front of the bar counter.

Birth

The alcohol behind the counter was also scarce in choices. There were a few people inside throwing darts, a couple more drinking beer while talking about their times in the military, four farmers playing poker at their table, and a loner off in the corner staring into his shot glass as if he'd find the answer to life in it. Then it occurred to Cloukora the reason why it was almost empty: it was still day time, on a Tuesday at that. The bartender behind the counter was a bit taller than the average female. She had long black hair and brown eyes, and was dressed in a red tank top and a short black skirt that only reached mid-thigh.

"What will you guys hav-wait, no minors allowed." She reminded, pointing at Cloukora.

"Oh no, he's just short for his age." Brev replied.

He didn't know if he should have been offended by that statement. He decided it was best to just ignore it.

"Uh-huh, ID please." She put out her hand, gesturing for a badge.

They both took the badges out and presented them to her. The bartender studied them closely, as if she thought there was something that would give them away. He hoped she wouldn't be able to notice anything, if there *was* anything.

"Alright, so what will you be having?" she finally asked as she handed the badges back.

"Nothing, ma'am. However, we do have some questions for you."

"About the missing person no doubt. Well, not much to tell, he was a drunk, and a party animal just like his friends. But he was also sweet; he never hit on the ladies like his friends did, he always left a tip, even if he didn't order anything, and he'd make conversation with me from time to time to keep me from being bored. He was a true gentleman. His closest friend, Dylan, is actually right over there. He might know more about what happened last night." She pointed to the guy sitting in the corner by himself.

"Thank you." They pocketed their badges and strode over towards the table. "Mind if we ask you a few questions?" He gestured to the chairs in front of him for them to sit in.

His eyes were red from crying and he looked as if he couldn't care if the place caught on fire. There were a few empty shot glasses to his side. "Let me guess, you're here about Zack?"

Brev folded her arms on the table and leaned forward. "Yes, and we're terribly sorry to ask you, but what did you guys do after the bar that night?"

Dylan shook his head and took a sip of whiskey before going on. "We were drunk, and stupid. We thought it would be fun to head out to the old farm a few miles down. The farmer just seems like a creep and we wanted to screw around with him a little, you know, just pranks. But nothing harmful, though. Anyways, after we were done throwing toilet paper over his yard, and painted on his house, we ran through the orchard there and into the forest. And-And, I don't know, it's all too hazy, but I remember hearing noises behind us, like something chasing us. I think it was one of his dogs."

"What kind of noises did you hear?"

"Growling, snarling, but we didn't see anything, only Zack did. Next thing we knew, he wasn't with us, and then we heard gunshots. But we didn't stop running, we couldn't. After a while, we did go back to see if he was on his way towards us. The only thing we found were claw marks, and it freaked the hell out of us. So, we hurried up and got out of there as fast as we could, and reported it the next morning. The police didn't believe us, they wouldn't even send out a search party. They think it's another prank, but I'm telling you, it's not. *Please*, find out what happened to him. I swear, we will never pull another prank!"

"We'll do what we can. We thank you for your time. You probably should go home and get some rest." When she got up, Cloukora followed her outside.

"What do you think happened?"

"I honestly don't know. Could be many things. What I do know is that we need to check out the crime scene, but first I need to contact HQ. For now, go do something." She walked away from him, towards the motel and leaving him on his own.

Cloukora was starting to get tired of the cold shoulder Brev had been giving him. He had done nothing to her, and yet she treated him

like dirt. "You can't leave me here like this!" She must have been out of earshot, even though he could still see her. "Great, what am I supposed to do?" He realized he hadn't eaten all day and decided to head to the nearest McDonald's to get something to eat. As he sat down in the booth, he unwrapped his burger, and began taking bites out of it while trying to go over the case in his head. *What the hell happened? I don't understand any of it, it's all so confusing. A grown man just doesn't disappear like this. There* has *to be some kind of explanation. Heh, now I know how CSI agents feel.*

"Hey, you'll never guess who I saw last night." He heard a girl near his table say to a friend.

"Who?" The other girl replied.

"Zack." This caught Cloukora's attention, but he played it off calmly by still eating his food as if he didn't notice them.

"Zack Zack?"

"Mhm, he was helping out the old farmer cleaning off the toilet paper. I thought it was really strange. He was all raggedy and...ew. Like I wouldn't even touch him with a ten-foot pole the way he looked."

"Did you report it to the police?" another friend of hers asked.

"Yeah, but they didn't believe me. They think this whole thing is just a huge prank."

So he's not missing then. Maybe it is *just a prank.* Brev walked in and sat in front of him.

"Our next stop is the old farmer's house."

"How was the call? To your 'HQ' I mean."

"It went fine. I just had to report your progress is all."

"Ah, how am I doing?"

"That's a secret. But we need to get to the farmer's house before it gets too late. Let's go."

"But, my food."

"Now."

"Ugh, fine." He quickly grabbed his food and followed her out the restaurant; he was too hungry to just leave it. "I heard the girls

talking in there, and I guess they saw Zack, and said he looked raggedy and that he was helping the farmer."

"Our Zack?"

"I think so. They told the police, but they thought it was a prank. Maybe he just got hurt on a tree branch in the orchard and the farmer helped him, and in turn, Zack cleaned up the mess him and his friends made."

"It's much more complicated than that."

"What? No it's not. He's alive and making up for what he did. What other reason could it possibly be?"

She walked around to the driver side of a black 2010 Toyota Corolla. "Just shut up and get in the car." She opened the car door and got in, slamming it shut as Cloukora did the same on the passenger side.

"Not a very fancy car for FBI agents is it?" He remarked as he buckled his seatbelt.

Brev ignored him and his remark, and pulled out of the parking space and drove on down the street, until they had reached the old farmhouse. Near the house was a small, grassy slope that led down to a dirt-covered apple orchard in a large dip in the ground, just shy of touching a neighboring forest. The house itself was horrible: it looked like it had been built in the 1800's, the paint was peeling off, windows on the second floor were broken, and shingles on the roof were missing. It was a complete disaster. Cloukora could never understand why people liked farmhouses. He thought they were too old and probably harbored ghosts inside of them.

"What a piece of crap." Cloukora commented as she parked the car in the house's driveway.

"We're not here for opinions. This is a matter of a person's life. His life, depends on us." Brev replied as she exited the car, with Cloukora once again following suit.

They strolled up to the doorstep and knocked on the door with the paint matching the house: white and peeling off. A man that was most likely in his late forties answered.

"Yes? Can I help you?" he asked politely.

"We're with the FBI, sir, and we have reason to believe a missing person was last seen on this farm." Brev explained as she displayed her badge.

"There were a few kids here last night, and they TP-ed our house, so, I let my dog chase them off, but that was it. If it's one of those kids you're looking for, one fella came back to help clean off the paint and take down the toilet paper. After he was done, he said something about taking off down to California, he got on a bus, and that was the last I saw of him. Aren't you a bit *young* to be a FBI agent?" He turned to Cloukora.

"The FBI recruits who they think is necessary, no matter the age. However, it would be nice to take a look around if that's alright with you?" Cloukora's tone showed a hint of impatience.

"Sure, go ahead." He seemed slightly offended by Cloukora's demand.

The farmer went inside as they walked down a hill towards the apple orchard, before Brev and Cloukora split off into different directions. After a bit of searching, spots of blood splattered on the ground had caught his eye. "Brev, blood."

"I also found the gun, it's an Enfield Revolver. These are really rare guns, and a few bullets are missing."

"Must have been the source of the gunshots then."

"That's what I just said." Cloukora only shook his head. Still the cold shoulder. When she walked over and dropped to a crouch over the crimson splatters, he noticed her bite her lip as she studied the blood. She leaned in closer, and Cloukora almost thought she was going to start licking it up off the ground, until she turned her head towards the forest, then back to a wooden shed on the top of the hill, at the back of the old farmhouse. "There's a trail of blood. It leads from the forest up to that shack right there." She pointed to it: it was as old as the house but even more broken down, if that was possible, and was just a little larger than the size of a bedroom.

"I don't see any trail."
"It's there."
"How do you know?"

"I just know." She started walking towards the shed until Cloukora seized her by the arm.

"Alright, enough. I want a damn explanation! I'm helping a complete stranger, who says there's a trail of blood when there clearly isn't, who works for someone that uses fake FBI badges, *and* has been practically stalking me for who knows how long. So, I'll ask this once more: Who. The hell. Are you?"

She sighed. "I work for a secret group. I cannot reveal too much, it would be against protocol and my boss' orders. What I *can* tell you, is that this case is a test, and if you pass, you get in. Trust me, this is a group you *want* to get in to."

"Join a group I know nothing about? You could be a group of…pedophiles or something for all I know!"

"I assure you we are not pedophiles." She gave a slight chuckle before putting on a serious face again. "We want you to join us because we have a few things in common with you. And, we also need your help." She seemed to regret saying the last part.

"My help? What exactly *do* you know about me?"

"We know what you're capable of. You know, the burning building incident? Again, I can't say much more, that's not my job, but you are a remarkable person, you just don't know it yet. Now, can we please finish this case so we both can go home?"

"Whatever." He started towards the shed until she spoke.

"Look, I get how you're feeling right now, but this is how we do things. If we told you everything and it turned out to be you aren't qualified to join, then you could spill all of our secrets. Something we can't deal with right now."

"It's not just the secrets; it's the damn cold shoulder you've been giving me all day!" He turned back around and gestured his hand at her.

"Then leave." She pointed away from the farm. "There's nothing stopping you from leaving. But I know you won't. You had many opportunities to go back home, but not *once* did you even make the effort try. You *know* why you're here, and it is *not* curiosity. It's the idea that you can finally do some *good* with us, to *save* people. To help

Birth

the helpless." The last bit sounded like it was meant to mean something to him. It did, it struck a chord inside him, but it would be impossible for her to even have an idea why. She dug in her pocket, pulled out her keys and dangled them in the air. "Here."

"What?"

"Take them. Take the keys to the car, and just go. You can even keep it."

"What's the catch?"

"Nothing. If you're really tired of the way I'm acting and all of this bullshit with secrets, then you can leave. We won't ever call or contact you again. You will never even see me again."

"You're not going to try and stop me? You want to recruit me, but you'll let me go? Just like that?"

"We dedicate ourselves to helping others, we're not the Mafia. So, I'm helping you. I'm helping you realize what you truly want. But it is up to you to decide. I cannot make this decision for you."

She's right. His whole life he had dreamed of helping others, of making a difference-of making the world, a better place. Now was his chance to do just that. *If I turn my back now, I'll be turning my back on Zack. I'll be turning my back on this one opportunity to actually do something worthwhile. Do I really want to give that up?* "Alright,"

"Alright what?"

"I'll stay. I'll at least see this mission through. Zack needs our help, I can't just abandon him."

"Good, now then let's not waste any more time. Oh, and by the way, if you actually looked closer at the grass, you'd see the blood." She said before starting up the slope once more, while Cloukora stayed and squinted at the ground. Moving a little closer, he finally saw the trail of blood leading up the hill.

"Oh…Sorry." He apologized before trotting up to join her halfway up the rise.

They carefully approached the shack before peeking inside, through the door that was opened just a crack. Brev pulled out her gun just in case and seeing this, Cloukora did the same. As they walked in, they saw a man standing over a cage covered with a large brown cloth.

"Master says we must. If we don't obey, he will kill us."

"Zack?" Brev asked as she pointed the gun at the man's head.

The guy turned around. "Is that him?" Cloukora asked.

"Yeah." Brev replied, still aiming the gun.

"If only you didn't interfere. Now, the hounds shall be released!" He pulled off the cover of a cage to reveal a hairy creature that was part canine, but looked part man. It snarled at all of them, and even tried biting at Zack. He walked over and uncovered three more. All snapping at Brev and Cloukora, as if they wanted to eat them.

"Those are huge sons of bitches." Cloukora commented, even though he was a bit freaked out.

"Do not refer to us as those!" Zack said angrily.

"Well, they are. They were born of female dogs weren't they?" Cloukora mocked.

"No, you idiot, these aren't dogs! They're werewolves! You know? The myths and legends? Well, they're *real*! And they're going to be the last thing you will ever see."

"Zack, listen to me. This is not you, it's not who you are. Just come with us, and we can help you. We can find you a cure, if there isn't one already. Please don't do this." He put out his hand for Zack to take. The werewolf took a step forward. "That's it. Don't give into this rage and primal instinct. We can help you."

Zack stopped mid-step and shook his head. "No! I don't need your help. This...power, this strength! I have never felt this much before. I feel like I could do anything." He looked down at his hands and was awe-struck by this realization. Until he rose his eyes to Cloukora and glared at him with a snarl. "Kill them." At that instant the four werewolves pushed the caged doors open and charged at Brev and Cloukora.

"Run!" Brev commanded and Cloukora sprinted out the door. She fired a few shots before she bolted out as well, catching up with Cloukora. "Cloukora, use your eye!"

"What?! My eye?! What the hell do you think I'm doing?!"

"No, focus, bring your energy forth."

"What?!"

"Just do it!"

He concentrated while still running, and the adrenaline started pumping through his veins again, just like before. He felt his eyes change, and things began to move slower, and he could focus more. He turned around and saw the werewolves running, but seemingly slower than they actually were. He raised the gun and aimed it at a werewolf. Pulling the trigger, it created a loud bang, and the bullet flew across the field, and into the werewolf's head, dropping the creature to the ground with a thud. He aimed at another, fired, and it dropped. Energy was beginning to flow through him. He charged at the third one and jumped up and punched it in the face then flipped over and spun around to shoot it in the back of the head as it tried recovering from the punch. All three lay before him, lifeless. Zack came out of the shed to see what had happened. The grin on his face from expecting Cloukora and Brev dead quickly faded.

"No, NO!" As he got more furious, fur appeared on his body, his body and muscles enlarged, his posture hunched over, and his head formed into that of a dog's. Zack had changed into one of them, a werewolf, and he howled. "YOU HAVE KILLED MY BROTHERS! FOR THAT YOU SHALL PAY!" He charged at Cloukora. Somehow, that flame-covered scimitar appeared in his hand once before. "Again?" He turned to face the werewolf and charged at it. Claws slashed at Cloukora's face, but sidestepping Zack's attack, he swung the sword at the torso and sliced the creature in half. The sword disappeared as the body hit the ground. "What the hell just happened?" He asked as he turned back towards Brev, who had a large grin on her face.

"Something amazing. Now, we'll head back and-" Cloukora's pistol quickly aimed past her, at the werewolf right behind her, and fired several shots into it. As soon as Brev saw the gun she dropped to the ground and rolled over on her back to see the bullets pierce the beast's chest as it howled in pain, and eventually fall to the ground. In an instant Cloukora hit the ground as well. "Come on, let's get you out of here." Brev said as she picked him up and put his arm around her neck to lead him to the car. She laid him in the backseat of the Corolla

Birth

and drove back to the motel room where Brev sat him on the bed, then dialed a number on her phone.

How? What happened? All that power, where did it come from? How...? While trying to make sense of everything in his head, his eyes closed and he dozed off into sleep. The next morning Brev woke him up.

"Your mom's on the way to get you, better get ready."

"She is? How do you know that?" he rubbed his eyes sleepily, and as soon as he opened them he saw a roach crawling along the nightstand, sending his body straight up and dusting himself off in case any were on him. "Fucking roaches." After his breathing returned to normal and he stopped panicking, he switched his focus to Brev.

"I texted your mom and said you were ready. I told her you were texting from your friend's phone." She said before he had a chance to ask.

"Ah...You know I have to admit, this was actually pretty fun."

"Good, because you passed."

"I don't know what that means for me now, but I suppose passing is always good." He slid out of the bed and went to change in the bathroom. He would talk to her more after he came back out, but after he stepped out of the bathroom, Brev had disappeared, and when he walked outside with his backpack over his shoulder, he noticed the Corolla was gone as well. He sat down on the curb, and waited for his mom to pick him up. Surprisingly, it didn't take long for her to get there.

"That was quick." He said as he got in.

"To tell you the truth, I didn't even go back home, I decided to stay at a hotel in the area. I thought it would be nice to get away from the kids for a bit. Lounge by a pool, eat some nice food."

"That sounds relaxing. I'm just glad to go home to my nice warm bed. Away from those roaches. Speaking of which, remind me to throw my backpack away." He buckled up and they drove off out of Tillamook, and towards home.

Birth

A cherry red 1969 Chevy Nova pulled in front of the farmer's rundown house. The same farm that Cloukora and Brev had investigated earlier. The man who got out of the driver side was tall and muscular, and the black suit he wore fit him well. The woman who got out of the passenger side was short, and had short brown hair that barely reached her shoulders. Her outfit was the opposite of professional: a low-cut V-neck top, jean short-shorts, and a pair of pink Converse sneakers. Neither looked that old, in fact, they probably hadn't even reached their thirties yet. "So, this is the place huh?" The man spoke with a British accent.

"I guess so. I don't get why we have to clean up the mess though. Why couldn't Brev and that...Cloud guy or whatever take care of it?" She said as they started up towards the house.

"You mean Cloukora?"

"Whatever."

"Brev said he passed out as soon as it was over, so she had to take him back to the motel. It would have been impossible for her to take care of both."

"He passed out? Do we really want someone like that working with us? I mean, if he can't handle a few werewolves, he's gonna have a hard time on other missions."

"Relax, The Executive says he has potential, that he can be the one we need to beat them. And I trust his judgment."

"Just because The Executive says it's true, doesn't mean it is." They had reached the farmer's door.

"Why don't you tell him that yourself then?" The man rang the doorbell.

"Hey, I may have opinions on things, but I'm not willing to get kicked out of the organization for them."

The farmer opened the door. "Hello there, how can I help you?"

Both pulled out and flashed their FBI badges to the man. "We're with the FBI, mind if we have a moment of your time?" The woman stated.

"FBI? Again? Well last I checked, you guys wore suits."

"Oh, you got a problem with the way she dresses? I didn't know clothing affected the way one does their job. I mean, you're not wearing overalls so you must not be a farmer then." The man pointed to the farmer's clothing which consisted of a button-up shirt tucked into a pair of jeans, and a pair of running shoes on his feet.

The farmer casually pointed to the man. "Oh, and he has a British accent, too. You guys couldn't even make it believable could you?"

"I told you, you should have worn the suit." The man told the woman.

"And I told *you*, I don't like suits. They're not very breathing. Maybe *you* should have hid your accent." She sighed before turning back to the farmer. "Well, you got us: we're not FBI. We're more unofficial." She accompanied the last word with a smirk. Abruptly the farmer went to slam the door in their faces, but with little effort the man gripped it by the side and forced it back open, pushing the farmer back. Not missing a beat, the woman dashed inside, grabbed the man by the arm and pushed him against the wall before pulling out a zip-tie and using it to cuff his hands behind his back. Firmly, she set him on the floor against the wall. "Now where are the bodies?"

"I don't know what you're talking about."

"Oh come on! You're only wasting everyone's time! The werewolf bodies, where are they?"

"I don't-" The woman's fist suddenly punched through the drywall behind the farmer, barely missing his ear. "In the shed! In the shed!"

"Thank you!" She stalked off towards the back door.

"Sorry." The man apologized before following the woman out.

The woman opened the wooden shed door to let out a terrible smell of death and decay. "Ugh. Next time we bring masks." They walked inside to find five long tables with a naked body on each one; one of the bodies being Zack's. "These must be it. Well, let's get to it." She stated as she pulled out a vial of a strange, blue liquid from her satchel.

"So wait, what do we do about the farmer? I mean, we can't arrest him and we're basically getting rid of the evidence right now." He reminded as he poured blue liquid onto one of the werewolves. The liquid immediately began dissolving and eating away at every single inch of its body until there was nothing left. Not even bone. Abruptly they heard growling from the direction of the house and when they looked, a large werewolf stepped out from the backdoor, wearing a ripped button up shirt and jeans. "Well, I guess that answers my question." He said casually as he calmly pulled a pistol from a shoulder holster and fired a shot at the werewolf. The single bullet hitting the creature right between the eyes. As the woman began dissolving the last werewolf, the man stepped out to do the same to the farmer. When both were done, they started back towards the Nova. The woman stopped short in her tracks, seemingly to be pondering something. "You alright?" The man asked when he noticed she had stopped.

"Yeah, just thinking. He took down five of those things. I guess maybe he will be alright." She said, grinning back at the shed. "Nah, he's gonna fail hard."

Birth

Angel's Gaiden

Experiment

June 24, 2010
Forest Grove, Oregon

 A few days had passed since the last mission. Were all the legends out there true? If werewolves were real, who was to say others weren't? He felt between the mattresses to see if the gun was still there, and jerked his hand away as soon as he felt the cool metal of the pistol. Even though he was all for people having guns in their home for protection, knowing that he shouldn't have it scared him, and knowing what it meant for him scared him even more. If the creatures of the night were real, that would mean danger lurked around every corner.

 He looked at his hand and frowned. *That sword....how did I do that? There must be some reason why it appeared. A connection, something!* He tried focusing again to see if he could make it reappear. Nothing. Since the day he got back from Tillamook, he had constantly tried to get it to return in his hand. Once, he thought he felt a spark, but nothing more. *I wish I would get some answers!*

 He heard a phone ring. Looking around, he couldn't see the house phone anywhere. Trying to listen for it, he heard an accompanying vibrating coming from the closet. Sliding the closet door to one side, he could hear it louder and coming from his dresser. Sifting through the drawers he finally found the source: one of his pants that he took along to Tillamook for backup clothes. Reaching inside, he pulled out a Droid 2 phone. The only thing was, was that it wasn't *his* phone; he could never afford one, much less a smartphone. "I have had a phone for an entire week and didn't even know it." Looking at the

name made him sigh. He pressed talk and put it to his ear. "You couldn't have just handed the phone to me?"

"Then that wouldn't have been as fun." It was Brev.

"What'd you want?"

"We got another job for you."

"Alright, before I go off on another mission, I want to know what this organization actually does!"

"We just make the world a better place."

"I mean job-wise! You didn't mention anything about werewolves before I went on that mission."

"You didn't ask, it's not our fault."

"Why didn't I ask?" he said mostly to himself.

"Because of your gut."

"My *gut*?! This is really pissing me off! I have no idea what the hell is going on and you tell me I joined some random organization and almost got killed by werewolves because of my *gut*?!" Luckily everyone was gone, otherwise someone would have come up and asked what the yelling was about.

"It's telling you that you can trust us, because you *can*."

"I don't give two shits about trust right now. Stop avoiding the question."

Brev sighed before she began. "I'm sorry, I can't explain much. It's not up to me. But our job is to take cases, whether supernatural or not, and get them done. When help is needed that no one else can give, we're there to help them. We save people, Cloukora, and we protect them, because that is our duty."

"So you guys are like heroes then?"

"Yeah, I guess you could say that."

He calmed down before he went on. "Look, I'm sorry. This whole thing has just been stressing me out. I do feel like I can trust you guys. I don't know why, I just do. So...What's the job?" He said half-reluctantly.

"A suicide in downtown Portland."

"Ok, and this concerns me how? I mean, it's sad and horrible and all, but it was a suicide, not a murder."

"The crime scene leads us to believe otherwise."

Cloukora sighed then finally said "Fine, I guess I'll do it. I've always wanted to help and save people."

"Alright, I'll pick you up in an hour, get ready."

"Oh, and uh, thanks for the phone. I appreciate the gift. I'll be careful with it."

"Don't worry about it. We designed that thing to handle any kind of force. You could chuck it at the side of a dam, let it fall in the water, pull it back out, and it'd still work like new."

"Great, so when I get pissed off at you guys I can chuck it at my wall without any worry." Cloukora half joked before he hung up, got dressed into dark blue jeans and an AC/DC Back in Black shirt, loaded the clip into the gun and put the pistol in between his waistband, and stepped out of his room to head downstairs. The upstairs hallway was narrow and filled with family photos and wall lamps on both white plaster walls. Walking out of his room at the end, and into the carpeted hallway, he passed by the four white, wooden bedroom doors, two on each side, and a bathroom door on the right near the stairwell. The bedroom he just came out of opposite of the stairwell was his, the first one on his left was the rec-room, and the other was his parent's. The other two bedrooms were his sisters' and his brother's, respectively. The balcony above and around the stairs was not made by traditional methods, but rather the railing was a short, thick extension of the wall, made out of the same material and plaster, providing better protection from falling over. The staircase went down a few steps, stopped at a landing, and then turned ninety-degrees downward. The stairs were covered in the same grey carpet as the upstairs and the rest of the house, with a wall to each side of him, and an easing on his right. As he neared the end of the steps, he accidentally hit his head on the low hanging ceiling that he almost always walked in to. Things like that are what made him hate his height a little bit, and the house too. Rubbing his head, he stepped down into the living room to go into the kitchen. The living room consisted of two tall, wooden, knickknack-decorated shelves to each side of a flat screen television on a wall opposite of the soft, brown couch that sat perpendicular to a same-colored loveseat.

More pictures decorated the walls as well as the television stand underneath the T.V. Next to the stairs on the right was the door that led into the kitchen, which in turn led to the dining room. On the other end of the living room was the front door, and to his left were two more doors: one for the guest room, and the other for the downstairs bathroom.

Entering the kitchen and getting into the cereal cabinet, he poured some Cocoa Pebbles into the glass bowl, followed by the milk, and began eating it by the spoonful. The cereal had turned the milk chocolaty, making it that much more enjoyable. As he was finishing up his breakfast, he saw the family SUV pull in and the people riding in it, come inside. They were carrying plastic bags into the house, of what, he did not know nor cared to know.

"Hey, where'd you guys go?" he curiously asked his family as they set the bags on the kitchen table. He saw that they contained groceries in them.

"We went to the store." His mom replied.

"Everyone?"

"Well, one person wanted to go, then another, then another, so I just said screw it and everyone went. We didn't wanna wake you, sorry."

"It's fine. Oh, I gotta go out again."

"Where now? Do I have to take you again?"

"Nah, they're picking me up. And downtown Portland."

"Who is it this time?"

"Another friend of mine."

"Ah, well, have fun." She said cautiously.

"You don't care that I'm leaving without asking you first?"

"You're seventeen, you gotta start doing things on your own. At least you told me, any other kid your age wouldn't have even *given* their parent that courtesy."

After an hour of watching T.V on the living room sofa, he noticed a black 2010 Toyota Corolla pull up in front of the house. "Alright mom, I'm leaving. Bye, love ya." He went to the back door and put on his grey skate shoes next to it. The shoes were decorated

with green and black here and there to give them more color and variation; he never liked wearing anything plain. On the tongue of the shoe, World Industries was woven in black. He decided to head out the back door since it was right there. As he strode towards the car, he noticed someone else sitting in the front passenger seat. *Another "coworker"?*

Opening the car's rear door, he sat down in the back seat of the car and put his belt on, and took notice of a sawed-off shotgun placed on the floor behind the driver seat. "Nice gun." He pointed out. Brev had on her FBI outfit just like last time: white shirt that wasn't buttoned up all the way, black blazer, black skirt that reached just to her knees, a pair of open-toed heels, and her silver-rimmed aviator sunglasses. He hoped he wouldn't have to wear that suit again.

"Cloukora… an honor to meet you, it truly is. Hopefully you live up to our expectations so that we may have more missions together. I can't *wait* to work with you." The man in the front seat said, making Cloukora feel uncomfortable. He felt like a celebrity who had just been approached by an obsessed fan.

"Um, what?"

"Oh, please forgive me, my name is Cal." He turned around to shake Cloukora's hand, who accepted it with a firm handshake. "Brev told me all about you and how you saved her life. Thank you for that…I don't know what I'd do if I lost her. We've been together for so long." The man was kind of stocky and he had a perfectly sculpted jaw with a pair of green eyes that would probably overwhelm any woman. In addition to his dirty blonde hair that was recovering from being shaved off, he had a light, kept beard and moustache attached to it. To mirror Brev, he wore a black FBI suit as well, except he wore pants and dress shoes instead of a skirt and heels.

"No problem. I didn't know Brev was married. I also didn't know that I was working with someone else today. Do you guys get a kick out of keeping secrets like this?"

"Honestly, you're the first recruit we've had in years. So we're not used to explaining things like this. *And* maybe seeing you freak out factors in a little bit." Cal joked.

Cloukora shook his head and grinned. "What's the mission?"

"Investigating the death of a teenager." Cal passed him a folder of pictures and information related to the crime scene.

After some reading he finally said "This looks like a suicide, nothing else. Why does it concern us?"

"We just want to make sure." Brev replied. "No harm in that, right?"

"Great, getting that mysterious organization vibe again."

"It'll go away with time." Brev assured as she pulled away from the house and drove towards Portland.

"I'm not gonna have to wear a suit again, am I?"

"No, Cloukora. You don't have to wear the suit." She said in a sing-song voice.

"Good, I hated wearing it."

Downtown Portland was a great sight to see. The tall skyscrapers and buildings towering into the blue sky, and the river flowing through the city gave off a beautiful vibe, but one thing always bothered Cloukora: Homeless people were always walking along the sidewalks, pulling bags upon bags of pop bottles and cans in carts. Sometimes one would walk up and ask for money or cigarettes, but get denied any. It was really a sad sight to see. Cloukora wished the world could be filled with better people: people who would be glad to help out the needy, and homeless who don't go around looking for people to rob. Though Cloukora had never actually seen anything go wrong in the city, but he heard about things that happened, so he always kept on his toes. He didn't want to end up as a news story. After all, despite its beauty, there was still crime in the city. Then again, what city *didn't* have crime? The world itself is vicious, and no one seems to want to fix it. And even if they tried, there would still always be someone greedy.

They parked the car next to a sidewalk near a house that had "Police Do Not Cross" tape surrounding it. There were still a few cop cars hanging around making sure the area was secure.

"We should wait a little while." Brev suggested.

"Yeah, we'll walk around for a bit until they clear out." Cal agreed.

"Wait, I thought you had access to this kind of stuff." Cloukora stated.

"It's complicated." Brev replied.

"Complicated. Heh, not only am I dealing with a mysterious group, they aren't even allowed access to the crime scenes."

"If we take these badges up there, and on the off-chance they look them up in the database, and they find no results matching them, what do you think they're gonna do?"

"Good point."

"So here, take this fifty and go find yourself something you like."

"Woohoo, I get to go shopping, what fun." He said sarcastically as Brev handed him the fifty dollar bill. "Why do I feel like I have another grandmother?" All three exited the car and stood outside as the sun's rays beat down on them.

"I'll call you when it's clear." Brev stated before her and Cal walked off, while he went towards Pioneer Square.

As Cloukora neared the Plaid Pantry store on the corner, he took notice of a matte lime green 2010 Dodge Charger R/T sitting out front. "Man, she's a beauty." Cloukora walked inside the store and the air conditioning felt so nice and cool on his skin. Around this time, the heat usually begins to build up until around July where it stops inclining, then stays around those numbers until August. *Going to be a hell of a summer. Maybe it'd help if I wore shorts instead of pants...* His first thought walking in was: *Energy drink*

He walked towards the refrigerated area and went to the energy drink section. "Oh energy drinks, if only I could marry you." He joked to himself. He was about to grab a Monster when he noticed a purple can on one of the shelves in the fridge. "Fountain of Youth. Never heard of that one before. Must be new." He continued grabbing the Monster and headed up to the counter with it in hand. On his way to it, a man bumped into him. This man had red hair that looked unnatural, covering

his left eye a little, and he was a little on the short side, yet he looked like he was in his mid-twenties. "Sorry man."

The man kept walking without saying a single word.

Cloukora shook his head and went up to the counter and paid. *Couldn't even say excuse me.* He exited out of the store and strolled along the city's sidewalks towards the mall. The heat hit his back quick and so hot, that two blocks down, he had already drunk half of his energy drink. Inside the mall, he felt the same cool breeze of the cooling system within. "Ahh. This feels soo good." He walked around the place, browsing through the merchandise in the stores that interested him. The mall was built with the shops on four different stories with walkways making up a squarish-perimeter, escalators going up and across the open area to the next levels, and a fountain down below in the center of the mall. For a while he couldn't find anything of interest. Until, he walked by Hot Topic. On the hangers, was a white hoodie stitched with a grey sword going up the middle where the zipper was and striking into an upside down rose with lightning bolts going out in different directions around it. Mirrored on each side of the sword was an eagle gripping the blade of its own sword; piercing it through a rose identical to the one in the middle, with one talon and gripping the rose with the other, with its wings spread. The same design was on each arm sleeve, the hood, and the back. He walked inside and had a thought. *Disguise.* He could save the world and hide his secret identity. *But, why? I'm not a superhero. Not yet.* That last part came from his subconscious. "I guess with the way things are going, I just might be." He said to himself. Then something else caught his eye. A mask. A dark grey metal one that would cover up the bottom half of his face, and make him less recognizable. He took the hoodie and the mask up to the counter and paid the thirty dollars for the items, getting a weird look from the cashier, of course. *Probably thinks I'm gonna murder someone. I don't blame him though, I probably would think that too.*

His stomach started to growl-he needed food-so he made a stop at the McDonald's established on the second floor of the mall. In the middle of eating, his phone went off. "Yeah?"

"It's clear, you can come back." It was Brev.

"Alright, I'm on my way." He hung up. "Again I get called when I'm in the middle of eating." He grabbed the food and ate along the way, just like last time.

When he returned to the Corolla, they were waiting outside the house for him.

"What'd you get?" Cal asked curiously as Cloukora threw the plastic bag containing the hoodie and mask in the back seat of the car.

"You'll see eventually. Shall we?" Cloukora reminded, gesturing to the house.

Brev led the way to the door and knocked on it, until a mid-thirties lady answered. Something didn't sit right with her, she looked shaken, scared. Not exactly something a parent would feel when their child died, maybe grief and sadness, but Cloukora could see pure fear within her.

"Hi, we're with the FBI and we were wondering if we could ask a few questions, if you don't mind." Brev politely explained.

"Well I already talked to the police about everything. Why does the FBI have interest in something like this?"

"It's just a precaution investigation. To see if there was a reason for his...early death and if anyone had forced or drove him to do it."

She frowned at them, probably in thought, for a moment before moving to create room through the door. "Here, come in, I made some tea." The woman said welcomingly as she turned to go into the kitchen.

They walked inside and sat on the couch in the living room. The furniture was fancy and elegant, and was soft to the touch, too, but the T.V. was small compared to most T.V.'s in a living room. The only thing that put off the fanciness, were the walls; they looked beaten and worn down, as if they went untouched. The woman walked back into the room with a tray and several cups of tea. Cloukora noticed her hands shaking while she put the tea cups on the table for Brev and Cal. When she tried putting Cloukora's in front of him, he waved it away politely. "No thank you, I'm not really a fan of tea. Thank you though." She set the tray onto the coffee table that rested before the sofa.

"Is there anything you can tell us about your son and why he might have did what he did?" Brev questioned with as much sensitivity as possible.

"He was a teenager, most of them keep to themselves. Even then, he was the happiest kid I knew, he was great at sports, had many friends, a girlfriend who he cherished most. But…."

"But what?" Cal asked.

"Oh it's nothing, my mind just…went off track for a second. Then one day, I come home, and I check up on him, and his…" She took a second to recover. "His wrist was slit open." She put her face into her hands and wept.

Cloukora thought he saw something out of the corner of his eye. He turned towards the stairs where it was, and barely noticed a foot disappear around the corner. He turned back to the grief-stricken- *or fear stricken* -woman. "Is there anyone else that lives here with you?"

"Just my little one, but he's sleeping upstairs in his room." She replied, wiping the tears and running makeup from her eyes.

"How old is he?"

"He's only one. I can't believe he's going to grow up without a big brother..." She looked as if she was about to cry again.

"I think we have enough, we'll leave you be." He said as he got up and began walking out.

"We are so sorry for your loss ma'am. We'll leave now, have a nice day." Brev said, trying to comfort her as they followed out the door. After they got to the car, Cloukora leaned onto the hood.

"Something's not right, she's not telling us everything." Cloukora commented.

"Why do you figure that?" Cal asked.

"Didn't you notice she was shaking? She was scared."

"Any mother would be like that if their child died."

"They wouldn't have fear, because what would there be to fear? And, I also saw something." Cloukora hesitated for a moment. Could it be what he thought it was? "I saw a foot go around the corner."

"Maybe the child was awake."

"He's one. He can't even walk yet."

Brev sighed as she looked up toward the sky, and then stopped short like she noticed something, and her eyes widened. "What is i-" Cloukora cut off as he turned to stare at the upstairs window. He felt his hair rise on his neck, his heart skip a beat, and his face turned white, when he saw what stood inside the window. It was a person, but it looked like it was rotting away, and its eyes were pure white. No human looked like that. At least, no live one. Without another thought, he took the sawed-off shotgun that had been lying in the backseat of the car, and ran towards the house before being stopped by Brev.

"Cloukora, wait!" He turned back around, anxious to go, as she handed a couple shotgun shells coated in purple from out of her pocket. "I've been meaning to test these out."

He went into a sprint, burst through the front door and up to that room, ignoring the mother's yells. As he ran up the stairs, loading the purple shells into the shotgun, he felt something change; he saw things more slowly and clearer. *Again? Why is it only certain times it happens?* He cocked the gun, and pushed his way through the bedroom door to see the creature standing over the young child's crib. He ran at it, grabbed it by its neck, and jumped out the window with it in his grasp, causing glass to shatter everywhere, as they fell creature first. While pointing the barrel at its face, he pulled the trigger and the pellets went through its head. But these weren't normal pellets, for they had a purple aura surrounding them when fired. When he landed onto the ground with the creature, black blood oozed from out of its skull. "The hell was that? Was that a...a ghost?" Cloukora asked, frantically standing up and away from the horrifying creature.

"I believe so." Brev walked over and poured a strange blue liquid over the corpse and watched as it faded into the sky. Cloukora thought he saw a glimpse of the spirit it once was before it went mad.

"Then, how was I able to grab hold of it?"

"It's all part of your powers, which you'll learn about soon enough. Now, we must leave, we have other business to attend to." Brev said as she walked to the other side of the car. Cloukora quickly got in the back as Cal and Brev got in the front before any more attention could be drawn.

Birth

Brev dialed a number as she began to drive off. There were a couple rings before someone answered, but Cloukora couldn't hear the person on the other end.

"I need Nole or Kaora to see if there were any reports of any strange activity at the victim's house. Alright, thank you. Oh, yeah he's doing fine, he's starting to get the hang of everything. Yes sir, understood." There was a silence after she hung up that lasted for a while.

"I'd ask what's going on, but I already know the answer: 'We can't tell you, it's not our job.'" Cloukora said in a mocking tone. He had always respected his elders, but this was starting to get a bit annoying.

Brev looked at Cal for a second. "We're sorry. We really are. I guess you deserve to know this much: We've been at war with another organization. We're not sure who exactly, but recently they have been causing problems for us. And our job is to clean up their mess. It shouldn't be our job, but it is. You're lucky, this case isn't as bad as our other ones."

"Another organization? Do you think they're behind this?" Cloukora asked.

"I'm not sure. We don't even know their motives, or their goal. We just know they exist, and that they're a pain in the ass."

"Oh yeah, we learned that the hard way after their stunt in L.A." Cal chimed in.

Cloukora leaned forward, interested to hear about this organization. "Wait, you don't mean the incident that happened last October, do you?" Cal nodded. "*They* were responsible for that?" He let him fall back to the seat as if the news were too much to handle. Anyone would do the same if they learned the people they were fighting against, were also responsible for that event.

"Yup. We didn't even know what was going on until it was too late. We couldn't stop them in time, and in turn we became the city's clean-up crew for about a month."

"Well shit, now I can see how they'd be a pain to stop. I do have another question though, why recruit me now? What's so special about *now*? Does it have something to do with this…evil organization-whatever their name is?"

"Honestly, I don't know. We were told you were important in some way, that something's coming, and only you can stop it. I'm not sure what that is though."

"Apparently you're not told everything either, considering you're now using 'I' instead of 'we.'"

"Only a select few in the organization knows what's going on and sometimes even they don't know. Our leader gives us orders, and we take them without question."

"I hate that. When a leader doesn't tell something he knows, it makes me feel like something's not right."

"It never is."

"One final thing. Can I at least know who I'm working for?"

"Wolfstorm. Maybe sometime we can give you a proper welcome." She tried to joke, but it sounded odd to Cloukora. Just a mission ago she was cold and distant, and now she's more loose and friendly. Then again, he *did* save her life. That could change someone.

A few seconds later, Brev's phone rang. After Brev answered, she said a few "Okay's" and "Understood's" then hung up. "Nothing unusual happened, other than one thing. One of the neighbors saw a strange man walk up to the door one day and go inside to talk to the victim. The one thing that stood out was that he had bright red hair. Not like the normal red hair you usually see, more like…I don't know, what's the word?"

"Like it was dyed?" Cloukora suggested.

"Yeah that. Why?"

"I think I saw him at the Plaid Pantry today. He seemed in a rush."

"Wait, I think I saw him too, he was standing outside the building earlier. Just staring at it." Cal added.

"Now, the question is, how do we find him?" Cloukora asked.

"They already found out his last location, a club not too far from here. He was last seen entering it about ten minutes ago. So he should still be there." Brev revealed.

"Alright then, hopefully it's not a gay club." Cloukora joked.

They turned and gave him a look as if he had just said something utterly stupid. Which, he in fact had.

"Hey, I have nothing against gays, I just don't want to be in a sweaty club with guys rubbing up on me. Drunk guys at that."

"You know, guys that say that are usually the most insecure about their sexuality." Cal pointed out.

"Yeah, well…Shut up." Brev and Cal chuckled at his failed attempt at a comeback.

A few moments later, they pulled up next to a decent looking building with the name "The Party House" in neon blue flashing on its wall. Cloukora dug out his hoodie and the mask from the bag and donned them both before zipping up the hoodie.

"So you got a disguise?" Cal asked.

"Yep."

"Seems a bit creepy for a hero, don't you think?"

"Want me to wear underwear on the outside of my pants?"

"No." Cal laughed. "Mask is good."

Cloukora sighed. "I realize I should present myself as a friendly hero, but I think striking fear into people, to make them scared to commit crime, is the most effective way to be a hero." *Isn't that the opposite of what I want? To not be judged by my looks?*

As if he read his mind, Cal said "How you look shouldn't be what scares people, it should be what you do that does. I think the fact that someone would kick their behind for committing a crime is enough to scare them. Regardless of how they look."

"And honestly, I don't think you could pull of scary. You've got too good of a heart in you. Don't make people have to judge different." Brev put in.

Birth

"Those are some good points. I'm still gonna keep the costume though, I think it makes me look badass." Cal and Brev only shook their heads.

They got out of the Corolla and strode up to the entrance to meet face to face with the bouncer. Cloukora could hear the muffled sound of the music thumping inside the club from where he stood.

"Names?" The bouncer asked without looking up from his clipboard.

"Does FBI ring a bell?" Brev simply stated as she displayed her badge. The bouncer's head shot up and his mouth went agape.

"Y-yes ma'am, go right on in." he frantically removed the thick red rope blocking the doorway and let them through the door.

As they walked in, the music abruptly got louder, and clearer. There was a lot of dancing that seemed sexual and invaded the personal bubble space. He passed a couple that were grinding their bodies up against each other. *Really* invaded the personal space. Strobe lights were flashing and there seemed to be a bit of a fog around everyone's feet as they danced to the music. Cloukora realized that the song everyone in the club was dancing to, was some pop song about a guy and a girl wanting to cheat on their lovers and have a one night stand.

Cloukora let out a groan. "Ugh, I hate this song, it makes me sick." He had to raise his voice a little so that it could be heard over the loud music.

"Why's that?" Brev wondered.

"If you listen to the words of the song, they talk about how their boyfriend and girlfriend are out of town, and they just want to mess around."

"I take it you don't approve of cheating?" Cal asked.

"Hell no, the only time I approve of it, is if it's because of love. If it's just to screw around because you're bored, then that's just stupid. If your loved one is not satisfying you, or you don't love them anymore, why not just leave them? It would hurt them a lot more if you didn't love them and slept with other people, than it would just breaking up. Plus it kinda bugs me that you can't tell if the person singing the chorus is a guy or a girl."

"Maybe it's Michael Jackson." Cal joked.

Cloukora laughed along with them. It still amazed him that they had some humor in them; they came off as the serious type to Cloukora. After a "split up" from Brev, they started scoping out the club to find the red-haired man. As Cloukora was moving through the dance floor, he took notice of a guy flirting with a girl next to the bar. The thing that drew his interest, though, was the ring on his left ring finger, and the lack of a ring on the girl's. He strolled over to the two and asked the man for the time. As the man looked down at his watch, Cloukora's fist went flying and hit him square in the face, with the force of the blow knocking him back and into the bar counter with a bloody nose. Cloukora wiped the blood on his knuckles onto his jeans and started back while the man called at him "You're crazy man!" But Cloukora only continued on, until he heard the man shout "You son of a bitch!" Cloukora stopped. *He just had to say that.* Spinning on his heels, he casually walked back to the bar area. Cloukora returning towards him, scared the man a bit. As he approached, the man tried to take a swing at him, and Cloukora, not taking his eyes off the man, knocked away the arm with his palm, and sent a fist into the challenger's face again. The man stumbled back towards the counter, and before he could recover, Cloukora slammed his face into the counter. "Don't insult my mom ever again." He said calmly before he turned around and headed towards the back where Brev and Cal were standing. Brev motioned for him to come over.

"Anything?" Brev asked after he rejoined them.

"To be honest, I was kinda busy."

"I saw that; you need to be more careful."

"I think I can handle myself."

"I'm talking about losing your focus. When you're not paying attention, anything can happen. Our guy could have snuck past you while you were busy 'brawling.'"

"I don't think so." He said matter-of-factly.

"Excuse me?"

"He's right there, and he's heading for the door." He pointed to the red-haired man from earlier pacing through the dance floor towards the entrance.

Brev only sighed before all three moved through the sweaty and smelly crowd swiftly, staying unnoticed.

After getting in range, Cloukora grabbed the man's shoulder and shoved him against a nearby wall, grasping the collar to keep him from getting away. "What the hell did you do to that poor kid?!" Cloukora felt something wrong deep inside of him, something he knew he couldn't let out. It made his stomach turn and his head swirl. His body felt tense and was aching to let loose on the man. He was like a rubber band cocked back just waiting to be released. What it was, he wasn't sure, but he tried to push it away and continue by kneeing the man in the stomach. That didn't help. It only made him want to continue beating him to a pulp. "Talk! Now!" Brev and Cal joined them and only stared at the red-haired man.

The man grinned. "Heh, you *know* what I did. I killed him!"

"What'd you say?" Cloukora pushed him harder against the wall.

"You heard me. I. Killed. Him. Do you have trouble hearing?" The man was obviously cocky and full of himself.

He wanted to tear this man apart, limb from limb. *Anger. That's what it is. But what would be so bad about letting it out. Why is something telling me not to give into my anger?* "Why?!"

"A test. The boss wanted to find out something."

"And it required a kid's life?!" Brev and Cal were still silent. Perhaps this was a lesson of theirs: learning how to interrogate. *A seventeen year old learning interrogation. What has the world come to?*

"Not really, but it was a way to make sure his results were a hundred percent."

Cloukora's grip tightened on the man's shirt. "What was he trying to prove?"

"That, I'm not sure of. Just like your organization, we're not always told everything."

"So you *are* working for that organization! Who do you think you are, going around and experimenting like you do?!"

"I don't know. Pioneers, I guess."

"Pioneers don't kill or harm people."

"Really? Pioneers killed Native Americans to create the most industrious country in the world: America. Just as in the Medieval times, doctors ended up killing people while trying to test their medicine. So you can't tell me that pioneers didn't kill people. Great things require great sacrifice."

"Shut up! Now, you're going to tell me exactly why you did what you did, and who the hell you and your organization are!" The anger in him just kept building up within. *What is wrong with me? I've never felt this angry before.*

"I told you, I don't know *why*, I just did what I was told. As for my name, it's Tayge. And our organization is-" At that moment, an explosion went off in the bathroom and as Cloukora turned to look, Tayge's fist hit him in the face and knocked him back into a daze, while Tayge quickly ran out the door before Brev or Cal could grab him. But as soon as the three made it outside, he was nowhere to be found. A red feather gently floated down onto his shoulder, but it was too light for him to even notice. As he walked away, the feather fell softly to the concrete sidewalk.

Tayge walked through a giant, elegant hall decorated with paintings that seemed to stretch throughout all of time. One painting was of a man wearing a crown standing on top of a ruined city barely the size of his foot, holding a blade in his hand with a dragon snaked around his body-it wasn't constricting him, more like protecting. Another was of a dragon sinking its teeth into a wolf howling in pain. All the other paintings were similar in theme: they portrayed some king and his conquests. He stopped at the great wooden doors at the end, and pushed them open into an enormous throne room. Almost everything, including the walls and ceiling, was decorated in gold, silver, and colorful jewels. Towards the back, in the throne, was a man with his

feet lifted up onto the throne's armrest. He was not much older than Cloukora, but his body was more built, his eyes blue, and his hair was straight, brown, and reached down to his chin. He donned a long, dark purple, leather overcoat with a plain black t-shirt underneath, black jeans, and knee high black leather boots. The leather on the coat was faded, and it fell just below his knees. It looked like something from out of a fantasy novel. There was a plate of fruit to his right he was eating from, sitting on a pedestal.

"Ah, Tayge. Do you bring good news?" The man asked with hope in his voice.

"Yes, my lord." Tayge answered as he gave a bow.

"So, is it him?" The man asked as he tossed a green grape into his mouth.

"Yes, but I don't think he knows his full potential yet. If he did, I don't think I would be here right now."

"Good, this is coming together perfectly. Soon the darkness inside him will take over and we'll have him on our side."

"Shall I prepare your plan, sir?"

"No, have Venn make the arrangements. You've been working hard the past few months. I don't need my group worn out and tired by the time the war starts."

Tayge grinned. "Thank you, my lord. I could really use a break." Tayge swept another bow, and then exited out the room. The door closing behind him.

When Cloukora came home, his house was dark and seemed to be empty. The family SUV was missing from the driveway. They must have gone out somewhere. He found the key in its usual hiding spot in an abandoned bird's nest, and unlocked the door. As he shut it, he turned on the light and noticed a note on the coffee table. He picked it up and it read:

Cloukora, sorry, we decided to go out for a bit again. Dinner's in the fridge. Oh, and your grandfather Aaron wanted me to tell you, there's a family reunion next week, and that you'll like where it's at. Love you! ~Mom

"About time. Maybe they'll finally explain what the hell is going on with me." Cloukora rubbed his eyes tiredly, and the image of the ghost earlier flashed into his mind, and his eyes shot open. "I'm gonna have nightmares for weeks from today." He took his hoodie and the mask he bought and took them up to his room and hid them underneath his bed. He came back downstairs, into the kitchen to grab something to snack on and eat, when he noticed a smell. It smelled familiar, but he couldn't place it. "Rotten eggs? That's weird." The lights started flickering and he was suddenly turned around and thrown against the wall by an invisible force, and he stuck to it like a fly trapped on flypaper, his back flat against the wall. He tried moving his arms or legs, but he couldn't even feel them. It felt like he was just a floating head.

He became aware of two people, a man and a woman, walking towards him, with the woman raising her hand as if she was holding him up. Then he realized she was. His eyes widened when he saw that their eyes were pitch black. "Demons."

"Ahh, it feels so good to do this." The woman said excitedly.

"Don't be too hard on him, Zela." The man said with some sarcasm in his tone. "You might break his skinny, little bones."

"He's the one, right? The one the boss is worried about?"

"Yeah, I see it in him."

The woman's grip tightened on Cloukora, and his breathing lessened. "Listen here, you piece of shit. We're not going to kill you, not yet anyway, but we're here to warn you, if you even *think* about meddling in our affair, we will personally have our master kill you!"

"Wait, what? What the hell are you talking about, you crazy demonic b-"

"Finish that sentence, I dare you!" The force on his throat increased and his breathing ceased. "Just don't get involved with anything we do! Understand?!"

The grip around his throat lessened, and after catching his breath, he asked "Wait, were you the ones behind the murder today?"

"What? No, that was someone else. Just be warned: we're watching you."

She let go and they both instantly disappeared into thin air as he fell to the tile floor.

"Is the world going insane, or is it just me?" He said as he stood back up, rubbing his neck. It felt like the grip was still there. Maybe some sleep would help. That is, if he could get any.

Angel's Gaiden

Reunion

June 30, 2010
Forest Grove, Oregon

    Cloukora was moving back and forth from his closet, packing his bags for the trip to the family reunion. He was usually like that; he would always put things off until the end rather than get it done as soon as possible. It drove his family crazy. After he got all the basic things shoved into his backpack, which barely held his stuff, he stared for a second at the bottom of the bed. He was deciding if he should take the disguise that lay hidden there. Hearing a "Hurry up Cloukora!" from Hayley, he quickly grabbed the hoodie and the mask, and shoved it below his other clothes before zipping up the bag. He threw the bag over his shoulder and practically ran down the stairs. After he got in the car, they pulled out of the driveway, and drove off.

    The red Durango pulled into his uncle's driveway behind his truck. They were told to meet there for a family breakfast before heading out to the campsite. Everyone was going to follow his uncle, for he was the only one who knew where they were going. Well, Aaron knew where it was as well, but they decided they'd just follow Daniel. They said it was supposed to be a surprise for the family, but Cloukora knew it was mostly a surprise for him. It made him curious as to where it would be.

    Cloukora wiped his feet on the doormat that lay before the back door of the farmhouse, a house that seemed like it was probably about

Birth

thirty or so years old. There was something different when he walked inside, something that he had never felt before. Especially not when he walked into that house. Though it was a new feeling, it felt like a sense of protection, like he had nothing to worry about or fear. And in a moment it was gone, yet Cloukora knew it was still there, lingering.

Almost the whole family was there; they still had to wait on his aunt because their alarm went off a little later than planned. Those that were already there were his grandma Serra, who was a sweet woman, but if allowed, could go on about anything for hours, his grandfather, Aaron, who was a calm and intelligent man, his aunt Cynthia who had inherited her father's intelligence, her husband Brian, a pretty relaxed guy that you could have almost any kind of conversation with, and then their two daughters Eris and Katy. And of course there was his uncle Daniel, who was usually a quiet man, but had a loud heart, his wife Patty who always had a cheerful smile on their face, and their sons Luther and Will. The family members not yet arrived were his aunt Jane, probably the most laid back of his aunts and uncles, her fiancé Chip who always had a joke to tell, and their kids Dennis and Chloe. He gave his younger cousins hugs before making a plate of golden scrambled eggs, mouthwatering bacon, crisp hash browns, and browned sausage links. He poured maple syrup all over the food and then poured himself a glass of orange juice. Afterwards, he sat on the couch in the living room and watched T.V. while he ate his plate of breakfast.

When he turned the T.V. on, the news channel was there.

"The manhunt in the Middle East still continues on for the terrorist Oushu Kan, the same man that had a hand in the attack on Los Angeles last October. Officials say they are closing in on him, but cannot offer any more details on the matter." The small square next to the anchorwoman changed from an image of the city of Los Angeles, to an image of 'The Party House.' "In other news," the anchorwoman began. "There was trouble at a dance club in Portland last week. A teenager, in what appeared to be a costume, got into a fight with another club-goer, followed by an explosion a few moments after." The news network rolled a clip of the club where Cloukora was at, including the

fight. "The victim was hanging out at the bar enjoying his drink, when the attacker randomly walked up and struck the man in the face. And as you can see here, the attacker *did* leave afterward, but not even a minute after the quarrel, he was right back at the bar for another go at the poor man."

Cloukora almost choked on his orange juice. *Glad I wore a disguise.*

"So John, what do you think of this...masked figure?" Questioned the anchorwoman to the anchorman after the video had ended. "I think he's just a nut job." She added.

Cloukora only stared at the lady on the television in disappointment.

"Well, Lynn, I think he looks like someone who could be in a gang. In fact, I'd put my money on him being the culprit behind the explosion. After all, cameras did see him leave the scene of the crime."

The hell is wrong with people? He took the remote and changed it to Cartoon Network. The Grim Adventures of Billy and Mandy were on. *Aww yeah. Cartoons bitches.*

"What was that about?" His uncle asked as he joined Cloukora on the couch.

"Oh, just about that guy in the hoodie in the club. Nothing important."

"Eh, I think it could be. He could be a superhero for all we know." Daniel looked at Cloukora with a grin. He was teasing him. "Plus I heard that the guy he beat up was cheating on his wife. I think that's any good reason to give a man a bloody nose."

"Yeah, I suppose." Cloukora grinned. Even if the news portrayed the incident wrong, and made the other guy look good, he knew the truth. And that's all that mattered to him. "I bet he goes around beating up unfaithful people who can't keep to their vows." He made fun of himself. "Heh, I bet he also calls himself 'The Protector of Fidelity'!" He mocked.

"That's actually not a bad name."

"Nah, I think it sucks. Smoke is such a better name for him. You know, because of his hoodie he wears." And he can summon a sword

of fire. But he wasn't about to include that as reasoning in case another family member overheard the conversation, then he'd have to explain how he knew that.

"Please tell me you're not serious."

"No, I was just joking." He *was* serious. "Do you think he was responsible for the bombing though?"

"No, of course not. If he punched a guy for cheating on his wife, he wouldn't put people's lives at risk. Anyone with any common sense would know that."

"That's the problem. How many people in this country even have that? I mean we're talking about a group of people that hurt themselves just to be funny on the internet, or to follow fads."

"Well, why would the opinion of someone who purposefully eats a spoonful of cinnamon matter at all? Obviously they're not educated enough to make their own."

After his aunt Jane had finally arrived, everyone piled into their cars and headed down the back country roads. The whole trip there Cloukora just stared out the window and watched the beauty of the world. The rolling hills passing by, the mass of trees that populated most of the wilderness, and the great, clear, blue sky with the sun, that was up just a little after sunrise, giving warmth to his face. He kept thinking about everything that happened recently, trying to make sense of it all, but could find no answer within. Even more odd, was that it all felt right to him. He couldn't place why, it just did.

After about an hour, the caravan pulled into the parking lot of a small store. Cloukora and his three uncles went inside. Cloukora grabbed the snacks his family members asked for, as well as a few things for himself. His uncle Daniel joined him in grabbing a few drinks from the refrigerated section.

"So, where are we going?" Cloukora asked as the two started towards the counter.

"Like I said, it's a surprise." His tone showed he wouldn't break.

"More secrets, of course." He put his items on the counter and pulled out the cash from his pockets to pay the cashier.

"Yeah..." His uncle seemed like he was staring off into the distance, outside the store, but Cloukora wasn't paying any attention. He was more interested in paying for his snacks. "Hey, do you have a bathroom?" his uncle finally asked, but at the cashier.

"Yeah, of course. It's out back. Here's the key." The cashier handed him a wooden board that had 'Bathroom' carved into it, with a key hanging from a drilled hole by a chain.

"Thanks. Cloukora, can you pay for me?" He asked as he handed a twenty dollar bill to his nephew.

"Sure." Cloukora started paying for the items, while his uncle went outside and behind the building to the restrooms.

Daniel stepped inside the bathroom, surprisingly neat and clean for a convenience store bathroom, and cautiously looked around as if expecting someone else to be in there with him. After checking the stall and finding no one, he sighed before turning around to see a man standing in the middle of the tiled floor. The man was tall, in his twenties, and had a somewhat-shaven face that matched his short, dark brown hair.

"What do you think you're doing? You have no business following him around!" His uncle shouted.

"You're right, I don't. But my boss does. He wants to make sure your *nephew* doesn't get in the way of his rise."

Daniel shoved the man against the plastered wall. "His rise? When? When?!" he shook the man against the wall, expecting to get an answer out of him.

"Soon, oh so very soon. And how joyous it shall be! All will bow before him, and those who defy will be crushed into oblivion!"

"That will never happen, and even if it does, we will stop it!"

The man laughed. "Pah! You humans. You are blind to so many things!"

Birth

"And yet you are so set on something that will never happen! I am *done* with you." As Daniel placed a hand over the man's mouth, his other hand was engulfed in a flame that oddly didn't burn him, but gave off some warmth. Immediately the engulfed palm went to the man's chest and abruptly caught fire to his clothes and the rest of his body. The "man" tried to let out a scream that was muffled by Daniel's hand, and his eyes turned from a normal brown to a pitch black that left no sign of white. Within a moment, he was nothing but a pile of ash that Daniel casually kicked down a drain. Seeing some dust on his hands, he gave them a quick wash before leaving the restroom, and taking the sign back in to the cashier.

It was about another hour or so of driving and rest stops before the caravan finally reached their destination. How he knew, he didn't understand. But he knew. He was staring outside through the car window when he thought he saw the world flicker as they turned down a gravel path just off the road, into the woods. *It's just my imagination. This whole mess of things must be getting to me.* They eventually came to a large clearing that would be big enough to park the cars, pitch up about six tents, have a campfire, and still leave a lot of space for the kids to play. They parked their cars, and someone from each car got out to meet up and talk. After some time, his step-dad came back and said they were camping at that spot for the night. Everyone got out of the vehicles, grabbed their tent kits and had set them up in a semi-circle next to a slope covered in trees so steep, that it could almost pass as a cliff. To the sides of the campsite was flat woodland that stretched far out deep into the forest, and even more on the other side of the gravel road that continued on past the clearing. After all the tents were set up and a fire was going, his uncle and grandfather motioned for him to follow.

They hiked up along a narrow, dirt trail along the steep slope. At the top, Cloukora looked out north to see a wide and calm lake less than a few meters from where he stood. The only thing that broke the surface of the water were jagged pillars of rock that seemed to be

arranged into a circle. Though there weren't many trees on this side of the slope, it was made up for on the other sides of the lake. He continued carefully following them downhill towards the edge of the lake.

They stopped at the mud-dirt bank, and as his uncle and grandfather were lighting cigarettes, Cloukora asked: "So, what're we doing here?"

"You want to know what's going on right?" his uncle asked.

"Yeah, as a matter fact I do. I swear I feel like I'm going through puberty all over again, just without the hair." Cloukora half-joked.

"Alright then, where do we start?" Before Cloukora could answer, his uncle continued. "What you're feeling is normal. It's part of your blood. Our blood."

"This is genetic?"

"Yes, for now the power only comes in heightened situations when your life, or even someone else's, is in danger. In other words, it's activated by your adrenaline. Which is why I gave you that necklace. You've been wearing it, right?"

"No, but it's been in my pocket all the time. Why?"

"Once you wear it, the power will come whenever you want it to come. You will be able to have full control over it." His grandfather explained.

Cloukora pulled out the necklace that was given to him at the hospital and looked at it. "What exactly *is* this power?"

"The power of the Atlantians. Well, specifically the Skyrells."

"Atlantians?! You mean from *Atlantis*?!"

"Yes."

"The Lost City?"

"Well, it's not really lost, but yeah."

"So, we're Atlantians?"

"Correct."

"Wait a minute," Cloukora had to take a moment to shake off the feeling of shock. "How do I know you're telling the truth? How do I know you guys aren't just messing with me?"

"That's why we brought you down here." His grandfather knocked a couple vines away from an object and revealed a small stone

square pillar with an indentation on top. "Place your hand on this, and you'll know."

Cloukora walked over to the pillar and hesitantly placed his right hand in the indentation. Five tiny spikes quickly shot up and pricked each finger before he had time to even escape it. He flailed his hand, trying to get rid of the pain before wiping the dots of blood onto his pants. The spikes withdrew and after a few moments the water began to ripple. "Um, what did I just do?"

"Just watch."

The circle of pillars in the middle began to rise and was discovered to be the top of an old tower. The tower rose through the water along with three others, with the three forming a triangle around the taller tower; the one that had been sticking out of the water. The towers were connected by huge walls that weren't very wide; only two people would be able to walk side by side. But the walls were tall enough to prevent anything, or anyone, from getting inside. Finally, the island, where the four towers sat on, broke the water surface.

"W-what is this?" Cloukora's eyes widened in amazement and his voice emphasized the excitement he couldn't contain.

"It's an Atlantis outpost." His grandfather explained. "It was built when King Relyt, your ancestor, came to North America. Inside, is a portal that leads to different places around the world."

"King Relyt? Ancestor? So, we're related to a king?" Cloukora folded his arms and put his hand to his chin. "Wait, why haven't I heard of him before?" He was more confused than ever, if that was even possible.

"He made sure everything that he knew, all the secrets the world shouldn't know about, were destroyed and only passed through the family. That included him and the family history."

"And what would happen if the world *did* find out?"

"After discovering that the things they thought were untrue, were actually true, even *more* people would be out there searching for them. And some of those secrets are just too dangerous for man to possess."

"Dangerous?"

"Yes, the world would be in chaos if even one of those secrets was revealed."

"Isn't *this* dangerous?" Cloukora gestured to the tower sitting above the lake.

"Yes, but this lake can't be found. At least not by a regular person."

Cloukora raised his eyebrow.

His grandfather sighed. He was asking too many questions. "There's a mystic shield that covers this whole area. It separates the lake from our world."

"Wait, we're in another world?"

"No, just separated from our own. No one can reach it, unless they're a member of one of the Four Great Families."

"Huh?"

"There were four groups that were the strongest nations all throughout the *entire* world. They were the Atlantians, the Vikings, Avalon, and the Reapers."

"The Reapers?"

"Not the kind you're thinking of. They were called Reapers because of their deadly skills in combat. Once you were locked in combat with one, you might as well consider yourself dead."

"Where are they now?"

"Most likely in hiding, just like the other families. They're probably waiting for King Relyt's reincarnation to reveal themselves."

"King Relyt's reincarnation?"

"Yes, he's told to-"

Aunt Cynthia yelled down from the top of the hill. "Dad! Mom says to come back to camp! We're gonna make dinner."

"Alright! We'll be there in a second." After his aunt turned around and walked away, his grandfather continued. "We'll talk more when everyone's asleep. For now, put that necklace on."

"Wait, if you have to be a family member to enter this area, how did Jack and everyone else who aren't a part of the family get through?"

"Well, they can still enter this area, but they can't see this lake. If they looked over that hill they'd see a large field, or something of the

like." Cloukora still looked confused. "Let's use the world example you came up with: They're still in their world, which doesn't include the lake, but in ours we can see the lake as well as the family. We're more in between both of them. Again, they're not different worlds, they're just…I don't know. Relyt's technology was tricky, and a lot of it was hard to grasp and understand. Our biological family can't see it either, except us three, because their power isn't…awakened…yet. Which is another story for another time."

"Ahh, I kinda get it now. Not completely, but I got the idea."

"Good. Now, the necklace."

Cloukora locked the necklace around his neck and felt a rush. First came a surge of energy, and then a massive amount of pain, sending him crashing to the ground. His head swirled and it felt as if he was just thumped on the head with a rock. The pain made him nauseous, but instead of vomit, he spat up blood. In a few moments, everything was "normal" again. He felt fine. Except, things seemed to move more slowly, and in a sense, become clearer. Everything seemed to return back the way it was as he calmed himself. There was no longer a rush of energy.

"Sorry, first time's always painful." His uncle remembered. "Which is expected since you've had ten times the amount of adrenaline you would normally feel rush through your mind and body all at once. But at least now you can control your powers, by controlling your adrenaline. The adrenaline heightens your eye movement, perception, and brain processing, allowing you to see things more quickly, and think quicker, which helps greatly in battle."

"Battle? Are you saying I'm going to be fighting?!"

"Maybe, maybe not. It all depends on what fate has in store for you." His grandfather replied. "Let's head back before your grandmother comes down here herself." Aaron joked as he started back up the path.

The moon illuminated the three Skyrells sitting in the camping chairs around the crackling fire. The stars twinkled brightly in the dark

sky. Everyone else had gone to bed a half hour before, so the only noise came from the forest that surrounded them and the fire in front of them. Cloukora had just finished roasting a marshmallow before putting it on a graham cracker to complete the s'more he had been making. "Ok, start from the beginning. The history of our family up to now."

"There were four great 'groups' at a point in time. There were the Atlantians, who ran with wolves. Then there were the Avalonians, who fought alongside dragons. The Vikings flew with gryphons, and The Reapers slew with gargoyles.

"Wait a minute, Dragons, gryphons, and gargoyles? Are you serious? Those things are real *too*? And Avalon? As in King Arthur's Avalon?"

"Yes, very much so, which is why man must not ever find out. If they did, they would try and harness the power to control them. And yes, King Arthur."

"Woah…Oh, sorry, please continue." He took a bite of his s'more to shut himself up.

"It started in between the ninth and tenth century: King Relyt, who hadn't created the fabled City of Atlantis yet, had a kingdom established in Europe. Which itself was named Atlantis. Yes, I know, let me finish and you'll understand. Anyway, both he and King Arthur had controlled most of the land at the time. They ruled in peace, both kingdoms, and they helped each other whenever one needed the other. Their alliance grew even more when the rise of the Vikings began. After realizing their great skills in combat, King Arthur thought they would be good to have alongside in battle. But King Relyt wasn't a hundred percent on it, because of their brutal nature and behavior, but he agreed nonetheless. Then, they had discovered The Reapers, although it's unsure how exactly, but both kings recognized their abilities and sought out their alliance, to which they had agreed. Together, nothing could tear them down. Every time, whenever one of the kingdoms was threatened, the others were there to support as quickly as they could. However, that all changed when a threat arose in the world. Down near South America, a race known as the Mayans had grew, and they needed to be stopped."

"The Mayans? Why? What did they do?"

"They found a great power: the Fountain of Youth."

"The Fountain of Youth? Ho-"

"Anyways, all four kingdoms knew they needed to be stopped. Only one problem, there was no way to get across the Atlantic Ocean. Except, King Relyt had been experimenting, creating things. He had invented some sort of aircraft. This was no ordinary aircraft though; he managed to create one with advanced technology, even more advanced than what we have today. Some family members even believed it was similar to a spaceship. He presented the creation among the other three leaders, and when they all agreed, they headed out for the Mayan Capital, Tikal. Both sides fought ferociously, neither side would give up, and it seemed as if there were no end in sight. The Mayans fought alongside giant creatures that, hopefully, no longer exist. These creatures were told to be very strong and powerful, so it was hard for them to be killed. Then King Relyt had finally devised a plan to end the whole war. The specifics are unknown, but Relyt and Arthur had somehow managed to make it to the temple to face the Mayan ruler. Only, their ruler had already drunk from the Fountain of Youth. Now nothing could stop him, he threw Relyt and Arthur around like ragdolls. But the two would never give up, they couldn't. During the fight, Relyt was stabbed and on the verge of death. So, Arthur did what any good friend would do. He revived him. He poured some of the Fountain onto Relyt, and when Relyt awoke, he had possessed enormous power, power unimaginable. None of his descendants could match their power with his. With his new-found abilities, they managed to destroy the Mayan Kingdom. Their leader fell, as did the kingdom. Relyt used his powers to obliterate the creatures, and after everything was cleared from existence that could allow the Mayan Empire to rise again, they returned home. Everything seemed to be the way it had been before. But King Arthur changed, he began to seclude himself from the rest, and the three kingdoms grew suspicious. Finally, Relyt decided to find out why. King Arthur had taken some of the Fountain of Youth, and he had already spread it amongst his people. The difference between Relyt and Arthur though, was that Arthur drank from the Fountain because

Birth

of greed; greed for power. In turn, it changed him into a 'monster'. This caused war to break out between the four. The Vikings were promised power from Arthur if they joined his side, so of course, they agreed. The Reapers didn't approve of Arthur's goals, so, they sided with Relyt. The battle was completely devastating. Tens of thousands of people died between the four nations. Even with Relyt's technology, and The Reapers deadliness, there was no hope for them winning. Of course, they cut Arthur's army down greatly, as well as the Vikings, but it wasn't enough to win. After the leader of The Reapers thought it was best to retreat and hide out, King Relyt decided to take his people away too. He fled to North America and built Atlantis within the Pacific Ocean. But Arthur wasn't done. He followed Relyt here, the place we now know as Oregon, to finish him off. In fact he came through that tower you re-surfaced. After realizing what he must do, he and his wife Aurora made sure there was no chance of anyone finding his kingdom by destroying every invention of his, and sinking Atlantis. While Relyt faced Arthur in a great battle, his people fled here, to this lake, to end their reign, so Relyt could guard the portal and prevent anyone from using it again. Relyt *did* manage to defeat Arthur. But, the fight drained most of his energy, and he only had enough to return to his people, and to die among them. Once he passed away, most of his kingdom decided it was time to part ways and lived amongst the Native Americans. Eventually the Skyrells themselves thought it was best too. They figured it's what he would have wanted. Before leaving, they sunk the tower as well."

    Cloukora opened his mouth to say something, but was speechless. All that came out was "Wow."

    "Any questions?"

    "Wait, my history may be fuzzy, but wasn't Atlantis during sometime in B.C.? But you said Atlantis was in the ninth and tenth centuries? That doesn't add up."

    "What Plato wrote, was because of a dream he had, a vision. He saw Relyt and his city in the future and thus wrote it down. Then again, it's possible that Relyt named both Atlantis because it was told he had a fascination for Plato's work. So it may not even be *the* Atlantis, but it

was *a* Atlantis. At least, that seems the most reasonable, because Relyt and his kingdom *were* during the ninth and tenth centuries. Perhaps we may never know the truth."

"Huh…So, Atlantis is in the Pacific Ocean? I guess that rules it out as the source of the Bermuda Triangle. Where is it at exactly?"

"I suppose it does. But, it is still Atlantian technology that causes the incidents that happen down there. There was said to be a ship that had malfunctioned and crashed into the ocean in the middle of the Triangle. Why it does what it does, I don't know. As for Atlantis, well, if you look closely towards the west, up at the stars, with the family's power you can see that the stars make out a wolf howling in the middle of the crest of the Skyrells."

"The crest?"

"It's the symbol on your necklace."

Cloukora "activated" the power by getting his adrenaline going and stared up at the stars, and he was able to pick out the wolf howling in the crest. "I see it, but what's so important about it?"

"Below that group of stars, is where Atlantis lies."

Cloukora calmed himself again and finished his s'more. "What about our powers? Did we get that from Relyt being infused with the Fountain of Youth?"

"Correct. The powers vary greatly from person to person. Some people may get one ability, some two and even some more than *that*. No one knows where it originally came from, so it's hard to tell how it works. It depends on the person though, and whether or not it's a part of them, or they drink it. One who simply drinks it, may not become as powerful as one who already has it in their DNA. Some get flying powers, or some get a huge increase in intelligence or strength. Some also get flying powers *and* heightened intelligence or strength. Why Relyt and Arthur were powerful as they were just by drinking it, I'm not sure. Maybe the power of the Fountain is wearing off. However, there are some powers that are not exclusive to the Fountain of Youth. Atlantians in general, even if not a Skyrell, were somehow able to wield elemental swords. And Skyrells ran alongside wolves long before the war with the Mayans."

Birth

"So that fire sword that's appeared in my hand is normal, too? Okay good. I thought I was going crazy. But if we can tap into our power, what about the rest of the family?"

"Everyone in the family has it in their blood. But it's dormant, so it has to be activated in order to use it. That necklace you're wearing, that's the... trigger you can call it. It has either technological or mystical properties to it, and any family member that puts it on can use the power that's inside them. Where the necklace came from, it's been forgotten, but I believe Relyt made it as his last invention, in case anyone should need it. There have been a *few* cases though where a member had tapped into their power without the necklace. Such as yourself. But those are *very* rare cases."

"It sounds like Relyt was a great man."

"He was, and he created a great family, too."

"Well," his uncle started. "I think it's time for bed." He got up and went into his tent.

"Night." His grandfather got up and did the same.

"Wait, one more question." Cloukora started.

"Hm?"

"You mentioned something about Relyt's reincarnation earlier. So he's supposed to come back?"

"So the prophecy says. Relyt himself even believed he would be born again."

"Do you believe it?"

"Honestly, I'm not sure quite yet. I respect Relyt enough to know that he wouldn't fool anyone. But even the smartest people can be fooled by themselves. So until I see something that hints at his return, I don't think he will." He took a sigh before returning to his tent. "Goodnight now."

Cloukora sat there staring into the fire. He was trying to run it all through his head and believe it all. Relyt, Avalon, King Arthur, Atlantis, mythical creatures, and reincarnation. They were all things that would be in a fiction novel. His thoughts were interrupted when he heard a noise by the coolers and looked over, but nothing was there. He shook his head and dismissed it as his imagination. *I better get to bed*

as well. He let out a yawn, then walked to his tent and lied down in the sleeping bag. After a while, he heard a noise outside the tent again and saw dog-like shadows moving around. One of the shadows knocked over the cooler, while a few smaller ones went through it, dragging food out. Cloukora quietly unzipped the tent and his mouth dropped as he saw what the shadows were. *Wolves.* There was an adult and four pups around the cooler. The adult was helping the pups get the food out, until it noticed Cloukora. It motioned for the others to follow it back into the bushes. *Must be their mom.* Cloukora decided to walk out and picked up the package of raw bacon. He took a strip out. "Hey, it's ok, you can have some. I won't hurt ya." The mom looked back at him. He threw the pieces towards them, and they immediately started chowing down on the bacon. Eventually the whole package was gone and there was no more to give. "Sorry guys, I think that's enough, we still need breakfast for tomorrow, and you just ate the best part of it." The wolves went back into the bushes. Cloukora was about to go back into the tent, when one of the pups ran up to him. "Sorry little guy, but that's enough. Go back to your mom." The pup wagged its tail and let out a small yelp. Cloukora started towards the bushes where the mom was at as the pup followed. The pup walked back towards its mom until she pushed the pup back towards Cloukora. The pup ran back over and sat in front of Cloukora. As he kneeled down the pup jumped on his knee and started licking his face. Cloukora saw the mom's face and thought she had nodded to him before she turned around and ran off. Cloukora scratched behind the wolf's ear. It seemed to enjoy it. But what dog wouldn't? "So, she wants me to take care of you then? Well, I've always wanted a wolf. Promise to be good?" The pup yelped happily and continued licking his face. "Alright then, you can stay with me. Now, to name you...How about Rhain? With an h?" The pup wagged its tail even more, if it was possible. Cloukora led it back into his tent to lay next to him and fall asleep.

The next morning they had packed up the tents and were ready to make the trip back home. Cloukora already explained about the wolf,

Birth

which his mom was uneasy about at first, but after some convincing, she eventually agreed. As he walked towards the car with Rhain right behind, he felt like he was being watched. Rhain abruptly stopped and stared towards the bushes. Cloukora looked as well and saw the pup's mom at the edge of the shrub. He knew Rhain was male from how it urinated earlier this morning, which Cloukora only noticed it right when it started, then looked away. "Go ahead." Rhain ran over to his mom, and she rubbed her nose against his head before nudging him away. After Rhain returned, she let out a howl that was followed by a smaller one from Rhain, and his family jumped at the sound and all but his uncle and grandfather freaked out and wondered if the wolves were going to eat them. Pushed by that fear, everyone hurriedly got into their cars and put on their seatbelts. With a "Let's go, Cloukora." from his mom, Cloukora got in the Durango, with Rhain resting on his lap, and they drove off.

Birth

Angel's Gaiden

Wolfstorm

July 2, 2010
Winchester House, San Jose, California:

"John, I don't know about this. We're gonna get caught!" Kayla shined the flashlight at John as he began climbing over the black metal fence that kept people out of the giant mansion's backyard. She was a little short for her age, had smooth, almost perfect skin, blonde hair, and blue eyes. She wore a loose, white blouse similar to those that were worn in medieval times, jean short-shorts, and a pair of green sneakers.

"Come on Kayla, don't bail on us. It's just one night. I mean, maybe we'll actually get to see if there are any ghosts here or not." Jackie said excitedly as she climbed the fence as John put out an arm to pull her up and over. She had dark skin, black hair and light brown eyes. She wore a white and purple striped V-neck, black short-shorts, and grey sneakers.

"Don't worry Kay. Me, John, and Mike got both yours and Jackie's backs." Kyle was a little built- he played football for a couple of years while he was in high school -had short blonde hair and blue eyes. His outfit consisted of a plain white t-shirt, jeans, and black sneakers. He was also Kayla's older brother. Mike on the other hand wasn't as buff and his hair was brown and his eyes green. And he wore a black t-shirt, basketball shorts, and basketball sneakers. Both were tall though. After giving Kayla a boost over, they jumped over it themselves, with John already at the window trying to pick the lock. He wasn't as built as Kyle, but he had done some wrestling during his freshman and sophomore years of high school. He had black hair and

Birth

dark brown eyes. Like Mike, he wore a black t-shirt, but instead of shorts he wore jeans, and for shoes he wore black sneakers. The room they climbed into was rid of dust, meaning someone still took care of the cleanliness. Short of the window was a bed with a canopy dangling over it. Beside the bed was a night stand on each side of the headboard. The wall across from it had a vanity mirror, and the far wall, near the door, had an old wardrobe closet.

"This place would be a lot scarier if they didn't dust it." Jackie joked.

"Let's just get this over with, alright?" Kayla hugged her shoulders and looked worriedly around the room. "Is it me or is it really cold in here?"

"Maybe it's the ghost of Sarah Winchester, watching us." Mike mocked, fluttering his fingers in his face.

Kayla shuddered at the mere thought. Ever since the incident at the house she had lived in when she was a little child, she couldn't take ghosts lightly. She felt her left shoulder where the scars were underneath her shirt. She remembered the pale, decaying creature grab a hold of her shoulder and try to drag her out of the bedroom. Shuddering again, she put her hand back to her side. Why the creature let go, Kayla never knew. All she knew right now was that she wanted to just go home. But, reluctantly, she continued following the group as they walked down the hall.

"See? No ghosts! I knew this place was just a hoax." John said aloud to everyone.

Behind them, a shadow dashed across from room to room. Kayla heard the movement, but when she looked back, there was nothing there. "I feel like we're being watched you guys. We should go."

"Sis, that Christian stuff is just getting to your head. Ghosts aren't all that bad as people make them out to be. I remember we lived in that one house in Los Angeles and there was a ghost, and it didn't even hurt a *fly*." He didn't know about what had happened that night. In fact, she hadn't told anyone about it, nor did she ever wear anything

less than a shirt. People would ask questions about those scars. Questions she didn't want to answer.

"Here's mine and Jackie's room. Goodnight." Kyle flashed a wink that was meant at John, but Kayla saw it. He took Jackie into the room and shut the door. Kayla heard giggling coming from Jackie from inside the room.

John picked the room right across from Kyle and Jackie's. "Find another room Mike."

"Yeah I know, I know. I'm gonna go around and take a couple of pics throughout the house, see if I can pick up any 'orbs'." Mike mocked again as he laughed and walked off down the hall. John shut the bedroom door after Kayla followed in to lay on the king sized bed.

Kyle sat at the head of the bed, his arm wrapped around Jackie who was lying on his chest, circling a finger on his stomach. "So, we're alone, in this supposedly haunted house, on this perfect bed, yet you haven't made a single move on me."

"You know I'm not like that. I'll do it when the girl is ready, not when I am." He flashed a grin.

She grinned back. "Well, tonight, I think I'm ready." She pushed her soft lips against his and started passionately making out.

Mike was walking down the hallway when he decided to try a door and opened it, but instead of it being a room, it was a brick wall. "House is a damn maze." He went to the next door, and this time, there *was* a room. He took a couple pictures of the room with his camera, until he noticed a dot on one the camera's screen. Trying to rub it off, thinking it was a smear or dirt, he found that it was a part of the picture. "What the hell? That's not a-is it?" He looked up to take another picture, and standing in front of him was a tall cloud of black smoke, with thin yellow eyes piercing his own. Mike let out a yell and then felt something stab through his heart, before his lifeless body fell to the floor.

Birth

John and Kayla were lying on their bed; John holding Kayla, giving her comfort as best as he could. "You know they're only messing with you Kay. There aren't any ghosts in here, it's all a bunch of stories that got out of hand. Now, take your mind off it, and just relax." John was moving his hand up her thigh towards her waist.

She pushed him away and sat up. "No, John. I want my first to be special, not like this."

He placed his hand on her thigh again. "Come on Kayla. We still have a year left of high school, then you're off to college. We might not get another chance like this." He flashed a grin but she knocked his hand away again. "Dammit Kayla!" He got off the bed and stood up. "What the hell is with you tonight?!"

"I told you, I'm scared. Sorry if that's keeping *you* from having fun!"

They both heard a yell. "Stay here. It's probably Mike playing a prank like always." He peeked through the door before starting out, but stopped short. Kayla wondered why, until she saw blood suddenly begin to leak out from where his heart was, and almost screamed. She covered her mouth. "No, Please no. This isn't real. It can't be." John's body fell to the floor, revealing a cloud of black smoke with yellow eyes. Kayla dashed to the window to try to get out, but it was shut tight. She turned around to see the thing right in front of her, and she let out a scream.

Forest Grove, Oregon

Cloukora lay in his dark room on his bed, with Rhain lying at the end, fast asleep. He, on the other hand, was wide awake. He had thoughts about his past, present, and future, trying to piece it all together. Things that people believed weren't real, actually were: Werewolves, Atlantis, King Arthur, ghosts, and monsters. What else is real? On top of everything else, he had found out he was a descendant

Birth

of King Relyt, the king of Atlantis, which meant he also had special powers. Then he remembered that night in the burning building, and how his eyes seemed to change. Quietly, he got up, walked silently to the bathroom, shut the door behind him and locked it. He didn't want anyone walking in on him. He placed his hands on the countertop, closed his eyes, let out a sigh, and raised his head. As soon as he wished it, adrenaline surged through him, and he felt more powerful than he ever had before. How he could bring it out so easy, he didn't know, but he loved the feeling it brought with it. It was also somewhat painful, but he was told that would ease up later on. He re-opened his eyes. Looking upon his reflection in the mirror, he saw that his eyes *did* change. They were no longer that of a normal human's, but of a product of an ancient power. His pupils were now a glowing green three-triangle triangle with a gray circle on each of its sides and a smaller gray triangle on each point. The upside down triangle in the middle was brown. It was the same symbol as his family crest. He stumbled back and almost tripped over the bathtub behind him, but had managed to catch himself in time on the towel rack nailed to the door. He calmed himself, letting the adrenaline seep away, and made sure his eyes were returned to normal. He walked out into the hallway and back to his bedroom. Rhain was still sleeping. He had took Rhain to the vet the day before to find out how to take good care of him, and found that he was only about four months old, and it shouldn't be long until he was full grown.

    He threw himself softly back on his bed and closed his eyes, hoping tomorrow would be an easy day. As soon as he was about to drift into sweet, sweet sleep, his phone rang. *The hell?* He picked it up off the nightstand and the caller ID said *Brev*. He answered it. "It's two o'clock in the morning, what do you want?"

    "Got another case for you." She replied.

    "Can't I do it tomorrow?"

    "No. Besides, you need time to meet the rest of Wolfstorm, right?"

    She got him there. He had been wanting to meet them ever since he found out about the organization. "Dammit. Meet me at the end of

Birth

my street." He hung up and put on his white and grey hoodie, grabbed his mask, his gun and put it in the back of his pants, and put on a pair of fingerless gloves. The gloves, he figured, would add a nice touch to the costume. He snuck over to the window in his hallway, took off the screen, and hopped out the window onto the low-sloped rooftop, carefully and quietly making his way down the roof before jumping off a few feet above the ground; the ridge of the roof only covered the first story of the house, so it wasn't that high up. He then headed towards the meeting place where Brev was supposed to be. After a half hour or so, Brev finally showed up in the usual Corolla.

Cloukora got in the passenger seat of the car as she handed a small backpack. "For your costume. You're not gonna need it for a while." After taking it off and stuffing it in the backpack, Brev made a U-turn and began heading eastward. Cloukora thought it was strange though: She didn't have on her suit. Instead she wore a light, black cotton wax jacket, a grey V-neck tee, a pair of jeans, and heeled dark-brown riding boots that reached up to her calves. It was weird seeing her in normal clothing rather than the fancy suit. *Does Brev have a twin?*

They eventually ended up in downtown Portland once again. "So where *is* your HQ?"

"Right here." She parked in front of a tall business building with a "Hero, Inc." sign on the highest story and the name stickered on the glass doors.

"Here? Really? I pictured something a little more high tech and fancy. Not a normal office building."

They both got out of the Corolla, with Cloukora throwing the backpack on his shoulder. "That would draw a lot more attention than we need." She unlocked the glass door and opened it for him to walk in. The lobby seemed like any other normal lobby, only this one was dark from being closed. Nothing out of the ordinary. They stepped inside the elevator and Brev pushed the *30* button. He felt the elevator thump and start to move upward towards the top. When the doors opened again there was a huge room before them. It was like it came straight off of the set of a science fiction movie. Almost everything was a bright white: the tiles, the walls, the ceiling the computer panels

Birth

around the monitors, and even both hallways that were to either side of him. Not a single wire or pipe was in sight. There also weren't any windows. Probably for safety reasons, Cloukora assumed. The fluorescent lights made it seem to shine even brighter. If he didn't know better, he'd think he was in Heaven.

"Wow." is all he could say as he took in the marvel of the room. There were three people at a giant computer area with several monitors screwed into the wall just ahead of them. Two were working at the controls while Cal was overlooking their progress on whatever it was they were working on.

"You've met Cal," Brev gestured to him. Cal was wearing a suit that looked like it cost him an arm and a leg to get. The two at the computers turned around to face them, while Cal still observed the monitors. The woman wore a dark blue blouse tucked into a black skirt that barely reached her knees, and had on a pair of black high heels. The man wore a regular blue t-shirt, and a pair of jeans, and had on his feet green Converse sneakers. One of them, the square-faced man, had short dark hair, dark skin, and green eyes with glasses over them. The other, the beautiful oval-faced woman, had long black hair that was put up into a pony-tail, dark brown eyes, and had dark skin as well. But unlike the man, she didn't wear glasses. "Meet Nole," she gestured to the man. "And Kaora." Then gestured to the female.

"Ah, you must be Cloukora. Brev has told me a lot about you and your success on your past few missions. I'm very impressed." Nole stood up and shook Cloukora's hand.

"Well, I try my best." Cloukora gave a half-smile. It was Kaora's turn to get up and shake his hand.

"Wow, a member of the Skyrell family...I'm sorry, I don't mean to be rude; it's just...I admire the history of your family, their powers, their tactics, and, and-"

Before she could get too carried away, Cloukora put up his hands to stop her from rambling on. "It's alright, it's alright. Weird to have a...fan...but I'm cool with it."

"I think Cloukora best be meeting the rest of the group. You two should be getting back to work." Cal interrupted, before anything

else could be said. "Speaking of which..." He twitched his arm to look at his watch. "I gotta get going as well. You two keep working on it." He told Kaora and Nole as he walked up to Brev to peck her on the cheek. "Bye hun, I'll be home later." He continued on towards the elevator.

"Where are you going?" Cloukora asked curiously.

"An undercover assignment. I'm gonna be just like James Bond. Some werewolves and witches may be involved, too." He pushed a button in the elevator. "It's gonna be fun. Too bad you can't come." Cal gave him a wink just as the doors closed.

"Come on, I want you to meet Bowe and Erro. Yes you heard right." She added as Cloukora opened his mouth to say something about their names. She led him down a hall to the right, as Kaora and Nole returned to their work, and then stopped at a door with a sign Cloukora didn't get a chance to read. "Might want to cover your ears."

"Why?-" The door quickly opened and immediately he heard a gun being fired from inside, barely giving Cloukora a chance to cover his ears. Cloukora then realized what he had walked into: it was a firing range. There was a woman in a black tank top, army cargo pants, and army boots firing at a sheet of paper at one of the stations. Her long, brown hair pushed behind her ears and her bangs swept to one side of her forehead, covering one of her deep-set hazel eyes, with a button nose in between them on her smooth, diamond-like face. She then took notice of them walking in and stopped firing as she pushed the button for the paper target to come closer. Cloukora saw that there was only one shot, located right on the forehead. "Lucky shot there."

The woman unloaded the clip from the gun and loaded a new into it before she cocked it. "Shots, and I wasn't lucky; it was skill." She said as she put the pistol- which looked to be a M9 - in a holster on her right leg. She also had a bit of a British accent.

All of those shots hitting one spot? Holy-.

"Name's Erro. You must be Cloukora I presume? Welcome to Wolfstorm: the Protectors of the World."

"Protectors?"

"Yeah. Brev should have mentioned it to you. We make sure man-made disasters don't happen, or at least keep them from being worse than they were intended to be. Remember the assassination of George Bush?"

"He wasn't assassinated." He said as if she were crazy.

"Exactly." She said matter-of-factly

Cloukora seemed a bit confused, but decided to just go with it. "So I'll be preventing assassinations and the likes?"

"Yep. Everything from werewolves to ghosts to assassinations, to sometimes even wars. Sounds like the perfect job huh?"

"Well, I've always wanted to be a hero. Guess now I get my wish." He said half-heartedly. Despite his desire, he wasn't sure if he was ready for that kind of burden yet.

"That's the spirit." She slapped him on the back, making him wince. The slap may have meant to be friendly, but it still hurt a little.

"Where's Bowe?" Brev changed the subject.

"Oh, he's helping Winter and Avenorra train in the Mat Room."

"Alright, thanks Erro. Keep up the good shooting. Don't wanna be rusty when it comes mission time." She said as she began out with Cloukora following her.

"Will do."

"Just three more to go, Cloukora. Then we'll brief you on your mission."

Cloukora followed her once more down the hallway, to another door. When this one was opened, he couldn't believe what he was seeing. There were two girls and one guy. The girls were either really young, they looked like teenagers, or they were just short for their age. The man seemed to be in his mid or late twenties. One of the girls was wearing a dark green shirt, tight jeans with a couple holes ripped into them, and just had a pair of white socks on her feet and her dirty blonde hair was pulled back into a ponytail. The other girl wore a white Hollister tank top, jean shorts that showed a lot of her legs, and pink Converse sneakers. Her light brown hair barely reaching past her shoulders. The man was well built and had short light brown hair. He wore a dark blue shirt that hugged his muscles and broad shoulders,

and had black cargo pants on with black combat boots. Cloukora thought he could pass as a CIA agent. But it was what they were doing, and their speed, that appalled Cloukora. The blonde-haired girl rushed up to the man and swung her fist at him, but even though it should have clearly hit, he managed to dodge her and swing his leg at hers - which were still in mid-run- sweeping her feet off the ground, bringing her face down into the blue leather mat. The brunette actually ran across the wall that was right behind them, and jumped off spinning herself to kick the man in the face, but his arm came down on her legs while she was in mid-air, dropping her to the ground. As soon as he knocked her down, the blonde swung her feet and swept *his* feet. As he was falling backwards, the brunette stood up and then leaped at him, her fist aiming for his face. When he hit the ground, he quickly rolled to the side; dodging her blow at the last moment, her fist striking into the dark blue mat. The brunette glanced up to see Cloukora and Brev watching.

"Alright, I think that's enough for today. We have company." The brunette said, standing up. Cloukora noticed her chest heaving heavily all the way from where he stood. "Thanks for the help Bowe."

"No problem. You just gotta work on your attacks. The speed is great, but the moves are just predictable." He replied, before going over to a side of the giant room, and picked up a holster with a gun, and wrapped it around his right leg.

The brown-haired girl came up to Cloukora and Brev. A playful grin showed on her strong squared face as her protruded honey eyes studied Cloukora. "New recruit huh? This must be…Cloud-something-or-another."

"Cloukora, actually. You girls were actually pretty good with those moves." Next thing he knew, the back of his leg was pushed down on the ground, his arm pulled back, and a foot on his back. She was so quick, he didn't even see her move. Brev was standing there, just watching. "Help? Please?" Pain was shooting up his arm; he felt as if it were about to be ripped off.

"What did you call us?" Her voice definitely showed she was pissed off. "We're not 'girls' thank you very much. We're two young - and beautiful - women."

"Oh Winnie, let him go. He didn't know." The blonde-haired girl joined them with a white hand-towel around her neck, wiping the sweat off her face with part of it. The brunette- Winnie she was called - let his arm go.

"Only warning you're gonna get buddy." Cloukora stood up and tried moving his arm around, making sure it could still move, and wasn't broken. *Geez, temper problem much?*

"Cloukora, this is Winter," Brev gestured to the brunette. "And this is Avenorra." She gestured to the blonde. "As for Bowe, he's the one on his way over here. He's our other marksman specialist. Haven't seen him miss a shot yet." The oval-faced blonde had up-turned light green eyes that complimented her hair color.

"Cloukora, right? Pleasure to meet you." Like Erro, he had a British accent as well. With his strong, chiseled jaw line, short black hair, and dark brown eyes, he gave off an intimidating vibe. As if he could kill Cloukora with one finger. He shook Cloukora's hand with a tight grip when he joined them. "So Brev tells me you're good with a gun. Maybe one of these days, I'll see for myself if that's true or not." He turned to Brev. "Well, I'm gonna make sure your ride's all good to go then hit the shower. See ya later Cloukora." He waved as he walked out the door, and headed down the hallway.

"I'm gonna take a shower and then head to bed. Night Avy." Winter said before walking out as well and headed down the hallway, the opposite way Bowe went.

"Night Winnie. Sorry about that. Are you alright?" Avenorra asked with a sweet, sympathetic voice.

"Yeah, I'm fine." He was rubbing his arm, trying to make it feel better. "Why'd she do that though?"

"She doesn't like it when someone thinks she's a little kid. I don't like it either, but then again, I don't have her temper. You just gotta watch what you say around her. The littlest thing can set her off. Hell, I once saw her beat a guy to a pulp for checking her out. It was horrible; blood was everywhere, there was an ambulan- Sorry, I seemed to have gotten side-tracked. Anyways, as long as you stay on her good side, you'll be fine. Now, I'm gonna go take a shower as well. Night."

It was nice meeting you Cloukora." She added as she walked out and went the same way as Winter.

"We should probably get going on the mission." Brev reminded as she began out of the room.

"You never did tell me what the mission was about." Cloukora asked as he followed her out. "Would be nice to know what I'll be doing."

"We're going to San Jose, California."

"California? Cool, can't wait to see what it's like. I bet it's like in the movies...gorgeous babes in tight bath-err I mean, why?"

"A couple teenagers were found dead inside the Winchester House."

"Are they sure it wasn't a murder or anything of the sort?"

"They think that's what it is. The way they died though...it just doesn't seem right... We want you to investigate it and find out what exactly happened inside that house. And if it's anything unnatural, we want you to take it out. Bowe, is the chopper ready?" She questioned when they reached the control room. Bowe was walking back from the hallway right across from them, wiping his hands on a small orange oil rag.

"Yep, all fueled up. Running perfect." Bowe replied.

"Thank you Bowe." Brev led Cloukora down the hallway Bowe just came from and eventually they came to a door.

"What if it's not unnatural? What if it was a killer?"

"Then you can either try to find the killer or come back home. Though I'm not sure you'd be able to track one down. Werewolves and ghosts are one thing, you know they're one when you see them. But killers, they can hide in plain sight and you won't even know it." She opened the door and outside on the roof was a helicopter landing pad. On that landing pad was a pitch black Black Hawk helicopter that almost blended in with the color of the sky.

"Wait, this is *yours*?!" His eyes were wide in amazement. "How were you even able to get your hands on one of these? These things are like, military grade shit!"

"Doesn't matter. Now c'mon, let's go." Cloukora climbed into the side of the helicopter and slid the door shut. Brev got into the cockpit and started the engine up. Cloukora buckled the belt and grasped the rope hanging from the ceiling as if he were hanging on for dear life. He had never ridden in a helicopter, or an airplane for that matter, so he was really anxious. After a while though, he was able to get himself to look out the window of the left side door, and his mouth went agape. The view from above wasn't like any other. The cities and towns twinkled and dotted the land down below while business buildings and large hotels thrust up towards the sky. The people walking around really did look like ants. This high, he could see past Oregon into California and a little of Idaho, and even less of Nevada. Through the other window, he could see the Pacific Ocean crashing along the shoreline, under the bright full moon. He laid his head back and just watched out the window as the chopper made its way to their destination.

San Francisco, California

After an hour or so, the chopper landed on a helicopter pad on top of a skyscraper, and by the time it had, the sun was already starting to come up in the east. He slid open the door and hopped out with his backpack over his shoulder before closing it back up. Brev opened the cockpit door, but didn't get out.

"Aren't you coming?" he asked. The sound of the helicopters rotors forced him to raise his voice, and the wind produced from them threw his hair all over, messing it up to the point it didn't look like a normal hairstyle.

"Not yet, for now you're on your own." She handed him a manila envelope. "The job information and keys to your car is in that package."

"And where is the car?"

"On the third level of the parking garage across the street. Parking spot number is twenty six."

Birth

"Alright. I'll make sure to do the job right."

"I know you will." She closed the door and the helicopter lifted off and flew back to the north, and his hair settled back down. It was still messy though, he just didn't know it was.

"I can do this. Shouldn't be *that* hard." He walked towards the rooftop door and proceeded down the stairwell, eventually coming to another door that led to a huge office area. Grey cubicles were side by side with people working rapidly at whatever it was they were doing. He almost bumped into a woman carrying two trays full of coffee. When he said sorry, she just ignored him and kept moving on. Eventually, he came face to face with the elevator and pushed the down button. It took a couple minutes until it finally arrived, and when it did, he was almost trampled by ten people pouring out of it. After some pushing and shoving from both him and the people, he finally made it into the elevator and pushed the lobby button. Before it went down though, about five more people flooded in. It took a good half hour or so before the elevator finally made it to the lobby. He stepped out and looked around. The lobby was the opposite of what it looked like upstairs. There were small little plants here and there, a couch and chairs facing a plasma screen T.V. hanging on one of the walls. Cloukora thought it a ploy to pull people in to the company thinking it would be a peaceful career choice, when it was really full of chaos and hurry. He noticed the exit to his left and went out the doors. Luckily the receptionist didn't notice; he didn't feel like dealing with that kind of situation.

Outside, the roads he could see were packed with cars moving ever so slowly. Few people were walking along the sidewalk due to how early it was. *Speaking of time...* Cloukora pulled out his phone to check what time it was and found it was only seven in the morning. *Damn, what kind of excuse am I going to give mom for this now?* He decided to cross that bridge when he got to it. For now, he was on the job.

He jogged between the cars in the road to get to the multi-level garage on the other side, and then took the elevator up inside to the third level. After figuring out which way to go, he finally found the spot

number twenty six. In that spot was a grey Toyota Prius. "Please don't let this be the right car." He pulled out the keys from the envelope, pressed the unlock button on the miniature remote that hung from the keychain, and sure enough, it was. "Really? Couldn't have picked a better car? At least a Camry would have sufficed. No use in crying over spilled milk I guess." After getting in the driver seat, and tossing the backpack in the back, he pulled out the info on the job:

Place of Incident: Winchester House, San Jose, CA
Time of Incident: Between 10pm-1am on Tuesday June 29, 2010
Suspects: None
Victims: Kyle and Kayla Nedly, Mike Long, Jackie Herbven, and John Ghent
Description: Five local teenagers had apparently broken into the attraction most likely to attempt to record some kind of evidence of any ghosts in the house (A video camera was found. It has been sent to Forensics to be viewed and dusted for prints). Four were found dead: Enormous scratches all over their bodies from what seems to be some kind of animal, and two of the victim's heads were separated from their bodies. An escaped animal such as a cougar or lion are possible explanations. Kayla Nedly has yet to be found. Theories of her being the killer are running around between the detectives on the case.

"I doubt a teenage girl would be able to kill four people. I guess it's possible it *could* be an animal. But I'm not sure if there were any reports of escaped animals though. Another problem with that is: how did it get in the house? The report didn't say anything about broken windows or unlocked doors. Only the window they came through. He put in the address of the house into the GPS on the dash. After putting his seatbelt on, the car was put into reverse, and then driven out of the garage onto the packed roads. "Where am I anyways?" He glanced at the GPS and saw that it said he was in the San Francisco area. "All the way down in San Francisco? Hopefully there won't be any earthquakes." He joked to himself.

After about an hour drive, he pulled onto the side of the road in front of a huge and beautiful house, that was about 4 stories high and

the windows were elegantly gilded. It was a house that could only look the way it did from thirty-eight years of constant building and remodeling. And of course a large amount of money. *Well, this is it.* He unbuckled his seatbelt and got out before noticing there was a van already parked outside. Taking out his disguise from out of the backpack, he zipped up his hoodie, put his mask and gloves on, and threw the hood over his head. He had almost forgotten about his gun that was hidden in the back of his pants. *I should ask Brev for a holster when I get back.* As he walked up to the house, he saw the side of the van with "Ghost Hunters plastered on its side door.

"Of course they would be here." He shook his head and continued for the house. A window was slightly open on the second story floor. *That's weird.* He climbed up some vines and carefully peered in through the window. No one was there. He quietly pushed open the window and stepped inside and listened for anyone on the second floor. It sounded like they were all downstairs. He could hear some yelling and freaking out coming from below. *Probably just pissing themselves over nothing.* He thought he should still check anyways. Almost tip-toeing he moved down the hallway towards the stairs. There were more yells and screams. Legitimate screams; not the kind you'd make just by hearing a weird noise. Immediately his gun was pulled out from his lower back, and he was dashing down the stairs to the sounds of the screams. At the bottom of the stairs was an unmoving body lying on the hardwood floor. He bent down to check for a pulse on the neck of the man's body that bore claw marks all down his chest and face. Nothing. "Shit." He couldn't hear anymore screams. The house was silent. He walked past the body to another doorway, and looked in it to find three more bodies laying there. All three pulses were gone. *Dammit.* He ran his hand through his hair in frustration. Frustration from not making it in time to save them. *I know it's partly their fault for this, but still. It's not right. I should have saved them. I should have came down here when I first heard them...* He turned to walk out of the room. Standing right in front of him was a shadow-like being. It didn't seem to have any feet, only a smoky bottom-half that resembled a Genie's, but had claws in place of hands, and its eyes were bright

yellow, piercing through his soul. Cloukora aimed his gun, but it was immediately knocked away, and he was thrown against the wall. Out of instinct, the fire scimitar appeared in his hands, and in a split second, it went through the thing's chest, causing it to fall towards the ground and disintegrate. He almost made the sword disappear until three more phased through the walls. His sword was readied for the attack.

All three lunged at him. They seemed to move slowly though in mid-air, and he could see how it would turn out; where they would land, where they would strike. He took this opportunity and spun, calculatingly slicing through each one, causing their "bodies" to disintegrate just as the first. After a moment of making sure there were no more "surprises" jumping out at him, he made the sword vanish, and his adrenaline was gone. His eyes felt like they were back to normal, but he was ready for anything else to pop out at him. In the corner of his eye, he saw a shadow move past the doorway to the kitchen, behind a staircase. Cloukora quickly picked his gun up from off the wood floor and moved into the kitchen to the staircase. When he looked behind it he mumbled "That can't be right." All that was there was a refrigerator next to the stairs. He glanced up the steps. "No, I'm sure it went behind the fridge." Grabbing a hold of it, he pulled it away from the wall and rotated so it would give room for a path to the wall. The bottom of the fridge had left black skid marks across the tile floor. "Oops." He went to the wall and studied it. There were no more doors, nor any creases or cracks that could signify one, just wall. He felt along the wall and noticed a part of it that felt different than the rest of the wall. Giving a slight push, it swung open, revealing a stone stairwell. "This must be one of Sarah Winchester's secret passages." Before he could take one step onto the stairs, he heard muffled crying coming from his left. Slowly, he began in the direction the sound was coming from, until he came upon a closet door. Leaning his ear against the door, he could hear whatever it was in there crying. Carefully, and hesitantly, he turned the door knob, and as soon as the door was open, he aimed his gun inside to find a blonde-haired girl huddled in the back. "Kayla?"

"Please…Please don't hurt me." The sight of his costume must have frightened her. When she spoke, her voice caught him off guard.

There was something about it. It was quite feminine, but it had a hint of masculinity in it, and it sounded forced. *Stop it; girls can have manly voices too.*

"Don't worry, I'm not going to. I'm actually here to help you." He lowered the gun and put out a hand for her. She grabbed a hold of it and hoisted herself up. "What happened?"

She was still shaking and scared, and most likely overwhelmed by grief. Tears had been running down her face ruining her mascara and makeup. "I-I don't know. The ghost killed all of my friends and…and my brother…and it tried attacking me, but when it touched me, it…it screamed in pain and ran off. I don't know where it went, I just knew I wanted to get out of here. I tried every door and window I could but it locked me in. If it couldn't kill me the easy way, it was going to let me die slowly. So I did the only thing I could: I found this closet and hid in here, and probably wait out my death, until you showed up."

"You said it yelled in pain when it touched you?" She nodded her head. "I'm not a ghost expert, but I know that doesn't usually happen. Ghosts being afraid of a human? That's just unheard of."

"It's not the first time that happened…"

"What do you mean?"

"I...Nothing. It's nothing."

"Kayla, I want to help you, but you have to help me first. Especially if this isn't the first time this has happened to you."

She sighed. "When I was younger, we lived in a house in Los Angeles. And…we didn't live there alone. We all knew there was a ghost living there, but no one cared because it hadn't harmed anyone. Until one night it came into my room, it scared the hell out of me. Just standing there next to my bed. It grabbed me by my shoulder and tried dragging me away, but it did the same thing the ghost here did. It screamed and fled, and left me to live with these scars." She pulled the neck of her shirt off her shoulder a little, showing three long, noticeable scars that made their way down to her chest area. The sight of it made Cloukora cringe. "I didn't tell anyone about it, not even my brother, and we are-were…close. You're the first person I ever told."

"How did you get out of the house then?"

"My parents wouldn't listen to me when I told them how scared I was living there. So, I used desperate measures and infested the house with roaches, my mom's biggest fear, and well, we hurried up and packed our stuff and got out."

"Good. Who knows what would have happened if you stayed. Now, let's get out of here. But first, we have to take a detour."

"Where?"

Cloukora strode back into the kitchen where the stone staircase was as Kayla followed right behind him. "Down here."

"Why?" She asked when she joined him at the top of the stairs. When he turned to look at her, he could see a small, almost unnoticeable lump in her throat. *Nah, there's a lot of girls that have an Adam's apple.*

"Because that thing went down there. And I need to stop it."

"Do I *have* to go?"

"You can stay up here if you'd like." Cloukora suggested.

"I'll go." She knew anywhere else was better than staying up in that house.

They were hesitant at first, but had finally pushed themselves to go down the stone staircase. It felt like being in an old tower from the medieval times. There were even torches lit going down along the stairs. Eventually, they came to a cave-like area with a low roof, but it was made out of dirt instead of rock. He noticed a dusty book sitting on a wooden table over to the left side of the cave with a lantern near it, and started towards it. As he walked closer, he heard a voice speak from behind them.

"You must be Cloukora, I've been looking for you." Cloukora and Kayla turned to see a pudgy old man roughly in his sixties or seventies. The man wore clothes that were worn in the 1800's and a black bowler hat on his head.

"Who are you? And how do you know who I am?" Cloukora was ready to defend themselves with either the gun or the sword of fire, even if that meant showing Kayla who he truly was.

"My name is Oliver Winchester. And I know many things."

Birth

"Oliver Winchester? You created the Winchester rifle, didn't you?" Cloukora relaxed a little bit and lessened his grip on the pistol in his hand.

"Yes, and I have been meaning to speak to you."

"Speak to me about what?"

"First off, that book over there." Oliver put out his hand and the book flew right into its grasp. "This book, is the Book of King Relyt. There is a great deal of information in this thing that I think you may find useful."

"I thought all evidence of Atlantis was destroyed?"

"Well yes, but one of Relyt's descendants thought there should be at least some record of themselves. So, they wrote this book, explaining a lot of the mysteries of the world, as well as the enemies Atlantis faced, and the life of King Relyt."

"I'm sorry, Atlantis?" Kayla asked curiously. Cloukora thought she was probably thinking he was crazy now. Or even perhaps she thought *she* was going crazy.

"W-why are you giving me this?" Cloukora asked cautiously.

"Because you're going to need it in the future. That includes the near future as well." Oliver seemed to grimace at the last part.

"What do you mean?" Cloukora asked.

Oliver sighed before continuing. "I'm not really supposed to tell you this-"

"No one is lately."

"-But… The end of all is drawing near, Lucifer is coming back, and he's going to rain hell upon the Earth to try and take it for himself. For some reason the Angels aren't mobilizing yet. And I don't know if they will either. The apocalypse is coming, Cloukora, and you're the one to stop it. This book will help you do just that."

"Of course it's me…I don't see why I'm so important, but I guess I am. May I ask you something though?"

"Sure."

"How do you know all of this?" He asked curiously.

He was silent for a moment. "I am one of the Four Horsemen. The Horseman of Conquest." Cloukora almost summoned the fire sword

until he quickly added: "Don't worry, I'm not here to harm. I do not wish to see the apocalypse happen. I already made the mistake by creating the vile weapon that I had made."

Cloukora relaxed himself once again. "Conquest…I guess that makes sense. Your rifle *had* technically conquered the world. You have my word that I *will* prevent the apocalypse from happening. I swear, on my life, that the world will never fall under the hands of evil."

"You don't need to promise me anything, I already believed in you from the start. However, before you go, I must show you something that will help achieve your victory. If I'm not mistaken, you can summon a sword of fire, can't you?"

"Yeah, that's right." Cloukora replied. Kayla had a confused look on her face and looked as if she was about to run back upstairs and away from this nonsense. But she stayed; curiosity is a powerful thing.

"That sword is called Fyron. It is one of four swords that when combined, can stop Lucifer from taking over the world. I will show you how to summon Terra, the sword of earth. First, put your hand over the ground." Cloukora was uncertain about it, but he did as instructed. "Now, concentrate. Connect with the earth and feel it flow through you, and then form the sword in your hand." Cloukora closed his eyes, and calmed himself. Trying to connect just as the man- or ghost- said, he thought he felt something for a moment. "Clear your thoughts, connect with the earth, form the sword." Cloukora kept his eyes shut. This time he definitely felt something, and when he did, he felt the earth begin to move. He opened his eyes in shock and lost both the concentration and connection. The ground sunk back into the earth. "Calm, connect, form." Cloukora nodded, and tried once more. This time, the earth moving didn't bug him. He felt earth flowing into his hand, hardening, becoming a solid form, and after a moment, he opened his eyes again. In his hand was a longsword that seemed solid, but at the same time, it seemed like it could fall apart at any time. "You can let it go now." When he did, the sword broke apart into chunks of dirt and fell back into the earth. "For the other two swords, I cannot say how to obtain them, or if you even can."

"Why wouldn't I be able to?"

Birth

"Apparently, few were able to wield all four elements. One would have been lucky to have been able to wield two."

"So, wait. Did you have those people killed just to bring me here?" If Oliver said the wrong answer, Fyron would be in his hand in an instant and through the ghost's body.

"No, I wouldn't do such a thing. I didn't even know you'd be here today, I was going to appear at your house, but you weren't there. And if a spirit did it, I *would* know about it. I'm sorry to cut things short, but I must go now, I have stayed longer than I have been granted. But before I do, Kayla. I am terribly sorry about your friends and your brother, and I wish I could bring them back, or at least kill whoever or whatever did it, but alas I cannot. It pains me to see ghosts going mad and killing innocent people. What I want to tell you though, is that there is a gift inside you. A divine blessing. What powers come along with it, I am not sure. Perhaps one day you will find out what it exactly is and what your purpose is. For now, I would be careful. Do not tell anyone of this power. There are beings that would try to harm you or use your powers for evil. You mustn't let yourself get in their hands. Understand?" Kayla nodded and Oliver handed Cloukora the dusty old book before he took a step back away from them. Cloukora hurriedly put the gun back into the back of his pants so he could accept the book from Oliver. "Goodbye Kayla. Goodbye Cloukora, and I wish you luck and safety on your quest." Oliver's image flickered, and then disappeared.

"Heh, with my life, there's no such thing as safe." He summoned Terra into his hand. This time, he did it with ease. "So they have names then, huh?" He made Terra fall to the ground before he turned to head out up the stairs.

"Who are you? *What* are you?"

"I could ask the same thing." Cloukora remarked. He took a deep breath. "I am someone who has a special gift, just like you, and I have to use it to protect people, to save them. And I would do it with my life, without a second thought. I am someone who would bleed for strangers, and I would even shed blood for them. I am what you would call a hero."

"A...hero?" She raised her eyebrow as if he were crazy. Maybe he was. Maybe this was all one huge hallucination.

"Yes, and I ask you not to tell anyone about what you saw. It would endanger me and my family. As it would yours if you told anyone about your gift."

"Don't worry, your secret is safe with me. Can we get out of here now? I can't handle being in here anymore." Cloukora nodded and they walked back up the stairs and outside; Cloukora broke a window to create an exit.

"Need a ride?" He asked as they walked through the clean-cut green lawn to the sidewalk in front of the house.

She shook her head. "No thanks, my house isn't that far from here, I'll be fine."

"You sure?"

She sighed. "Yeah...after all, I am going to have to get used to not having a big brother to protect me..." She frowned. Cloukora felt bad for her. He wished he could do something for her, to make her feel better. He wanted to hug her, but he didn't think a hug would be enough. Plus he thought that would be a little awkward. "I hope you do complete your quest, Cloukora. For the sake of the world."

"Yeah, I do too..." She started off down the sidewalk before turning back around and wrapping her arms around him.

"Thank you."

"It's no problem." The hug felt weird. He thought breasts would be softer, but her chest felt hard, almost as if she wore a bra with nothing there for it *to* support. They both let go and turned their separate ways; her walking the way she had started, and him towards his car. As he was about to pull on the door handle, it dawned on him. "Son of a bitch, I knew it." He looked back at Kayla, who was already a house down. *Should I say something? I mean, what if she's not? Or what if she is and she doesn't want it to be pointed out? But what if she needs support?* "Hey Kayla!" Kayla stopped and looked back. "Stay strong. This hard part of your life will *transition* into something beautiful." Before he could hear a hesitated and flustered "Thank you" he opened the car door and got in.

When he got in the driver seat, he opened up a page about King Relyt, and began reading some of it. What he read was what his grandfather had already told him: the powers, family history, and a little about Relyt. He turned the page and was shocked at what he saw. What he saw was neither a painting nor portrait, but a *picture* of Relyt. As if it had been taken with a digital camera. That wasn't what had shocked him though, it was Relyt himself. He was the spinning image of Cloukora. Hair, face, eyes, everything, the only thing slightly different was the age, and probably tallness. He closed the book and set it on the passenger seat. "Weirder and weirder." He pulled out his phone and called Brev. "I'm done, so whenever you're done doing whatever, you can pick me up."

"Alright, meet me back at the building I dropped you off at. Oh, did you get a chance to kill any ghosts with your gun?"

"I didn't get to fire a single shot off, sorry. Why?"

"I did something to your bullets to see if they would kill any ghosts, but it's fine. I'm getting in the chopper now so I gotta go. Bye."

The call ended, and he put his phone away, and then drove off back to Los Angeles as everything that happened in that house finally hit him. Oliver telling him the apocalypse is coming and only he can stop it. Only he could fight Lucifer. Something he wasn't ready to do. He wasn't strong enough. Worst of all, those bodies, those people dead in there. The people he couldn't save. He was supposed to be a hero, something he had even told Kayla he was, and yet he couldn't save them from a *ghost*. How was he going to save the world?

A shadow with claws and yellow eyes phased through the wall of the house, and to a purple-coated man standing in the street watching a grey Prius drive away. The shadow formed into a somewhat built man with long pitch black hair, with the bangs going to one side and covering his left dark brown eye. A Scottish claymore was sheathed behind his back. He wore brown cargo pants, a Slayer T-shirt, and a pair of black Airwalk skate shoes. "So that's him then?" he asked.

"Yes…Cloukora. The one who stands in my way." The purple-coated man said, watching the car turn around a corner and out of sight.

"He is a good swordsman. I hope to face him myself." Venn grinned

"That he is. I should know." The man grinned as well before walking away. "You will face him Venn, when the time comes. Be warned though, *I* am the one to kill him."

"What about the girl? Do you think she-he-or whatever will be a problem?"

"It's she."

"Look at you, being all politically correct. I admit, she's actually pretty hot."

"I wouldn't let Ava hear you say that. And no, she won't be. All she has is a gift to keep spirits from harming her. Nothing more. There's no need to deal with her." Suddenly, dragon-like wings spread out from his back, and he flew up and into the air before Venn could say another word to him.

"Cloukora, you have no idea what's coming to you." Venn turned and walked the opposite direction before spreading brown angel-like wings and taking flight into the blue sky.

Birth

Angel's Gaiden

Blood Thirst

July 5, 2010
Forest Grove, Oregon

    Cloukora had been sitting in the wooden oak chair on his front porch when Brev's Corolla pulled up. He had a cigarette in between his lips and fingers, puffing smoke out every few seconds. He wore a Van Halen: Hot for Teacher shirt, with a woman probably from the sixties on it, lying somewhat provocatively with an apple in her hand. His eyes said that he was far off somewhere else in his mind, thinking. Debating whether or not he was cut out to be a hero, if this was the life for him; the life he was meant to live. The rugged and worn book sat a few feet away from him on the porch couch. He had been reading it a lot since he had received it from Oliver Winchester. There were so many things that he never knew of. Or knew the truth to. The sun stood high in the clear, blue sky with not a cloud to bother it. The church bells rang from across the baseball field across the street. He knew that meant it was around twelve in the afternoon. Taking the cigarette out of his mouth, he exhaled some smoke, and flicked the ashes on to the ground.

    He only glanced at her as she walked up the narrow path to the porch steps. She was wearing a grey V-neck tee, short green cargo shorts that reached down only to her mid-thigh, and a pair of Converse sneakers. And of course her aviator sunglasses shielding her eyes. Her outfits seemed to be getting more and more casual. "Why haven't you been answering my calls?" She stopped short of the steps and crossed her arms. She shook her head when she noticed the cigarette and continued up the steps to sit on the porch railing in front of him. "You shouldn't smoke, no matter the reason. It's not good for your health,

Birth

and it doesn't help like you may think." Cloukora didn't answer, just took another drag and watched the sky. "How did you even get a hold of it anyways?"

He snapped. "You just don't get it." He threw the cigarette angrily at the ground and stood up. "Maybe you've seen a lot in your career, but what I saw- what I saw in that house, it wasn't right. The way that thing *butchered* them…I wasn't even able to kill the damned thing! Sure I got Kayla out of there, but that doesn't change the fact I didn't save them."

"It wasn't your fault. You know as well as I do, that they shouldn't have been there in the first place-"

"But they *were* there, Brev. I can't get those images out of my head. They're gonna haunt me for the rest of my *life*. I could have saved them, but I didn't. If I had went downstairs the first time they screamed, maybe they'd be alive."

Brev sighed. "May 17, 2001." Cloukora looked at her, a little confused as he sat back down on the wooden chair. "I was with the FBI at the time, before I joined Wolfstorm. I was working on a case tracking down a psychopath serial killer. We didn't have much to go on, not even a pattern; he killed anyone he wanted to, without leaving a single print. Until, he slipped up and tried to kill a lady in front of a store. Luckily, that store had a camera that saw the crime, and caught his face, so we were able to track him to a cabin in the woods. What we didn't know, was that he had kidnapped a young boy, and by the time we got there…the boy was…he was gone. He must have somehow known we were coming, because the coroner said that he was killed just five minutes before we had got there. Even though we had finally caught him, I still blame myself for that kid's death. To this day, no matter how many people I've saved in my line of work, it cannot make up for that boy's death, or any other that I've failed to save. However, I've come to realize, that I've prevented uncountable casualties, and that…that has slowly made me feel better. It has made me feel at peace with myself. It's the reason why I keep going. It's why I'm still with Wolfstorm. Why I still save people." She waited for something, but

Birth

after no answer, she stood up and went towards her car, shaking her head again.

She was right, and he knew it. Just because he lost a few people doesn't mean he shouldn't give up on everyone else. He suddenly felt as if he were a child that had thrown a tantrum because things wouldn't go his way. As she was midway to it, he finally said: "Heroes don't turn their backs on the world. No matter how small the threat is. They don't take a day off of saving the world just because they're not feeling so great. They're there to risk their life for the life of another, no matter the condition they're in, or the risk. If I'm going to be a hero, then I'm not going to do any different. I will be there whether it's a small house fire, or, Heaven forbid, an evil villain threatens the world. My life will be dedicated to this Earth, and everything on it. I, Cloukora Skyrell, swear on my life, that I will never turn my back on anyone, or anything, no matter how dire the situation."

Brev turned to him. "Cloukora…"

Sighing he said "I guess what I'm trying to say is, I'll help you." He got up, picked back up the cigarette and put it out in the ashtray, grabbed the book, and went inside to grab his disguise and gun. As he walked to Brev and her car he said: "And by the way, I got it from my step-dad. He doesn't know though, so don't tell him. He'll kick my ass."

"Don't worry, I won't tell." Brev said mockingly and with a smile. "Good to have you back."

"I didn't go anywhere." He gave a half-smile and sat in the passenger seat of the Corolla. "So, what's the case?"

"There's been a string of disappearances from a club throughout the past few months. At first it didn't seem like our type of case, until someone wound up dead in the middle of the dance floor last night."

"So how does that make it our case?"

"Not *one* person in the club cared or even tried to help."

"How did they even find the victim then?"

"Her mother called the police to check out the club to see if she was alright, because she hadn't come home that night."

"Ahh. So where is this club?"

"Salem."

"Well, that's a bit of ways, isn't it."
"Yep."

They pulled into the open parking space in front of a 7-11. She grabbed the key and before turning it off, asked if he wanted anything.

"Eh, I'll go in with you." He unbuckled his seatbelt and got out of the car as she did the same.

As soon as they walked inside the store, there was a rush of cool air. Even though they were only outside for a second, it felt as though the heat probably could have cooked an egg. There were several rows of short shelves in the middle of the store: one had products for electronics such as batteries and video games, another had magazines and other miscellaneous items, and the rest had food stocked on them. The left wall was lined with fridges to keep items cool. Half of the back wall had a small section for deli sandwiches and the sort, and the other half had a slushy machine. The right side was taken up mostly by the cashier counter. Cloukora went to the fridges and got a bottle of Dr. Pepper and grabbed a small bag of chips from one of the aisles.

"Is that everything?" the cashier asked.

"Yeah, that's it." Brev answered as she laid her stuff down on the counter which only consisted of a Gatorade and a bag of chips as well.

"That will be eight ninety six." She handed the cashier a ten-dollar bill, and he traded her the change. "Thank you, have a nice day."

"You too." Brev said as she and Cloukora grabbed their things off of the counter.

As they walked out the door, Cloukora's phone rang. It was his grandfather calling him back. "Hey, grandpa."

"You said you needed to talk to me?"

"Yeah, you wouldn't believe what I found." As he got in the car, he grabbed the book from off the floor. "It's a book that has every record of the Atlantis history. The wars, Relyt, Avalon, The Reapers, everything." Brev got in and turned the key before pulling out of the small parking lot.

"Where did you find it? There shouldn't be *anything* that tells the truth of Atlantis."

"Apparently someone wrote about it. You know how I asked about the inconsistency of Plato and the era Relyt lived in? I found something on it."

"Oh really? What does it say?"

"I guess the author visited a descendant of Plato and asked them about his writing of Atlantis. Turns out, it was a vision after all. And Plato knew it was a vision too, but he didn't want to risk being called out as a witch, so he made a story out of it. To still get what he saw out there, but without the danger. The Hercules' Pillars he mentioned aren't literal, but metaphorical; America and Japan are two of the strongest countries in the world, and Atlantis lies right between them. It goes on about it more and clears it all up, but I didn't call you because of that. I called you because I found something else. Listen to this: And when Relyt's soul shall return, he will take his place upon his throne as the true king, and shall exercise his judgment upon all those who oppose him. His might will flip the Earth onto its head. His presence will cleanse and purify the world, purging evil from the hearts of man. His intelligence will unite the people. His blade will strike down his enemies. And rivers of blood and death shall flow from where he stands." Brev looked at him, confused. "This sounds like something out of the friggin Book of Revelations. Was Relyt a god in his time or something?"

"No, but some people looked up to him as one, because of the immense power he held."

"Well, it sounds like he's supposed to return, just like you said. I haven't found anything on when though. I'll keep looking into it. It's weird though, he looks *exactly* like me."

"And how do you even know what he looks like?"

"There's a picture of him in the book. Not a painting, but like, a digital photo."

"Really? Hm, guess they were more advanced than we had thought. I gotta go now, your grandmother's home. Bye." The phone on the other end clicked and he hung up as well.

Birth

"Something the matter?" Brev asked sympathetically.

"What? No. No, I'm fine. Just thinking." He turned to watch outside his window for the rest of the drive.

Salem, Oregon

They finally reached the city after about an hour of driving. They parked in front of a building with a –what would be lit in the night - neon sign that said: The Lair.

"A bit of a weird name for a club." Cloukora remarked as he knuckled his back and stretched when he got out of the car. They didn't stop at all on the way, and it hadn't been all that comfortable for him. "So, FBI agents again?"

"Can't risk it. First sight of law enforcement, and we'll probably end up at the bottom of a river."

"It's just a club?" He asked as if nothing else should be expected, as he zipped on the white and grey hoodie and put on his mask that covered the bottom half of his face, his gloves, and the holster he recently got from Brev.

"Doesn't feel that way." She seemed a little eager to go in, and perhaps a little angry. Cloukora thought it best to just listen to her. She was, after all, the leader.

"Do we got a plan?"

"The plan is to follow me." She checked her gun, and cocked it before she put it back in her holster. Cloukora put his hood up, and did the same. Cloukora followed her in, and made sure to stay close.

The club music was loud, despite the lack of it outside. The bartender was serving drinks, of course, and people were dancing in the middle of the dance floor to some kind of techno music. It looked like any other club to him, and when he mentioned it to Brev, she just ignored him and kept walking towards the back. There were two big, burly guys guarding a door that led further to the back. One of them put their hand up, and said, "You guys aren't allowed back here."

Brev simply said: "The bat takes flight when the moon shines upon the night."

Cloukora didn't understand what it meant, but they were let in. "Brev, what's going on?"

"I'm meeting an old friend." They were led even further back, through a large, empty, concrete room that Cloukora wasn't sure what it could be used for, to another door, which opened to a staircase leading downwards. At the bottom, was another room. This room had a grey marble floor, and blood red wallpaper. On the other side of the room, was a bed which was already occupied by man with two beautiful women that were in only their underwear. It made Cloukora a little nervous being in the same room.

The man slid off the bed and strode towards them both. "Brev! Long time no see. It's been years, hasn't it? How have you been?" As he got nearer, Cloukora could make out his appearance. He was tall, and had short gray hair, but a younger looking face, and his eyes were dark brown. He sported a dark blue suit, with the tie loosened. "So good to see you again." He took her hand and bent to kiss it, but it was pulled away from him before he could.

"Cut the crap, Nathan. What the hell do you think you're doing?" If her eyes were swords, they would have pierced right through the man's skull. She was furious, and Cloukora was glad he was not the other man.

"I believe I'm trying to enjoy my life. And my birthday, if you don't mind. What do *you* think I'm doing?"

"I don't know, maybe supplying our blood to innocent people, making them disappear, along with a chain of murders." She said as if he should know

"I have no clue what you're talking about." He said sarcastically with a smug face as he went over to a small bar to pour himself a glass of whiskey.

She reached into her pocket, and tossed a syringe with a red liquid inside of it to the ground. It must have been made out of a special glass because it didn't shatter when it hit the concrete. "Then what the hell is that?"

"I honestly have no clue. That is not mine. That's not even blood!"

"It sure as hell looks like it."

"It sure as hell isn't! As I said, I'm just living it up, before my time expires. Whatever this is," He pointed at the needle. "This is not mine nor my people's doing."

Brev sniffed. "Before your time expires." She shook her head. "Dammit, Nathan! Enough playing dumb! I *know* what kind of man you are! My team ran tests and your blood showed up! It's a perfect match."

Nathan took a sip of his drink. "You know, I recall…helping a little girl in need when she was on the verge of death, and now, she stands here and disrespects me like this!? Even though I've done *nothing* to her. If you really knew me, you would know that I wouldn't do something as stupid as give humans our blood-Oh that bitch."

"What?"

"Not long ago, I met a girl here at my club, a nice blonde hottie, and well, we kinda seduced each other and came down to the bedroom. We might have had a few too many drinks and a little too much drugs because I felt a pinch like a needle at the back of my neck, and I felt it, but I didn't even really think about it until now. That blonde bitch stole my blood!"

"Oh c'mon Nathan, you think I'll fall for that? That wouldn't have been the first time you put the blame on someone else. How dare-"

"No, how dare YOU bring a human into *my* territory and turn around and accuse me of such crimes!" His eyes turned pitch black and fangs appeared as he strolled over to Brev. Cloukora tried to stop him, but was held back by a guard he hadn't noticed before. Brev was also grasped in the arms of another guard as Nathan's hand slapped across her face, and Cloukora struggled even more to get out the guard's hold. *How is this guard so strong?* Cloukora's adrenaline flowed through his veins, and his pupils formed the Skyrell crest as always when his adrenaline pulsed inside of him. He noticed Brev's eyes changed too, but they were pitch black, like Nathan's, and she had protruded fangs instead of normal teeth coming out of her gums.

"Wait, you two are *vampires*?!" Cloukora asked with horror.

"Whoever is giving humans that crap, it is not me. I'm telling you they stole my blood! For what reason, I don't know. What I do know, is right now I have a price on my head from betraying a vampire mob a few months ago. I would rather crawl into a hole before going and doing something like pollute the human population. I am trying to stay as low as possible."

"All the more reason for you to create an army. If you had enough soldiers, you could kill the mob and be free from the bounty." Cloukora remarked.

Nathan pointed at Cloukora. "This guy. This guy is smart. Where did you find him?" After noticing Cloukora's eyes, he took a step back, shock appearing on his face. "He has the Skyrell eyes." Cocking his head he said. "Wait, I know why you picked him." He turned toward Brev with a grin on his face. "That is just beautiful Brev. That is *beautiful*."

"Shut up, Nathan. That has nothing to do with why we chose him." Brev bared her teeth. Whatever it was, he had pissed her off.

"Oh he - he doesn't know, does he?"

"I said shut up."

Nathan put his hands up. "Alright, alright. I'll honor your wish. As for the blood, ever thought maybe it's that organization you've been going at it with? Hm? No, you just want to point the finger at me."

"How do *you* know about the organization?"

"As someone who can't leave his own home, the only way to know about what's going on in the world is through my eyes and ears. And some of my guys overheard some people mentioning you and your organization."

"What did they say?"

"I don't remember, something about how you're more of a nuisance than a problem. I wasn't paying attention."

"I think you're lying."

"I think you're a bitch." Brev got loose of the guard and swiped long fingernails across his face. Cloukora forgot vampires get claws too. Holding his face, Nathan commanded the guards. "Take these two out of here!" He commanded the guards. Both of the men grabbed their

Birth

arms and led them out. As they were in the concrete room upstairs, almost to the door, Nathan had followed up. "Actually, I got a better idea. I'll kill them." The guards turned Brev and Cloukora to face Nathan, who held an ornately decorated bastard sword in his hand. As he neared, Cloukora concentrated, making Terra appear in his hand, and quickly caused the earth by the wall to sink, creating a hole in the wall and allowing sunlight to shine through right on Nathan. He then elbowed the guard in the ribs, and proceeded with a swift elbow to the head, knocking the man unconscious. Cloukora gave Nathan a smirk.

"AH! AH! IT BURNS!!!NOOO!!NO! No oh ho ho. Hehehe. You really thought that would kill me? Oh, you fool." Nathan's hand pointed at Cloukora and suddenly his hand moved towards the outside of the hole, causing Cloukora to be thrown in that direction, Terra disappearing while flying through the air. When he hit the ground, he rolled a couple times before stopping in the middle of the street. Surprisingly, the impact didn't seem to be as painful as he thought it would be. In fact, it felt like he had only just fell off a bicycle, or a skateboard, nothing more. Though that's not to say that there weren't any cuts or scrapes on his face. Nathan stepped out through the giant hole in the wall, onto the pile of rubble, and shook his head. "Ancient vampires like me, have become immune to the sunlight over-" Cloukora had quickly got on his knee, drew his gun, and fired three shots into the vampire's chest. The man didn't even flinch as he pulled out one of the bullets that struck his heart. The other two bullets were pushed out of his body as it regenerated and healed itself. "You're getting annoying."

Despite the failed attempt, Cloukora was a little relieved he wore his disguise, for there were people standing around them. Most of them were on phones; most likely talking to either people they knew like family and friends, or calling nine-one-one. Others just stared and watched, but all had made sure they stayed back a safe distance. "Guess there's only one thing left I can do." He didn't have to try very hard to get his adrenaline pumping even more; his eyes still that of the Skyrell crest. Cloukora put the gun back into his holster, and made Fyron appear in his right hand. The scimitar was enveloped in fire, so much

that it was a wonder to Cloukora that it didn't burn his hand. He gripped the hilt with his other hand, and charged at Nathan, his sword ready to swing, and when it did, it met with Nathan's. They both were pushed off of each other, and Cloukora went for another swing, clashing with Nathan's and bouncing off, then another swing, and another, until Cloukora was kicked backwards by Nathan's foot. Both had sweat dripping down their faces, from both fighting and the heat radiating from Fyron, and both of their chests were breathing heavily.

"I haven't had a challenge as good as this in a long, long time. This is quite exciting." Nathan's pitch black eyes seemed to stare into Cloukora, and those fangs...those fangs looked like they wanted to taste his flesh. Cloukora readied his sword, in case he made a move. In a split second, Nathan was right in front of him and Cloukora swung Fyron, but it only sliced air. He quickly whirled and swung behind him. Again, only hit air. "Not fast enough." He felt his neck hairs rise, and it made him have Terra reappear, and he quickly spun the sword, blade pointing backwards, then thrust it behind him. He could feel the sword pierce Nathan, and he heard a sword clatter to the ground. Cloukora let go of Terra, and turned to face the man, or rather vampire. Nathan yelped in pain as he strained pulling the sword out of his abdomen. Before it could be drawn out, Fyron had slashed through his torso. His body transformed into ash and fell to the ground as it was picked up by the wind.

Cloukora had Terra and Fyron dissolve, and he started to feel the adrenaline slowly settle down until he felt normal again. He saw all the eyes of the people around him, staring, wondering. He thought they probably harbored some fear towards him. *They must be horrified. Then again, who wouldn't be? I mean, they just witnessed me kill someone. It doesn't matter if it* was *a vampire, they didn't know.* He saw Brev in the shadows of the building, and he nodded to her, turned around and paced off down the alley. They would have to get back home a different way. Too many people were there; someone would notice the license plate of the car.

Cloukora sat at a table in the Starbucks on the corner a few blocks down from The Lair. He had turned his hoodie inside out, for it was the only way to not draw attention without throwing the thing away. His gloves, holster and his mask were in the pockets and his gun in the back of his pants. He wasn't about to throw those out either. Brev came through the glass door, and walked towards him, barely having to look around for him. He didn't know if he would be able to get over the fact that she was what she was.

"I didn't know you were a coffee person." She said as she sat down.

"I'm not, it's hot chocolate." Part of him didn't even want to talk to her.

She sighed. "I'm sorry. I probably should have told you. But I didn't want to scare you off. We need you, Cloukora."

Cloukora shook his head. "I don't even know what to do. Part of me says I should kill you right where you stand." She didn't even flinch at the suggestion. "But a small part of me, says to be rational about this. And…I guess if you were going to kill me, you would have done it by now." He was silent for a moment, and so was she. Even though she was so still, he was sure she felt like she was waiting to hear her sentence: Life or death. He sighed heavily. "You're in the clear…for now."

"That's what makes you so great, Cloukora. You have a heart, you give people second chances. And that makes a good hero."

Cloukora nodded in agreement. "I suppose."

"So, are there any questions you have?"

"Nathan said ancient vampires are immune to the sunlight, and you seem to have no problem with it. I'm guessing you're one too, right?"

"Yes, I am. So is Cal."

"Cal?"

"Yes. Nathan, Cal, and I grew up together in the early 1300's. We were all such great friends. Without each other, we wouldn't have ever survived. Then, the Black Plague hit, and I wasn't strong enough to overcome it, and it took my life. Nathan, having already been a

Birth

vampire, couldn't deal with my death. So he dug up my grave, and turned me. I was grateful for what he did, I really was, but I had fallen in love with Cal. Jealous as Nathan was, he killed Cal. I couldn't believe what he had done, and I didn't know why he killed him at the time, so I told him I never wanted to see him again. Then, he left, and I never saw him again until the early 1900's."

"And I'm guessing you turned Cal, too. Right?"

Brev nodded. "We should probably get to the car before it's too late, and cops show up."

"Wait, before we go, what was Nathan talking about?"

"What do you mean?"

"He said he knew why you chose me. The way he looked at me…It's been bugging me."

"It's nothing, just Nathan being…Nathan. Don't worry about it."

"If we're going to be working together, I have to start trusting you. So, I trust you. I figured it was nothing anyway." They got up and walked out the door, Cloukora holding the door open for Brev. "Hey, at least you don't sparkle, 'cause then you *would* be dead by now." He gave a smile to show it was a joke, and she only laughed and shook her head. The trip back to the car and on the way back home was quiet, but peaceful.

Angel's Gaiden

The King Reborn

July 7, 2010
Forest Grove, Oregon

    Cloukora sat at his desk, chair leaned back and feet out, while Rhain lay on the floor in the sunlight, as he read over Relyt's biography for the fifth time:

> *King Relyt Skyrell was the king of Atlantis as well as a pioneer in technology and warfare. Few have dared to challenge him and his country, and each nation that tried, failed in doing so. Relyt wasn't a merciless leader, he let his challengers go, but with a warning: if they ever so much as looked like they were to go against him again, they would be crushed in an instant. He made sure everyone in his land got what they needed: food, money, shelter; the basic things. His nation was one of the Great Four: Atlantis, Avalon, Vikings, and Reapers (Origins unknown).*

    Most of it was what his grandfather already told him. But what kept eating at him, was the part about Relyt's powers. According to the book, Relyt was not only the only one to be able to control all four elements, but the only one to control the wind element. It also states that a sword he had created sank along with the city of Atlantis. The sword was meant to be all of the four elemental swords put into one, and it was made out of the strongest metal ever known: Orichalcum. When Relyt wished it, it would disappear, and when he wanted it, it would appear in the same spot where it was last. The power was mostly

Birth

used to make Relyt's enemies think he was unarmed, and weak, so he could have the upper hand in small fights, such as tavern or street fights.

He put the book down, propped his elbows on his desk and ran his fingers through his hair. *What if I-*. He shut the thought out before he could finish it. "I must be going crazy. Thinking I'm some king reincarnated just because he looks like me." He half-believed what he told himself. Something was keeping him from giving up the thought. It wouldn't let him deny the fact completely, no matter how irrational it seemed. *More irrational things have happened.* He shook his head, trying to shake the idea away, not wanting to think about it anymore, at least for the time being. Getting up out of his chair he walked down the stairs to the fridge to take out a soda. He leaned back against the washer in the kitchen area, opened up the can of Coca-Cola and watched the world outside. The sun had to be high in the sky, or at least more to the east, because he wasn't able to see it through the window. The sky was bright blue and no clouds were in sight. The Rocky Mountains rolled off into the distance. He saw birds zip across the backyard back and forth, from one tree to another, and to another, and so forth. His eyes came across the huge above-ground pool sitting out in the yard. After hesitating for a moment, he said "Worth a shot." He exited through the back door and headed towards the pool.

For being twelve in the afternoon, it was pretty hot. Luckily, there was *some* cool wind that blew and immediately took away the heat. He took a sip of his soda, before setting it down on the ground next to the pool. "Energy is needed for fire; focus for earth. What would be water…?" He thought about it for awhile, trying to figure it out. "Calmness." He took a deep breath, put his hand over the water, and let his thoughts drift away, bringing him peace of mind. Water began to form into his hand. It took most of his effort to keep the thought of being Relyt's reincarnation away. Finally, his mind was at peace, and the sword took shape in his hand, but it was oddly shaped. The grip was wrapped in aqua blue cloth-like material with light gold thread making wave forms around the grip several times. The hand guard was on a side of the grip, rather than above it, and it was fashioned into a curved blade, almost like a butterfly sword. Instead of a pommel, there was

steel sharpened into a dagger. The weirdest part of the sword was the blade itself: it was in no way sharp. In fact it was thick, and it curved at the end to resemble a kind of hook. It was as if someone smelted a long crowbar with the rest of it. He realized what kind of sword it was: a hook sword; he remembered reading about them in the book. They weren't meant for slicing, but more for disarming and breaking bones. Of course, this wasn't a traditional hook sword; those are usually flattened instead of being thick, but it was close enough in form to be called one. Suddenly, an identical one appeared in his other hand. These twin blades, he remembered, were called Vesi and Neró. "Three elements…Maybe I am…" His thoughts were interrupted when he remembered his mom was on her way home, and quickly, he made the swords disappear. Of course, similar to Terra, they turned into water before they fell to the ground. He grabbed his soda and walked back to the house. As he was, he pulled out his phone and began dialing his uncle's number.

"Hello?" his uncle answered.

"Hey, I'm guessing grandpa told you about the book I found and what I learned from it, right?"

"Yeah, why?"

"Well, I have a crazy theory." It took him a moment to come out with it. "Maybe I'm Relyt's reincarnation."

"Relyt's reincarnation? It's not so crazy, considering the prophecy in the book. But are you *sure*?"

"No, but if I'm able to control the wind element…then I am. Which brings me to my next question; you can't teach me to use it, can you?"

"Sorry, I can't. No one can. Relyt was the only one who could manipulate it."

Cloukora sighed. "Damn, I figured as much. Alright, I'll try to find another way. Thanks anyways."

"Although…there might be someone…I'm not supposed to really be talking about it, but this is an exception."

"Who?"

Birth

"He hides out in Scotland somewhere. Some mountains I last remembered. I don't know the names of them though."

"That's good enough for me; I can probably figure it out from there. Thanks."

"Yep, good luck."

Cloukora hung up and dialed Brev's number. "Brev?"

"Yeah?" she asked. Cloukora could pick out sounds from other cars, she must be driving.

"I need a favor. I need you to fly me to Scotland."

"Sorry, I'm a little busy today. I'll contact HQ and have them arrange something. They should be able to help you."

He let out a sigh. "Fine, just don't get Winter to do it. She scares me." She said bye with a slight chuckle, and then hung up. His mom pulled up in the red Durango as he almost made it to the back door.

"Hey mom, I found somewhere to go while you have your, uh, baby shower thing."

"And where's that?" She grabbed a couple of bags before hopping out of the driver seat.

"Jake's house." He hoped she wouldn't catch on that they never hung out in the summer.

"You're always going to a friend's house lately. You have a ride there, right?"

"Yeah, I think so. I'm waiting to hear back from them to see if they can pick me up." Cloukora followed her into the house.

"You know if you had a driver's license…"

"I know, I know, I've been working on my driving as best as I can. Besides, I don't have enough at the moment to pay for one."

"That reminds me. I want you to find a job. You're seventeen, you need to get out there and look for one."

"Yeah, work at McDonald's? No. Never going to happen."

"You can't be picky. No one likes their first job."

"I know I'm not going to like my first job. I just don't want one that I'm going to hate and dread going to every morning."

His mom sighed, and before she could say anything, Cloukora's phone rang. He answered it, and as expected, it was Brev. "That's him."

"Someone's on their way to pick you up. They'll be there in a half hour or so."

"Hey, you wouldn't happen to know anyone who could give me a job do you?" He hoped she knew what he meant.

"We might be able to work something out. I gotta go, I'm at a friend's baby shower." She hung up before he could speak anymore.

A car door closed outside, drawing his mom to the door. "Has to be a coincidence." He said quietly to himself. He went to the door as well. When the door opened, Brev was right at the door, almost about to knock on it. Cloukora's eyes widened with shock, yet hers were calm and cool. She knew. Of course she knew. She *had* picked him up from his own house a few times already. *First being a vampire and now this?* His mom let her in and motioned for her to sit on the couch. This time she wore the same casual clothing she did when she picked Cloukora for the mission in Salem: V-neck, cargo shorts, and sneakers. Only thing she wasn't wearing were her sunglasses, but she held those in her hands.

"Cloukora, this is Brev Heart, she's my friend from high school."

"Brev Heart?" He asked, almost about to chuckle.

She threw her hands up. "Don't look at me, my parents named me. If anything, that movie's name was inspired by mine."

"Oh, Cloukora, did you find out if you're getting picked up?" his mom cut in.

"Yeah, they should be here in a half hour." Cloukora replied, glancing at Brev nervously.

"Okay. Brev, I'm gonna go in the kitchen and finish things up." Brev nodded and his mom walked off.

"So, why do you need the chopper?" Brev whispered to Cloukora.

"I have a theory, and to prove it, I need to visit Scotland."

"What theory?"

Cloukora shook his head. "I don't want to say a whole lot, it might be nothing. I'll tell you how it goes when I get back." Cloukora glanced at the kitchen to make sure his mom was still in there as Rhain

Birth

trotted down the stairs. Bending to his knee, he petted Rhain's soft fur as he told the wolf what to do. "Go upstairs, grab my hoodie and wait until I call you." After getting a quick ruffle on his head, Rhain ran back up the stairs to do just what he was told.

"So that's Rhain."

"Yeah, I can't believe I have my own wolf."

"He's a smart one."

"I know, I think it has something to do with the connection between my family and wolves."

"Most likely." Cloukora's mom returned to the living room and sat on the couch perpendicular to the one Brev was on as Cloukora sat on the floor.

The next half hour or so was a little awkward, hearing Brev and his mom share stories from their past. Stories about places they went, things they did, boys they liked, girls they hated, teachers and classes they dreaded and liked. He wished he knew they knew each other beforehand. Then he'd at least be able to prepare himself a little bit. Eventually, another car arrived, and it was Bowe who came to the door.

"Hi, I'm here to pick Cloukora up for Todd. He's too busy to drive out here himself." He explained to Cloukora's mother. "Ready?" he asked Cloukora.

"Wait, I thought it was Ja-"

"Yeah. Mom, I'm taking Rhain with me." He whistled and called Rhain, who came running down the stairs with the hoodie between his teeth, and followed him out the door to the car, Cloukora shutting the front door behind him, all before his mom could say another word on the matter. The car parked out front was a cherry red 1969 Chevy Nova.

"Nice ride. At least someone in the organization has a good taste in cars." Cloukora complimented as he got in the passenger seat and Rhain got in the back to lie down.

"You should see Avenorra's car. It's a freaking Lambo. The thing is a monster. I tell ya, she knows her cars."

"Speaking of Avenorra, I noticed Brev and Cal are together, you and Erro are together, and I assume Kaora and Nole are together. Right?"

Birth

"Yeah, and?"

"Are…Winter and Avenorra…you know?"

He chuckled. "We've been trying to figure that out since we first met them. It's just one of those mysteries that no one's ever going to figure out."

"Stranger things have happened."

Bowe laughed a little bit. "That *is* true. So, Scotland then?"

"Yeah. I gotta find someone who can only be found when he wants to be."

"Sounds easy enough. Alrighty, Scotland it is." The car pulled away and roared down the street.

Somewhere over Scotland

The sight above Scotland was breathtaking, it was almost indescribable. The green hills rolled on for miles and miles. The mountains peaked high above the clouds, and then there was the most incredible scenery: the Scottish castles. All were crumbling from the wear and tear from standing for so many years. Cloukora wished they could stand throughout all time. It's a shame that in five hundred years, they'll probably be gone, and the people in the future won't ever be able to see and experience the beauty of the Scottish history.

"So, where are we heading?" Bowe asked.

"To be honest, I'm not exactly sure. Some place where one can't be found, I guess."

"I think I know a place. People have reported major snowfall in a range of hills, causing them to get lost and forcing them to turn back. Some have also said that while in the snowstorm, they saw a grey sasquatch-looking creature."

"Sounds perfect, take me there."

"Over the hills we go." The chopper turned to fly over the land below, eventually landing at the base of thick-forested hills. "Here we are. I'll be at a fuel station not that far away." He tossed an earpiece to Cloukora. "Signal me when you're ready."

Cloukora and Rhain hopped off the helicopter. "I'll make sure to. Thank you for the ride." They both started off toward the forest as Bowe took off somewhere to the north. "This is gonna hurt in the morning." He said half-heartedly. The forest was just like any other forest. The only thing that stood out really, was the massive amount of moss it had on the trees and the forest floor. And the fact he felt eyes on him, but he couldn't see anyone. For some reason the feeling brought him comfort, like he was safe. Besides, Rhain wasn't growling, so they were in no danger for the moment. He kept himself ready though, just in case. After about an hour or so, it started getting colder, as they got higher; almost freezing cold. Then, snow began to fall slowly. "We're in the right area Rhain. We're not turning back." Snow fell more heavily, and Cloukora zipped up his hoodie to protect from its cold touch; he didn't think throwing his hood over would be necessary just yet. Not too long after that, the snow started coming at him on high winds, pelting him in the face. The snow on the ground was probably three feet high by now. The rate it was both falling and piling up was incredible; it was unnatural. But no matter how hard it kept falling, he kept moving forward, as did Rhain. "We can do it Rhain. We have to." Suddenly, the feeling of safety was gone, and he saw things scatter out in the distance. They were dog-like, and ranged from black, to white, to grey. He realized what they were: wolves. That's why he felt so safe, the wolves somehow knew he was a Skyrell, and it explains why Rhain wasn't affected by their presence. *But wolves were supposed to be extinct over here, they had killed every last one of them. Unless...they didn't.* Then he saw something tall and grey in the distance. His heart beat a little faster, and he let adrenaline flow through him. His body felt a little warmer from the adrenaline, not by much though. The figure got closer, and closer, and Cloukora could make it out. It looked like a Sasquatch, but had grey fur instead of brown. He remembered reading something on a creature called the Grey and how it was pretty much the Scottish version of Big Foot. "Who are you?" It didn't answer, and it didn't stop coming towards him. Instead, it moved faster.

Cloukora made Vesi and Neró appear: some of the snow below him melted and then flowed up to his hand to create the two swords. "Last chance." Nothing. He darted towards the creature with the left sword horizontal in front of him, and almost dragging the right sword. Rhain charged in as well and met the Grey before Cloukora could, biting into the flesh of the creature. The Grey roared in pain before throwing Rhain off into the snow. "Rhain!" The wolf got back up and steadied itself. Cloukora knew that Rhain would stand by him as long as he lived. And so would Cloukora stand by Rhain. Cloukora swung the sword in his right hand at the Grey, but the creature grabbed the blade with its fist as the other met Cloukora's face. The force sent him flying backwards, hitting a nearby tree. "Damn, this thing's strong." An idea came to him as he stood up, and he focused on the snow around him, melting it, and forming it into a wall of water about six or seven feet high. He sent the wave crashing towards the Grey, surrounding it with the water. The creature struggled to break free as the water hardened, until it was encased in a giant block of ice. Not a single part of its body could move anymore, and it would probably be stuck like that forever, unless the snow actually slowed down. Which didn't seem very likely.

    He continued walking, Rhain following right behind him. As the adrenaline faded away, the cold returned, and his body began to shake. He thought it must be below freezing by now. "I should have brought warmer clothing." He threw on his hood to try and keep his ears as warm as he could. His legs grew tired and sore, and he noticed Rhain was slowing down too. Not to keep the pace with his human friend, but because he was getting tired too. Abruptly his legs gave out and he would have fell face first into the snow if he had not caught himself with his hands. "Can't…give…up…" His arms finally gave way and his body collapsed into the cold snow. The snow numbing his ears and face. His arms and legs were too weak to get back up, and he could see Rhain on the ground too, panting. Cloukora could see the wolf's breathing began to slow. "I'm sorry, Rhain. I'm sorry." He reached out with the little strength he had to place it on his companion's fur head. He looked ahead and before his eyes blacked out on him, he

caught a glimpse of someone walking towards them, with what seemed to be wolves following right behind.

His sight slowly came back to him as he opened his eyes. He felt himself lying on a bed, and warmth, most likely coming from a nearby stove or fireplace. His eyes were blurry but he could make out some objects and a dog-like creature eating out of a bowl on the ground. As he sat up he rubbed his eyelids and closed and re-opened them. The blurriness was gone and he could clearly see that he was in some kind of polished wood-cabin, and the "dog" he saw was Rhain. Cloukora tossed the heavy blankets to the side before slowly getting out of the bed, and stumbled out into the living room area; his legs were still a little weak, so he had to hold onto some of the surfaces and objects he passed by. The place seemed old, yet still furnished. The owner kept the oak walls and floorboards polished and smooth to the touch. He had to walk through a hallway past several doors before he made it to the living room. There was a couch on the wall immediately to his left, and a fireplace crackling across from it on the other wall, with three wolves curled up next to it. From what he could see, there was no sign of electricity; only candles and oil-based items that dotted the cabin. Then there was a man, standing at a table to Cloukora's right, next to the kitchen, pouring soup into a bowl. He was kind of big, and scruffy looking. Cloukora couldn't put an age on him, but he thought he was probably in his fifties or sixties. Though it seemed like he had quite a bit of energy in him, something an old man would not likely have. Cloukora supposed living up there one would have to push himself and not let age and lack of energy get the best of them. Or else that could mean death. Behind the man was a door next to a window that showed the dark, snowy night outside. An escape if anything should go south with this strange man.

"Hey, you're up. I saw you out there, and couldn't help but bring you back here. I want people to stay away, but I don't want them to die either." The man put his hand out with a bowl of what looked like stew towards Cloukora. "It's just regular stew, no human added."

He chuckled as Cloukora hesitantly took the stew. "I know people like you get all worried about that kind of stuff. So, what's your name, kid?"

"Cloukora. Cloukora Skyrell." The man stumbled as he walked to the couch with his own bowl.

"Skyrell? I haven't heard that name in *years*. So what brings you up here?"

"I'm looking for someone." Cloukora sat on the couch, next to the man, and took a bite of the stew. It tasted fine. In fact, it was delicious.

"And who would you be searching for up in *these* mountains?"

"I don't know his name, but I know he can help me with something."

"With what?"

"You're going to think it's crazy."

"Trust me, I've heard crazy things. You can't outdo any of them."

"I..." He was still having trouble coming to terms with it himself. "I think I'm a king reincarnated, and to prove it, I need to see if I can control the wind."

"Hah, I guess maybe you can." He slurped the rest of his stew broth and turned to face Cloukora. "Well, I'm the guy. And the wind element isn't just something you can learn. It has to be in you already." He lightly poked Cloukora's chest.

"So, if I really am Relyt, I should already be able to do it?"

The man nodded his head. "Just like the others, focus."

Cloukora placed his bowl on a nearby end table and stood up in front of the couch. Concentrating on the air around him, he felt air swirl around his hand, and he could see a faint katana start to form; it wasn't a strong form, but it was there. It was hard to relax, and focus at the same time. Finally, the sword became solid. The katana was simple in shape, but what wasn't so simple about it, were the four diamond shaped stones floating around the circular hand guard. All four moving in perfect motion, neither moving too high or too low.

The old man stood up in awe. "The sword Gaoth. You *are* his reincarnation." The man looked like he wanted to bow down in front of

Cloukora. Composing himself, he went on. "You know what to do next, right?"

"Yeah, head to Atlantis."

"This also means the apocalypse is coming, doesn't it?"

"Yep, that's what the First Horseman says."

The man frowned. "Well I hope the outcome doesn't turn out as bad as the prophecies say. This also means I'll have to fortify my home. Just make sure you kick Lucifer's ass for me."

"I will." He had never actually thought about the fact he would most likely have to fight Lucifer to stop the apocalypse. That sent chills through him. He would have to come face to face with God's biggest enemy. *I guess I should have known it was implied. How would I stop the apocalypse without having to go near Lucifer?* "So, what's the deal with you, and the wolves, and living way up here?" Cloukora said as he glanced around the room.

"I like to live close to home."

"Home?"

"Yeah, didn't you know King Relyt first established his kingdom in Scotland?"

"Really? I didn't know that. I knew it was in Europe but I didn't know exactly where. You know, I bet if people knew about the Skyrells and the wolves, they would never have killed them off."

"Yeah, it's a real shame. All those wolves…That's one of the reasons I live up here, because no one can harm the wolves that live in these hills. People fear these creatures, when they have no reason to. They're quite beautiful."

"They are, aren't they?" Rhain came up next to Cloukora and got his ears scratched by his human companion. "Well, I should be heading back. Is there a short way to get to the bottom, so I can call in my ride?"

"Yes, I'll have Lass and Aurora guide you down. It's easy to get lost in that storm by yourself." He whistled, and both wolves got up, one was an Arctic wolf, and the other a Timber. Together they went to the door, where the man now stood to open it.

"Aurora…That was Relyt's wife's name, wasn't it?"

The man nodded. "She was said to be one of the most beautiful women during her time. She was also good with a blade too, if I remember correctly. Which was rare for her time as well."

"If only most girls were like her and weren't so dependent on men. Our society would be much stronger."

The man chuckled. "If we had more women like Aurora, every guy would be standing in the back, keeping their mouths shut while the women ran the world. You wouldn't catch me saying that in front of a woman, though. Dependent or not, they'd give you a nice smack for talking like that." The man said as he walked towards the door, Cloukora following right behind.

Cloukora laughed. "Alright, well thanks for everything uh... I never got your name."

"And you never will." He chuckled and opened the door.

As Cloukora started out, his eye caught a long, thick white walking staff resting against the wall by the door. It wasn't an ordinary staff, though: it had tiny, barely noticeable, metal inlays in the shapes of various snowflakes covering almost all of the staff. In the middle of the stick was a metal grip that had been carefully and elegantly crafted around it. Dead center of the grip, was a Skyrell crest smelted right into it. *Why would he-Ohh...* Cloukora's mouth turned into a grin before continuing out. *Another Skyrell.* "C'mon Rhain." Rhain got up from the other wolves he had been resting with and followed Cloukora outside. Snow surrounded the cabin still, and it wasn't anything less than it was before. At least it had stopped falling; Cloukora could also see the stars in the sky now. It had passed a day already. Along the side of the small cabin was a stack of firewood that stretched all along it. The man was going to have enough fire for quite a long time.

"Hey, Cloukora. Good luck."

"Thanks. I'll never forget you or how much you've helped me."

"At least forget where I live." He laughed as he closed the door behind him. Lass and Aurora led Cloukora and Rhain down the mountain. When they reached the part of the forest where there the snow had ended into several streams, the wolves had turned back towards the cabin. Even without the two guides, it didn't take long for

them to walk the rest of the way, and when they got to the bottom, he signaled for Bowe on the earpiece. However, getting picked up took quite a bit of time; Bowe had a hard time finding Cloukora even with him waving Fyron around.

As he and Rhain got on the helicopter, he told Bowe: "I need your helicopter again tomorrow, I have something else I need to get."

"No problem. Are you gonna pay for gas?" He said jokingly, and took the helicopter back towards the United States.

Birth

Angel's Gaiden

FALLEN CITY

July 8, 2010
Somewhere over the Pacific

    The helicopter hovered over the Pacific Ocean, right where Atlantis should be. The sky was clear, and dark, with the stars twinkling brightly above them. There was a small hint of sun off in the distance. Besides the small ripple from the helicopter, the ocean was calm; they were nowhere near the beach. Brev tried handing Cloukora an oxygen tank in case he needed it. "Are you sure you'll be all right?"

    Waving away the oxygen tank he said "Don't worry, I got this." Cloukora made Vesi and Gaoth appear, and the water below separated and formed a circular tunnel that went straight down to the bottom of the sea. Cloukora took a deep breath, and then stepped off the helicopter. He didn't fall, the wind actually held him up.

    Brev gasped. "This is incredible."

    Cloukora gently floated down through the tunnel, and landed on the soft, wet sand. In the deep blue ocean, he could see all kinds of fish, turtles, jelly fish, and aquatic plant life all around outside of the tunnel. There were sharks close enough for him to touch! But of course, they wouldn't be able to pass through the invisible wall of air. He made sure of that by making the force of the wind strong enough to keep everything in the water; the "tunnel" was formed by manipulating the water. Of course he could have just used one, but he felt safer using both elements. Plus it stressed his abilities more, thus making him better at controlling the elements. It was like anything else: the harder practice you put upon yourself, the better you would be at whatever it is you were practicing.

The most glorious sights of the ocean though, were the structures sticking out of the ocean floor. The architecture was amazing, so intricate and carefully carved. The pillars and walls were made out of white marble gilded with gold, bronze, and silver metal, while the buildings were only made out of the white marble. It was fairly similar to Greek architecture, except, Cloukora noticed street lamps along the streets. They weren't candle-lit street lamps, but in fact were similar to modern street lamps. There were also what looked like billboards along some of the rooftops. Besides the marble, it could pass as a modern day city like New York. But what caught Cloukora's eye, was a wide spire that almost reached the surface of the water in the middle of the whole city. Most of it was covered in seaweed, algae, starfish, and other ocean plant life. Another tunnel leading to the ruins was cleared away, and he continued on towards the giant spire. When he reached the golden gates, he noticed that they had fallen and had become rusty from both time and being soaked in water. As he neared the walls, he could see that they were worn, despite their beauty, and looked like they could crumble with just one touch. He continued clearing water out of the way, forming a tunnel so he could get through the city. Finally, he reached the spire. Outside the door was a stone column that was identical to the one at the lake. Sighing in annoyance, he stuck Gaoth into the sand, and placed his hand in the bowl. Sure enough, the spikes came up and pricked his fingers, and then were gone within a split second. The giant doors slowly opened, and abruptly a rush of water poured out right at him. But before the water could get close to him, he stopped its flow and the water stood still, as if there were an invisible glass that had kept the water from moving any further. Slowly, the water that was inside the building, poured out, went above him, and joined the rest of the water in the ocean.

    Not long, the water had finished draining out, and he grabbed Gaoth and stepped inside. As he did, his mouth went agape. He turned around full circle, struck in awe by the room. Inside, the water-dripping walls were made of stone similar to that of a castle, but what had caught his attention was the technology everywhere. Television screens and computers lined the walls, and in the center was a plastic or glass

surface surrounded by controls and small computer screens. "Oh shit, is that a hologram projector?" He tried messing with a few buttons and switches until miniature digitized people appeared on the small surface. The people were rushing out the door, most likely evacuating the city. "Sweet." He messed with a few of the screens, which he found were to be touch screens, and rewound to different times of the day. "Relyt was a smart motherfucker. He even waterproofed all of this." He switched off the hologram, admiring it for a moment. "If only we had this kind of technology." He turned and headed down a hallway out of the room.

Cloukora came to a doubled-door, and readied Vesi in case he needed to control water from flowing out again. He opened the door, and to his luck, there was no water waiting for him. Before him was a large room made up of stone blocks, dimly lit by only a few lights along the wall, not torches but lights, and above him was a ceiling that extended high enough to where Cloukora couldn't see it. In the room were four statues upon large square stone pedestals, two in each row, each to be several meters from each other, and at the back was a katana sticking out of a smaller stone pedestal, which he wasn't able to make out from where he stood. Each statue was some kind of creature, or animal. One of them was a European dragon, with its wings folded, another was an ogre type creature holding a club on its shoulder, the third was a snake coiled up like it was ready to attack, and the last one was a man holding a spear upright. The ogre stood one and a half his size and the dragon three times. Unlike the man who only stood about a head taller. As he began towards the katana, he heard stone crumbling and breaking; the statues were coming to life. The snake, apparently made out of water, sprung out at him from the left. Quickly he rolled out of the way, back near the dragon statue, and faced the snake, sword pointing out. The dragon huffed behind him, breathing its warm breath on his back, and on instinct, Cloukora quickly spun, surrounding himself with water, creating a shield from the fire that had just shot out of the dragon's mouth. Steam surrounded them for a moment, from the collision of the opposing elements, and Cloukora used that as an advantage to move out of the way, giving him time to assess the situation. When the steam cleared, the ogre and the man stepped off of

their pedestals. Each one seemed to be made out of an element; the dragon: fire, the snake: water, the ogre: earth, and the man was wind.

The ogre's dirt club swung at him at unbelievable speed, and he was barely able to dodge it as the club crushed the stone where he had just stood. The dragon quickly darted towards him from above, and was about to send a ball of fire until Cloukora shot a blast of water at it, making a hole all the way through it. New fire immediately replaced the hole, and when the fiery beast was about to impact, Cloukora side stepped, and sliced through the body with Vesi. The dragon crashed into the ground, and the fire steamed until it was nothing but evaporation. The snake was the next to attack, springing at him once again and Cloukora swung Gaoth before the snake reached him, blowing it away with the wind until it was no more. As soon as he had Vesi and Gaoth disappear, Terra and Fyron were in his hands. The ogre swung his giant club horizontally at Cloukora, with too much speed, preventing him dodging it, and knocking him against the wall. As it swung again, Cloukora was fast enough this time and rolled out of the club's way towards the ogre's side, stood up, and stabbed the ogre right through the neck with the flaming scimitar. Immediately, the flames of the sword burned the ogre into a crisp, leaving only ashes, blackened dirt and stone.

The last one left was the man with the spear, who stood unmoving. He was waiting for Cloukora to make the first move. "Guess it can't be helped." Cloukora made Fyron disappear, and ran towards him, Terra ready. The sword would have hit, but the man blocked the attack right at the last second with his spear, despite it just being made of wind. "Of course you're fast, you're *wind*!" Cloukora struck, and was blocked again, but this time, pushed back by an invisible force against the wall. Grunting, he got back up onto his feet. "I know earth supposedly beats wind, but how the hell do you *eliminate* wind?" He charged again, and this time, when their weapons met, stone shot up and out of the ground, and pierced through the man made of wind. However, the man reformed himself, rendering the attack useless and pointless, wiping Cloukora's smirk off his face. "Dammit! How do I beat him? Wait, I may not be able to destroy him…" Cloukora charged

once more, forcing the man to focus on him. Right before he struck, stone abruptly rose up around the man and trapped him inside a small, tightly sealed dome. The dome barrier had no creases or cracks for the elemental to escape. Catching his breath, he turned around, and walked towards the katana vertically thrust into the pedestal. As he got closer he saw that it was the magnificent blade King Relyt had once wielded. The handle was wrapped in blue-green cloth, and the hand guard was smelted into the Skyrell family crest. On the silvery Orichalcum blade was inscribed *Pugnare pro honore, amore et fide,*. There were four slot holes surrounding the pedestal in the floor. One of them was a small linear slit, another was a very thin diamond slit, a third was a linear slit, but slightly bigger than the first, and lastly, was a wide horizontal slit.

    Cloukora immediately knew that these must be for each element, and put Terra into the diamond slit. The sword stuck out quite a bit, but he figured it only needs to be in enough to be recognized by whatever device was down there. He then made Gaoth appear, and slid it into the small linear slit. Then Fyron went into the bigger linear slit. The last to go in was Vesi and Neró. He wasn't exactly sure on what he was supposed to do, so he toyed with the idea he had, and tried combining the two back to back, and before he could put them together, they pulled to each other by themselves as if they were magnets. "Well, that's neato." He slid it into the wide slit, and stepped back. The element from each sword flowed out of it in colorful streams, and into the katana in the pedestal, causing it to give off a rainbow glow until the elements were done transferring and connecting with the sword.

    He gave it a few moments, before pulling it out from the pedestal; which made the flat surface of it split apart and bring up a vertical-standing scabbard with a back strap for the katana. The scabbard was blue and had an etched white tribal wolf down the middle of it. Cloukora thought it was a beautiful casing, perfect for the blade it was meant to shelter. After he took it out, a large television screen he didn't notice before flickered on, and a man appeared inside it. It was Relyt Skyrell, and it was like looking into a mirror for Cloukora.

    "Hello? Is this thing on?" Relyt sat down in a chair. "My name, is Relyt Skyrell, and I am the king of Atlantis; one of the four great

nations. I am recording this for whoever ends up finding this city. I had not originally planned to sink Atlantis when I first built it. In fact, I was going to further my research on diseases and plagues so I could find cures for both present and future illnesses. I was also going to even create a space program, for I know there is more life out in the stars. We can't be the only ones in this vast universe. But… events have happened recently that weren't expected. Arthur had…had let greed get the best of him. All he wanted was power and control. He was a strong willed man, and I fear if he can give into it this easily, then there's no telling what a normal person would do with this technology. I don't think mankind is ready for it, or ever will be. That is why I am sinking it. To prevent unnecessary mass warfare and destruction. Whoever ends up finding this, I cannot stop you, but unless man has realized the things that are more important than greed, I ask you, please do not re-surface this city. It will be your undoing. I do hope one day humankind *can* discover this technology and put it to good use. I would also like to note that energy from Atlantis will continue to emit, and keep the coast area safe from any kind of attacks and disasters. I don't know how far it will extend, but it should be far enough. I can at least give the future *that* much." He took a moment before continuing. "This will be the last record of me at all. This is Relyt Skyrell, signing off."

The screen went black, and Cloukora stood there for a moment, thinking it over. Weighing the good and the bad that could come out of it. *I either let people die from disease and other natural killers, or I let them die by a massive world war. No matter what I choose people will die, people that I could have saved.* A hidden door near the screen opened up and revealed a long tunnel, made mostly of glass that allowed the view of the ocean, much like the one Cloukora created on the way in. However this one had something solid keeping water from bursting through rather than thin air, and instead of sand to walk on, it was stone. After grabbing the swords out of the slits and making each one disappear, he sheathed the katana and put it on his back as he headed down the tunnel. But not before taking one last look at the room. So much good could come of this place, but yet so much evil. He turned around and strode through the tunnel, and after quite a walk, he finally

made it to a rock cavern formation. Through a glass wall, he could see water bursting through a hole like a geyser, then retreating back in, before bursting out again. When he stepped on a part of the rock, the glass moved and swung inward, blocking the hole the water came from, while pushing the rest out, and kept more from coming in. Steps leading up to the top were revealed. They were carved out of the rock, and when he walked up them, he came out on top of a cliff overlooking the ocean. He realized he was at Thor's Well, and quickly got clear of the geyser, because in the case of a high tide it could get dangerous. The moonlight helped him see where he was walking. When he made it to safety near a road, he called up Brev, told her where he was, and waited until the chopper picked him up and returned them to the Wolfstorm building.

Portland, Oregon

The chopper landed on top of Wolfstorm HQ. As he stepped out he saw his grandfather standing on the helipad. "Grandpa Aaron?" Cloukora asked as he walked towards him. "What're you doing here?"
"I'm the real leader of Wolfstorm. I first formed this group in 2001, and I've been running it ever since. Now, I want to pass the legacy on down to you."
"What? Me? Why? I don't understand."
"Because you're Relyt's reincarnation. It's your right to take over leadership against Darkstar. I knew it would end up being you. That's why I had that building set on fire, to test your skills. To help you acknowledge them."
"Wait, what the hell? You could have killed innocent lives, that child could have died if I didn't save her. What if *I* died?"
"If I didn't do it, you would have never developed your powers, and you would have never came this far. I know what I did was wrong, but I had to do it. For the good of the people. You'll understand some day that as a hero, there will be decisions you have to make. Decisions that you may not think are right."
"So, what exactly *am* I supposed to do?"

"Whatever you think is necessary. Keep a look out for strange things that go on, and investigate them. Just make sure the world is safe from any kind of evil. That is your primary job. If you can't do that, then anything secondary won't matter."

"I will. I will give my life for this world, and everything in it, just to keep it safe."

"I know you will. Ever since you were born, I knew you you'd go on and do great things, and *become* someone great. So far, I have not been proven wrong, and I don't expect that will change either. After seeing the things you've done in such a short amount of time, I didn't hesitate when I found out you were Relyt's reincarnation to put the organization into your hands. Heck, I think you will become an even better leader than me." Cloukora wiped his eye. "Are you crying?"

"What? No. Of course not." Cloukora turned slightly red and his grandfather just laughed.

"Alright, let's head home. I think you took in enough for today." They walked towards the door on the roof leading inside the building.

Venn opened the chamber doors that led into the throne room. "My lord, I bring good news." He knelt onto one knee.

"And what news is that?" The man in the dark purple overcoat asked, who sat in his throne messing with a tablet device, researching recent events. He took a grape out of a bowl and tossed it into his mouth. So far nothing out of the usual had occurred; he had been keeping an eye out for strange activity ever since he found out the apocalypse was nearing. He wanted the world destroyed and in chaos, but by his hands, not someone else's.

"The government is close to finding him. Your plan can be set into motion now, my lord."

"Good, make the preparations Venn."

"Understood." He turned and walked out of the throne room.

Angel's Gaiden

FORTUNATE SON

July 9, 2010
Forest Grove, Oregon

    Cloukora woke up in the middle of the night, with a sudden urge to relieve his bladder. He tossed aside his blanket and walked down the pitch black hallway, half-asleep, towards the bathroom. After he finished his business, he exited the bathroom and headed back to his room. Halfway down the hall, he felt a hand grab his shoulder. The touch shook him wide awake, and on instinct he grabbed the intruder's arm, twisted it, spun around, grabbed the dark figure's shoulder and pushed their face against the banister. Before Cloukora could ask who the person was, he felt someone come up behind him and wrap their arms around his torso. Cloukora quickly swung his head back, hitting the person behind them in the head, which hurt like hell, leaving his head a little woozy. From the corner of his eye he saw another shadow coming toward him from his right side, and elbowed their neck, spun the person he was holding, and kicked them into the person he just head butted. He flicked on the light near him, and saw about seven men in military grade armor, plus the two he took down. One was closely to the right of him, three were in front near his room, the one he just elbowed in the neck, and two walking out of his sisters' room to the left. *Seems like Avenorra and Winter's training is starting to pay off.*

    The one to his right moved first, and as they swung at him, he leaned back out of the way, pulled the arm, bringing the man closer, and karate chopped him in the neck. One of the soldiers in the front came at him, but before the man could get close enough, Cloukora kicked him in the chin, sending the man flying backwards. Cloukora spun the man he had a hold of, and smacked his face into the banister,

knocking him out cold. Another charged at him from the front, and Cloukora stepped aside, grabbed the man by the vest he was wearing, and threw him over the banister, onto the stairs. He turned around to get a punch right in the stomach, and bent over from the pain. The man's other fist flew towards his face, but he knocked away the blow with his palm, countering with an uppercut to the man's chin. A fist coming from his left hit him square in the face, knocking him to the floor. As the man who just hit him stepped in his direction, Cloukora swept the man's legs starting from the right leg, forcing him to fall and hit his head on the banister, falling unconscious on top the man already down next to the banister. Four left. Cloukora stood up, and made Neró appear in his hand. He wanted to hurt them, not kill them. They all pulled out batons and rushed in at the same time. After he swept the leg of the man closest to him with the inside of the hook, knocking him over, Cloukora blocked the first attack with Neró, pushed the baton downwards, and quickly pulled his sword up, smacking the man in the face with the back of the sword. The man fell and was knocked out too. He kicked another man that was in the middle of swinging his baton at him, pushing the man backwards to the ground. The last man standing drew a pistol and aimed it at Cloukora. But before the trigger could be pulled, Cloukora quickly grabbed the arm with the gun, pointed it upwards in case it fired, and kicked the man in the stomach, and then slammed his head into the nearest wall. Cloukora turned to walk out and see one of the men getting up, and he took the blunt edge of Neró and slammed it into the man's leg, dislocating it; maybe even breaking it. He made Neró disappear by also using wind to turn it into vapor, headed down the stairs, and grabbed the man lying on the stairs landing by his shirt.

"Who are you, and who do you work for?" Cloukora asked irritably. The man wouldn't answer. Agitated even more, he threw the man down the stairs, sending him into a roll on the floor down below. The sword on Cloukora's back appeared, and he unsheathed the katana as he continued down the steps. Ready to interrogate him more. When he stopped at the man's feet, he heard guns cock and saw red laser beams piercing through the darkness, aiming at both his chest and his

head. The light flashed on, and he saw men in uniforms, like the ones S.W.A.T. use, with MP5's, UMP's, and G36's raised, aiming at Cloukora. He saw his family tied up in chairs by the far wall.

"Drop your weapon, now!" One of the men shouted. He could probably take them all out if he wanted to, but that would require endangering his family, something he wasn't about to risk. Cloukora dropped the sword onto the floor and raised his hands above his head. One of the men opened the front door, letting some kind of General in, with medals decorated on his left breast.

"Cloukora Skyrell. We finally meet." The General walked in, took off his hat, put it in between his arm and torso, and sat on the arm of the loveseat. "It took a long time to find you."

"How *did* you find me?" Cloukora still had his hands up, but tried to seem unaffected by what was going on. A couple men went upstairs, probably to investigate his room.

"Well, not many people can fall out of a four story window and survive. I'll admit; it was still a little difficult even with that. Someone tried really hard to hide your location." *Thank goodness for Wolfstorm.*

"Cloukora, what's he talking about? What's going?" his mom asked.

"Yes, why don't you tell her? Tell your family who you really are."

Cloukora glared at the General, he hated him already. "Nothing. Just know everything will be alright." The men came back down.

"Sir, we found this." They held up Cloukora's pistol. "Eight men are also upstairs, badly injured."

"Cloukora? Tell us what's going on. Why do you have a gun? What was with the sword?" His mom pleaded.

Cloukora sighed. "I...Well..." He took a deep breath. "I'm...a superhero."

Jack laughed a little. "A superhero? Really?" Cloukora just looked at him. "Prove it." Cloukora looked at the General for approval, who nodded. Cloukora put out his hand, and let air swirl into his hands, forming Gaoth. "What in the hell? How long has this been going *on*?"

Birth

"About a few weeks." Cloukora replied, making Gaoth disappear.

"Why didn't you tell us?"

"Because I didn't want to endanger any of you. It's rule number one as a superhero: never reveal your identity to anyone. Even family." *Wait, why* can't *they tell their families? Unless their family runs their mouth off and spouts every secret, there isn't really any danger...*

"We came here for a reason, Cloukora." The General cut in. "We need your help to catch a target of ours."

"And who would that be?" Cloukora spoke as if his family wasn't in the same room.

"Someone we've been trying to catch for nine years now: Oushu Kan. We actually found him, but his base is fortified, and we could really use you for help."

"And what if I say no?"

"Well, if you don't, then we'll report who you really are to the authorities and have you arrested for being a vigilante. Your choice if you want your enemies to track you down a lot easier."

Cloukora glared at him. "Fine. But I get to write a list of conditions, and you have to agree to them."

"Done. We'll see you in the morning, Cloukora. An escort will pick you up." The General got up, put his military cap back on, and walked out the door with the rest of the men just behind him, and carrying the injured men from upstairs as well. The last soldier to go out was the one who cut the ropes loose around his family's hands.

Before they could say anything, Cloukora went back upstairs and went to his room. He suddenly realized Rhain had not done anything to help, and went to check the wolf's pulse. He was still alive. Cloukora heard a honk outside and opened his window. The General was getting into a Humvee. "Don't worry, your…pet…is alright. He was just sedated. Good night to you all." Cloukora shut and locked the window, turned around, and crawled into bed.

Military base, Western Oregon

Cloukora pulled the light military vest over himself. He wore a black Slipknot t-shirt underneath, a pair of jeans, and his usual skate shoes. He thought it would be much cooler if he wore casual clothing, since they were going into the desert. Plus he wasn't much of the uniform type. The room was a military hangar, and in front of him was an Airbus A400M military transport airplane, which hasn't even been available to the nations yet. It's not surprise though, America *is* known for getting around things.

"Hey newbie, I don't think you're gonna survive in that kind of gear." He heard someone behind him say.

Cloukora cocked a Beretta 93R pistol that fires three rounds in a burst, and placed it in his holster. "I'll be fine. You should worry more about yourself." He turned around as he cocked a second 93R and saw three men. The middle one, the one most likely talking, was almost as tall as him, and had thin brown hair that went just below his chin. He also wore a heavy vest with magazine pockets all around the abdomen area filled with magazines. He had two forty-fives in holsters, one on each leg, and a M4A1 assault rifle, with a red dot scope and a fore grip attached to it, on a strap that hung off his shoulder. The one in the middle looked young though, almost Cloukora's age. The one on the right looked about twenty-two or so, and had an almost shaved head, with some black still along the top. The one on the left had the same haircut, but had blonde hair, and looked around the dark-haired man's age. The other two wore the same gear as the man in the middle, but had Scar-L assault rifles, instead of a M4.

"So it looks like you finally met the Black Ops that'll be joining you on the mission." The General walked in with a few other soldiers that were ready to go. "Are you ready yet?"

"Just about." Cloukora grabbed a UMP 45 submachine gun and shoved a magazine filled with rounds in it, into the bottom of the gun, and placed it over his shoulder. Then he readied a L115A3 sniper rifle, and slung it over his other shoulder. "Now I am."

"You will be deployed with five Marines, along with these three Black Ops being led by Tomi Pendra." Cloukora's eyes darted to the man in the middle; he remembered that name.

"Tomi Pendra? Did you, by any chance, hang out with a boy and a girl when you were younger, like about six or eight?" Cloukora asked.

"Yeah, why?" The guy in the middle replied curiously.

"It's Cloukora. Cloukora Skyrell."

"Cloukora? Son of a bitch it's been a long time." They grasped each other's hand, pulled close, and patted the other on the back a couple times, then let go.

"You guys can catch up on the flight. We need to go, right now." The General commanded before getting on the plane.

Cloukora went over the plan again. "So, we're getting dropped in the middle of the Iraqi desert? And then the plan is to get to the base, and then bust our way through? Alright, well that sounds like a good plan. Let's go."

Somewhere in the Middle East

The military airplane was in flight, en route to their destination. Cloukora had no idea where they were. Everyone was buckled into their seats, readying their guns. "So, Tomi, how did you end up in the Black Ops?"

"Well, you know how my dad was always extremely strict and disciplinary?" Cloukora nodded. "One day, it got out of hand, and he hit me square in the face because I didn't want to do what he asked me to do. I got pissed off and pushed him. He fell back. Hit his head on the corner of the counter, and bled to death. The neighbor's heard the commotion and called the cops. I was taken away from my mom and sent to a foster home. My new father had connections with the government, and he saw strength in me, so he got me recruited into Black Ops."

"We didn't even know he was joining us until today, when we first met him." One of the other Black Ops soldiers put in as they readied their pistol.

"It was a last minute thing." Tomi replied.

"I'm sorry about your dad. I didn't know what he did to you until it was too late." Cloukora sympathized.

"It's alright, man. It's not your fault, and there's nothing you could have done about it."

"But if you hate your dad, why do you still use his last name?"

"Just because I'm not proud of my dad, doesn't mean I'm not proud of his family. They did great things in their lifetimes, and I hope to do the same in mine."

"Ahh. That makes sense."

"What about you? Why are you here?"

"Hah, well you see that's a funny story," He couldn't think of an excuse. What reasonable explanation could he give for being there? He had to tell him. "I'm actually the hero that's been running around and fighting bad guys, and the government ended up finding me out and needed some extra firepower, and so yeah. Now I'm here."

"That's *you*?"

"Yup. Something happened to me recently, something amazing, and I've decided to use that new gift for good. If I have the power to help people, what's the point in sitting around and watching the world burn?"

"Sometimes, cold people like to feel the warmth of destruction because that's the only warmth they can feel. Anything else is blocked out by numbness. Numbness from pain and agony they have suffered from long ago. It's the only way they can feel *alive*. To feel like they matter. And, after all, living is the ultimate goal in life, is it not?"

"No." Tomi seemed taken aback. "Suffering is no excuse to cause pain to others, or to let it happen. *Everyone* has the power to choose. Instead you should take that pain, take that anger, and put it towards helping others, to keep them safe. To try and change the world and make it a better place. So that they will never have to suffer as you did."

Birth

"That's easy for you to say, Cloukora. You haven't had a terrible life. When people treat you like dirt or stab you in the back, if even it is only but a few, that will change your whole perspective on people in general. You'll start to lose compassion for them and gain a deep hatred in place of it. You know, many tend to hate on the villain without even giving thought to *why* he's a villain. Traumatic events can create a villain just as much as they can a hero. And it kinda makes you wonder. Who's the real villain? The villain? Or the ones who made him a villain?"

Cloukora opened his mouth to counter what he said, but could not come up with the words. "That's not what happened to you, is it?"

"Oh no, of course not. I'm still the same ol' Tomi. If I hated people do you think I would be helping to kill the most notorious terrorist today? Or do you think I would actually be working with him?"

"Good point. Speaking of which, anyone know where we are?" The soldiers shook their heads, and Cloukora unbuckled, got up and asked the pilots.

"We're just about to pass over the location of the target." The co-pilot replied.

"Alright, thank you." Cloukora walked back, but not to his seat, to a button on the side of the plane.

"Cloukora, what're you doing?" The large cargo door of the back of the plane opened up. Wind quickly swept up in the plane, making it a little hard to hear, and made Cloukora have to hold on to something.

"I'm not waiting! It's now or never!" Cloukora readied his sniper rifle, and ran off the ramp of the door into the open sky, no parachute on his back. He could see the compound below as he was falling. There were three main buildings: one to the North, one to the East, and one to the West. The rest were just small walls from a past building to the south. As he fell towards the base, he pulled the scope of the sniper rifle to his eye, aimed high above an enemy soldier that was walking along a balcony and took the shot. He cocked the gun. Aimed high above another soldier and shot at him. Cocked. Shot again. Cocked again, and fired. Cocked once more, and then shot one last

time. Cloukora let go of the sniper rifle, letting it fall through the air, and put his arms to his side, making him fall faster, and at an angle towards the southern part of the complex. He rolled as he hit the ground, to carry his momentum, and as he pulled out his UMP 45, the bullets he shot in the sky fell and pierced the five men he shot at in the skulls. Cloukora brought up his gun, looked down the iron sights, and fired at a man on a balcony. As Cloukora ran to cover behind a short wall, he turned his gun a little to the east, shot another guy, and waited behind the wall for the enemy to run out. Sure enough, about twenty or so more men came running out of the buildings. He peeked around the corner, and shot down one running out of a door with an AK-47 his hands. Suddenly, the gates behind him to the compound burst open from an explosion; most likely C4. The rest of his squad came running in to get to cover, suppressing fire on the enemy at the same time. Tomi crouched behind the wall across from Cloukora.

"Alright Tomi! Just like when we were kids!" Tomi nodded and they stood up, aimed their guns, and fired on the enemy soldiers, making sure to fire in short bursts to prevent loss of accuracy. The sniper rifle he let go of earlier, hit one of the men, butt end first in the head as Cloukora popped out to put rounds into a man running towards them. Aiming his sights up on the balcony across from him, he fired at the several soldiers, forcing them to duck behind the metal slates along the railing. Unfortunately for them, they were armor piercing bullets, so they ripped easily through the metal, and flew into their chests. Tomi tossed a frag grenade near three soldiers behind a barricade, and before they could get away, it exploded and sent them flying. Changing out the gun's magazine, he took a deep breath, then swung around the corner and spread fire on the rest of the soldiers on the building to the North, with Tomi doing the same not a second after. Before the enemy could even fire their guns, they were knocked back by the bullets piercing their bodies. As they stood there, waiting for more enemy soldiers to show up, there was complete silence. It felt eerie to Cloukora: one second there was so much noise that you couldn't hear yourself think, and the next there was no sound at all. It felt maddening that chaos brought peace. It wasn't natural.

Once they realized it was clear, the squad stood up as Cloukora said "Marines, take the western building! Black ops take the eastern, and I'll take the North one." They all split into the buildings they were commanded to investigate. Cloukora opened the door slowly, and peeked around the corner while aiming a 93R- he ran out of ammo with the UMP. No sign of anyone. He carefully stepped inside, checking for anything that would trip explosives. As he reached the end of the hallway, he heard footsteps walking his way. He peeked around the corner and saw a man with a turban on his head, holding an AK-47. Cloukora quickly rounded the corner and fired a three round burst into the man's chest, dropping him to the ground. He continued on and heard shouts coming from down the hall. "I knew I should have used a silencer." He whispered to himself. Three men with guns appeared from a door, and before they could raise their guns, Cloukora put several bullets through each of their chests. That must have been the last of them because the rest of the search came up empty, and he decided to head back out. The five Marines were standing outside in the middle.

"Where's the other squad?" Cloukora asked.

"Still in there. We would go in, but we thought keeping an eye out here might be best." One of the soldiers stated as Cloukora ran in to follow the Black Ops squad.

Tomi and the two Black Ops were deep into the building; they had gone down a couple flights of stairs and found a secret floor. They eventually came to a room occupied by three men in it: two looked like guards, and the other looked like Oushu Kan. The two guards were taken out immediately; all that was left was Oushu.

"Tomi, what are you doing here?" Oushu asked.

"What the hell? I knew there was somethi-" Tomi pulled out the two silenced pistols he was carrying, and shot both Black Ops members at the same time in the head, before the blonde could even finish his sentence.

Birth

"I'm here to save you from the U.S. government. They're here to kill you. But first, I need a favor from you." Tomi tossed a gun he had carried in between his jeans and his back to the Oushu. "Use that on me. That way he'll think I'm dead." Before Oushu could ask what Tomi meant, Cloukora ran in, and as soon as he did, the gun in Oushu's hand went off, the loud bang roaring in his ears and leaving a ringing sound. The bullet exited the barrel and flew through the air, and all Cloukora could do was watch, wide-eyed as his heart sunk down to his stomach. The bullet piercing Tomi's vest. The force knocking him back. The bullet tearing through his friend's chest and exiting into the wall behind him. The moment may not have actually been long, but it felt like minutes to Cloukora. It was as if Death was toying with him, making him watch the incident as long as possible. Tomi's body lay so eerily still, not a single rise of the chest showed. Cloukora waited for him to get back up. He couldn't be dead. He couldn't. It was his best friend. He couldn't die, he didn't deserve to. How could fate be that cruel?

"NOO!!" Cloukora ran to drop by Tomi's side. He checked his pulse on the neck. Nothing. "No." Anger flowed through him. Anger he could not control. "No, you can't be dead Tomi. Come on, get back up." He could feel it spreading through him. Something deep down told him, *yelled* at him, not to let the anger out, to keep it suppressed. But he couldn't stay calm. He didn't *want* to be calm. He didn't care that it was taking him over; his best friend had just died in front of him. He had every right to let it out. A tear began to form at the corner of his eye. His head started to swirl, his muscles tensed up, forcing his hands into fists, his heart rate increased rapidly, and his breathing became heavy. He stood up to face Oushu. Dark purple armor had begun to replace his skin all the way up to his mid-neck. Purple-black spikes ranging from as small as a few centimeters to several inches long began to grow along his arms, spread to his shoulders, his back, and then to his legs. The larger spikes being fewer in numbers. His hands formed into demon-like claws. His eyes changed too. The Skyrell crest in his eyes changed form. It rotated onto the tip and the colors inverted: the green in them became a magenta and the brown a sky blue. Only the

gray had stayed the same. The armor even changed his build; it had made him more fit and muscular, but it didn't change his slender shape, it actually emphasized it more and added to his height. He didn't look weak or as frail as he had before. In fact, besides his head, he didn't look human at all; he looked more like a monster. A creature you would see in the shadows of the night. If people were scared of the way he normally looked. They would piss themselves at the sight of him now.

Cloukora was on Oushu in a split second, pushing him up against the wall with just a claw around the neck. "You killed him!" He snarled. Even his personality was no longer human. "You killed my friend!"

"I-I-I was just doing w-what I was t-told to do. Please d-don't hurt me."

"You don't deserve to live." Cloukora's claw squeezed harder on the man's neck, and then shoved the other claw through the man's chest, and ripped out his heart. He let the man's body drop to the ground, threw the heart down next to it, and as he began walking out, he started losing some of the anger. As it was fading, it made him feel dizzy and nauseous. He felt weak too, and he could barely stand. A part of him didn't want to let whatever it was go. He liked having that much power; he didn't want it to go away. He wanted more. Despite his reluctance, the anger, the power, was gone when he got to the door. By the time he reached outside, he was fine, and his body normal. A little shaken up and weary, but fine. A chopper with the five marines already in, waited for him. "Tomi's down there. Dead. And the two Black Operatives, too." Three medics and several soldiers hopped off and rushed down into the building. After a few minutes, they came up with nothing.

They only brought up the two Black Ops members and Oushu. "He's not down there, only neutralized tangos. Look on the bright side though, we got Oushu. It's a hundred percent match. The bastard's finally dead. His cause of death is odd, but whatever you did, good job."

Cloukora was silent on the flight back. Despite the rewards he would get for the mission, despite killing one of the most notorious criminals in the world, it couldn't replace Tomi.

Birth

Tomi watched as the U.S. helicopter flew off, as he hid in the shadows of a building. Venn walked up next to him.

"My Lord, how did it go?" Venn asked, handing Tomi a dark purple leather overcoat.

"Perfect. I've awakened the dark power within him." He replied as he took the coat from Venn and pulled it over his shoulders. He had already tossed away his vest and military gear.

"How did you even do it?"

"I used a special bullet and a special gun. The gun gave the bullet enough force to pierce through the vest and through me. That way I would actually die. But, the bullet contained specially engineered stem cells that were released as the bullet passed through me. They were designed to heal slowly enough to stay dead for Cloukora, but quickly enough so I couldn't be found by the soldiers."

"That is brilliant. But I've been wondering: what will this accomplish? I'm not sure I see a point here."

What was *the point?* "It hits two birds with one stone." Tomi began, fixing the coat's sleeves and smoothing it out so it looked more fashionable. "That power gives him an edge against Lucifer, creating a better chance of winning, and if he's in the form long enough during the fight, he'll succumb to the darkness. Once that happens, he'll be willing to join us. Making everything that much easier."

"But what if that doesn't work?"

"Then I'll just kill him. And I mean *me*. If your blade so much as goes near his heart, mine goes through yours and you can join him."

"Ah. That makes sense. Kinda. And of course, my lord. Your wish is my command." Venn probably thought he was a bit crazy. Sometimes he even thought that himself; that he *was* crazy, and his plans *didn't* make sense.

"So Oushu's finally dead?"

"Yeah, Cloukora killed him."

"Was that also part of your plan?"

"Yep."

"Good. That guy was a total prick. What he did back in L.A. was just- it was wrong."

"Yeah…" Tomi changed the subject. "Tell me how your mission is going."

"Eh, it's going. The town doesn't suspect a thing. But if Cloukora is stronger, doesn't that make him more of a challenge?"

"I'll let you find that out for yourself." A helicopter landed in the middle of the compound, and Tomi and Venn strode towards it. Tomi began to faintly remember a memory deep in his past.

Spring, 2001

Three young kids lay out in a back yard on a hill, looking up at the sky. Clouds dotted very little of the atmosphere, but they still tried to make shapes out of the white puffs. Tomi had shorter hair back then, and wore a t-shirt and cargo pants.

"I still can't believe you're leaving, Cloukora." Tomi told the other boy. Cloukora's hair wasn't that much different than now, and he was wearing a t-shirt as well, but jean shorts instead of cargo shorts.

"I know. I don't want to move either, it sucks. I'm never going to forget about you guys, though. You two are the closest friends I've ever had, and that's a memory worth cherishing for the rest of my life." Cloukora replied.

"Do you think we'll ever see each other again?" The young girl asked. She had blonde hair that fell just below her shoulders, green eyes, and wore a dark green tank top, and shorts that fell short of her knees. Tomi thought she looked beautiful, and he knew Cloukora thought so too.

"Yeah Ashley, I think so. No, I'm sure we will." Cloukora sat up, leaning back on his hands. "Let's make a promise: when we get old enough, let's all look for each other and never stop until we succeed."

Ashley and Tomi both said "Promise."

"Cloukora! Your parents want you!" Tomi's mother yelled to them.

Birth

"Alright!" Cloukora got up and turned to them. "This is it. I'll miss you guys, I really will." He gave Ashley a hug, and Tomi a fist-bump, and walked out to the front through Tomi's house. He wished the goodbye could have been longer, but Cloukora truly seemed bent on seeing each other again. So he knew the goodbye didn't mean forever. One day they'd be together again.

"Let's go see him off, Tomi. It's what any good friend would do." Ashley suggested, and Tomi nodded. They started walking towards the back gate.

"Tomi! I need you in here for a minute. I have something for you to do." His dad poked his head out from the back door of the house.

"Alright dad." After his dad went back inside, he turned to Ashley: "Please, don't leave me alone with him." He begged her.

Ashley gave him a confused look. "Why? You'll be fine! Trust me." She pecked him on the cheek and went out the back gate. Tomi walked inside through the back door into the kitchen.

"Tomi, down to the basement. Now." His father commanded.

"Yes, dad." Tomi followed him down. When he reached the bottom of the steps, his dad held a vial of a purplish liquid.

"You need another dose."

"No! I don't want to drink that stuff anymore! It's making me feel weird."

"Tomi. Our ancestors fought for the Fountain of Youth! For this!" His father held up the vial. "You are going to drink it, and *like it!*"

"I don't want to!"

"Tomi! Now!"

"NO!" A longsword appeared in his hands. The hilt was made out of dark gold, and the blade had sharp curves that went downward near the bottom, and went upward towards the middle.

"My son, do you have any idea what you're holding?! You're wielding Excalibur!! The blade of our great ancestor!"

"I'm tired of your sick experiment! I'm your son! Not a test subject!"

"Tomi, you're the only one who's ever held that sword besides King Arthur himself!" He went to his workbench where the rest of his supply of Fountain of Youth was stored. "If we're gonna awaken your full potential you're gonna need a lot mor-" Excalibur pierced through his heart.

"I told you! I'm done!" He pulled the sword out, and watched as his father turned to face him. His eyes stared back at Tomi's in shock and disbelief, blood beginning to drip from the edge of his mouth. As his lips quivered to say something, his body collapsed to the stone floor, where he lay gasping for air-for life. Life his son had just taken from him. No longer did his mouth move, and Tomi now only stared at the dead body of his father. A mixture of sadness and guilt and happiness filled him. He wasn't sure what he was supposed to feel. His father *did* treat him like a guinea pig, but it's still his father. He must have stared for an hour before he went upstairs to his mom, hands dripping in his father's blood. His heart broke when his mom let out a scream and backed away from him. She acted as if he were a devil. How could killing evil make him evil? He didn't understand.

A couple days later, he was sent to a foster home for killing his father. Not because of the abuse inflicted on him; which wasn't even been brought up in the court hearing. The dark government-owned sedan pulled up to a beautiful white two-story house in a normal, suburban neighborhood where every house looked practically the same. Apparently this was the only family that would take him in. Tomi anxiously walked up to the door, nervous to see what the family looked like. He hoped he could start anew, and live a happy life here: Go to school, make friends, play a sport or two, get a nice girlfriend, and maybe go off to a nice college. The front door opened, and a couple stood in the doorway. They looked like they were extremely happy with each other. A good sign. The man had his hair a mess while the woman contrasted with him. If anything, the man looked like a rock n' roll star and the woman a sweet motherly type.

When he got up to the door, he received a bent hug from the woman. Did they even know what he did? "Hi! My name's Annie and this is Chris. He'll show you around while I go make you some lunch,

okay?" She straightened and went off into the kitchen. The child service folk had went back to their car and drove off as Tomi stepped inside the house to follow Chris. The tour didn't take that long and what he saw of the house was amazing; it was such a gorgeous but normal home. It has an elegant feel to it, but it wasn't too elegant. It was just right. And it made him feel safe, too. He felt like this was a new start for him, for his life. Finally, he was led to his room.

"This is where you'll be staying." Chris pointed out all of the belongings they had got for Tomi. "Your TV is against the wall there, which gets shut off at nine o'clock by the way, your toy chest in the corner there, and your closet is behind you. Oh and of course your bed which you're standing next to." As a grinning Tomi began unpacking, Chris continued. "I know what you're capable of Tomi Pendragon. Yes, I know your real name." The grin on Tomi's face faded, but his unpacking didn't slow. "After all, I was a friend of your father's. I can't see why you would hate the gift that was given to you. You could change the world, maybe even control it. And I can help you achieve it, Tomi. I can help you become the most powerful man on this planet. The way your father was going about it, was all wrong. He shouldn't have forced it on you like he did, but rather showed you its true potential, to train you to become something great. To live up to your family name. But he wasn't bright enough; his head was stuck on the idea of creating a monster. You're proof of his idiocy." He turned to leave the room. "You'll start tomorrow. Welcome home." Tomi was wrong, this wasn't going to be pleasant; this was going to be Hell.

Military base, Western Oregon

Cloukora walked outside the hangar with the General to a car that sat on the runway. It was a ruby red 1971 Plymouth Hemi Cuda with the stock Hemi decal towards the rear of the car on either side. The wheels in the back were bigger than the ones in the front by at least an inch, giving it that hot rod feel to it, and it had a small wing on the trunk. It was one of the few things he asked for as a condition. Cloukora

ran his hand along the smoothly-painted car. He could not believe this was his first car; he felt like he was in a dream.

"Managed to get a hold of one huh? What about the rest of my stuff?" Cloukora opened the car door and sat in the driver seat. The general handed him a driver's license with all of his information and picture on it, and the keys to the car. Cloukora turned the key and the engine roared to life. He turned on the radio and Foreplay/Long Time by Boston came on. "Newer radio, just like I asked."

"Yep, and your immunity to the law has been notified to every police station. Your alter ego's immunity of course, not your real identity's." The General stated. "You're legally a vigilante. You should be honored."

Cloukora closed the car door and put on the seatbelt. "Never ask me for anything again. Ever." He put it into drive, and peeled out, zooming off, with the loud music colliding with the engine's roar.

Angel's Gaiden

Summer of Monsters

July 14, 2010
Connor Lake outside of St. Paul, Oregon

    Torches were lit all around the dock and bank of the lake, allowing for the large group of people to see in the dark as they downed all types of alcohol and danced to the loud music coming from the vehicles parked nearby that added even more light with their headlights. In the middle of the lake, a large boat drifted on the calm, dark blue water. The partygoers on its deck contrasting with its peacefulness. Some of the guys wore just swimming trunks, and some girls wore bikinis, or at least had the top showing, but almost all of them had some kind of glow stick around their wrist or neck. After all, they were drunk. They had to have some way to be found easily.

    Nicole grinned when she pulled up in her fairly new hatchback next to an old, beat up pick-up truck. She knew tonight was going to be amazing. She turned off the car's engine before stepping out to get a better view of the party. She was somewhat short, had short black hair that didn't even reach her shoulders, and wore a tank top and a pair of short shorts. A young woman not much shorter than her ran up to her with a red cup in her hand and wrapped her arms around Nicole, causing some of the drink to spill out of the cup. "Hey Raspy, how's the party?" Nicole asked the other woman. That was her nickname given to her by her colleagues because of her slightly raspy voice.

    "It. Is. Amazing! So many hot guys, so much booze, and the lake is *so* much cooler than I expected." Raspy replied before taking a sip of the red cup.

Birth

"Is Sean here?" Nicole asked, glancing around the party to find him.

"Yeah, he went to take a piss. He'll be right back. Tonight are you gonna…" She gave a fake cough to hint at what she was talking about.

"Raspy, I'm not like that!"

"Soo that's a yes?"

"Are you kidding me? Miss the chance to sleep with the hottest guy at school? Nuh uh." That was somewhat of a lie, she wasn't sure what she would do if she was given the opportunity.

Raspy laughed. "Speaking of hottest guys, I'm gonna go back over to Steven. Have fun." She said the last part in a sing-song voice. After Raspy turned to leave, Sean had walked up to Nicole. Sean was quite a few inches taller than Nicole and had a muscular body to even it out. His hair was a light brown that matched his eyes. Like almost every guy there, he wore just swim trunks around his waist.

"Hey, what's up?" Sean said smoothly with a smile.

Nicole brushed back her hair. "Not much, just got here from my house. I snuck out; I'm not actually supposed to be here." That was also a lie.

"That's pretty badass." That smile of his was getting under her skin, but she thought it in a good way. "Hey, wanna go for a walk around the lake? There's a nice spot in those trees on the other side we can sit at."

Nicole bit her lip before saying "Sure." She took him by the hand as he led her around the lake. When they got to the other side they took a seat down on the muddy bank, the trees giving them some privacy.

"So uh, we're here all alone. Surrounded by the trees. No one to bother us." Sean said, moving a little closer.

"Mhm." She looked into his eyes. "Well, do I gotta make the first move?" She wasn't sure where that came from; she had never been straight-forward like that. He really *was* under her skin, but she liked it. It felt right to her. Perhaps it was just hormones. Either way, she wasn't backing out now. Sean leaned forward to brush her hair back

and gently press his lips against hers, slowly starting to make out. This excited her, and her body felt like it was being electrified, and in the heat of the moment, took off her tank-top to reveal her green bikini top. Sean put a leg on the other side of her, positioning him above her. Nicole leaned back on her elbow, still kissing passionately.

Sean let out an "Umph" and took his lips away from hers.

"What's wrong?"

"I don't-AGH." His back arched forward. "W-what's happening?" Scales began to cover his body and gills formed on his neck. "What's happening to me?!" Nicole moved her body backwards away from him, unable to turn her head from both curiosity and fear. His eyes turned yellow, and his pupils narrowed as if they were the eyes of a reptilian. His body became a dark green, his teeth sharpened as they elongated, and his mouth transformed with them to fit their size and shape. His fingers grew longer and formed sharp claws at the end of them as a long, wide tail grew out from his tailbone. The transformation of his body shape and size caused his clothes to rip off his body. A body that was no longer human, but reptilian. As soon as Sean was no more, the creature took notice of Nicole and lunged at her as she let out an ear-popping scream.

The scream brought attention from the party-goers on the boat, and when they looked in the direction it had come from, all they saw was a splash in the water by the bank. "What the hell was that?" One of the guys asked.

"I don't know." Another replied.

"We should check it out." But before they could start up the boat, they felt something hit its bottom. "What was *that*?"

"Probably just the wind picking up." The bump came again, only this time it was rougher, and they all ran to hold onto the railing around the boat. One last bump moved the boat, but this one was much bigger, causing the boat to tilt until it had flipped over bottom side up. As the boat began to sink, a giant reptilian creature broke through the water's surface. It was what Sean had turned into, but now bigger than a three story house. Its roar had everyone on the bank screaming in panic and running to their cars to escape the ferocious monster.

Birth

Hours earlier
Forest Grove, Oregon

Cloukora lay in his bed, just staring at his wall without a care in the world. A care *for* the world. Brev had been constantly calling him, most likely to go on another mission, but he ignored every single one. He had on jeans and an Iron Maiden shirt that had the band mascot, Ed, on it: A man holding a hatchet with his skin missing. Cloukora's mind was blank except for one thought: Tomi was dead. That was all he could think about since he left that airbase. He wished it was all a dream; he wished he could just wake up and he'd be alive. His mother walked into the room and crossed her arms.

"Cloukora, you've been in your bed for almost a week. Ever since you got back." When he didn't give a reply, she sat on his bed and put her hand on his shoulder, trying to give comfort. "Is it about that mission you went on? Want to talk about it?"

"No." Cloukora curtly replied.

"You have to get out or something. Go for a walk."

"Mom, just please." He was starting to get irritated.

She shot up off the bed and put her hands on her hips and looked at him. "Hey! I don't know what your problem is, but you need knock it off." Cloukora didn't answer. She shook her head and headed out his door. "When you finally feel up to it, your stepfather wants to show you something." She sighed and walked off, shaking her head again.

Not too long after, his phone sitting next to him went off. Caller ID said Brev, but he didn't pick it up. The ringing stopped, and then started again. Cloukora decided to answer it just so she would finally stop. "Yeah?"

"There was a murder in St. Paul. I thought you might want to check it out." Brev replied.

He sighed. "And why would I?"

"A man murdered his wife in their own home." She said it like it was hardly anything. He wondered how some people could take death so lightly.

"Maybe he just had something wrong with him. Like Multiple Personality Disorder."

"No history of violence or anything wrong with his brain. Right after he killed her and the cops arrived, he realized what he had done and ran to her side, *crying*."

"Like I said, Multiple Personality Disorder."

"I don't think that's it." She let out a sigh. "Some say he might have been possessed."

Possessed. Cloukora hated that word already. It meant having to deal with demons more than he had to. He just wanted to fight Lucifer and get it over with. It honestly didn't matter whether he won or not. He let out another sigh. "Alright fine, I'll do it."

"You still have your badge right? You're gonna have to pose as an agent again. It's turned into a crime scene."

"Yeah, I still got it. Alright, I'll head there now. Bye." He hung up, rolled over onto his back, and ran his hands down his face in frustration. "Great. Just fucking great." Cloukora got up, packed up his hoodie, gun, mask, ammo, badge, and some clothes into his backpack, and picked up his sword which he had at the corner of the front of his bed and the wall. The sword disappeared into thin air when he put it around his back.

As he walked down the backdoor steps, he noticed his stepdad working on a car that looked like a late 60's or early 70's Pontiac GTO. The car looked as though it had sat for a few years, never being driven. There wasn't any rust, but there were spots of paint wearing out here and there. He placed his bag by the 'Cuda and walked over to him. "Nice car, Jack. When did you get this?"

Jack, his stepfather, was in the process of replacing the old spark plugs with new ones. "I got it while you went on that mission for the government. It's a 1969 Pontiac Le Mans. I was gonna tell you before you went, but I wanted it to be a surprise. Then you came back, and you wouldn't even leave your room." Cloukora walked to the back

Birth

workbench of the garage and noticed a small throwing knife holster with five knives in it, lying on the bench surface. He took one out and started fiddling with it as he started back towards the front of the car.

"It looks a lot like a GTO." Cloukora pointed out.

"Yeah, but this car's better." His stepfather joked, still occupied with it.

"It's a beautiful car, I'll say that much."

"Yep, she sure is. But all muscle cars are beautiful."

"Oh of course."

"So where are you going?"

"Well now that you all know who I am…I'm going on a mission over in St. Paul. It's about an hour or two away so I don't think I'll be gone for long." He spun the knife in his hand. "So what *do* you think of my situation?"

"I'm not really sure. It's great you're saving the world and all, and having super powers must be really awesome. But, I don't want to end up having to attend your funeral." He said straightening from working on the plugs and wiped off his hands of grease onto a rag.

"Eh, I'm sure I'll live for a long time. No villains have popped up yet." He laughed, but it was partly forced, because he remembered of his appointed fight with Lucifer. A fight he wasn't too keen on fighting. "If I go down though, I won't let myself go down as anything but a hero. I'll make sure of that…But, as I said, you won't have to worry about seeing me buried six feet under."

Jack only nodded, but wasn't convinced. "I never got to check out that sword of yours. Mind if I look at it?"

"Go ahead." Cloukora pulled the sheathed sword off his back as he made it appear, and handed it to him.

His stepfather unsheathed half of the blade, studying it as he ran a finger across its edge. "What does this say on the blade?" He flipped it over, and the inscription was on the other side as well.

"Pugnare pro honore, amore et fide. It's Latin for: Fight for honor, love, and faith."

"How'd you find that out? Did you take a Latin class or something?"

Birth

"Google."

"Ahh." His stepfather noticed Cloukora messing around with the knife. "Know how to use those?"

"Kinda. I know I'm supposed to throw them, but not sure how exactly."

"It's not hard, really. He sheathed Cloukora's sword and handed it back to him, before holding out his hand for the knife. When Cloukora gave it to him, Jack held the blade upside down. "You hold the end of the knife that's the lightest, put your weight on your main leg, and keep the weight off your other leg. Angle the blade in your hand, and ..." Jack flung the knife into the drywall at the back of the garage, blade sticking into the wall. "Throw. Just like that. Remember, it's not about the force you use to throw them, but *how* you throw them. It takes dexterity, not strength." Jack turned to go back to his car. "Take 'em with you, maybe you can find some time to practice with 'em."

Cloukora picked up the knives off the bench, and the one from the wall, and headed to his car while sheathing his sword before making it disappear. "Might wanna fix the wall before mom sees it." He threw his bag in the back, and almost got in the driver seat when Jack spoke.

Not looking up from the engine, he said: "Cloukora. Whoever you lost on that mission, don't blame yourself for it. Trust me, that's a route you do not want to take, and it only makes things worse for you and everyone else. Just…keep pushing on. It's what they would have wanted." Cloukora didn't reply, even though he knew Jack was right, only stared off at the ground for a moment before silently getting in his car and driving off.

St. Paul, Oregon

He pulled in next to the curb in front of the house. It had looked like any other suburban house: two stories, one-car garage, perfectly painted white siding and a garden of flowers in the front yard. The police had arrived already, taking notes on what the neighbors reported. Yellow crime scene tape blocked off the inside of the house; it being

the only difference from the other houses. A cop was already taking a man to the police cruiser when Cloukora walked up to him. "Excuse me, officer; may I have a word with the man?"

"And who are you?" The officer stopped and looked at him. The man he held by the arm only looked down at the ground, not paying any attention to what was going on around him.

"Agent Jordan, FBI." Cloukora went to pull the badge out, and felt that it wasn't in his pocket.

"A little too casually dressed to be FBI aren't you?"

He patted his other pockets feeling for it, until realized he had left it in the car. "Excuse me a moment." He walked to his car and shifted through the glove box until he found the identification badge, then went back to the officer to show it to him. "Sorry, I'm a little new. So what happened here?"

"This *psycho* murdered his wife with a butcher's knife. Then he had the nerve to act like he didn't do it." The officer replied with disgust.

"That's what I heard. I'm just curious why he's still playing the part of the innocent man. Even though he's going off to jail."

"It doesn't matter, this man needs to be locked away. For good."

"I think I'll be the one to decide that. So, can I have a word with him?"

"Go for it. I can't even stand to touch him." He obviously hated this man with a passion.

Cloukora pulled him off to the side and sat down on the curb. "I want to hear *your* side of the story. What's your name?" The man didn't answer. "It's okay, it's just your name."

"It's Marcus." Marcus still hadn't taken his eyes off the ground.

"Marcus, my name's agent Jordan, and I can help you. But you have to tell me what happened."

The man was still in shock. "I-I'm not exactly sure. Everything was going fine: we were in the kitchen making dinner, pot roast. She made the best damn kind too. She asked for the butcher's knife and then when I turned to grab it, I blacked out and…When I came to, Megan was…" Abruptly, he broke down and started crying and sobbing into

his palms. Cloukora patted him on his back and frowned. He knew what it felt like to lose someone close to him. Maybe not as close as Marcus and Megan were, nor was it his fault for Tomi's death, but he still felt the same pain.

"It's alright, I believe you. Is there anything you can tell me that might help me figure out what went wrong, and prove you innocent?" The man shook his head. "Alright, well, until I figure this out you're going to have to stay in the cell. Don't worry, I'll take care of this. Okay?" The man nodded. Cloukora helped him up and took him to the police cruiser. "I'm gonna take a look at the crime scene." He told the officer. "Hold him in jail until this investigation is over." The officer nodded as Cloukora strode up the sidewalk path and into the house. Almost everything was nice inside: the furniture was made of dark, polished wood and soft, milk-colored couches and chairs, and the grey carpeting felt comfortable under his shoes. Along the white walls were scattered pictures of family members and of the couple. The kitchen was the only place that looked horrific: the dead woman was being zipped into the body bag, with blood splattered on the floor and the cabinets and walls near where she lay. Cloukora felt some empathy for the man that killed her. He most likely didn't know what he was doing when he murdered her. He couldn't imagine blacking out and murdering the woman he loved. Nor did he even want to.

"May I help you sir?" A detective, who was zipping shut an evidence bag with the knife inside, asked curiously.

"Yes, I'm agent Jordan of the FBI. I was assigned this case." He showed the badge.

"Well there's not much of a case. The man stabbed his wife, and the neighbor ran to the house when they heard the screaming, saw him murder the victim, and then called the police. Hell, he even admitted to doing it. It's a pretty cut and dry case if you ask me."

"Mind if I still have a look around?"

"Sure, the master bedroom still needs to be checked out. Everywhere else is being taken care of."

"Thank you. Oh, do you have a pair of extra gloves on you? I seem to have forgotten mine." The detective pulled out a pair of white

gloves from his jacket pocket and tossed them to Cloukora. "Thanks." Cloukora put the gloves on and headed towards the back room to begin investigating. When he walked in, he noticed a purple energy drink on the vanity mirror near the door. "Fountain of Youth..." He turned it to the back and read the description: "'Tired of feeling old? Well drink Fountain of Youth and you will think you're a teenager again, and will be rushing to get all the things you need to get done, done.' Sounds like a load of crap to me." He continued searching the room, going through the closet, drawers, and the dresser, but couldn't find anything of importance. No pills, no drugs; nothing that could have caused him to up and just kill someone. Cloukora walked back out to the living room. "Nothing, but a can of an energy drink. I guess you could run toxins on it, to see if it was drugged, but no drugs or pills that I can see."

"I told you." He said with an I-told-you-so tone. "I'll have the can sent down to forensics. See if they *can* gather anything on it." The detective chuckled. "Can. Get it?"

Cloukora shook his head. Any other time he would have thought that was a little funny, but today wasn't any other time. He noticed the body was gone. "Is the body down at the Coroner's?"

"Yeah, you can head down there if you'd like."

"I will. Thank you." Cloukora walked to his car and sat in the driver seat for a moment, thinking. *What would make someone do that? It doesn't make any sense. It didn't look like he was possessed. But I also don't see anything proving otherwise. Maybe he really was...* He put the Cuda in drive, and drove to the police station.

Down in the autopsy room, the Coroner, Sheriff, and Cloukora stood around the body, studying it. The autopsy had already been done before Cloukora had gotten there. The room was just like it was in the television shows and movies: Tiled, cold, and drawers of bodies along the wall. Cloukora was still in deep thought.

"This is the *fifth* death in *two* weeks. In this small town, that's unusual...What do you think of this, agent Jordan?" Cloukora was half paying attention, not realizing the Sheriff was talking to him. "Agent

Jordan? Agent!" Cloukora snapped out of it, remembering where he was.

"Sorry, was, um, spacing out. You said there were four other deaths, right? What happened?"

"All horrible, and some disturbing, incidents. One woman was killed in the woods, brutally mutilated. Two had their blood drained from them. And the other was killed in some kind of sacrificial ritual."

"Did you find any suspects?"

"Only for the ritual case. One of their friends tipped us off, letting us know what they were gonna do. But...we didn't make it in time to stop the sacrifice. At least we got the sons of bitches."

"Is it possible that the woods attack was a wild animal and the victims drained of blood were due to natural causes?"

"There are no wild animals that are in those woods that could do something like that. And as far as I know nothing natural could cause a sudden loss of blood."

Then maybe it's something unnatural. *But that wouldn't make sense. Vampires and werewolves happening to be in the same location? It doesn't seem right. Unless they are somehow getting along. If that was the case, then what was with the ritual?* "Have you noticed any...hostility in this town? Like townsfolk hating each other or being bitter towards them?"

"No, not that I know of. Why?"

"Just curious. And the ritual. Do you know why they were sacrificing the woman? Or who or what they sacrificing her to?"

"Look, we don't look into that kind of stuff. We try to stay out of the crazy department. If you want, we got one of the cult members locked up here. The others have been transferred already. If you wanna talk to him, go ahead."

"Show me." The sheriff led him out the door and up the stairs to the upper floor, and then down a hallway to several iron-barred jail cells that were lined up. In one of the cells a black-robed man sat on a bench, head in his hands. "Excuse me, sir. I have a question for you." The man didn't even lift his head. "That ritual. Why did you sacrifice that woman?"

Birth

That got the man to look up and stare at Cloukora, brows furrowed and looked as if he was on the verge of tears. "You don't understand. We didn't want to. She didn't deserve to die. But we had to do it. We had to. This town is cursed; it's being overrun with monsters and creatures of the night. Creatures that are taking people from their own homes and killing them! They can only be the work of the spirits. They are angry at us. And you know why? Because this town hunted and burned 'witches' long ago, and now their spirits have come to take revenge. To kill everyone and everything in this town! I know because I read it in the book of the town's history. Those creatures we thought weren't real: ghosts, werewolves, and vampires. They are all real. That's why we sacrificed the woman. In hopes of calming the spirits and freeing this town from their wrath."

"That's enough crazy talk." The sheriff began.

"I saw them with my own eyes, sheriff. I saw a werewolf rip someone to shreds. My own friend!"

"Being delusional about your friend's death doesn't honor him. Get some sleep."

"No… it was my *friend* who did it. My *friend* tore that man open." This caught Cloukora's attention, who was about to walk away.

"Your…friend turned into a werewolf?"

"You believe me don't you?"

"That's enough, we need to focus on solving this case. Let's go agent Jordan." Cloukora followed the sheriff away from the cells, and when he looked back he caught the man watching him walk away. *So, there are werewolves and vampires then. Is it really witches though? Why would a bunch of dead witches suddenly start offing people? Why now? Nothing is adding up.* The sheriff's phone went off and when he answered it, said a couple of "Mhm's" and "Okay's" before hanging up. "Welp, they didn't get anything off the toxicology report. Now what?"

Cloukora rubbed his hand down his face. "I don't know. This case is just. I don't understand what's going on-"

"Sir, we just got a call of a domestic disturbance on Hazel Street." An officer alerted, sitting at a nearby desk with a phone to his ear.

"I'm on it." The sheriff assured as he hurried out the door.

"I'll go too, but I'll take my own ride." Cloukora told the sheriff as he followed him out. The sheriff got into his own cruiser and sped off down the road with his lights flashing and siren blaring, and Cloukora following a few seconds behind.

When both cars had pulled up in front of the house, Cloukora stepped out and told the sheriff to wait outside in case the suspect tried to get away, and before the sheriff could protest, Cloukora was already at the door, gun ready and aimed inside. The lights in the living room were off, in fact all the power seemed to be shut off, and the furniture thrown everywhere. "FBI, come out with your hands up!" No answer. He slowly crept through the doorway and living room, careful not to step on the shattered glass covering the wooden floor. "I'm not going to ask again. Come out with your hands behind your head." As he moved towards the hallway, an old television set flew from the end of the corridor and into the wall of the living room.

"Get out of my house!" A woman walked out of the darkness of the hallway and into the light of the setting sun that shone through the window. "This is my home. You can't take me away!"

"Look, lady. I'm just here to help. Obviously you're going through something, and that something needs to be fixed before anyone gets hurt." With not even a single moment consideration to what he just said, she had sent a ball of blue energy at his chest, knocking him into the television screen mounted on the wall, and onto the floor. Before he could get back on his feet, a half a dozen of pots and pans flew directly at him; she most likely had used some kind of telepathic powers. Quickly he used the wind to prop the nearby wooden coffee table in front of him on its short end, so that it stood tall above him to block the flying objects. After the barrage ended, Cloukora had the

Birth

wind turn around the coffee table so that the legs faced the woman, and sent the table at her, trapping her behind it.

"Let me go."

He grabbed his gun from off the floor and started towards her. "No, not until you surrender."

"Never!" The coffee table was sent right back at him, and with Fyron in hand, Cloukora sliced it in half, and made the sword disappear as soon as the split was made.

"I don't want to have to use force." Her breathing was heavy while his was surprisingly still normal. She looked at the ground a moment, deciding on what to do. Suddenly a knife flew into her hand and she lunged at him. On instinct Cloukora brought his gun up and fired three shots into her chest until she fell to the ground, and lowered it again. *Now* his breathing was heavy. "Great, witches are real too." At that moment the sheriff burst through the door.

"What happened?" The sheriff asked, aiming his gun around the room in case anyone else was in the house, before putting it back in its holster.

"She came at me with a knife. I...I couldn't do anything about it. It was on instinct." The sheriff put his hand on Cloukora's shoulder.

"It's alright, agent Jordan. Things like this ha-"

"What the hell is going on here?" Cloukora turned to face the sheriff. "That was a *witch*. She tried to kill me with friggin pots and pans! You didn't want me to listen to that guy locked up in the cell not because you thought he was crazy, but because you know it's true. You know those were werewolf and vampire attacks, don't you?"

The sheriff sighed. "Yes, I do. The whole police office knows. We're just trying to keep it under wraps; we don't want to freak the locals out. Or anyone else for that matter. It also makes us feel a little saner. We didn't even put those murders into the official database."

"When did it start? These murders?"

"About a week or so ago."

"So this hasn't been going on for a long time then?"

"No, it all started around the same time the locals saw a strange man walking through the shadows of the town."

"A strange man?"

"Yeah, they say he moves swiftly through the night. But that's not all that's strange. They also said it feels like he *wants* them to see him."

"It might be him causing all of this. Call up one of your officers. Tell him to cross reference any events that happened around the time this all started. And I mean *any*." The sheriff nodded and began to dial his phone while Cloukora walked around the house to search for clues. When he finished, and found nothing helpful, the sheriff was just hanging up his cellphone as he entered back into the living room.

"All the officer could find was a shipment of supplies to a local convenience store."

Something caught Cloukora's eye sitting on top of the kitchen counter by the sink. "Let me guess," Cloukora began as he walked towards the counter. "The new Fountain of Youth energy drink."

"Yeah, how'd you know?" Cloukora held up a half-empty can of the energy drink that sat by the sink as he turned back around. Cloukora's face frowned as he crushed the can in his hand and hurled it the fridge door, letting out a yell of frustration.

"Son of a bitch!" Cloukora strode towards the front door when the sheriff's two-way radio went off.

"We need a dispatch at Connor Lake. We're getting reports of a giant lizard attacking everyone! All available units report to the vicinity. I repeat: all available units!"

"I'll take care of it; you go get those drinks recalled from all of the stores." Cloukora didn't wait for a reply and continued out the front door to his car. Night had already come, and the moon illuminated the starry sky.

The crowd ran away from the lake and into their cars, screaming as the giant reptilian creature behind them roared. Its sharp-toothed mouth went for a woman who had unfortunately tripped over an unseen cooler. But before the mouth could get close to her, bullets pelted the monster's face, calling its attention to where the shots originated from.

Unfortunately, the bullets weren't strong enough to go all the way through. "Hey fuckface, over here!" It was Cloukora wearing his disguise, adrenaline pumping through him, making his eyes that bright green color, and smoke coming from the barrel of his gun he had aimed at the beast. As the reptile looked at him, he had a moment of regret for drawing its attention. *I suppose it's better me than them.* Cloukora rolled out of the way of a large foot that came down right where he stood and ran towards the beast, as a pillar of the earth shot out of the ground to strike the creature's jaw, causing it to stagger, Cloukora ran up a thin, sloping path made of earth he had formed, only about two feet wide, that went up and over the monster's back. Jumping off the path and onto the creature's scaly head, he struck his sword into its skull, and aimed his gun to fire into it, but the bullets still bounced off. "Dammit." *Got one other option.* Cloukora pulled his sword from out of the skull and ran towards its front and leaped off and into the air. Spinning around mid-fall he aimed his gun, calculating the wind speed and angle from where he was and would be when the trigger is pulled, all in one instant, before firing the bullet into the beast's eye and into its brain. Cloukora landed on his back and somersaulted backwards onto his feet to watch the creature fall into the lake, unmoving.

He turned back around to walk towards the crowd that was now gawking at him. *That monster had to have been too big to hide in this lake unnoticed.* "Was anyone here drinking the new Fountain of Youth energy drink?"

A woman hesitated before answering. "Yeah, my friend Sean was."

Cloukora sighed. "I'm sorry to be the one to tell you this, but that was Sean. Which brings me to my next point: don't *ever* drink that energy drink brand. Not unless you want to end up like Sean and have me come back to kill you as well." Saying that had made himself feel a little terrible. Threatening someone with death is not a good way to present as a hero, but he needed to scare them. People had to stop drinking it or else he *would* have to kill them.

"Wait, if that was Sean…Oh my gosh!" A different woman ran off around the lake and towards the other side with a man following

close at her heels. When his eyes went back to the crowd, he saw a silhouette standing in the middle of corn field before it vanished into the stalks.

"Excuse me." Cloukora apologized as the crowd moved out of his way when he walked towards them and continued into the field of tall corn stalks. "Who are you? Why are you doing this?" A man stepped out from behind a group of stalks. He had long black hair, wore a Metallica t-shirt, denim jacket, black ripped jean shorts, and sneakers. When Cloukora saw the sword on the man's back, he drew his own.

"Cloukora, we finally meet." The man said.

"Who are you?"

"I'm sorry, my manners. My name is Venn, and I'm with Darkstar. The organization you've been at war with."

"So that's your guys' name. But what does *Darkstar* want with this town?"

"We need an army, Cloukora. The apocalypse is coming and we alone cannot stop it. We need help."

"And how does creating monsters with an energy drink help?"

"You still haven't figured it out have you? It should be obvious to you what it is, we put it on the can for crying out loud! It is no energy drink. No, it's from the actual Fountain of Youth."

"What? But I thought…"

"Our leader found it down in Central America. Your ancestor didn't destroy it, he couldn't. So he simply hid it instead. Just not as good as he thought he did."

"But how did it change those people into monsters? They were good people!"

"No, I was careful about choosing my test subjects. They all had a dark secret to them, which meant there was at least a sliver of darkness in their hearts. The man that killed his wife? He cheated on her a few days ago. That Sean kid? Heh, he bullies kids that are younger than him! They were not as good as you thought they were."

"It still isn't right! They didn't deserve to die!"

"Then join us, Cloukora. If you did, then we wouldn't need an army, because we would have you. We could give you *so* much power,

Birth

Cloukora. Enough to easily wipe Lucifer off the face of the Earth, and then help us take it for ourselves!"

"Not gonna happen."

Venn sighed. "Your loss." He drew the sword from his back; a Scottish Claymore. "Too bad I'll have to kill you. You seem like a pretty cool guy, and you're a living legend. Plus it looks like we have the same taste in music." Venn pointed to Cloukora's Iron Maiden shirt. "Last chance, dude."

Cloukora rushed towards Venn, sword ready to attack, and as it was about to hit, Venn had morphed into one of the ghosts he had seen at the Winchester House, and in an instant there were about ten more surrounding Cloukora. Despite some of them hiding in the stalks, he could still see where each one was. Luckily the moon was bright that night. The blade went through the ghost that had been Venn, and the ghost immediately evaporated into thin air.

"Wrong one." He heard Venn say, but his voice seemed a little altered from being a ghost, as if it were an echo.

"You bastard! That was you."

"Ya got me. Now, can you catch me?"

Cloukora concentrated on the ground, and had thin, sharp spikes made out of the earth pierce through every ghost. All of them vanished, and Venn dropped to the ground, bleeding from where the spike went through in his chest. "I don't have time to play your games." Venn grinned, and then vanished. Cloukora felt something behind him, and barely spun just in time. The claymore would have gone through his heart if he hadn't turned around, but instead, it grazed his right arm. He had never felt this kind of pain before. Pain that sent a shock throughout his arm and shoulder. "Agh!" Cloukora held his shaking hand on the wound, wincing, and blood dripping down as he turned completely to face Venn.

"I'm not that easy." The claymore swung at Cloukora, but was blocked by Cloukora's katana. The pain surged through his body as he struggled to keep the sword held up with both hands. "Come on, just give up already!" Cloukora pushed up harder, but it wouldn't move any further, and it looked like Venn wasn't even breaking a sweat.

Birth

Cloukora kicked Venn in the stomach, and as the balance was lost, Cloukora pushed downwards on Venn's sword, and elbowed him in the face. Venn backed up, wiping off the blood dripping down his nose. "I'll die before I give up." Cloukora attacked this time, and each time he swung, it was blocked by Venn, who after several more strikes, finally seemed to be getting tired.

"You are something, aren't you? But you're no match for my boss. He will cut you down like butter."

"As are you. And I don't give a rat's ass what your boss can do. I'm coming for him, and nothing will stop me."

Venn grinned, and charged at Cloukora, sword ready. In one swift motion, Cloukora pushed Venn's sword to the ground and sliced his side open. Venn fell to his knees, holding the side of his chest. He wasn't going to die any time soon, the wound wasn't that deep, but he would pass out long enough to put cuffs on him. "You're screwed Cloukora. He won't stop until he gets what he wants. He's a very ambitious man. If I were you, I'd start planning my funeral."

"Then let him try. Let him throw whatever he has at me. Because I won't stop either. I won't stop until the world is safe from evil like him. And when you see him, tell him...tell him King Relyt has returned, and he's the first on my list to bring the sword of judgment down upon his neck. Tell him, the true king has returned." Cloukora hit him in the back of the neck with the side of his hand, knocking him out cold. "Taking too long." Cloukora picked him up and dragged him to the car.

The sheriff heard a knock at the door of the police department. He had stayed behind while everyone else went home, waiting on agent Jordan to return. When he opened the door he found a man in a white-grey hoodie and metal-like mask on the steps holding another man by the arm. It was the vigilante that had been sighted in Salem and Portland. "You."

"Before you arrest me, this is the man you want. He was the one handing out the poisoned energy drinks to everyone. *He* is responsible

Birth

for all of the deaths." The vigilante handed the man in cuffs over to him before stuffing his hands into his pockets and started down the steps.

"It's no coincidence, is it? That both you and agent Jordan showed up around the same time, and he isn't anywhere to be found?"

The hooded man stopped and cocked his head to the side. "Don't tell anyone. If you do, I just might have to come back." The hero continued down the steps and along the sidewalk and out of sight.

The sheriff grinned. "Maybe having a vigilante around isn't such a bad thing." Remembering the man he now held by the arm, he led him down to the cells. "Let's get you where you belong."

Cloukora was driving towards home when his phone rang. His arm was still in pain, though not as much as before; he had patched it up with some bandages he kept on hand in his car for such occasions. It was Brev on the other line.

"Good work on your mission. How'd it go?" She asked.

"Bad. The other organization, which I found out are called Darkstar, was involved and apparently they're distributing an energy drink called Fountain of Youth to the public. And the kicker is that it's actually from the Fountain of Youth. It's turning everyone into monsters." He had explained to them awhile back about his family history and the Fountain of Youth, all of which his grandfather had already told them. In fact, all of Wolfstorm's members' abilities had come from the Fountain. It's what Brev had been testing the bullets with, too.

"If that's the case, then people are in danger. I'll get Kaora and Nole to search for any factory that could be manufacturing them so we can tear them down."

"Alright. Hey Brev…"

"Yeah?"

"I killed people today. Instead of trying to sedate them, and find a cure, I killed them. I mean, I killed people back in Iraq, but these were good people. They just weren't themselves."

Birth

Brev was silent for a moment. "Cloukora, even if you did try to find a cure for them, there's no sure chance that you could of. The Fountain of Youth is something no one can understand. I don't think Relyt even could have. They tried to kill you, you acted in self-defense. It's alright if you want to feel the way you do. But you can't let it get to you. Instead, learn from what happened. Remember the mistakes you made, and make sure you don't make them again. We all make mistakes, it's how we choose to live with them that matters."

"Heh, you always know what to say don't you?" He nodded as if she could see. "You're right. I gotta learn from these mistakes. Thank you, Brev. Let me know when you've got something."

"We will. Oh, and Cloukora. Check your bank account." Brev hung up and Cloukora did so as well before calling his bank.

"Hello, this is Oregon National Bank, how may I help you?" The operator asked.

"Yes, I need to check my account balance."

"Of course, what is your name and pin number?"

"Cloukora Skyrell, and it's 8675."

"One moment, please." After a few seconds, she came back on. "You have a balance of one thousand dollars in your account, the last deposit by a company called Hero International. Anything else I can do for you?"

"No thanks, that's it."

"Okay, have a good day."

"You too." He hung up. "Nice. Now I don't have to work at Safeway." He shifted gears, and sped down the road, the forest of trees becoming a blur.

Tomi walked along the sidewalk towards the police station. The sun was high in the sky; birds were chirping, and no cloud was in sight. He could smell fresh cut grass and feel a cool breeze roll in.

He opened the door to receive a "Hello, how may I help you?" from one of the officers. The place inside was pretty small, and only had a few officers working. After all, this was a small town. He heard

Birth

'Bad Moon Rising' by Creedence Clearwater Revival playing from a speaker somewhere.

"I'm looking for someone." He replied, looking around, before heading towards the jail cells.

"Sir! You can't go back the-" With a motion of Tomi's hand, the man's neck twisted and he fell to the ground. The rest of the officers, about three others, pulled out their guns and aimed them at Tomi. Excalibur appeared in his hand.

"Freeze! Put your hands in the air!" They tried to act with courage, but Tomi knew they were scared out of their minds.

"No thanks…" Tomi threw the blade at the officer to the right of him, and appeared in between the other two, right as Excalibur pierced through the man's neck. Tomi placed his hands on the two officer's faces, and a purple aura surrounded his hands. They began to bleed through their eyes, nose, mouth, and ears, as they screamed for their lives. In a few seconds they dropped to the ground, lifeless, eyes rolled to the back of their heads. Blood began to paint the floor around them. Tomi continued towards the back, towards Venn's holding cell.

"My lord! I'm so glad to see you." He held his side; it looked like he was injured. "I'm sorry, he caught me off guard and I couldn't capture him. Next time I'll get him." Suddenly Venn was pulled up to the bars by an invisible force.

"What is the policy about failure?"

"I-It's not tolerated, my lord." Tomi heard fear in his voice.

"So why didn't you kill him?"

"You said you wanted to kill him yourself!"

"That is no excuse."

Tomi could see confusion in the man's eyes. *Did* he say that? That thought was gone in an instant. Of course he said to kill him. "Please, my lord, give me a second chance. I won't mess up again!"

"Fine." Excalibur appeared in Tomi's hand, and pierced through Venn's heart. "In your next life, don't fail." He pulled Excalibur out, and Venn collapsed to the floor.

With his last breaths, Venn said "He knows he's King Relyt's reincarnation, and he says you're the first on his list to bring his sword

of judgment upon your neck." He coughed up some blood. Tomi didn't understand how he was even still alive. *Perhaps I missed.*

Tomi laughed. "It's all talk. He is nowhere near as powerful as I am."

"He is going to kill you. And everything you worked for will be worthless." Venn laughed, coughing up more blood. "I can see it now. He'll be standing above you, his sword at your throat, as you bow to him like a peasant and beg for mercy. And I hope he doesn't give it to you, you son of a bitch." Tomi turned to walk out as Venn made some more coughing and choking noises before turning silent.

"Traitor." He barely took notice of an officer at the end of the hallway with his gun raised.

"Who are you? What'd you do?!" He fired a few shots as Tomi walked towards him, each time missing.

Tomi finally reached the man, who was trying to fire bullets that were no longer in the gun. "I cleaned the place." Excalibur was swung at the man's neck.

Angel's Gaiden

VENGEANCE

July 17, 2010
Portland, Oregon

    The sun's rays beat down on Cloukora and Brev's backs as they bustled through the crowded streets of Portland. Even though it didn't show, Cloukora still felt Relyt's sword on his back. Not in a physical sense, more in a magical kind of sense. He just knew it was there without actually having to *feel* it, it was like a special connection. Today he wore an Aerosmith t-shirt, jeans, and his skate shoes. The necklace with his family crest -that amplifies his powers- dangled from his neck. He wondered how much longer he would have to wear it for. Eventually he should be able to use his powers without it. Brev wore a slightly formal white short-sleeved blouse, a medium length black pencil-skirt, open-toed black heels, and her aviator sunglasses. It was Saturday, so not only were there a lot of teens out of school for the summer, but adults had a break from their work as well. Walking through the crowd, he overheard people talking about the events happening lately; the things he had done. Most of what he heard were good things. The majority of people were actually excited to have a superhero exist, especially in their own area. One or two people had said that it was a bad idea, because that might mean a villain will reveal themselves and bring chaos to the world. Cloukora partly agreed with them on that part, but he was also confident in himself. He was sure he could take down any evil villain that showed their face. It was odd. He was never confident in himself, but once he started being a hero, he felt stronger, braver, and more confident. Perhaps he had found his purpose

Birth

in life. Brev pointed out a tall, fancy, and expensive-looking corner skyscraper at the next intersection across the street.

"That's where we tracked down the factory. It's where they're making those energy drinks." Brev reminded.

"It doesn't even look like a factory."

"There's a possibility they have it underground. We're going to stake it out though, just to be sure."

"Aww. That's no fun." He jokingly complained. "So where are we watching from?"

Brev gestured to a restaurant that had tables with umbrellas and chairs outside of its entrance. "Portland's Finest Burgers."

Before they could even reach a table, he was bumped into by a young woman in a business outfit in a rush to get somewhere. Cloukora turned around to face the girl, who met his eyes with hers. She was about a few inches shorter than him, her round face perfectly smooth and bright, her green eyes sparkled like emeralds, and her long brown hair pulled back into a ponytail. "Sorry-" He noticed a ring with an emerald stone on a silver chain hanging from her neck. He had a flashback from his childhood: Before he moved, he had given an emerald ring to Ashley, his childhood friend and crush. It was given both as a going-away present, and a promise to always keep her in his heart. The latter without her knowledge.

"I'm really sorry, I'm just…I don't know. I tend to walk fast, and I wasn't watching where I was going."

"Nah, it's alright. Don't worry about it." He was still focused on that ring, until he realized it was a little too close to her breasts, and brought his eyes to her face, a little embarrassed. "What's your name?"

"Ashley." She replied.

Could it be? "Cloukora. Nice to meet you." He held out his hand for a handshake. Instead she wrapped her arms around him.

"Cloukora!" He thought she was going to start crying tears of joy. "It's been so long! I missed you."

He hugged her tightly. "I've missed you too Ashley. I see you still kept that ring."

Birth

They let go of each other. "Of course I did! Why wouldn't I?" She fumbled with the keepsake. "This was given as a promise. Now all we need is Tomi!" So maybe he did promise her, it just wasn't exactly the promise he made in his mind.

Cloukora's joy vanished. "About that…Come sit with us, so I can explain."

"What's wrong?" She followed him and Brev to a table and sat down with Cloukora.

"I'll go get us some food." Brev said before entering the restaurant. She knew that they needed to talk by themselves.

"Tomi…well…he…" He wasn't sure how to go about telling her. Should he say the full truth? Folding his hands on the table he said it: "He's gone…" It needed to come out sooner or later, and he was stalling enough as it was.

"What do you mean? Did you talk to him recently?"

"Yeah…under some unusual circumstances, but the point being…he's no longer with us." He stared down at the table, if he ended up shedding a tear, he didn't want her to see.

"Did he leave to another country?" Cloukora shook his head. "He's not…dead, is he?" Cloukora didn't lift his eyes from the table. "Tomi's *dead*? How do you know? What happened?!"

"I just do…and I don't really want to talk about it. I'm sorry Ashley…I didn't want to tell you. I wish I didn't have to…"

She couldn't help herself from crying, and covered her face to keep people from seeing her, but Cloukora thought that made it a bit more obvious. Regardless, he sat in the chair next to her and held her in his arms while she cried into his shoulder. Brev came out with the food, placed it on the table, and sat down in a chair as Ashley straightened in hers, wiping tears from her face.

"Thank you." She said, but she didn't reach for it, only stared at it. Cloukora felt bad for telling her, he didn't like seeing her like this, but she deserved to know. His grandfather's voice spoke in his head. *You're going to have to do things you don't want to do. That's the life of a hero.* He pushed that thought out of his head. *It's not the same.* He told himself, but a voice in the back of his mind told him it was.

"So, what's with the business outfit? Did you get a job or something?"

She picked up the hamburger and contemplated on taking a bite. "Yeah. When I was in middle school I got to skip a grade and instead of eighth grade, I joined the freshman class of my high school. So I got a year's head start and graduated in June." She finally took a bite and chewed it before continuing on. "And about a week ago I landed an internship at a fashion design firm, which I was on my way to now to drop off a couple of things." That seemed to lighten her mood a little. Everyone enjoys talking about themselves from time to time. Even Ashley.

"Congratulations, on both the graduating and the job. I wouldn't have expected any less; you *were* the smart one out of the three of us. But fashion design? I thought you would have gone into science or something."

"I actually plan to do something in the science field, not sure what yet. I just couldn't find a better position than the one I found."

"Ah, well I'm proud of you Ashley."

"What about you?"

"I start my senior year in September, and then after that...I don't know. Maybe go off to college." He honestly didn't know. With the recent events, he wasn't sure where he'd even be by the time school started. He could be dead for all he knew. "As for a job I...well I-" Brev tapped Cloukora's shoulder and pointed towards the building for Cloukora to look at. A man in casual clothing had walked inside.

"Now why would a working class man like that just walk into a building with that much prestige?" she asked rhetorically.

"Ashley, I'm sorry to leave you like this, but I gotta go take care of something. Do you have a paper and pen?" Cloukora asked.

She pulled out a business card from her purse that read Beaverton Salon & Beauty. "You can just write on the back of that." She then took out a pen and handed it to Cloukora, who jotted down his phone number on the card.

Birth

He gave her a hug before leaving. "It was nice seeing you again. Next time we'll talk on better terms." Cloukora let go, before walking across the street with Brev towards the building.

Before they went inside, Brev commanded: "Look for anything that would lead to a downstairs." Cloukora nodded, and they walked in. The lobby inside looked just like any high class building that would employ blue and white collared workers. The air was nice and cool inside and it smelled like someone had baked an apple pie. No doubt that was originating from candles. Unless they had an oven in there. In that case, Cloukora wanted some.

"Can I help you?" The lady sitting at the front desk nicely asked.

"Yeah do you have any app-"

"I'm looking for a Mr. Donald Lemway." Brev leaned on the counter. "I have an appointment with him for an article I'm working on."

"Ah, yes. He's on the Executive Floor, number fifty-four." The lady said politely. Cloukora wondered how Brev got the right name, then noticed a board on the wall behind the lady with names listed on it. One of them being Donald Lemway. *Oh.*

"Thank you." Brev straightened up and they walked towards the elevators until Cloukora noticed a door to the building's stairwell.

"Going down?" Cloukora opened the door and gestured to the stairs leading downward. After they reached the bottom of the stairs, Brev opened the metal door as they each drew out a pistol, loaded a magazine into it, and cocked the chamber. The basement on the other side of the door was just a long hallway with pipes and wires lining the concrete walls. They held their guns ready as they started down the corridor. The closer they got to the end, the louder they heard metal clanking and machines moving. Suddenly an alarm went off, and red lights flashed down the hallway. They must have realized Brev wasn't a journalist. Their presence was no longer a secret. "That was fast." Not long after, footsteps ran up the stairs and the people that accompanied them wore tactical gear: Face masks, bulletproof vests, black clothing, and held M4's with red dot sights and grips attached to the guns.

Birth

"Drop your weapons and put your hands behind your head, now!" One of them shouted. *Four men, about fifteen feet away. I got this.* Cloukora tossed the pistol at them, and as it flew in the air, adrenaline surged through him and he quickly had Neró and Vesi appear in his hands and charged at them. Bullets fired at him as he ran, each one flying through his path, being blocked with the two hook swords and deflected back at the walls. Within a few seconds he was right in front of them, smacking the middle two in the stomach with the back sides of the swords. In an instant, the two swords disappeared, and in one swift movement, Cloukora drew two knives from the sheath, one in each hand, and drove them into the other two's chest, and pulled them out. Sheathing them again.

"You've gotten better." Brev stated as she walked towards Cloukora, who picked up his gun off the ground.

"I've kind of been training whenever I can." He replied modestly. He had been shedding blood, sweat, and admittedly even tears each training session.

"Well, good. It seems to be working. You need to get as strong as you can before the big fight."

"Yeah…We should keep moving." He had been trying to keep from talking about the fight as much as he could. It would only stress him out more.

At the bottom of the stairs at the end of the hall were roughly ten more men waiting for them. Machines that had stopped running took up the majority of the floor space, and the ceiling went up about ten feet higher from the stairs, which itself was about twenty. All the workers apparently had escaped. "Brev, let me see your gun for a second." She handed it to him and Cloukora ran and jumped onto the railing as the enemy rained bullets on him, every bullet miraculously missing. Half way down the railing, he jumped off and as he was in the air, aimed the two pistols, judging when and where to shoot each bullet within seconds, and fired back at them, precisely hitting five men; killing three, injuring two. As soon as he landed on the hard cement, he ran to hide behind one of the machines, while trying to return fire at the same time.

He placed the guns on the ground, and pulled Relyt's sword from the sheath on his back, allowing it to appear. Focusing on the ground, the earth began to shake and five blunt spikes shot out of it, hitting each of the remaining men in their chests, knocking the breath out of them, and they fell backwards onto the ground. After they all stopped moving, signifying their death, Brev walked down the steps. "Did you really have to kill them?"

"They were trying to kill *me*. Not even that, they work for Darkstar, and I'm sure they know full well what they're guarding and who they really work for. I mean, I do feel *some* remorse, but they should have chosen a different side."

Brev only shook her head. "We need to destroy this place somehow. Any ideas?" Cloukora gestured to a barrel with a flammable symbol on the side.

"How about that?"

"That would work, but how would we set it-" The ground tilted the barrel and spilled the oil all over.

"We should probably get out of here." Before Brev could ask why, air swirled around inside a machine that held coal set ablaze, picked up one of the pieces of coal, and dropped it onto the ground where the oil was slowly snaking its way towards. They spun and ran towards the exit in the back, and barely made it across the street before flames had burst through the basement windows, sending glass shards flying everywhere as far as the asphalt. The fire alarms inside the building went off and employees poured out in panic. They didn't understand what was going on, but of course they wouldn't, only the higher-ups would know what had just happened in the basement.

"Think we made an impression?" Brev asked.

"Yeah. They know this means war."

"Do you really think so?"

"If your supply factory was destroyed, wouldn't you be pissed?"

Brev didn't answer, and they both turned opposite directions and walked off through the awe-struck crowds. Cloukora saw that

Birth

Ashley had her hand over her mouth unable to believe what had just occurred, but only kept moving. *If only she knew…*

A woman burst through the throne doors. She was a thin woman with long pitch black hair and icy blue eyes. She wore a black Metallica t-shirt over a light grey sweat-shirt, ripped jeans, and black heeled boots. A broadsword was sheathed on her back and a silver-plated heater shield rested over it. The top of the shield curved into a point, instead of being flat across like most heater shields. "Where the hell is Venn?!"

"Ahh Ava, how have you be-" Tomi started. He wore his usual black shirt and purple overcoat, and his leather boots.

"Cut the crap, Tomi. You sent Venn on a mission and he hasn't come back! Where is he?"

Tomi sighed and put on a face filled with sorrow. "I've been trying to figure out a way to tell you this…I sent him on a mission to kill Cloukora, our biggest threat of late. And unfortunately, I have received word that he had killed Venn. In cold blood, and in front of a bunch of police officers, too! They he killed soon after. I can only imagine what you and the families of the fallen officers must be feeling right now. That Cloukora, something's not right with him. I'm so sorry, Ava."

She was silent for a moment. "Cloukora huh? Do you know where I can find him?"

"Well there's a fair tonight, and he recently met a girl…So I would start there." Ava allowed nothing else to be said as she quickly stormed out of the throne room. Chris, Tomi's foster-father, walked through just as she left. His hair was a tad messy, and he wore a blue suit with the blazer unbuttoned and a white button up shirt underneath. His outfit also lacked some type of tie.

"What was all that about?" Chris asked.

"I told her Cloukora killed Venn." Tomi simply replied, as if he didn't just put a death sentence on Cloukora.

"I'm guessing that's not true and your blade was the one that ended his life. Why did you do that?"

"Well for one, if I told her the truth, she would attack me, and I would have to kill her."

"And the other reason?"

"Love drives strength in people. They go to great lengths to get what they want. She just might kill him for me." Tomi turned around to look behind the throne at the wall. There were multiple screens of places around the world playing live footage, with one displaying the Portland factory exploding. He tossed an apple slice into his mouth.

"But I thought you wanted him to join our side?"

"I do…I did…I change my mind. It'd be easier if he was just dead. Now please, leave me be." Tomi tossed another slice of apple into his mouth as Chris turned to walk out of the room.

Hillsboro, Oregon

The sun was setting and the breeze was cool. The fair was alive with people, the smell of fair food filled the air, and the lights had already been turned on to light up the whole fairground. A local band playing a cover of "Wanted Dead or Alive" that was originally played by Bon Jovi sounded off in the distance. The music and the sounds of screams coming from people on the rides oddly mixed in together. Cloukora and Ashley strolled through the crowds, Ashley eating pieces of cotton candy off a stick. She had changed from her business outfit to something a little more casual and easier to breathe in: jean short shorts, blue tank top, and a pair of black flats. Cloukora wasn't actually sure she would say yes when he called her a few hours before, asking her to the fair. But he was glad she did.

"Thanks for taking me here, Cloukora. It's nice hanging out with you again." Ashley commented.

"Yeah, it really is. Hey, I heard the Ring of Fire is pretty scary, wanna try it out?" Cloukora asked.

"Sure, then we'll get something to eat. I'm starving." As they were waiting in line for the ride, Cloukora had a sudden strange feeling he was being watched. He glanced around behind him, but didn't see anyone watching. "Something the matter?" She asked.

"Oh nothing, I just…it's nothing." Cloukora shook his head. *Just getting a little paranoid, that's all.* It was their turn for the ride. The Ring of Fire was like a roller coaster, but it was a single loop. The carts would start moving back and forth along the loop until it gained enough momentum to reach the top and then begin going full speed around the loop, making it feel like it was out of control. During the ride, he felt the eyes again, and as the ride reached the top of the loop, above everyone else, he looked around and saw a woman with long black hair, arms crossed, watching the ride. No, watching *him*. The ride went down, but when it came back up, she was gone. After they stepped off the ride, Cloukora bent over, holding his stomach. He felt like he was going to blow chunks at any moment. He didn't think he'd ever ride on it again. "Let's get some food now. I probably won't eat right away, but I'll get you something." At the concession stand, he felt the eyes again, and turned to meet eyes with the same woman he had seen. Able to get a good look at her now, he saw that she had a black Metallica shirt on over her grey sweat-shirt, and wore ripped jeans. But what made her stand out was the broadsword and shield on her back. It felt as though she was staring at him like she was angry at him, but he had never seen her before in his life. His stomach still felt queasy and before he knew it, she started towards him.

"Cloukora! I will kill you, you son of a bitch!" Not giving him a moment to react, she kicked him in the stomach, sending him back into a group of empty picnic tables. She drew the broadsword from her back and pointed it at Ashley's throat. "You killed Venn, now I will kill your little girlfriend!"

"Venn? I don't know who you're talking about." That feeling of anger began to form inside him, like it did when he encountered Tayge, and back in Iraq. It took all he had to keep it suppressed. *I can't let it out, not here.*

She strolled over and kicked him in the stomach again as he lay on the ground. Pain surged through his abdomen, not helping his nausea and worsening the urge to vomit. The feeling of anger got stronger, too. "You don't even know his name? You bastard. He went on a mission down in St. Paul and you killed him *and* the police officers in the town!" Ashley tried to attack the woman, but the pommel of the woman's sword swung at Ashley's head, knocking her out cold. The woman's eyes not even straying from Cloukora. This didn't help the rage building up inside him.

"What the hell are you talking about? That must have been someone else. I only put him in jail. Maybe sliced his side open a tad, but that's it."

"Don't lie to me! Our boss said it was you!"

"Don't you think maybe your boss is *lying*?" He had to do something, but his stomach made it difficult to even move. *Damn my weak stomach.* He tried focusing on the ground, but nothing happened. He quickly swept her leg with his and as she fell backwards, he stood up, drew Relyt's sword from his back and pointed it at her. Getting up that quick was a bad idea, though. It made his queasiness feel worse. "I don't know who you are, but I don't want to have to kill you. So I ask you, please go before this goes any further."

"Shut up!" She lifted her left leg and kicked him in the chest, sending him flying into a booth, knocking everything inside over- luckily the booth attendant moved out of the way in time. He saw her get up, but it was difficult for him to follow suit. Even with his adrenaline pumping, he couldn't focus. He managed to make a couple earth spikes shoot out of the ground where she stood, but they weren't quick enough and she simply walked around them. Next thing he knew, after he had finally stood up, a fist had hit him in the chest, and sent him flying at an impossible distance into a building, breaking through the green-painted brick wall. The impact sent a shock throughout his back. The man that hit him had tanned skin, blonde hair, and had enormous muscles. He looked like one of those preppy guys from school that always worked out and acted like he was better than

everyone else. In fact, he even wore preppy clothes. The pain in his back made him forgot about his stomach.

He was starting to get tired of being thrown around like a ragdoll now. "Who the hell are you guys?"

"My name is Cairne, and this is Ava. Venn is her lover, the one you killed." The man replied.

"For the last time, I didn't kill him." The man and Ava charged at him and Cloukora kicked his sword up from off the ground with his foot, and managed to block Ava's attack just in time. As he was about to wonder why Cairne hadn't reached him, Winter appeared and punched Cairne in the stomach and in a split second, kneed him in the face and kicked him back. She wore jean shorts that ended mid-thigh, and a thin white Hollister long-sleeve shirt that almost covered her shorts.

"We put a tracker in your cell when we gave it to you. We usually just track your movements off and on, but today Brev had us monitor you all day long. She knew after the explosion, they might come after you. Apparently she was right." She explained.

"Well they're not after me for that. They think I killed one of their members in St. Paul."

"You didn't. We saw the footage, someone else offed him."

"Who?" Ava asked.

"It was-"Cairne tried to grab Winter by the arm, but she grabbed *his* arm, stepped to the side, twisted his wrist, and then used the side of her other hand to hit the back of his neck, knocking him out all in one swift motion. "Don't you ever interrupt me again." She smoothed out her shirt. "We don't know who exactly. But he is very powerful…I think Venn knew him, at least it seemed like he did. There was no sound to hear what Venn had called him, but the man scared the living shit out of your boyfriend." She told Ava.

Ava sighed. "I know who it was." Cairne was already getting up; he was a tough son of a bitch. "Let's go, Cairne. Cloukora, I'm sorry for threatening you like that. My anger had blinded me from the truth." Suddenly, Angel-like wings spread open on both of their backs. Ava's

Birth

being brown, and Cairne's orange. Then they were up in the air and gone.

Cloukora looked at Winter. "What the hell was *that*? We're facing people that can fly? We're screw-" Winter had spread green wings from her back, too. "The hell? Does everyone get wings but me?!"

"C'ya Cloukora." She flew off into the sky as well.

Cloukora walked over to Ashley, picked her up, and carried her to the 'Cuda.

Beaverton, Oregon

Cloukora pulled up in front of Ashley's house, and she finally regained consciousness. "So now you know what I do for a living, huh?" It was an attempt at a joke that didn't seem to work.

She rubbed her eyes, and put her hand on her head. Cloukora handed her a towel with an ice pack he picked up from the store on the way. She replaced her hand with it. "So today at that building…that was you?" Cloukora reluctantly nodded. "I'm guessing that's also how you knew about Tomi, right?" Cloukora nodded again. "Why didn't you tell me?"

"You know the code: 'Don't tell anyone your secret identity.' Apparently it's a lot harder to keep a secret than I thought." He leaned on the steering wheel.

"I am your *best friend*, we're supposed to tell each other everything!"

"Look, I'm sorry. I didn't want to endanger you."

"Did a fine job at that didn't you?"

"How was I supposed to know someone would mistake me for killing someone?" He let out a sigh. "From here on out, I will be perfectly honest with you. I promise."

"Then be honest about this: Police found burned bodies in the basement from the explosion. People died in there, Cloukora. And they say the burns were post-mortem; they died before the fire. Did you have anything to do with that?"

Cloukora was silent for a moment. "I didn't have a choice, Ashley. They were trying to kill me—"

"Only because you broke into their facility!"

"They were also part of an evil organization. They were working for the bad guys."

"Is that what you're telling yourself? So you'd feel better at night? Cloukora those men had families, people that cared about them." She shifted in her seat to face him better. "I want you to picture their faces when they find out their son, husband, father, whatever died in that fire. Feel their sadness, their rage. What would you do if someone killed your dad for just doing his job so he could support his family?"

Cloukora ran his hand down his face and propped his elbow on the car door as he glanced out the window. She was right, and he knew it. "I...I'm sorry. I acted on instinct, I did what I thought was right at the time. There are decisions I'm going to have to make that I won't like."

"Look, Cloukora, I *know* there are going to be times when you have to kill. I don't like that fact, but it comes with being a superhero. All I ask though is to put more thought into it before you go killing them. Think about why they're firing at you. Think about their families and those you will end up hurting. Do that for me, please."

Cloukora didn't say anything, just continued to stare out the window. Ashley opened the door irritably and got out before shutting the car door and starting up the narrow brick path to her house. "Ashley wait!" She ignored him. "Ashley I need to tell you something."

"No, just leave me alone."

"It's about Tomi." She stopped in her tracks halfway up the path. "His...his funeral is about a week from now. Do you..."

"...Yeah, let me know the time, and I'll be ready for you to pick me up."

Cloukora waited a few moments after she was inside her house before driving off.

Birth

Ava kicked open the throne room doors, and walked in, sword drawn and shield ready. "Tomi! You piece of shit! You killed Venn!" Cairne followed her in. He wasn't going to stand for this either.

"So you figured it out? Bravo, bravo." He clapped his hands mockingly. "Now what? Are you gonna try and take revenge out on me?"

"I'm not going to *try*, I *am*!" Ava rushed at him, and swung her sword at his chest, but was blocked by the sudden appearance of Excalibur in his hand. It didn't even seem like he was putting any effort into the block. Tomi kicked her in the chest, and as she flew back, Excalibur unbelievably sliced her shield in two. The impact of the wall shook her whole body, sending a shockwave of pain all throughout her body. She felt like she couldn't move as Tomi walked towards her. She felt like a paralyzed animal waiting for her predator to lunge. Cairne just watched, he wanted to help, but he knew Tomi was too strong, even for him.

Crouching, he looked into her eyes. "I should kill you right here and now for this little stunt." Ava's eyes widened. He was serious; he really was going to kill her. "But, I realize my mistake killing Venn. He could have been helpful…No matter; you will make up for it." He stood up. "But don't even think about betraying me again." He started out the throne room. "Cause it won't just be your life that pays the price." He shut the doors behind him. Cairne looked at Ava, then at the doors, then back at her, contemplating what he should do. In the end, he decided to leave. Ava understood why, though. *Tomi would kill Cairne in an instant, because he also had Eve, so it wouldn't be a huge loss. I, on the other hand, am vital now that Venn is gone.* Tears fell out of her eyes as she sat there and began to sob. "Venn, I'm sorry, I tried. Please forgive me. I wasn't strong enough to avenge you…" She rested her head against the wall. It was going to take quite some time for her to even get up on her feet.

Angel's Gaiden

Old Acquaintance

July 21, 2010
Tualatin Hills Nature Park, Beaverton, Oregon

    A man and a woman moved excitedly through the forested area during the cool summer night. The man was somewhere in his early twenties, he was a bit on the short side, had an almost-shaved head, and slightly large tunnels in his ears. He wore a loose, black tank top, long denim shorts, and sneakers. The woman was slightly taller than him, in her early twenties as well, and had long blonde hair. Her outfit was quite revealing: She wore a short, summer dress that pushed up on her breasts, and showed a little more than what should be shown, and wore flip flops on her feet. They had been flirting with each other and talking dirty all night long until finally, they couldn't wait any longer: they ran into the forest to find a quiet and private spot to ease their hormonal rage.

    "Tiff, come on. It's cool. There aren't any animals in here except birds." The man assured the woman, who stopped for a moment to glance nervously around the forest.

    She hesitated before continuing. "You're right, Greg. I just feel like we're being watched is all." She said half-convincingly as she continued to follow Greg deeper in. They eventually came to a spot next to a tree and began their little make-out session. All of a sudden, Tiffany heard a branch rustle from somewhere nearby. "Did you hear that?" She asked as he was kissing her neck and moving his hand along her belly.

Birth

"It's nothing, Tiff, we're fine." He said irritably. Another tree rustled. This time, he heard it too. They stood for a moment, watching the trees. Waiting for something to pop out at them. Waiting for a creature of the night to spring out of the darkness and snatch them up. Their heartbeats were racing, their fear building up with each passing second. Suddenly a large grey-feathered creature swooped down straight towards them. On instinct they threw their hands up to protect themselves, but it had no quarry with them, and instead it directed its flight to the next branch. After realizing it was only an owl, they let out a short laugh at themselves for being so scared, before continuing their passionate kissing next to the tree.

Tiff opened her eyes for a moment to see someone walk behind Greg. The man wore all black, so it was difficult to see what he looked like, but what she could see were pitch black eyes and long, sharp fangs. She let out a scream as the man sunk his teeth into Greg's neck. His body and face turned pale white as the blood was being drained from him and into the other "man". She quickly turned to run back the way she had come, or rather where she could remember. She glanced back to see if she was being followed, and when she turned her head forward again, the man was standing in front of her, forcing her to skid to a halt. From the moonlight shining on his face, she could see it was a vampire, something from the legends, now real. She let out a scream as his teeth sunk into the skin of her neck.

Cornelius, Oregon

Cloukora pulled up next to the gas pump in his ruby red 'Cuda. After he paid the attendant the thirty bucks, the man went to put the gas hose into the fuel tank at the back of the car, as Cloukora shut off the engine and laid his head back on the leather seat, and waited for the pump to finish. Today he wore a black t-shirt that said Pantera in yellow-orange font, and his usual dark blue jeans. His phone rang in his pocket, breaking the sweet silence. Pulling the cellphone out, he found that it was Brev who called.

"Hello?" He asked, resting his arm on the leather car door with the window rolled down.

"Got another case for you, Cloukora." She said, getting straight to the point.

"Well that's a surprise." He said sarcastically. "What is it?"

"Two bodies were found in Tualatin Hills Nature Park. They were drained of their blood."

"Vampire?"

"Most likely. They found bite marks on their necks identical to those of a vampire. But of course, they're not gonna say it's a vampire."

"When do you want me to meet you there?"

"Now. But you won't be meeting with me. I got other business to take care of. Winter will be going on this mission with you. Be at the Beaverton Police Department. You two have to view the bodies; you guys know more than they do."

"Winter? Why not Erro, or Cal, or Avenorra?" He really did not want to work with her on this case. He thought Winter seemed like a bossy kind of person that would push him around the whole time. He didn't like being pushed around. He liked calling his own shots. Or at least be ordered by someone who wouldn't break your arm if you called them a girl.

"Half hour, Cloukora. Be there." She hung up the phone, which Cloukora did right after, and had put it back in his pocket. The gas attendant was finally done, and Cloukora started up the engine and drove off towards Beaverton.

Beaverton Police Department, Beaverton, Oregon

Cloukora walked through the doors of the coroner office to find the bodies of a man and a woman lying on trolleys, with only their pale, lifeless faces shown. Winter and the coroner were standing over them, talking. The coroner was an old man, probably in his fifties. He had thinning grey hair, wore glasses, and despite his age, was tall. His clothing was the standard white coat and a plastic apron over it. Winter

wore jean short shorts, a light blue Hollister-brand tank-top, and pink Converse-brand sneakers.

"Hi there, can I help you?" The coroner asked politely as soon as he saw Cloukora walk in.

"He's with me." Winter quickly assured, before Cloukora could even say a word.

"What's with the lack of professionalism with you two? I thought you were FBI. Did you *just* get the call or something?" The coroner asked nosily.

"Something like that." Cloukora replied, walking over to the bodies. "So what can you guys tell me about the bodies?"

"Well, all I can see wrong, is their blood had been drained from the body, and what appear to be two teeth marks on their necks. I think we have a psychotic vampiric serial killer on our hands." The coroner let out a slight chuckle and Cloukora and Winter put out the best fake laugh that they could muster up. "The guy-or girl if you will-must have a huge obsession with vampires. So I'd start there. Though, that's a long list. With the whole vampire and werewolf fad going around."

"Trust me, we're pretty good at our job. A little scrap of clue can go a long way. Thank you for your help." Winter thanked. "Come on agent Smith, we'll check out the crime scene." She said to Cloukora.

"I thought your supervisor said his name was agent Jordan?"

"Yeah, that's what I said." Before he could say another word they both walked out the doors and out the department building. Winter walked over to her car in the parking lot, which was a 2009 Ford Fusion, as Cloukora walked over to his own car. They both got into their respective vehicles, and drove off towards the scene of the crime: Tualatin Hills Nature Park.

Tualatin Hills Nature Park, Beaverton, Oregon

Both cars pulled up into the parking lot of the park, and both drivers got out and started along the blacktop path that split off into a worn asphalt path winding through the forest. "You're gonna need

this." Winter tossed a magazine to Cloukora, when he looked at the top bullet, he noticed it was silver.

"I thought silver didn't kill vampires?" Cloukora said, slightly confused.

"In Europe, no. In North America, yes. Vampires are different all around the world, and have different weaknesses and traits. Kinda like humans. Don't worry, in the case that it's a migrated European vampire, those bullets were dipped in Holy Water. So either way, it's dead." Winter loaded her magazine into her gun, cocked it, and held it ready as she headed into the forest along the asphalt path with Cloukora following right after, loading his gun. Trees consisting of Redcedar, Pine, and Fir made up a canopy over them. A variety of bushes, flowers, and other plant life covered most of the forest floor. Cloukora could smell a marsh not far off from where they were.

"What about sunlight then? I thought it kills them." He was ready to aim his gun if needed as he eyed the woods for any sign of a vampire lurking about. Luckily the park was closed for maintenance, or else they would end up running into trouble with tourists.

"*Direct* sunlight. They are in a wooded area where it's filtered, so they'll be fine to run around in here. A little sun doesn't kill them. Or anyone for that matter." She was talking about someone else now.

"Right? Like the kids these days."

"Exactly. On their iPods and game systems all day. What happened to imagination and going outside and playing?"

"I guess technology happened. People had always wanted to advance with technology, so we could be lazier. Well, it looks like they got their wish. Let's just hope it doesn't get any worse." Winter and Cloukora both broke their straight faces and burst out laughing.

"Good one, Cloukora." Winter realized she was laughing, and abruptly tried to hide it along with her embarrassment. Cloukora thought she must like to be serious all the time.

They went quiet, and for some time, there was silence in the woods. "Hear that?" Winter asked.

"Hear what?"

"Exactly, not even a bird." She looked around more warily now. "Be sharp." They heard a rustle coming from behind them, and they both pointed their guns in that direction of the noise and watched to see if anything moved. Nothing did. They lowered their guns and turned back around to see a man right in front of them. His eyes quickly turned black and fangs protruded from his gums. Before the vampire could do anything, Winter kicked it in the stomach, gave it a right hook, sent an uppercut with her left, and then pushed it away with the bottom of her foot. As it flew through the air, she shot at the creature three times, before it landed on the forest ground. Both slowly walked over to the corpse to confirm its death. It had three bullet holes in it: two in the heart, and one in the head.

"Nice shot." Cloukora complimented. He fired two more shots into it. "Sorry, just to be safe." Winter didn't protest or argue. Cloukora looked back at Winter to see a vampire appear behind her. "Look out!" He shouted, and before he could stop it, it grabbed Winter by the waist, jumped onto a tree branch, and headed deeper into the forest with her struggling to get out of its grasp. Cloukora fired a couple rounds at it, but missed each time. "Dammit." He lowered his gun, staring into the forest. "Don't worry Winter, I'll find you." He started off in the direction it went, but walking along the path near a pond, until he heard footsteps in the mud along the bank. Cloukora quickly hid behind a nearby bush next to the bank and tried to peep through it to see who it was. It was a woman, a woman that looked familiar to him. Then he remembered her: it was Zela. That demon that came into his house and threatened him to stay away. Oddly, that night made more sense now. They were referring to the apocalypse. *Guess they weren't crazy after all.* He almost charged at her, but then saw someone else appear through some kind of door of light. It was a man, and he had giant white wings on his back and a light, golden aura about him. Cloukora thought he looked like an Angel.

"Nyx." Zela acknowledged as the angelic man approached her.
"Zela." Nyx bowed to her. "How is our master?"
"He's…anxious to get out."

"As am I. This world needs control. It needs someone to straighten them out and show them their true place in the universe. A race that is destroying its own world doesn't deserve to be that high on the food chain. Soon they'll realize they're not as high as they think they are. Soon."

"Yes, they will. But your part. How goes it?"

"I'm still working on the preparations."

"Good, do any other Angels suspect you?"

Nyx shook his head. "If they did, I would know about it. After all, I'm not the only Angel trying to bring Lucifer back."

He *was* an Angel. And he was working with a *demon*?

"Things are almost ready on our end as well." She assured.

"And what of this Cloukora boy? Is he going to be a problem?"

"I honestly don't know. Lucifer thinks he might be." She sighed and hesitated before continuing. "He has the Sword of Atlantis."

"King Relyt's sword? I have not heard, nor spoken that name in a long time..." He looked like he was basking in some kind of nostalgia. "No matter. That sword will only hurt Lucifer. It can't kill him."

"Speaking of which, what of the Blade of Michael?"

"It is in Heaven, guarded heavily. And watched by one of our own. He will never get it. And besides, he needs Death's Sword to wield it anyways."

This was all confusing to Cloukora. Death's Sword? The Blade of Michael? So many swords. And they were worried about *him* walking through Heaven's gates and taking the blade? That was impossible.

"So tell Lucifer he has nothing to worry about. The world will be in his hands with very little resistance." Nyx half-commanded, and then begun walking away. Cloukora couldn't let him escape. He darted around the bush to where they both stood and aimed his gun at Nyx.

"Don't move!" Cloukora commanded.

"Are you freaking kidding me? You're making me look like a liar!" Zela said defensively. "Even after I told you to stay out of our business!"

Birth

"Yeah, telling a hero to stay out of something he knew nothing about at the time that would inevitably destroy the world is something you should do." Cloukora was unsure if that even made sense.

"Wait, what?" Zela was confused, but Cloukora didn't think she was that bright anyways.

"Is this the boy?" Nyx asked.

"Yeah, this piece of sh-" Nyx interrupted her before she could finish her sentence.

"Cloukora. My name is Nyx." The Angel moved towards Cloukora. "Nice to meet you." Cloukora wasn't going to fall for it. When Nyx got close, he lowered his voice so only Cloukora could hear. "I'm not really working with them. I'm undercover, and I'm trying to take them all down. Especially Lucifer. But you aren't letting that happen. So just go, I got this." Cloukora could believe it, after all, why would an Angel betray God? So he lowered his gun. "Dumbass." Before Cloukora had a chance to react, Nyx knocked Cloukora back into a tree with just his arm as Cloukora's gun flew out of his hand. A golden broadsword appeared in Nyx's right fist. "Don't worry, you won't be going to Heaven where you can tell on us. Or Hell where you can kill all the demons. No…I'm sending you somewhere better. I'm sending you to Purgatory. Where you will rot and suffer for the rest of eternity." Cloukora was on all fours on the ground, holding his chest with one hand.

"No, *you* can go to Purgatory! I won't let anyone get in my way to stop this thing. Not even an Angel. Hell, you don't even deserve that title."

"You think that's supposed to be an insult? Hah! I don't give a rat's ass about being an Angel, because when Lucifer rises, he will give me a place in his world that is worth a whole lot more than playing God's little soldier." Nyx's foot went for Cloukora's face, but right before it hit, Cloukora grabbed it mid-swing. Adrenaline was pumping inside him now, and he could focus more. "How-?" Nyx saw Cloukora's transformed pupils staring straight into his own. Cloukora pulled out a knife from his shoe with his other hand and stuck it into Nyx's leg. Before Nyx could counter, Cloukora stood up knocked the

sword out of Nyx's hand with his left fist, and with his right, punched the Angel as hard as he could in the ribcage. Cloukora brought Nyx's head down, and kneed it with his right leg. As Nyx stumbled backwards, Cloukora drew his sword from his back, and as always, appeared *after* he had grabbed it. He drove it into Nyx's chest, blade going out the other end, but it didn't affect him at all. "Man-made blades don't affect me." Nyx smirked and grabbed the blade of the sword in his chest, pulled it out with a force that knocked Cloukora back. Catching himself with his hands, he landed on the muddy ground next to Nyx's sword. Cloukora quickly grabbed the sword, spun on his knee and when the Angel appeared over him, drove Nyx's own sword straight into Nyx's chest. "N-no. I can't die…" Nyx looked fearfully at Cloukora. "Perhaps you *will* be a problem for Lucifer…"Nyx burst into a flash of light that forced Cloukora to shield his eyes, and the golden sword disappeared with its owner as Cloukora's sword fell to the ground. Cloukora picked up his sword and noticed Zela was still standing there in awe. She *wasn't* very bright. When she snapped out of the trance and saw Cloukora, she started running, but Cloukora motioned with his arm upwards, and a thin spike made of the earth pierced through her leg, the force knocking her onto her back. She screamed in pain as she lay there holding her leg.

"P-please. Don't kill me." She begged as Cloukora sauntered over to her. It wasn't just the fear of getting killed, it was the fear of getting killed by *him*. Those eyes. That sword. His bloodline. It scared her. "I'll go rogue. I won't do any more harm- agh! I swear!" Cloukora didn't answer, and just flipped his sword around, so that the blade was pointing behind him. He stopped next to her. She was trying to pull out her leg from the spike, and she almost got it off, but Cloukora made the spike continue on and then turn back into the ground, creating an arc so that there was no way of getting it free. "Mercy! Please!" Cloukora drove the sword into her chest, and she screamed even louder, and then…nothing. Cloukora only wore a blank expression, and when he realized what he had done, he took a few steps backward away from his sword, in shock at himself, and sat on the ground, staring at his hands. How could he just do this, without any emotion? Even if it was

Birth

a demon? Was he just getting used to killing? *Maybe Ashely's right...* Whatever the reason, Cloukora didn't like it. He didn't want to be that kind of person, he wanted to have a conscience, to stay human. He stood up, pulled his sword out from her, found his gun, and said an "I'm sorry" before continuing on to find Winter.

"Let me go, you bloodsucker!" Winter commanded the vampire. She was tied up tight from rope around her wrists and legs. She was in some kind of hidden underground cave. Her restraint was somewhat elaborate: Not only was she bound by rope, but both wrists were also handcuffed to thick tree roots coming out of the dirt wall above her head, and her legs tied to roots by more rope. She hoped Cloukora would find her, because she knew there was no way out of this. The vampire just continued walking away from her, and towards the giant hole in the ground above, and jumped back out into the woods. When he was gone, she threw herself forward in anger. "Fuck!" Dirt fell on top of her head and as she looked up, she noticed the handcuffs were starting to pull the root out of the dirt. She tugged harder and harder until it finally let her pull the other end of the handcuff on her left wrist off the root. She pulled the handcuffs off the root on the other side, and used her teeth to loosen the rope and get it off. She got the rope off of her legs, and went over to her pile of things on the ground, which just consisted of a couple knives, her phone, and a pistol magazine; she lost her pistol when the vampire had kidnapped her. Taking out a hairpin from her pocket she unlocked the handcuffs and rubbed her wrists from being bound for so long. "Vampire was a dumbass. Didn't even take my hairpin." She then grabbed her pile of things, put them in her pockets, and climbed out of the hole, and into the forest. She didn't know why they had kept her alive, nor did she *want* to know. Winter heard yelling coming from somewhere nearby; it sounded like Cloukora. She rushed through the forest over to where the sound came from, and saw that it *was* Cloukora, with the vampire right on top of him! A knife was pulled out of her pocket, and she drove

it into the side of the vampire's neck and it fell on top of Cloukora, who rolled it off of him. "Bloodsucking bitch."

"Thanks." Cloukora said as Winter helped him onto his feet.

"No problem. Let's go, I'll treat you to some ice cream." She patted him on the back.

Cloukora laughed. "Still think I'm a kid? Well, I guess I can't argue with free ice cream, can I?"

Winter laughed too. "Nah, I think you've actually grown since we first met." She gave him a re-assuring smile. "I was kidding about the ice cream though." Cloukora wasn't sure to laugh or be sad about that, because now he *did* kind of want ice cream. They walked back to the parking lot, and their respective cars, and drove off.

Devil's Tower, Wyoming.

A man stood up on top of the mountain, looking out onto the forest and grassland all around him. He was tall and muscular, but had some age to him, perhaps in his thirties. His short hair was jet black, and he had a thick, rounded black beard, and thick sideburns that connected with the beard, which also connected to a thick black moustache. He wore a charcoal black jumpsuit, similar to what you would wear in a prison. Another man appeared on the rock. He was young, maybe in his mid-twenties, clean shaven, average height but a little thin on the weight side, and had short brown hair. He wore a simple grey t-shirt, dark green cargo pants, and boots. It was the other demon that Cloukora encountered before, along with Zela.

"My Liege." The younger man knelt on his knee, and bowed his head.

"Rulx." The man turned to face him.

"I'm sorry, my lord, Zela and Nyx are dead."

"I know. I saw it."

Rulx stood up. "I found out she was meeting Nyx when it was too late. If I knew before hand, I would have gone with her."

"It wouldn't have mattered. He would have just killed you too."

"If you don't mind me asking, master, if you saw it, why didn't you stop it?"

Surprisingly, he took the question lightly. "Because. All I can do at the moment is influence, and appear in people's minds. I can't intervene with anything. If I could, Cloukora *would* be dead by now."

Suddenly a blue-purple oval portal opening appeared with a purple-coated Tomi stepping out of it and joining them on the mountain. "So I heard Cloukora killed two of yours today, including an Angel." He looked at the two of them, who were giving him looks of contempt. "I know, you hate me, but yet you know you can't kill me right now. Because for one, you're just a hologram." He turned to the bearded man. "You can't touch me." Tomi mocked the other man's inability by walking through him, causing the image to flicker, and looked out onto the land below. "And you know it's pointless to sick your hound on me, because you know I can kill him in a heartbeat."

"What do you want, Tomi?" The bearded man asked impatiently.

"Why did you pick this mountain? Of all places to meet?" Tomi asked in return.

"Because anything with my name in it gives me power in that place or thing. Or wherever my name is mentioned. A power that seems small, but can go a long ways. At places like this, I can project an image of myself, as I am doing now."

"I thought the naming of this place was a mistake though? So it's not really yours."

"It may have been a mistake, but it is still known today with my name a part of it."

Another man appeared on the mountain, and quickly knelt before Rulx. "Sir, your presence is needed for a matter."

"If you'll excuse me, I must take care of this business." Rulx bowed before the bearded man. "I await your return, Lucifer." Rulx followed the new man, and both disappeared into thin air.

"Now that we have privacy, what is it that you want?" Lucifer asked.

"You're not ready to return, and you know it."

Birth

"Heh, and why do you say that?"

"It is way too soon. Your power hasn't reached full potential. It's not what it used to be, or can be."

"And what of it? With the power I have, I could easily take over the world."

"You keep telling yourself that, but do you really believe it?" Tomi turned to face Lucifer. "You know that between Wolfstorm and Darkstar, you have no chance. Especially with me and Cloukora."

"I thought you wanted to *kill* Cloukora?"

"I do. But as the saying goes: 'The enemy of my enemy is my friend.'"

"Until a knife is driven into the friend's back."

Tomi shrugged his shoulders. "Well that's his problem, not mine." He walked over to the other side of the mountain and opened up a portal, just like the one he arrived through. "Now if you excuse *me*, I have business to take care of myself. Catch ya later." Tomi waved to Lucifer without even looking, and disappeared through the portal." Lucifer sighed, and then disappeared as well. The mountain top was empty, and silent, except for the cool wind blowing across the mountain rock.

Angel's Gaiden

Honor

July 23, 2010
Local jewelry store, Portland, Oregon

    The security room was dark but warm, and the only light came from the security camera feeds on the monitor screens. Two security guards watched the monitors with dull expressions. One was a bit on the plump side, while the other was on the more built and sturdy side. The stocky security guard stood up and stretched his arms, letting out a yawn. "I'm hungry. I'm gonna go down to the donut shop and grab a few. You want anything?"

    "Sure I'll take one or two. And a coffee." The other guard didn't take his eyes off the screens.

    The hungry guard patted the other guard's shoulder and walked out of the room and out of the jewelry store, into the city, locked it up, then headed towards the donut shop that stood a few blocks down. On the roof of the building adjacent to the jewelry store, separated only by an alleyway, knelt a man in a blood-red cloak with the hood over his head, watching the guard stroll down the sidewalk.

    After the guard disappeared out of sight, the hooded man dropped down into the alley below. He was tall, built, and bore lightweight, black metal armor on his body and a black metal mask that covered his whole face. The mask was designed in a way that it gave off the illusion of hollowed cheeks, and two red lines started at the middle of the forehead, curved across his eyes, and stopped at the cheekbone on each side. The lines mirroring each other perfectly. Hanging on his shoulder, but under the cloak, was a small black satchel.

Placing his armor-gloved hand on the brick wall, a red cloud of energy appeared from his hand and it began to eat through the wall until it had formed an archway big enough for him to walk through. Not a single scrap of the wall cut out remained; it was as if it had disappeared out of existence! A large wave of red energy pulsed out of his body, and was sent in every direction, shattering the glass counters that held the jewelry inside. As the alarm began to ring, he quickly moved from display case to display case, pocketing as much jewelry in the satchel as he could. As he was still looting the store, the guard from the security room appeared and aimed his gun at the intruder. "Freeze! Put your hands behind your head!" The cloaked man turned and shot a small blast of energy from his hand through the guard's chest. The man fell to the ground with the hole in his chest, dead as soon as the blast had impacted him, as the masked man finished filling up his bag, exited through the entry he made, and jumped onto the other roof just as soon as the other guard came running through the door.

Hillsboro, Oregon

Cloukora laid himself down next to Ashley in the shade of the tree on top the blanket they had brought with them. Today he wore a t-shirt that represented the band Scorpions and his usual jeans. Ashley wore a white summer dress patterned with all kinds of colorful and beautiful flowers. The day at the park was beautiful too: the sky was a clear blue color, the sun was shining brightly, the birds were singing, and the ducks in the pond were quacking for more bread to be thrown at them. To make it better, she had calmed herself since he had dropped her off after the fair. She was starting to come around to her senses. It felt perfect to him. He felt like he could lie there all day as long as she was there next to him. As if she was thinking the same, Ashley said "I could lie here all day with you. Because it's nice out, of course. Not because I want to be with you or anything, cause I don't. I mean I do. But as friends." She stumbled on her words nervously, before finally sighing and giving up. He glanced at her and saw that she was trying to

Birth

hide her blushing. Cloukora already had a feeling she liked him, and he wondered if he had feelings for her. He always liked being with her, it made him feel good and happy inside, and he even liked her. He just wasn't sure if it was the right move to *be* with her; he wanted to, but at the same time it didn't feel right. His mind constantly conflicted on the matter, and he could never figure out what he truly wanted. It's why he hadn't said anything to her; why start a relationship you're unsure about from the start?

A ringing interrupted his thought process, and he reached into his pocket for his phone to put it up to his ear. "Yeah?" He asked, rubbing his forehead, as if to rub away the thoughts of Ashley.

"We got a case for you."

"Today was supposed to be a day off. I did one yesterday!" He sighed out of frustration as he sat himself up. "What is it?"

"Have you heard about this… Red Hood guy-"

"Red Cloud!" Cloukora heard Cal correct from the background. "Red Hood's a comic book character!"

"Sorry. Red Cloud."

"Yeah, I've been seeing him on the news a lot recently. A red cloaked man breaking and entering jewelry stores and stealing as much as possible. Even two to three times a night. Some reports say that he controls some kind of red energy. I think they're exaggerating things a bit much, you know with me and what's happened and all. But why are we worrying about him now?"

"No specific reason, we just think we need to find and stop him. He went up in his wanted list: he murdered a security guard last night during a robbery. Plus, it's boring here and we don't have many other interesting missions."

"Alright, I need to…make a quick stop, and then I'll be there." He said looking at Ashley.

"See you in a bit. Tell Ashley I said hi." She hung up. *How does she know what I do? They must have some kind of secret satellite they use to watch people.* Then he remembered the chip in his cellphone. *Oh yeah.*

"Who was that?" Ashley asked as she sat up.

"Brev. Apparently we're tracking down the Red Cloud." He had told her about Brev and Wolfstorm a few days ago. She took it surprisingly well. She even made him take her to meet them.

"The guy robbing the banks?"

"Yeah. I feel like she knows something. It doesn't make sense to suddenly go after him now."

"I don't think Brev would do something like that. She seems like a pretty open and honest person, she'd tell you the real reason."

"True, but I only met her, what? A month ago? She could be a vampire for all I know." That part was true; he discovered who she really was a few weeks ago on a job in Salem. Ashley didn't know that though, and he wasn't about to tell her.

"Yeah, right, and I'm the Boogeyman!" She laughed, and immediately it brought out a laugh in him. It was weird, when she smiled, he smiled. When she was sad, he was sad. It was some kind of emotional connection they had that he couldn't break free from, no matter how hard he tried. After a few seconds of silence she said "Cloukora, we need to ta-"

"I should probably get going." He knew what was going to come next, and he wasn't sure if he was ready for it. "Let me take you home." She nodded and began to pick up the blanket and left over food. After they both packed up, they got into the car and drove off to her house. The whole ride was silent, not one word came out of each other's mouths, even though they both wanted to say something. Pulling in front of her house, he watched as she got out of the car and walked towards the door of her house. Every step she took, his heart beat faster, and the more he wanted to get out of the car and run to her. To wrap his arms around her and plant his lips on hers and say those four words. "I love you Ashley..." He said to the air. But he knew that the life of a hero was no life for love. She was a strong woman, but not strong enough to handle what might come. No matter how much he wanted her, he couldn't have her. Pushing the thoughts out, he let off the brake pedal and drove towards Portland.

Birth

Portland, Oregon

Cloukora walked through the jewelry store doors to find a body bag being zipped up by a detective and Brev crouching by the entryway the culprit had made, studying it. "So, what do we got?"

"I honestly have no clue." Brev said as she stood up and walked towards him. She was of course wearing her FBI suit this time. "You tell me."

So she wants to test me. Alright, I'll play. Standing by the entryway, he looked it up and down. "Obviously this wasn't normally made. Not by anything we know of." He looked at Brev. "Or that I know of." Turning back towards the "door" he continued. "Couldn't be an explosive. No, that would send the bricks flying and there aren't any bricks. Couldn't be a saw. Not a laser either, otherwise there'd be at least be dust or residue on the ground. But there's not."

"So what was it?"

He lowered his voice so only she could hear. "My first thought was Darkstar somehow, but they wouldn't need to rob jewelry stores. They could rob the White House if they wanted to." That strayed his thoughts a little. *Why haven't they taken over the world already? I'm not strong enough to take them on yet, they could easily do it in an instant. So what's stopping them?* He switched gears, and it took a moment to actually say it. "But, I think it's someone who also has powers." That irked him. Another person with powers. Another person he'd have to fight.

"We're done here." The coroner said as they took the body away on a gurney.

"Thank you." Brev replied then went back to Cloukora. The room was no longer full with CSI agents; it was just him and Brev that remained. "What should we do?"

"Only thing we can: we wait. Do you have a map or something?"

"Even better." She pulled out an electronic tablet and placed it on a display case that got lucky and didn't get shattered. As she pressed a

map icon, a map application popped up on the screen, showing a complete map of Portland.

"Alright, how many jewelry stores are there in Portland?" Typing in jewelry stores in the search bar, twelve red dots popped up on the map. "Now, take away the ones he's already robbed." She made eight of the dots disappear. "So it's going to be one of these."

"Unless he robs one he already hit."

"The thing is about robbers, you can only rob a place once, and eventually, you're going to run out of places you can rob." He stated as he walked out the door.

"Where are you going?"

"To wait in my car until something happens." He walked on the sidewalk until he got to his car, and as soon as he slammed the car door shut, Brev was at his window.

"Alright, what's your problem?"

"My problem? Nothing."

"Bullshit. You're having some kind of distaste towards me, and the organization."

"Because being wary of an organization that I just met a month ago that deals with the supernatural isn't normal."

"You haven't had a problem with us before! Where is this coming from?"

He sighed. "I'm sorry, I'm just. I feel like there's something you're not telling me. About this case. Why now? Why are we going after him now, when we could have gone after him from the start?"

It was her turn to sigh. "I didn't want to tell you this, I didn't think you needed the pressure, but since the rumors started we have noticed a lot of Darkstar activity."

"You mean the rumors about the robber having the powers, which we now know are true?"

"Yes, we think Darkstar wants to get their hands on him and use his powers for their own purpose."

"They want to recruit him." He summed up.

Brev nodded. "We need to get to him before they do and stop him."

"You mean kill him."

Brev bit her lip and hesitated. "If it comes to that, yes. Under Darkstar's control...he can do a whole lot more damage than rob jewelry stores. What's one person to a city worth?"

He couldn't believe what she was saying. "Fine." And with not another word, he drove off to find a place to park and wait.

Night had fallen on the city and the only defenses against the darkness were the pools of dull city lights along the city streets. Cloukora had been sitting on the roof in his usual disguise, with his hood down, for the past few hours or so, listening to the police radio Brev had given him. She used the tracker in his cell to find him so she could, as well as say a few words of apologies. It didn't help how he felt, but then he also knew it wasn't the lie that made him edgy. He felt like it could be this life, the life of a hero, his friend dying before his eyes, and unsure whether or not he should be with Ashley. He had no reason not to, except for the small feeling inside that told him not now. *Maybe after all this apocalyptic shit is over I'll be able to tell her the truth. With demons as my enemy there's no telling what they'd do to her. Having her as my friend is bad enough right now...*He went back to the radio. Surprisingly, not much crime was going on tonight. There were only a few, minor reports: A husband and wife in a trailer park vulgarly arguing over who drank the last beer in the fridge, the arrest of someone's ex-girlfriend who vandalized his car, and then a drugee resisting arrest for dealing drugs. Cloukora thought he could probably settle each report himself and prevent others from getting hurt. Except maybe for the drugee: he had called the cop a pig, hitting a nerve in Cloukora. That guy might leave with a few bruises. But he didn't have time for any of that, he had to wait for the Red Cloud to make a move, which Cloukora was starting to think wouldn't happen.

Not too far off, a loud ringing sound went off: a store alarm. The nearest jewelry store was about three blocks down, which was just about the right distance from the alarm source. Putting his gun in his holster, and hood over his head, he dashed towards the jewelry store, jumping across alleyways and pipes and vents on rooftops as fast as he

could. The first jump had scared him, since he had never done it before, but when he saw how he landed perfectly, it immediately became fun. He knew without these powers of his though, he would have most likely broken a leg or two. Without thinking twice he jumped off the last building and onto the street in front of the jewelry store. Seeing the red-garbed man, who also noticed Cloukora, he quickly burst through the doors, aimed his gun, and shot at the running Red Cloud. But he wasn't fast enough; the other man dodged every single bullet and made it through his entryway similar to the one at the last jewelry store, into the alley. Cloukora reached the alleyway to see the other man already on the roof of the next building.

"You're gonna have to do better than bullets." Red Cloud taunted as he ran off.

Cloukora manipulated the wind around his feet to give him a boost onto the rooftop. Red Cloud was about three buildings ahead of him, it would be impossible to catch up. Aiming his gun again, Cloukora fired several shots, each one missing Red Cloud as he jumped off a building into an alleyway. "Dammit." He kicked the ground and let out an "Aghh." He turned around to get down from the roof, when a small patch of red hanging from a vent caught his eye, he went to grab it, and found that it was a piece of cloth. The odd thing that stuck out though, was that it was both smooth *and* tough to the touch. He grinned as he put it into his pocket and pulled out his phone to dial Brev's number. "You might wanna wake up Kaora and Nole. I got something for them."

When he arrived at Wolfstorm headquarters, his disguise off for now, he saw Kaora and Nole already at the computer in their spinning chairs, both in their pajamas and holding a cup of coffee. "What was so important that you had to wake us up at ten at night?" Nole asked irritably as he rubbed his eyes.

"People actually sleep this early?"

"Normal people do." Kaora changed the subject. "You said you had something for us?"

Birth

"Yeah," He reached into his pocket and pulled out the piece of cloth. "I found this. I think it's off of Red Cloud's cloak."

Kaora grabbed it from Cloukora's hand and studied it for a moment. "Strange it's smooth, but it has a durability to it."

"I noticed that too. Is there any cloth like it?"

"No, not that I know of. Unless..." She rolled her chair over to a microscope and placed the cloth under it, and looked into the lens. "I don't know how exactly, but titanium was threaded with the wool. It was done so precisely that you would have to look through a microscope to tell. This is amazing. This could protect soldiers in battle, it could save countless lives. It's weightless but indestructible." She had a glow on her face; she wasn't so tired anymore.

"If it's indestructible, then how did it rip off his cloak?"

"You must have hit it when you shot at him, and the vent you found it on pulled it off. The bullets we use are very different than usual bullets. You saw what you did to that ghost with my shotgun." Brev explained. "The only metal that could beat ours is Orichalcum, which we don't have, except you and that sword of yours. Even though it would be great if we did, considering it's the strongest metal ever." She looked at Cloukora to emphasize what she was trying to say.

"For the last time, I'm not re-surfacing Atlantis."

"But imagine the amount of lives you could save, and how far technology could advance!"

"No Brev, and that's final."

Kaora interrupted. "While you two were at it, I searched up who could afford this in the Portland area, which is very, very few, since this sewing is near impossible, and would cost roughly several million dollars."

"How many suspects?"

"Five."

"Alright, print em out, and me and Brev will look into it in the morning. You guys need some sleep."

"Finally!" Nole got up and immediately walked out, not even waiting for Kaora.

Birth

"I doubt I'll get any. I'm too excited to sleep at all." Kaora handed the printout of the suspects and their addresses to Brev and followed Nole out. "How am I gonna sleep knowing titanium can be woven into cloth!" The two entered the elevator before the doors closed and headed towards the lobby floor.

Brev and Cloukora walked up the brick-laid driveway of the large, white-paneled manor, Brev in a black suit and white blouse, and Cloukora in a t-shirt with the band name Anthrax and jeans. "Who's next?" Cloukora asked. It was midday already, and the sun was high up. The other three suspects ended up taking over an hour for each investigation!

"Our fourth guy on the list. Victor Brennis, male, forty-five years old, and a Capricorn. Sounds like your type." She said jokingly, receiving a head shake and a laugh from him. "He's also the CEO of a local logging business for 14 years. Oh, and he lost his wife and teenage daughter."

"How'd they die?"

"Wife in a car accident and his daughter from a brain tumor."

"How long ago?"

"His wife died a few years back, and his daughter several months ago."

"I don't think he's our guy then. He's probably still grief-stricken from her death."

"Most likely, but it doesn't hurt to check him out." She said as she rung the large manor's doorbell and waited for a well-dressed middle-aged man to open the elegant wooden double doors. The man was tall, about an inch or two above Cloukora, and had a fit body to go with it, despite being forty-six years old. His hair was beginning to grey, but no wrinkles could be seen.

Inside was lavishly decorated: Paintings and photos hung up on the bright, white wall while antiques, vases, and plants rested on stands all throughout the house. Right behind the man was a grand staircase that split off on both sides and turned back around to the second floor.

On either side of the room, Cloukora could see a doorway that led to another room.

"Hello? Can I help you?" The man asked.

"My name's agent Heart and this is agent Jordan. We're with the FBI and we've been investigating the recent Red Cloud incidents." Both she and Cloukora presented their badges to the man. Victor then pointed his finger at Cloukora and opened his mouth to say something, most likely about not looking professional, but Brev only answered the gesture with a "Don't ask."

"Ahh. And you think I'm a suspect?"

"Well, no, not really. But you know, we gotta follow every lead. Mind if we take a look around your house?"

"No, of course not. Go for it." He gestured them inside, and they followed him into the yellow-walled living room. The air inside felt clean and calm, but at the same time empty.

"Lovely house." Cloukora complimented. "Not many people get to have such a nice home."

"Thanks. My wife, Elena, designed it while she was pregnant with Astrea. Heh, no matter how many times I told her she was overdoing herself, she just kept at it. She was one stubborn woman..." His smile faded and he stared blankly for a moment before catching himself and shaking his head. "Anyway, I got a roast in the oven, so you guys go ahead and do your thing." He turned and strode towards the kitchen.

Brev went off to another part of the house while Cloukora strolled around the room, studying it and trying to find any evidence. Though, he wasn't sure how he'd find any in a living room. He figured there could be a hidden vault or switch behind one of the many paintings, but after looking behind them all, he didn't see anything of the sort. He even tried moving the elegant silver rapier hanging above the fireplace. "Nice sword." He said to himself. "But mine's better." Grinning he turned to go to another room when Brev walked in.

"I can't find anything. He's clean."

"That was fast."

"It doesn't take much for me to notice something's out of place, and, well, everything seems in order here."

Birth

"So that's it?"

"It's all we can do right now."

"So what's the verdict?" Victor asked as he walked in, wiping his hands on a kitchen towel.

"You check out. You're in the clear." She started towards the door as Victor went to open it. "Well, thank you for your time. We'll let you get back to your roast. Have a nice day."

"No problem." He said as Cloukora and Brev exited the house. "And you have a nice day as well." Victor added before the door gently shut as the two started for the next house.

"Then the next person's gotta be Red Cloud."

"Well we'll find out when we search his house, which is the next house down." She pointed down the hill to a wooded area where you could barely make out another manor through the trees. It was only a short walk from Victor's house.

After ringing the manor's doorbell several times, and no answer, they realized that the owner must have been out. "Great, now we have to come back later."

"Not really." Brev gave a devious smile as she pulled out a hair pin and worked at the keyhole in the door knob.

"Let's get arrested for breaking and entering. That's a great idea."

"We're posing as FBI agents."

"Yeah, I suppose we'd probably get away with it."

"No I meant that breaking and entering will be the least of the police's worries." She grinned as she unlocked the door and opened it.

"That makes me feel totally better." He said sarcastically as he followed her in.

"You check upstairs, I'll take down."

Cloukora nodded and headed up the staircase. Unlike Victor's house, this one felt darker, and clumped with antiques and collectibles, and the staircase didn't split off, or was as fancy. He walked down the long, red-rug, dark hallway towards where he assumed the master bedroom would be. Hearing something move behind him, he spun and aimed his gun in the direction of the sound. "Who's there?" No answer. "I know I'm not going crazy." He said as he lowered his gun and

hesitantly continued the way he was going. His guess was right and he found the master bedroom. He went straight for the dresser across the room and began rifling through all the clothes and drawers, throwing some of the clothes out in the process. After going through the bottom drawer, he felt as if someone was behind him in the room, watching him. He froze for a moment as the hair stood on the back of his neck. Snapping it out of it, he turned around and had Fyron in his hand, pointing it at the door Brev had just walked into.

"Are you alright?" She had a worried look on her face.

"Yeah..." He looked down at his hand as he made Fyron disappear. "Just hearing things." Suddenly the bottom drawer popped out of its track and onto the floor, revealing a pile of garb underneath where it was.

"Must have pressed a switch." Brev said as she walked over to him as he took it out to reveal it was the same clothing Red Cloud had worn.

"It's him alright." At that moment they heard a car pull into the gravel driveway and they both got their guns ready as they headed towards the staircase, and as they reached them an old man in his fifties had just walked through the door.

"Put your hands above your head, and don't even *think* about trying anything!" Brev commanded, pointing the gun at the old man, who dropped the paper bag of groceries that was in his arm and put his hands straight up. Well as straight as he could for his age.

"Wh-what'd I do? I have a license for that weed in the yard!" He pleaded.

Brev walked down the stairs to handcuff the man with a zip tie. "Don't play dumb with us."

"Wait, where's my wife? What did you do with her?!"

"Your wife's been dead for years, now go." She tightened the zip tie and pushed him out the door.

Wait, if he thinks his wife is still in the house, and she's dead...Then...

"That's not the man you're looking for." A womanly voice whispered behind him, but no one was there when he turned around.

"Cloukora, are you coming?" Brev asked, just noticing he wasn't following her.

"That's not him." Cloukora said, turning back to the door.

"We found the costume in his bedroom, and he has the motive. He lost his job several months ago, and his house is about to be foreclosed in a week."

"Brev, stop. I know how bad you want to catch Red Cloud, but if this was him, don't you think he would have just killed us, or at least broken out of that zip tie? That costume was planted. He's not the real Red Cloud."

She took a moment and looked at the old man. "You're right, I'm letting this get to me." She sighed at herself, took out a pocket knife, and broke the restraint. "I'm sorry, sir. We'll leave you be." She headed out the door and Cloukora began to follow.

As he was walking out, the old man grabbed his arm. "Is my wife...is she really...dead?"

Cloukora frowned at him for a moment. "No, not in the spiritual sense. Physically she may be gone, but she is watching over you now. Your wife must have- no...She *is* a good woman, and her love for you goes beyond her death. She'll always be there for you when you need it. Her *soul* is forever attached to yours."

The man had tears flowing from his eyes, and a large smile appeared on his face, then he suddenly surprised Cloukora with a huge embrace. "Thank you."

Hesitantly, he returned the hug and let go. "Just don't piss her off." Cloukora said half-jokingly as he walked out and met up with Brev.

"So what do we do?"

"We wait for him again." They both walked off towards the car that was parked in front of Victor's house.

Cloukora stood on the roof in his usual hoodie and mask disguise, as the bell rang in the jewelry store, and Red Cloud jumped onto a rooftop across from his. This time, Cloukora noticed, Red Cloud had an elegant, silver rapier rested on his waist. Upon seeing Cloukora, he quickly turned around and tried to run the other way, but immediately had to hold up his hand over his face when a giant wall of red-hot flames rose up in front of him, and when he turned back around, the fire had spread, and made a large square arena around them as Cloukora stood holding Relyt's Sword in his hand. And in case he tried dropping into the alleyway, fire flowed between the two buildings. Of course the fire was controlled, Cloukora made sure of that, so that it wouldn't damage the buildings. However, he knew he had to make this fast: it wouldn't take long for the fire department to arrive. Red Cloud charged at Cloukora, throwing a ball of red energy right towards him. The sphere wasn't a solid shape, but always moving and never perfectly round. Barely side stepping, Cloukora sliced through sphere, splitting it into two. Each half tearing through the building's roof. Luckily they didn't hit any of the support beams that held the roof up. Another ball came flying at him, but was casually knocked into the wall of flames, creating a small explosion. Returning the favor, he sent several fireballs at Red Cloud, who sent three balls of energy right back to collide with them. In an instant, Red Cloud disappeared in a shroud of red energy and then appeared in front of Cloukora, rapier drawn and going right for his neck. While deflecting the rapier upwards and away, the force of the attack itself almost caused Cloukora to lose his balance and sent him stumbling backwards a few steps.

"Nice blade." Cloukora commented.

"Thank you." His voice was muffled; the man was smart. "It was passed down through my family. It belonged to the great D'Artagnan, captain of the Musketeers."

"Wait, the Musketeers were real?"

"Um, yes? How do you not know this?"

"I'll be damned. This blade was actually from one of my *own* ancestors. But where it came from is an entirely different secret." Cloukora swung his sword vertically at Red Cloud, missing his target when it stepped to the side to quickly bring a fast rapier across his chest. Cloukora screamed in pain as he knelt to the ground. The wound wasn't fatal, but it still hurt like hell, and blood began to stain his hoodie. *Ignore the pain, Cloukora. C'mon, get up.* Noticing the rapier coming

for another attack, he somersaulted to the side, and with enough force he knocked away the other sword. As Red Cloud lost his balance for a moment, Cloukora swept Red Cloud's leg to bring the thief to the ground and drive his own blade into the man's shoulder. Though he missed the actual shoulder, he managed to pierce through the armor and graze the arm underneath when Red Cloud rolled out of the way. Red Cloud was back on his feet, and about to hit with a spin attack, until Cloukora had blocked and trapped the other blade, and slid his sword upwards, slashing at Red Cloud's chest, and cutting through the plate armor and some of his skin. "Wound for wound." Cloukora swung his sword downward to hit the shoulder but missed, again, before Red Cloud followed up with a quick flurry of attacks, each one harder to block than the last.

Both of them were of equal skill. Each hit Red Cloud made was quick, but created a minor wound, while Cloukora, if he could even manage to counter an attack, got in a more-than-minor-wound. It was a battle of speed versus strength, and it seemed like the fight could go on forever, until Red Cloud managed a stab in Cloukora's lower abdomen, producing a great amount of blood. Falling into the gravel on top of the building, Cloukora barely kept himself from collapsing completely. The pain was too much. Red Cloud began to walk away when he turned to Cloukora. "You were a worthy opponent, and though I wish I could finish you off, I must leave now." He turned and shot a ball of energy from his hand, creating a hole in the roof of the building. "Thank you for the challenge, hero. Perhaps we will meet again." He disappeared through the hole.

Water splashed on Cloukora and he could feel steam coming from water being sprayed onto the fire; the fire department finally showed up. "About time." Forcing himself to stand up he began to stagger towards the alley side of the building. If he stayed they would find him, and with his wound, he wouldn't be able to fight them off from seeing who he really was. Making it to the ledge, he had the flow of fire stop and then dropped down into the alleyway. Slammed would have been a better word. Gathering the small amount of strength he had left, he got up and staggered further from the jewelry store, and eventually into

Birth

his car. Reaching into his glove box he pulled out a first aid kit, and grabbed rubbing alcohol and a needle and thread from inside the kit. Taking off his blood-soaked hoodie and shirt, he poured alcohol on the wound in his stomach, which stung like a bitch, to disinfect the gash and rinse off the blood so he could begin stitching it up. It was no easy or painless process. He had never before been in this much agony, even when Venn cut his arm. "It always looks so easy in the movies-AGH" Both the needle piercing through his skin, and the tightening of the gap were the sources of the pain. He poked one more hole, and pulled it hard enough to close the final part of the gap before cutting the excess string off with a pair of medical scissors. Leaning back, he let himself have a couple of breaths before wiping up the blood with his hoodie, putting his shirt back on, and driving off.

Red Cloud opened Victor's front door and stumbled inside. That hero guy had done a number on him. He needed to treat his wounds as quickly as possible. Running all the way to his house didn't help at all either. On the stand next to the door, he placed his mask, and pulled the hood back as he headed to the nearby closet, pushed the coats that were hanging up to the sides, and his heart skipped a beat. The lights along the hidden staircase were already on. "I was sure I turned them off." He put his hand to his rapier as he carefully, but swiftly, continued down. Reaching the floor, he saw a teenage boy standing over his daughter who lay in her bed with a machine hooked up to the vein in her arm. His daughter had long, black hair; deep blue eyes under her closed eyelids, and though it was hard to tell, she was tall for just turning seventeen. Some of the strawberry cake was still lying next to the bed in case she woke up; he didn't want her to think he had forgotten about her on her own birthday. The room was pretty small, about the size of an average bedroom, but it had a concrete floor and there wasn't much lighting or even decorations; the room was plain. Except for the bed, which was a carved wood bed frame painted white, and pink blankets to make up the bedding. It was the same bed she had before she was

admitted to the hospital, and he brought it down here for her to feel safe and at home. "Who the hell are you?"

"It all makes sense now." The teenager turned around, and Red Cloud recognized who it was: it was the FBI agent from earlier that day, and that wound he held was no coincidence, nor the blood covering the shirt: this was who the superhero really was. "Your daughter slipped into a coma before they could remove the tumor. Desperate, as she was hanging on for dear life, and being as rich as you are, I'm sure you knew someone who could cure her, or at least keep her alive until she woke. So you pulled some strings, faked her death, and had her running on whatever it was since then. And I'm assuming it's not just one dosage, so you have to continually buy it, and it not being cheap, you began to run low on money. With no other option, you resorted to robbing jewelry stores to sell the jewelry and pay off the dealer." The teenage boy pulled out a pouch of needles from his pocket and showed them to Victor. "As for your powers, you must have also found someone to develop some kind of super power for you in case you were cornered by someone else with powers, like me, and injected yourself with it. I tell ya, my co-workers are gonna have a field day with this stuff." He said as he put the needles back into his pocket.

Victor sighed. "How'd you know it was me?"

"Your blade, the one you used against me, I remember seeing it on the fireplace. It was a bit difficult putting together the motive, which it wasn't even provable, that is, until I saw *her*. Then I was sure. Oh, and my name's Cloukora." He awkwardly added as an afterthought.

"Anyone else know?"

"No, just me."

"Good." Red energy appeared in Victor's hand and was flung across the room at Cloukora, who instantly had a katana appear out of nowhere and slice through it. As Cloukora was distracted with hitting the ball of energy away into two different walls, Victor teleported in front of Cloukora, fist going right for his face. With ease, and hardly paying attention, Cloukora quickly grabbed Victor's arm, pulled him in, and kicked him back across the room. "You...You were holding back weren't you?"

"Yes. As a hero, I shouldn't do it, but when I fight an opponent, I fight on equal grounds."

"That *is* crazy. If you have so much power, why not use it?"

"Because I fight with honor: I give my enemy as much of a chance to kill me as I them. There is no honor in slaughter. Just because you have so much power doesn't mean you should take advantage of it."

"Alright then. Let's have a rematch, but this time we both go all out."

"Sounds fine to me."

"Meet me upstairs in the mat room. I'll be waiting." Not wasting any time, Victor teleported out and into the mat room where he had always practiced his fencing and fighting techniques, and waited for Cloukora.

Cloukora walked into the bright room and onto the large white mat Victor already stood upon. The room looked and was furnished like any other room in the house. It looked very similar to that of the living room, except the theme was white, whereas the living room was more yellowish.

"I apologize for this; I'd rather not kill you. But unfortunately, it must be done." Victor drew his sword and pointed it at Cloukora. "No one can know about this."

"No, it doesn't. You don't have to kill me." Cloukora tried convincing. "You can join Wolfstorm. We will help your daughter! We could really use someone like you. You could clear your name and become a hero. It's what your daughter would want!"

Victor seemed to be thinking it over in his head, he even almost lowered his sword, but then shook his head and kept the sword pointed. "No, I have a good thing going. I won't mess it up, and I won't risk my daughter's life!"

"If you die, then who will keep her alive?"

"I *won't*." Victor quickly let his red energy flow out of him and cover his entire body, then flung a ball of energy the size of a couch straight at Cloukora.

Making Relyt's sword appear in hand, he sliced through the energy ball as if it were butter, and both halves flew to the sides of him, creating two giant holes in the wall and leaving two small trenches out in the yard. Victor threw several more energy balls at him, each one easily deflected by Cloukora's sword, going through the plastered walls. The house wouldn't be standing much longer at the rate it was going. As soon as a barrage of energy blasts were thrown at him, Cloukora made the sword disappear and instead had Vesi and Neró in his hands, dashing towards Victor. Right as he was about to meet the red barrage, he spun around, one sword in front, another in back, knocking away each blast in different directions of the room as if he were a mini tornado. As he went to swing at Victor, Victor instantly had his sword drawn to block his attack, but it didn't slow Cloukora's pace. Rapidly he swung the hook swords, moving too fast for Victor to push back, thus pushing the man closer and closer to the wall, with Cloukora not breaking a single sweat. Before Victor could get on the offensive, Cloukora used the hook of Vesi to grab Victor's blade and pull Victor towards him to push back again with a kick, sending Victor against the wall. There was a sudden rumble underneath them, followed by a blast of water that shot out from under the floor, hitting Victor, and with the extreme pressure, pushed him through the ceiling and onto the second floor. Cloukora quickly jumped into the fountain of water to get to the second floor as well, doing a backflip out of it and over Victor just as the man was getting to his feet. "Great, now I'm soaking wet." Feeling his damp hair, he added "And my hair's messed up too! And I really hope that was clean water." He looked down at Victor as he made Vesi and Nero disappear. "One more chance, you can join us, or I finish you off."

Victor took a moment before answering. "Alright, alright. I'll join you guys." But as he got to his feet, he sent his rapier into Cloukora's shoulder before the hero even had a chance to dodge it.

"Agh." After pulling out the rapier, Cloukora threw a punch at Victor's face, knocking him back, followed up with a knee kick to the stomach, stepped around to Victor's back, pulled on the man's arm and stepped on his calf, quickly bringing Victor to his knees, and tossed

him across the room into the wall, and before Victor could blink, Relyt's sword pierced his heart. "I'm sorry, I didn't want to do this. I didn't want for this to happen." Cloukora took his blade from Victor's chest and slumped against the wall next to Victor, disappointed in himself for what he had just done.

"I wish I could have honor, just as you do, Cloukora. I think my daughter would have wanted that...instead of...robbing people to keep her alive. Heh, you know it's funny. My ancestor's would have given their lives for royalty...They gave this family honor, and yet I ruined it all through Red Cloud."

"No, you have honor, and it's no different than mine. I fight to protect the world and the innocent. That is what I honor. It's my duty. Yours is your daughter. You did what you could do to keep her alive; you risked your life and your freedom for her. *She* was *your* royalty. Any father would have done what you did. You know, usually I don't condone criminal's actions, but I see now why they do what they do. I always thought big shot executives like you were corrupt, and were what was ruining this country, this world. But now I see, everyone is corrupt. Hospitals and insurance companies let people die because the patient can't afford the procedure, so they're left to slowly wait for their heart to give out. Rich employers and executives don't give out enough pay to their employees just so they can drive a new Mercedes-Benz. Then the poor and homeless become corrupt, and they rob, steal, and even sometimes kill because they can't afford their rent. And it's all because of money. Money will be mankind's downfall. The piece of green paper can already drive a man to rob a bank, what will it do in ten years? It has created a dog eat dog world, where everyone fends for themselves, and no one else. And everyone is just too damn selfish to care."

"I don't think that's true."

"What do you mean?"

"You're not corrupt, nor selfish. You are a good man, Cloukora. And if you can be a selfless person, then there must be others out there that are uncorrupt, just as you. There is still hope for the future. I think you just have to show them the way."

"Perhaps you're right...Hey, can you do something for me?"

"Sure."

"You were my first actual villain, so I was wondering if you could say 'Curse you Cloukora for foiling my plans!'"

Victor painfully chuckled, and coughed up blood. "Yeah, no. Now, it's time for you to get going. So I can at least do one honorable thing before I go. I pushed the silent alarm button when you arrived, so the police should show up any time soon, and unless you want to end up in a jail cell, you should get out of here. It was nice meeting you Cloukora."

"And the same to you, Victor. Go in peace, descendant of D'Artagnan." Cloukora got up, patted Victor on the shoulder, and began walking out and noticed his wound had opened up. He'd need to fix it up better when he got back to headquarters. As well as the rest of his wounds. "I'll make sure your daughter gets treatment and the help she needs." He said, looking back at the dying Victor one last time.

"Thank you...now go..." With that he closed his eyes and his breathing slowed to a stop as he fell into a deep dream that would last forever.

"Brev? I need a favor from you." Cloukora began on his cell as he walked to his car down the street.

The Portland Police Department's forensic team was scattered across Victor Brennis' house, all trying to find some clue as to what had exactly happened to him. Detective Hearl, an old, but sturdy man, stood over Victor's lifeless body. "So let me get this straight, Victor Brennis, a renowned, and very wealthy I might add, CEO, turned out to be Red Cloud, and the hero that's been going around town offed him?"

"That's how it looks, sir." His partner Detective Ryans replied, a much younger man who had no muscle to him.

"Well looking isn't the same as being." The detective looked up and saw a security camera bolted up in a corner of the ceiling. "Anyone get on that yet?" He said pointing towards it.

"Yeah, in fact IT should be done with it by now." Without another moment wasted, the detectives walked quickly down the hallway to the security room, led by a forensic agent. As soon as they entered the room, the IT specialist pressed play on the giant screen, giving them a view of the hero finishing off Victor with a magical sword. And as the hero got up from a moment's rest and turned around they saw the true face of the hero: Cloukora.

"I want a facial scan on him right no-" The screen suddenly became static.

"I can't get it back. Someone remotely deleted everything off the hard drive!"

Behind them, a forensic agent had watched the video play and had a sly grin on his face the whole time. The man, who went by the name Damian Hawthorne, was in his 50s, wore glasses, and was a weak and frail fellow, but his brilliant mind substituted for the lack of strength; he had solved over twenty murders during his career. *So, the hero was here. Hopefully he left me some kind of evidence.* The man strolled to the door that Cloukora had walked out of on the security footage, and found what he was looking for. Bending down with a test tube, he scraped a small drop of blood on the floor into it. *With this, I will become a revolutionist, a visionary! No...I could be even better.* Making sure no one was looking, he stuck the test tube in his pocket, and then continued on to try and find other evidence that was left behind. *Whoever you are, hero, enjoy your last days, because I, the soon-to-be god, am coming for you.* The man did all he could to keep himself from laughing hysterically.

Cloukora sat in the Wolfstorm headquarters rubbing the area where his wound was. He still couldn't understand or believe how the balm Brev had used on him made it disappear. Now it was just a scar, which itself would also disappear in about a week. According to her at least.

"The tapes on Victor's hard drive were erased. Your identity is safe." Kaora assured as she turned around.

"Thank you."

"Oh no, I should thank you." She grabbed the needle of red liquid. "For bringing me this. The question is though, who made it?"

"I don't know, he didn't say. I didn't ask." He turned to Brev. "By the way, did you get Astrea a hospital room?"

"Yeah, I did. But her uncle called as soon as he heard, and he's coming to claim her tomorrow. We can still pay for her treatment, but it's his choice whether or not to continue it." Brev replied.

"Ah...I hope he makes the right decision."

"As do I."

Astrea slowly opened her eyes to see a white-tiled ceiling, and a woman in green scrubs off to her side checking the machines that were hooked up to her. "Ma'am...where am I?"

The nurse jumped. "Astrea! Hold on, I'll be right back, I need to get a doctor." Without giving Astrea another chance to speak, she ran out to fetch a doctor.

After the doctors had finished checking her vitals and asking her a few questions to make sure she was okay, the same nurse came back in. "Astrea, I have someone here who wants to see you."

"Is it my father? Where is he?"

"I'm sorry, I wish I knew, but it's your uncle. He's flown all the way from Los Angeles for you. Shall I send him in?" Astrea nodded and sat up as the nurse went to retrieve her uncle from the hallway.

Astrea heard an "I'd like to have a moment alone, if that's alright." from a man and a "That's fine." from the nurse. But the man that walked in was not her uncle. Instead it was a tall boy about her age, with chin-length brown hair, and blue eyes. His clothes were more on the gothic side: He wore a long, dark purple, leather jacket that had all the shine taken out of it, and a plain, black t-shirt underneath. On his legs he wore black jeans and knee high, black leather boots. "Do not scream, I just want to talk."

"Wh-who are you? Where's my dad?"

"My name's Tomi, and that's why I'm here." He sat on the edge of the hospital bed. "There's no easy way to say this. Your father is...he's dead."

"What? You're lying! Why would he be dead?"

"Your father was a great man, who had great power, and with that power he did what he could to keep you alive. But there was someone who didn't agree with what he was doing. And despite your dad's intentions, that person killed him in cold blood."

Tears started to fall out of her eyes, and then in a moment, those eyes became an icy blue glare. "Who was it?"

"Cloukora Skyrell."

"When do I get to kill him?" Her fists clenched the bed sheets until her knuckles went white.

"I was hoping you'd ask that. First, you'll need to be very powerful in order to defeat him." Tomi pulled out a black pouch and unzipped it to take out a needle with a red liquid inside. He flicked the needle. "Something I can help you with."

Angel's Gaiden

Double-Edged Sword

July 25, 2010
Rood Bridge Park: Hillsboro, Oregon

    The sun in the open blue sky shined down on the park as Cloukora pulled the 'Cuda into a parking space. Ashley was with him, holding a rectangle-shaped gift wrapped up in balloon decorated wrapping paper in her lap. After Cloukora put it in park, and took the keys out of the ignition, they both got out of the car and felt the immense heat from the sun; it was supposed to be almost a hundred degrees today. Cloukora grabbed the Book of Atlantis, something he had started calling it, from the back seat, and they slammed the car doors shut, and walked over to the large group of people all around a table that had food, drinks, gifts, and balloons along the top of it. Cloukora wore a black Murderdolls t-shirt with the band's red logo on the front, and of course, he wore his regular jeans. Despite how much hotter it made him feel. Ashley had her hair down, and wore a pink tank top, jean short shorts, and a pair of wedges: raised sandals that look similar to high heels.

    The park was quite large: A playground stood near the parking lot, but it was not too close so that the children wouldn't get hit by a careless driver. Beyond the playground lay a large, green, hilled field that was meant for large team sports such as soccer or football. To the east side of the playground was a forested area, with a creek running along the outskirts of it, and into the woods. Trees dotted all along the park, except for the field of course.

    Ashley walked over to where most of the group was hanging out, and handed the present to Cloukora's cousin Dennis, who would be turning ten today. Today was his birthday, and Dennis' parents had

Birth

decided to celebrate it at the park. Cloukora wished it could have been a different day, when it wouldn't be as hot. Then again, he should have also worn shorts. As he was walking towards the group he said: "Sorry I'm late, I had to take care of a werew-uh whereabouts of a friend." He needed a break. He was getting way too used to his missions. *If I'm not careful, I'm gonna say the wrong thing in front of the wrong person, and end up getting myself killed.* Cloukora walked over and sat in a camping chair next to his grandfather, who was sitting next to Cloukora's uncle, Daniel. The chairs were arranged into a semi-circle, and off to the side, a little away from the rest of the family. It gave them some space to have their conversations. Cloukora was actually glad they weren't near the family so he could talk to his grandfather and uncle without being heard. They both were smoking when Cloukora opened up the book to the page with Relyt's biography. "Hey grandpa, I was wondering if you could help explain something to me. I can't seem to understand what they're talking about. I know it has to do with his powers, or ability, or whatever. It's just in terms I don't know." He handed it to his grandfather who began reading it.

"Heh, the irony." His grandfather said after a few moments.

"What?"

"It's saying Relyt's brain was like a calculator. He could calculate and predict things using just math and physics. He could accurately judge measurements and use that to his advantage, such as how fast a wind was exactly blowing and its direction. He could fire an arrow at a precise spot and do it all so fast the arrow would barely touch the string of the bow before it was let loose. Some believe he literally saw the measurements: the angles, the speeds, the distances, and so on, all within his mind, and within an instant. Sounds a bit absurd, but with everything going on recently I wouldn't be surprised if it was true."

"Could he calculate when and where a burning piece of wood in a building would fall?"

"I suppose it's possible. Using the rate of the fire burning, how hot the flame was, the angle the piece of wood was sitting at, I'm sure he could."

"Could he control it? His ability I mean."

"It says he could, to an extent. A lot of times it was done subconsciously, without him even trying. Why?"

"I think I have his powers. When I was in that burning building, I saw the burning piece fall *before* it fell. Then, while in Iraq, I somehow was able to calculate where a bullet would land when I shot it out of a sniper rifle, after I jumped out of a *plane*. It's happened other times, those two instances were just more impossible than the others."

"Well, you *are* his reincarnation. And with what I just read, I wouldn't doubt you having the same powers as he did." His uncle reminded. "But as always, with great power comes-"

"I know, I know. Great responsibility. I've watched the movie." Cloukora interrupted. He didn't know that quote was also in the comics. "I just realized something. This ability must be why I'm so good at math." He joked. "Oh, another question. When your guys' adrenaline starts…you know…flowing, do your eyes-your pupils I mean…do they change?"

"No." They both answered.

"Weird. Cause apparently mine does; they turn into the family crest. It's really weird."

"We noticed that at the lake, too. We weren't sure why at the time. But now that we know you're Relyt's reincarnation that could be why. That's the only theory I could come up with anyway."

"Ahh. I mean it's cool, but it's also kinda weird."

"I have a question for *you*." His uncle leaned in, and put out the cigarette in the ground. "Are you sure you want to do this?"

Cloukora thought for a moment. "Yeah. I do. What have I done with my life up until now? Get good grades? Never screwed up my life? That's pretty much it. But this…this is my calling. I can't see my life going any other direction other than down this path. This is my destiny; it's what I'm meant to do. And you know what? I love it. I love being a hero. I love the power. And most of all, I love being able to be to jump in and save the day. The feeling I get when I save people, it's the best feeling I have ever known. I have a purpose now, and if I quit, there would be a hole, an empty space in my life, and no amount of a normal life could fill that void; I wouldn't have a reason to *live*. And honestly,

I would die before I went back to a normal life. I couldn't handle sitting behind a desk after everything I've been through so far. It just wouldn't feel right. Not like it does now." He took a moment before continuing. "Besides, I haven't had to fight any villains so far, so I'm good for now. It's only been creatures of legend." That was a lie that he covered up with a grin. Cloukora didn't want to make them worry. But his grin faded when the image of Victor bleeding out in the mansion popped into his head. Darkstar was still out there too.

"What about Darkstar?" Cloukora forgot his grandfather had been Wolfstorm's leader.

"Oh, and them too. But they haven't really come after me."

"Do not take them lightly, Cloukora. I haven't actually fought against them face to face. But I know how dangerous they are. Don't let your guard down with them; you might end up with a knife in your back."

"I suppose I should be more careful with them. Other than them though, it's just been the supernatural. And besides, I'm living every kid's dream. I'm a friggin superhero!" He gave them another grin. Part of him wanted to mention the transformation in Iraq, to figure out what happened, but another part told him it had to just have been his imagination. That what had happened wasn't real. "Alright, well, I'm gonna go for a walk in the woods. I need to think some things over. Be back later." Cloukora got up. "Keep an eye on the book." An obvious statement. He headed into the woods and took his time walking along the paths, admiring the scenery. This is why he loved Oregon; the beauty of the nature all around, it was just breathtaking. The lush plants, the colorful flowers, and the gentle wind that brought the smell of the flora. He eventually came to a calm, unmoving pond, where he sat down, legs crossed, on its bank. He looked around to make sure no one was looking, and made small motions with his hand and fingers. The water near him and the bank began to move, and then started to look like it was dancing. It wasn't anything big though. Maybe about as much as a couple drops worth of water was moving. It spiraled upwards a little, split into four streams at the tip, and intertwined with each other again as it went back into the water. He continued making it dance for

a little while longer. This was how he usually practiced his abilities. He had also done the same with fire, made tiny tornadoes that would only seem large to ants, and moved tiny chunks of the ground.

"That's a cool trick." Cloukora recognized the voice, spun around, and in a split second, Relyt's sword was in his hand pointing at her throat: Ava. She wore a red tank top with the word Slayer in black font, with the letters slightly resembling lightning bolts. She wore black jean short shorts that had a couple holes in them, an unbuttoned blue flannel, and black high-heels that were opened at the toes. Her hair was down and pulled to her left, and her sword rested on her back. Her shield seemed to have been missing. "Put that thing down. If I wanted to kill you, I wouldn't have even said a word to you." She said condescendingly.

Reluctantly, Cloukora lowered his sword. "What do you want?"

Her face became grim. "You were right, I'm sorry I accused you of killing Venn." She looked down, kicked a rock casually, and looked back up. "It *was* our leader. He even told me he did it. He didn't even..." She was starting to tear up. Cloukora was unsure of what to do. She was an enemy, how do you comfort an enemy? Hesitating, he gave her an awkward light hug, and then let go. It felt weird.

"Are you still with him?"

She looked away, wiping a tear. "Yeah."

"Why? You should come work for Wolfstorm. They're better people than the ones you work with!"

"Honestly, I don't know. I know he won't kill me, and I wouldn't even care if he did. Part of me wishes he would, though…But I just can't bring myself to leave..." She brushed her hair back as she looked down at the ground again.

"Don't say that. I didn't know Venn, or the kind of man he was, but I know that if he loved you, he would want you to live on and do something meaningful with your life!"

She looked up at him, sighed and gathered herself. "You're right." She nodded in agreement. "It's what Venn would want. He'd do the same for me. I'll work for you guys. But I'm not gonna leave Darkstar, I can help you guys take them down from the inside." Cloukora nodded

as well. Suddenly, the pond water moved, and the earth shook beneath their feet. The water in the pond slowly drained down a large hole in the pond's bed, as if it were a drain in a sink. What emerged out of it, they could not believe. It was a giant serpent or dragon-like creature: its body was long, green, scaly, and had the form of a snake's body, but it was wider than a concrete pipe. Near its head, which had scaly horns that matched the rest of its scaly body, small dragon-like wings came out of its sides. Slithering all the way out of the hole where the pond used to be, it towered over Cloukora and Ava. They heard a thumping sound behind them, and the earth started shaking again. They turned to see a giant hippopotamus-like creature walking towards them. It had a brown, muscular body, a tail on its rear, and two small tusks protruding out of its mouth.

"This isn't good." Ava remarked, gaining a worried look from Cloukora. "These things are the Leviathan and the Behemoth, and they're only supposed to show their faces when the end of time comes near."

"Can we even beat them?" Cloukora focused on the Leviathan again, while Ava still had her attention on the Behemoth.

"I don't think so."

"Guess we'll just have to find out." Cloukora went back to back with Ava, and readied his sword at the Leviathan, while Ava drew hers and readied herself against the Behemoth. "Let's do this!" Both of them charged at the monsters they were facing, ready to swing their swords.

The Leviathan swung its tail at Cloukora, who managed a flip over it, and brought his sword down on its tail. It didn't affect it at all; Cloukora's sword just bounced off of it. The tail swung at him again, and Cloukora hopped onto the beast and began running up its body toward its head. Suddenly, the serpent took off into the air, making Cloukora lose balance until he struck the sword between the scales and planted his feet on the creature's body, holding onto the sword for dear life. It kept flying through trees, trying to make him hit one of them and fall off, but Cloukora was able to dodge them, although barely, and with difficulty too. It turned upright and flew into the sky high above the

forest. Looking down, with a little regret for doing so, he could see all the people down there, in the park, looking back up at him. Watching the "show." It swerved downward to the park, and flew right above the people. He needed to slow it down somehow. An idea came to his head: He pushed down on the sword, and the Leviathan went downwards, straight into the play structure, crashing through it and into the ground. Cloukora jumped off with his sword, in front of the creature, and wasted no time in charging at its face, but right when he was about to hit, it opened its mouth and swallowed him whole. He slipped and fell down, before rolling into its stomach. It must have taken flight again, because Cloukora started going deeper down the tract a lot quicker than he should have. For some reason, he started to become angry at himself. He noticed that had been happening quite a bit lately; he would get angry at things somewhat easily, even the smallest of things, and sometimes for no reason at all.

His body started changing like it did in Iraq: a purplish armor with varying spikes on his arms, spine, and legs; only his head wasn't covered with it. But of course his eyes changed: The Skyrell crest flipped on its head and the green and brown colors became magenta and sky blue colors, respectively. Only the gray remaining the same. Relyt's sword in hand, Cloukora jumped towards the stomach lining and sliced his way out of the side of the beast's belly with only one swing, falling out of the air and landing on the green field, as the beast roared in pain and fell to the ground before him. Believing the creature to be dead, he began to walk away until its body suddenly regenerated and was perfectly healthy once again. It saw Cloukora, and darted right at him. But with ease and grace, Cloukora stepped aside and split the beast horizontally down the middle, from head to tail. The two halves then lay still, unmoving. It was finally dead.

  Cloukora finally noticed that people were looking at him, watching him, and on instinct, he quickly dashed into the wooded area, surprisingly taking only but mere seconds to reach its edge, despite the amount of distance there was in between. His anger-induced armor faded and he fell to the ground, feeling all the fatigue from the fight all

at once. He was amazed at himself and the fact that he hadn't yet passed out from exhaustion.

"You *have* grown stronger." Ava said, walking towards him, holding a blood-stained flannel. She had scratches, cuts, and bruises all over her body. She noticed Cloukora noticing them, and said "Oh these little things?" She lifted her arm to take a look at a cut going all the way down the length of it. "They're nothing, I've had worse injuries." She seemed to space out a little, as a hint of sadness showed on her face for a moment, but she quickly shook her head, shaking whatever it was, off. "I'll be fine." She gave a smile.

"Are you sure?" She nodded her head. "Well, for the record, it was a pleasure fighting alongside you. Even though we weren't actually fighting *next* to each other."

"Same to you." She agreed. "Oh, yeah. I need to get back to the base. I almost forgot we have a meeting tonight. I'll contact you later." She waved goodbye, spread her brown wings, and flew off into the sky. Which direction she went, Cloukora had no clue. He stood up and ambled tiredly towards his car; hoping most of the people had left. He noticed a large cut on his left upper arm, bleeding; one of the Leviathan's teeth must have nicked him when he was swallowed. As he walked through the woods, he saw the Behemoth ripped to pieces on the pathway. She didn't show it any mercy. He held the cut and continued towards the 'Cuda as Ashley ran to him. He also saw his uncle and grandfather looking at him. With looks as though they expected answers from him. How Brev was going to cover this up he had no clue.

Ava rushed the massive beast in front of her, sword ready to swing, and when she got close enough, swung the blade, but the beast charged at her too quickly, knocking her against a tree, pressing her body against it. Using her sword, she barely kept the tusks from going into her stomach. It was difficult, she would admit, but she didn't give up. She couldn't. She saw Cloukora was nearby fighting the Leviathan, and ended up in the air on its back. She focused on her enemy again.

"Why am I not strong enough?! I can't even fight a fatass hippo!" The Behemoth was unaffected by this insult, obviously. "Venn, why am I so weak?!" She shut her eyes, trying to keep tears from falling out. Then...then memories flooded in her mind. Venn playing football with the boys of Darkstar. Venn in the kitchen helping her cook dinner. Or rather showing her *how*. Venn standing before her, in front of her apartment building, on the night of their first date when he planted a soft, gentle kiss upon her lips. Tomi standing in front of her, admitting to her face he killed Venn. Her eyes shot open in anger. She lifted her leg and sent a kick to the beast's face, pushing it backwards so she had room to move.

She gritted her teeth. "I will avenge you Venn. I swear on my life I will kill Tomi!" She stabbed her sword into the Behemoth's eye, causing it to roar. She didn't let up; she slashed at the monster's face, putting a huge gap in it. She sliced again, and again, and again, until there were nothing but chunks of it covering the pathway. Its body started piecing itself back together until she sent her sword deep into the beast's skull. Blood had now covered all of her clothes and face. Blood of the monster. She also found she had a couple injuries all over herself, including a cut down her arm. "Bastard got a few hits out of me." She kicked the Behemoth's head into a group of nearby bushes. "Bitch." She sheathed her sword and walked towards the park, assuming Cloukora would be there as she began to clean off the blood splatter with her flannel. "I will avenge you Venn. I swear..."

Tomi sat in his throne room upon his throne when Ava barged through the chamber doors. She also noticed Tayge was in the room as well. They had obviously been talking, and Ava had just interrupted them. She didn't care though. "It's done." She said.

"He thinks you're on his side?" Tayge asked. "Wonderful job. Can we just blow him up now?"

"You and your damn bombs."

"I prefer to call them my babies." Tayge corrected and Ava only shook her head.

Birth

"No." Tomi said sharply, accompanied by a just as sharp look at Tayge. "We need him to fight Lucifer. He may grow stronger from it, and he may even grow stronger than me, but that's a risk we need to take, because he's the only one that can defeat Lucifer."

"He's a double-edged sword." Ava summed up. Tomi nodded.

"Why can't *you* just kill Lucifer?" Tayge asked.

"Because only The Blade of Michael can kill him." Before Tayge asked another question, he continued. "And because of my evil nature, I cannot wield it. Only one with a pure and good heart can hold it."

"Sounds cheesy."

"It is." He turned to Ava. "Go. There's a demon lurking around NYC that I need you to interrogate."

Ava nodded and walked out. *Why* does *he want me to play double agent with Cloukora? What is that going to do to help us? Maybe Path is right, maybe he* is *going crazy.* After the doors shut, and she exited out the main doors, she stood in the mansion courtyard and said to herself: "Cloukora, I'm counting on you to help me. My life and fate are both in your hands." She spread her wings once again and took flight.

After Ava left, Tayge turned back to Tomi. "My lord, it appears that many people, including news stations, caught today's fight on camera. What do you wish to do?"

"Delete them. Erase every piece of evidence of today." He commanded.

"Sir?"

"I can't have someone going off and killing him before I get a chance." That wasn't his reason. It was the reason of a voice inside his head. A voice that he left behind long ago. A voice that didn't want Cloukora to die. "I need you to go to Japan and lower the demon infestation there."

"Of course, my lord." Tayge let out a bow and walked out of the room, leaving Tomi in silent thought.

Angel's Gaiden

An Ally Discovered

July 26, 2010
Berlin, Germany

    A dark-haired business man moved swiftly through the crowds of people on the city sidewalks, bumping into anyone that happened to get in his way, constantly glancing back over his shoulder. He felt as if he was being followed by someone. Who, he did not know. But what he *did* know, was he had to keep moving, or else he could very well end up dead. Abruptly he took a hard right into an alley. He figured if he could see his stalker, he might have a chance to defend himself. Halfway down the alley, he spun around to see if his follower had come down as well, but there was no one there. Just an empty alley, with garbage skidding across the ground from a small breeze rolling by. His hair on the back of his neck rose and before he could turn around to see why, he felt something stab into his chest. A man cloaked in black stood over the dead business man's body, as he wiped the blood from the blade of a knife.

Beaverton, Oregon

    The sky was strangely cloudy for a summer's day when Cloukora pulled up in front of Ashley's house in the ruby red 'Cuda. He wore a black suit, which he wore reluctantly, and a solemn look on his face. Ashley walked out wearing a black dress with the straps on her shoulders, a medium cut that wasn't too high or too low, and a hem that fell to her knees. She had her brown hair hanging loose, but pushed

Birth

behind her shoulders. Of course, she wore the emerald ring around her neck, just as Cloukora still and always will wear the Skyrell crest around his. He decided, even if he eventually didn't need it, he would still wear it as a representation of his family. After she put on her seatbelt, Cloukora drove off to the funeral. The whole trip was silent, apart from the sound of the car's roaring engine.

    The ceremony went as any other, except for the fact there was no body to mourn over. There was still a casket, however, but it was closed. All the attendees there walked past the casket to say their goodbyes and someone said a few words about him during the eulogy. Not much was said, just the usual "He was a good kid" and "He didn't deserve to go so soon" kind of speech. Cloukora wasn't able to say anything about him, because up until recently, they hadn't even spoke to each other for nine years. Then it was time to bury the casket in the cemetery outside of the church. Rain began to fall from the grey clouds as Ashley clung tightly to Cloukora as the coffin was lowered into the ground. A few tears fell from her eyes, and Cloukora almost let out one as well. But he knew he couldn't show any weakness for her; he had to be strong.

    Tomi stood far off, hidden in the trees of a nearby forest, watching the funeral from afar, wearing his own black suit. He rested against the trunk of a maple tree, hands in his coat pockets. A woman with long, wavy red hair approached him from behind. Her hair wasn't as eye-popping as Tayge's though, in fact it was actually quite darker than his. She wore a plain grey t-shirt with a dark green cargo jacket over it, black cargo pants around her waist, and dark brown boots on her feet. On her ring finger she wore a diamond ring, around her neck she wore a silver cross, and she wore diamond earrings in her ears.

    "How'd you find me?" Tomi didn't turn his head to ask the question as she leaned on a tree near his.

    She grinned. "Hah, good one. Well you already know the answer to that: I'm a tracker. I can find you from *nothing*." The smile

Birth

faded and she let out a sigh. "So, how does it feel watching your own funeral?"

"A little surprised that this many people would show up for me."

"Putting the fact you're an evil villain and all aside, and the fact you killed Venn, tried to kill Ava, and you trying to kill your best friend, you're really not that bad of a guy."

"You think?" Tomi lowered his head for a moment, and his mind started to ponder why he was doing this in the first place. *Why do I want to rule the world? That's not me. This is my father. I don't want to kill; I don't want to hurt anyone. I just want to be with Cloukora and Ashley again. I just want those days back...* Immediately pushing the thought away, he began to walk back into the forest. "We have work to do, let's go."

The woman started after him. "I still don't get why we have to help prevent Lucifer from rising. I mean come on. Shouldn't that make it *easier* to take over the world?" Tomi stopped in his tracks and turned to her.

"Many reasons why. First off, it *won't* be easier, because I'll have to kill Lucifer myself, and that's just near impossible without the Blade of Michael. Secondly, even if I somehow defeat him, by that time there won't be *anyone* to rule."

"I suppose those are valid points."

"Then are there any more questions, *Path*?" He asked with some irritation.

"Nope, I'm good."

"Then let's go." Tomi spread a pair of dragon wings as Path spread yellow angel-like wings and they both flew off.

Forest Grove, Oregon

Cloukora sat on the edge of his bed, staring down at the carpeted floor, the rain beating down on his window pane. The sound of the rain somehow made him even more miserable. *Tomi's...dead.* He had kept

himself from thinking about it all this time, because he didn't want to. He didn't want to face the fact that he'd never see his friend again. *You're dead, because I didn't make it in time. If only I had moved faster, if I had been better at what I do...You'd still be alive. If only Oushu Kan failed in L.A...* His eyes flickered. *Wait, Brev said Darkstar caused the attack in L.A. And if Oushu was a part of that then who's to say they weren't working together on the mission. It's all making sense now. When they found out I was joining the mission, they must have somehow pulled some strings to get Tomi on it as well so they could kill him. To mess with my head so that my emotions would cloud my judgment.* "Tomi, I *will* avenge your death. Darkstar will pay."

His phone went off, interrupting his thoughts, and to no surprise it was Brev. He took a moment to gather himself, and push aside the anger that just bubbled up inside him, before answering. "Yeah?"

"We have another case for you." She said. He hadn't told her about the funeral. What *was* surprising was that she didn't know from the tracker in his cellphone. Or maybe she did and she just didn't want to say anything about it.

"Alright, tell me where and I'll start driving." He didn't really *want* to do anything, he wanted to just lie in his bed and stare at his wall all day. But he knew that would be pointless, it wouldn't solve anything. Getting his mind off of the matter and doing something worthwhile, that *would*.

"Actually, you'll be going by helicopter. You're going to Germany."

"Germany? Why?"

"What do you think?"

"Murder? Well, aren't the police over there able to handle it?"

"That's the problem; they can't find any traces of anything. No DNA, no fingerprints, no clothing. There are even a few cases where they were murdered in the middle of a crowd during broad daylight. Hell, they even had to call the FBI, which is how we got the case. A buddy of mine passed it on to me. They would take it but they're still going crazy with the spy swap a couple weeks ago. The spies involved are still debriefing the agency."

"So do you think we're dealing with some kind of wandering vengeful ghost then?"

"I don't know. If it's not a ghost then they must be one hell of an assassin."

"Alright, I'll pack my bags."

"I'll be there in an hour to pick you up. Oh, and one more thing, you're going to have to wear your costume." She sounded a bit reluctant on the last bit. It was a slight hint, but Cloukora noticed it.

Cloukora almost didn't want to ask. "And why is that?"

"I might have told the police that I could get the 'new hero' to help them solve the case."

"Brev, I'm not a detective, I don't know how much help I will be to them."

"Then what was Victor and Red Cloud? If that wasn't detective work I don't know what is. Plus you would be doing detective work without them anyway."

"Well, you would have done most of the work. I would have just sat back and helped when I had to. But, I guess you're right. You always are." Before Brev had a chance to hang up, Cloukora continued. "Oh, and Brev, can you do me a favor?"

"That depends. What is it?"

"Can you look into the operation I did in Iraq? See who was a part of it all?"

"You think they had a mole?"

"Yeah, I do. Brev, if Oushu Kan and Darkstar were working together before, why wouldn't they now? I think they knew we were coming. And I think they *wanted* us there. They wanted me to watch my best friend die."

"Alright, I'll get Kaora and Nole to see what they can do. Until then, worry about the case you're on now." They both hung up, and Cloukora wasted no time in gathering clothes, from out of his closet, to shove into his backpack, as well as changing out of his suit into a casual outfit of a ZZ Top t-shirt and jeans. All that was left was his disguise. He pulled a large, black chest from under his bed, locked by a specially designed padlock that could only crack open through the pendant on

Cloukora's necklace. Both he and his uncle had worked hard on designing it so that the crest, and *only* the crest, around his neck could unlock it. It was done by sliding it through a slit at the bottom of the lock, only wide and thick enough for the crest to slip through, where it would fall into place in an inlet within the padlock that was cut into the exact shape of the crest. Underneath the inlet, were a number of springs, sensors, and switches all designed so that if the exact weight and pressure of a forged pendant didn't match the real one, the lock wouldn't open. This made it difficult for people to forge his pendant and break into the chest. If the lock accepted the real pendant, once it was unlocked, it would pop the pendant back out through the slot. Of course, if it didn't, it stayed trapped inside the lock so the burglar couldn't try again. When he unlocked it and opened it up, all that lay inside were his disguise, fake badge, gun, as well as ammo, and the Book of Atlantis. Although he didn't have anything worth stealing, except maybe the Book of Atlantis, he knew down the road he might, and that he'd need it safely protected. He emptied the chest and stuffed it all into his bag before re-locking the chest, shoving it back under his bed, and walking out of his room, shutting the door behind him.

Berlin, Germany

An orange 2007 Porsche Carrera GT slowly pulled into the palace driveway, driving alongside the courtyard of people cheering and screaming. Cameras flashed and recorded the vehicle as it headed towards the podium on the blue-clothed stage before them. They had been cheering ever since the car came into view; today was an important day. The car stopped in front of the entrance of the Bellevue Palace; the White House of Germany. The building was a rough U-shape: there was the main building everyone stood in front of, and then two long wings on either side of them, extending about half way down the green courtyard that they all gathered on. The courtyard itself was split in half by pavement that connected the driveway that looped around it. The car doors opened upward and two men stepped out, one

from each side, and into the sun's blazing rays. As soon as they were out, the crowds cheered even louder, if that was even possible. The driver waved to the crowd in acknowledgement.

"So, *Mr. President*, what're you gonna do first?" The man that had sat in the passenger seat whispered.

"I think I'm about to win over these people, my dear vice-president." The newly-elected president sauntered up to the pedestal, and waited for the crowd to die down, and cleared his throat before speaking. "Dear citizens of Germany, the world has seen hard times of late, some even believe the end of the world is near. I want to assure you that I will not let that happen. Not to this country. Not while I'm running it. In fact, as my first duty as president, I will lower the cost of *everything* in Germany, allowing for more people to buy what they need! And yes, I have a plan to do it without causing deflation!" The whole crowd immediately roared with cheers and excitement. He covered the microphone with his hand and whispered to the vice president: "See? Amazing how a simple thing can bring you so many followers."

"You're not really going to lower prices are you?" They were still smiling to the crowd.

"Oh, I am. That's the first step; the next will be poison all the food."

"Why not just poison it anyways?"

"Because, as I said, lowering the prices means more people are able to buy products; and even a few more people can go a long way in our plan in creating an army for Lord Lucifer." He uncovered the microphone. "I also plan to make Germany a greener environment, to replace electricity with solar panels, to plant more trees and plants, and anything else there is to do. Oh, and on the topic of green, I will make sure your Cannabis will not be confiscated, and you can have as much as you would like to have in your possession!" The crowd cheered again. He had done it; he won them over. But it wouldn't last long. Suddenly, a bullet went through his skull, the force knocking him backwards to the stage floor. The vice-president rushed to the man's side to check for a pulse, before receiving a bullet through his head as

well. The people cried out in horror, and began to panic as their newly elected leaders lay lifeless before them. The once cheery crowd had now become complete chaos.

    Cloukora was loading his pistol in the cabin as the helicopter flew over the ocean and land below. A suit-wearing Brev sat across from him; Bowe was flying this time.

    "I was thinking, if you can control all the elements, couldn't you just use your powers to find and eliminate all of Darkstar? Like communicate with the ground or air?" Brev asked curiously.

    Cloukora cocked and sheathed his pistol in the holster on his right leg. "For one, I can't talk to the elements like that, or at least I haven't tried. Two, believe it or not, using those powers actually tires me out quite a bit. It gets exhausting if I use them too much." Throwing on his white, eagle-, rose-, and sword-themed hoodie, he pulled the zipper up. *Maybe picking a hoodie was a bad idea for a costume in the summer.*

    "I had no idea it even did that to you. You do seem to be getting stronger though, so maybe eventually it won't tire you out. At least as much."

    Cloukora slipped on his fingerless gloves and grabbed his mask, ready to put it on when they landed. "Yeah, I hope so. Speaking of Darkstar, what is up with their name? It sounds very close to Wolfstorm."

    "Who knows? They probably weren't creative enough to think of their own."

    "I guess I'll just have to ask the next member that comes along why they chose it." *Before I kill em of course. Except Ava, though, she's on our side. Then again, she might have had a hand in the set-up. No. Even if she did, she's trying to atone for her sins, and I should give her a second chance.* "By the way, did you ask Kaora and Nole about my favor?"

    "Yeah, they're looking into it right now. They're working on other things, too. So it may take awhile."

"Cool, thank you." Cloukora looked down as he fiddled with his hands. Brev could tell he was anxious.

"It's about your friend isn't it? Tomi?"

Cloukora looked up. "I think it was Darkstar. At least it feels like the only logical group of people that would want to do this to me."

"What if it's just what it looks like? What if Oushu and his men gunned down Tomi and his-"

"No! Don't you dare say that. Tomi and the other two were Black Ops. There's no way they, especially Oushu, could manage to kill all three by themselves. They had to have help.

"Maybe you just want to think that."

"Bre-"

"Cloukora, all I'm saying, is it's possible your perception isn't seeing what's real."

"My perception." Cloukora said with a condescending chuckle and a shake of the head.

"I just think you're trying to find someone to take your anger out on. And that's normal: When there's no culprit for one's death but Fate's, you want to pin the blame on anyone you can. But right now you're letting your emotions get the best of you. You need to keep a cool head, Cloukora."

"So you don't think there's even a slight possibility Darkstar was behind it?"

Brev was only silent as she turned to look out the window, marking the start of a silent ride. And marking the truth behind Cloukora's words.

The chopper landed on the helipad of the police building, and Cloukora stepped out in his outfit, his mask on of course. He was greeted by a dark man in a trench coat with a detective badge around his neck, and a handshake. "Welcome aboard this investigation, mister..." His accent was, naturally, Germanic.

Cloukora had never really thought of an alias to use, so for now he went with "Creed. Just call me Creed."

"Alright...Creed. The death you were to investigate, you won't be. We have a higher priority case for you instead."

"And what would be more important than a murder?"

"The death of the German president."

"I didn't hear anything about this." Cloukora crossed his arms. "When did this happen?"

"It happened just this morning, it's fresh news."

"Ah, well to be fair, I didn't know Germany even had a president."

"Well, we do-did. He was assassinated. Most likely by a sniper."

"Do you think it's the same guy killing everyone else?"

"Possibly, but neither of the two victims have any connections to each other whatsoever."

"So either our killer is upping his game, or he's inspiring someone to kill as well."

"Both options are equally bad."

"Yeah, we gotta stop this before it gets out of control. I'm gonna need to see the crime scene."

"Of course. Right this way." The detective led Cloukora and Brev to the roof access door and down through the building, and onto the city streets of Berlin.

"So tell me a little more about these murders."

"That's the problem. We don't know anything. Just that there were victims and the victims' identities. Oh, and the killer has managed to kill without being seen." He added as an obvious statement.

"No one saw *anything*? How many murders so far?"

"This assassination makes thirty."

Cloukora stopped in his tracks. "Thirty?! The murderer is a ghost," *Or maybe even a demon*. "and has murdered thirty people, and you haven't even thought about asking for help from the FBI before now?"

"We're the best in Germany, and *we* couldn't even find a trace. We figured it would be pointless to call them in."

"Pointless? *Pointless*? People's lives are at stake, and you consider calling for more help pointless?" Cloukora shook his head and

kept walking. "I fucking swear…" Brev shook her head, most likely at him, and continued following them to a police car.

When they arrived in front of the Bellevue Palace, the police had cleared the area of citizens using their yellow police tape. Even though the tape was in German, he figured it had said "Police-Do Not Cross." Of course, there was a crowd on the courtyard watching the officers, and now Cloukora and Brev, at work.

"So, where's the body at?" Cloukora asked.

"About that, we moved it." The detective replied.

"You *moved* it?!"

"Well, uh, the crowd was getting freaked out after seeing their new president killed. We thought it would ease the mood a bit if we got them out of here and out of sight."

"Where are they now?"

"In the truck ready to go to the Coroner's office."

"You drew the outline for the bodies, right?"

"Correct."

"Put them back in their spots."

"But-"

"No buts. Now."

"Yes, sir." The detective walked towards the truck that had "Coroner" written on the sides, and started talking to a couple of the coroner officers. The two men began hurriedly pulling the bodies from the back of the van as the detective returned to the podium with Cloukora and Brev.

"Where did you guys find the bullet?" Cloukora asked, glancing around, hoping to find one lying on the ground.

"That's another problem. There wasn't one. But that *is* a bullet hole. It's like it disintegrated after it exited out."

"Not getting easier…" While the bodies were being replaced, Cloukora was studying the area around them to see where the shooter could have been. After the bodies were placed, Cloukora walked over

and looked at them. "By the looks of the holes on their forehead, they were both shot from the front."

"Well isn't that kind of obvious? The shooter couldn't have hit him from behind. That'd be too close." Brev pointed out.

"I'm just stating for reference." Cloukora studied them for a moment. "It had to be a sniper…" He propped the president up next to the podium, and faced his head facing forwards, gaining a look of disappointment from the detective, and some gasping and crying from the crowd. He looked at the bullet hole, and where it entered, then turned the head left a little towards the north wing. "That's your killer." He half told the body. "Or at least where he was."

"We checked the wings top to bottom. He wasn't there."

"Not the wing. On the way here, when we crossed over the bridge, there was a…elementary school, is it? That's where he shot from."

The detective's mouth went agape and he had the look of someone who thought another person was an idiot. "That's impossible. Even if he could somehow manage to get to a position in the school, with a sniper rifle I might add, the wing is right in its way. He couldn't have made the shot."

"Which direction was the wind blowing today? Around the time he was shot?"

"I don't see-"

"Just answer."

"South…Southwest I believe."

"And how fast?"

"I think they were in the thirty to thirty-five miles per hour range."

Cloukora stood there for a moment, looking in the direction the school would be, his mind lost in thought. "Son of a bitch."

"What?"

"This guy's smart. He knew exactly where to shoot. By using the wind, its speed, and adjusting for gravity he was able to shoot your president. Not only that, he was able to get in another shot right after the first." He wouldn't admit it to anyone, but he was scared now. A

man that could shoot from anywhere and hit his target? If he tried to chase the shooter down, he could end up dead before he knew it. *As much as it scares me, I have to think of the people that would die if I don't at least try.* That part of his thought got him, for he had been frightened of the apocalypse that was supposed to arrive. Just like with this killer, he needed to face the apocalypse and Lucifer and get over his fear. "Get some people over there to check it out."

"I still don't see how this is possible but alright. I'll get men to cover the borders too, so he doesn't skip town."

"Nah, this guy's smart. He knows if he leaves town that will make it all the easier to find him. Most likely he's still waiting at home. You can still set up patrol, in case he actually is dumb, but I doubt he will even go near the border."

"So how do we find him?"

"I don't know yet, start with the school and we'll go from there."

The detective walked away without another word to make the call.

A man in a grey t-shirt and dark sunglasses watched from the crowd, with his arms crossed, as the great new hero attempted to solve his crime. "He's smart. And quick about it too." He muttered to himself before strolling off towards the city area, away from the crime scene.

Cloukora walked out of the school building and onto the streets, still in his outfit. So far all that had been found was gun residue on the rooftop. The case was a dead end, and Cloukora needed a breather to try and think it through; to figure out if there was anything he may have missed. Brev had stayed behind to discuss the case more with the detective. The sun shined brightly, giving off a lot of heat down to the city, and on Cloukora. There was a strange smell in the air; he couldn't pick out what it was though. He just knew it smelled really horrible to him, and it had started to give him somewhat of a headache. He had

Birth

been smelling it ever since he arrived. Suddenly, he got the feeling that someone was following him. *Might be the killer. He was probably watching me investigate the crime scene to see what he was up against...* He remembered how most of the people that were murdered had been killed in alleyways, so he took a turn into the next alley that he saw. A couple steps down the alley, he quickly had two throwing knives fall out of his sleeves, spun around, where a man in sunglasses with a knife was about to stab him, and pushed the knife out of the way with his own, then socked his attacker square in the face with his other fist. The man quickly recovered, almost like it didn't affect him at all. Cloukora went for the face again with a right hook, but the man grabbed his arm before it reached, and twisted it in a way that made Cloukora face the opposite direction with his arm forcefully behind his back. In a split second though, Cloukora spun clockwise and went to elbow the man across the face with his free arm, but was blocked by the man's other hand. Then Cloukora gave a quick sweep at the man's right leg, causing the assailant to fall on the ground, and pulled out his pistol and aimed it at the assassin. "Who are you?" Instantly, the gun was kicked out of Cloukora's hand, and the man was up. But on instinct, Cloukora made Fyron appear and had it pointing at the man's neck before the attacker could make another move.

The man took off his sunglasses to reveal a face of shock. "No way. It can't be."

"What?"

"A Skyrell." The man immediately dropped to a knee before Cloukora. He could clearly see what the man looked like now: he had short, messy black hair, had a bit of muscle to him, and, when he wasn't kneeling, stood maybe about an inch shorter than Cloukora. He was also about Cloukora's age too, probably a little older, and had icy blue eyes.

It made Cloukora feel a little embarrassed. "Dude, get up, there's no need for that."

"It's an honor to meet you." He said, getting up.

"Come on, I'm not even a king."

Birth

"Still, you're a descendant of him." The man just stared at him, and then abruptly shook his head. "Forgive me, my name's Ezel, I'm a Reaper."

"Wait, a Reaper?!" Cloukora's mouth dropped. "If anything I should be bowing to you. You all went into hiding and were never seen again. *I'm* lucky to have met *you*." He lowered Fyron.

"From what I have been told by my family, my ancestors fled to Rome, and when the first Pope came to power, we decided to be his personal army. Anyone that The Church found evil, we took care of them. It's what we've been doing since, even now."

"So, you are the one who's been killing these people."

"No," Ezel began. "Not people. Demons."

"Demons?"

Ezel nodded. "They're preparing for the apocalypse."

"Then you know about it too?"

"All of us do, the Pope is the one that told us." He said as-a-matter-of-factly.

"How do I know you're telling the truth?" Cloukora brought his sword back up, and looked at him more intently.

"Wait, they look like normal people to you, don't they?" Ezel asked as if they shouldn't.

"Yeah, don't they for you?" Cloukora almost thought this guy was a little crazy. Almost. Or perhaps *he* was crazy. *What if I'm just imagining all this? Maybe I'm not really a superhero and I'm really in some deep coma and I created this world to cope with it?* He wasn't sure where that even came from. The smell had to be getting to him, as was the headache. He tuned back in to Ezel.

Ezel shook his head and grinned. "I thought maybe you would be able to, being King Relyt's descendant and all, but I guess I was wrong. Perhaps you need to be blessed then."

"Blessed? By who?"

"The Pope, of course. I'm done with my mission here anyways; I'll take you to him."

"Hold on, I'll have to call someone first."

An Ally Discovered

Cloukora dialed Brev's number, and then waited for her to answer. "Brev, I need you to cover for me. The killer isn't killing people, he's slaying demons. I need to go with him to see the Pope. Don't ask. Just please do this, I gotta go. Bye." He didn't give any time for her to answer before hanging up. Though with that story, he wasn't sure if she even could. "You better be right about this."

As they were walking further down the alley, Cloukora heard something swoosh over him, and when he looked up, all he saw was a gargoyle statue. Cloukora's heart jumped: the statue looked down at him. "I see you still use gargoyles." He said after he managed to calm himself down.

"Yep. That's Talon. Had him since I was a boy."

"Ah."

"What about you? Still use wolves?"

"Yeah, actually. Rhain's at home though. Now that I think about it, the rest of my family doesn't have one. They have dogs though…"

"Rhain. Beautiful name for a wolf."

"Yep, and there's an 'h' in there by the way, just so you know."

As they were walking Cloukora pointed out the terrible smell. "Oh, that. That's just people smoking pot." Ezel replied.

"Huh. Well it smells freaking horrible." Cloukora commented. Ezel laughed as they kept walking.

St. Peter's Basilica, Vatican City, Rome

Cloukora and Ezel walked through the open doorway of the basilica into something he never would have imagined in a lifetime. The building's layout was in the shape of a rounded-out cross. The ceiling was dominated by domes, metal carvings of Biblical beings, and words scribed along the sides all around the basilica. Words Cloukora couldn't read even if he wanted to. Not only because it would take hours to read them all, but also because it was in Latin. Holding up the building were wide, rectangular columns stemming from the main

walls by archways that created paths for people to walk through. In each of the columns, a statue rested in an inlet of the surface of the column that faced the main hall. The floors had been cut from marble and had been painted with square designs that covered most of the floor. Cloukora also took notice of small alcoves all throughout the building with statues, paintings, and even altars residing in them.

To his left, after walking in, he saw a recreation of Jesus' birth through statues. In front of him was a long, rectangular area enclosed by short red walls, barely reaching his abdomen, making somewhat of a walkway. Cloukora wasn't sure what it was for, but guessed it was probably for ceremonial purposes. Past that, in front of Saint Peter's altar with six candles and a cross standing on top of it, were two staircases that curved downward towards Saint Peter's tomb. Beyond his altar, was the Chair of Saint Peter. A black, gold-gilded chair that seemed to float against the back of a wall with chiseled golden clouds flowing upwards behind it, into a frenzy of angels surrounding a golden, stained-glass window. Below the chair were four statues of old men standing, with two on each side, and an altar below it. In between Saint Peter's altar and his chair, were rows of red leather-seated pews facing the chair, and two large organs to either side of them.

All of these things, Cloukora knew nothing about. In fact, Ezel had to actually point out everything to him. He wished he did though; the place was beautiful and he felt like he wasn't appreciating it as much as he could. As they walked towards the other end of the hall, to his right he saw an altar with a painting above it. The painting was of a group of people surrounding a half-naked bearded man who seemed to be floating in the air, while another man stood over him with some kind of candle. To his left, further down from Jesus' birth recreation, was a room with a choir group, practicing their vocals. When they reached the intersection of the cross, where Saint Peter's altar rested, they took notice of a Mass in progress in the pews in front of the chair, being led by none other than the Pope himself!

"…The Devil has managed to turn many of God's people over to his side. Most of the time, they are turned *unknowingly*! He uses the smallest things to change them, whether it is just a little lust for

someone or a lie about running over their neighbor's cat. Or even putting the Lord's name in vain! He's building up an army, and I have foreseen the End of Days! It is up to all of you to prevent it from happening. Look to God, ask Him for forgiveness, and follow His ways. Stray from the sharp-tongued Devil and do not give into his temptations!" The Pope noticed Cloukora and Ezel towards the back of the pews. "I leave you all with this quote of John 14:27: Peace I leave with you; my peace I give to you; not as the world gives do I give to you. Let not your heart be troubled, neither let it be afraid." He gently closed the Bible as the people got up to leave, and stepped down to walk over to Cloukora and Ezel. "Ezel, my child, how did your mission go? And who is this young man here?"

"The mission was successful, your Holy One. All the threats were eliminated. The rest of the demons should back off now. And this. This is Cloukora Skyrell. Descendant of the great King Relyt." Ezel informed.

Cloukora wasn't sure how to show respect to the Pope, so he decided to bow. "Rise, my child." The Pope replied. "There is no need for such things. Is it true what Ezel says?"

Cloukora nodded. "Ezel also said you can give me some kind of blessing to see demons. Is that true?"

"Of course. I would have thought you already could though, being a descendant of Relyt."

"That's what I said!" Ezel said in agreement.

"Let's head down to the tomb area. We can't let others see." Cloukora nodded in agreement, and followed them down the stairwell. When they reached the end of the narrow hallway, the Pope pushed a brick in, and the wall moved, making an entryway to another, bigger room. The room was the opposite of the halls upstairs. The walls and floors were made out of stone instead of tile, but it was lit by modern-day lights. On one half of the room, all kinds of people practiced sword fighting skills with each other. It was mostly men, but there were women there too. Even a few children practiced as well. The other half was of students listening to battle strategies, as well as other useful information for the looming war.

Birth

"What are they doing?" Cloukora asked.

"Practicing for battle." Ezel replied.

"Lucifer's building an army. I simply decided to build one of my own. For now, it's secret, but later this year, I'm going to openly recruit people from all around the world." The Pope explained. "With you though, I don't think that will be necessary."

"Well, it's always good to have one, just in case." Cloukora advised.

"Thinking like a good king."

"I'm a descendant of a king, but I'm not a king. And I hope it stays that way. I couldn't be someone like that. That kind of job comes with too much pressure, pressure that would break me in two." They walked to the end of the room, into a smaller room that was lit by hundreds of candles.

"Here we are. Kneel, Cloukora." Cloukora got down on one knee, and bowed his head. *"Dominus pugnabit pro vobis velim huic virtus. Da ei virtutem ad bellandum. Per laborem ad sanitatem dari et mentis viribus vincunt. Maxime mundare animam inimicorum eius et videre eum. Amen."* Suddenly, Cloukora felt something go into him, into his soul. Something that felt great, something enlightening, and it gave him a feeling he had never felt before. The feeling of being able to do anything. He felt like he could go through hell and back without even hesitating if he had to. Most of all, he felt as if a part of something divine and Holy now resided within him.

"How do you feel?" Ezel asked.

"Better than I have ever felt in my entire life." Cloukora replied, gasping for cool air. It felt like the energy in him was taken away for a moment and then rushed back into him.

"Now, I have another mission for you, Ezel. Cloukora, I'm sure you could be of some help as well."

Cloukora nodded as he stood up. "Of course I'll help."

"There's a man down in Uganda. His name's Brandon Forks, and yes, he is in fact a demon. Well, has a demon inside him anyway. He's been abducting kids in poor villages, forcing them to join his

army, and kill their parents. He also uses the young girls for...unspeakable acts. He's a monster, and he *must* be stopped."

"Brandon Forks? Never heard of him." Cloukora commented.

"Not surprising, he's been in the shadows all this time. He's been doing this for about twenty years or more. I've tried asking the government for assistance, but they refused. They said it wasn't profitable enough, and it's not their business."

"Twenty years? So this could have nothing to do with the coming apocalypse then. I'll still take him down though. Someone like that doesn't *deserve* to live. I might also be able to get the government to help us out with whatever we need."

"I'll get everything else prepared for you two." The Pope began to give people commands, as he spoke to Ezel about the details. Cloukora didn't stick around though; he went up to call an old "friend" of his. After a few minutes of convincing the United States' General, and reminding him that he still owes Cloukora, he finally agreed to help out. A few hours later, they were on a helicopter to Uganda.

Some village in Uganda, Africa

Cloukora and Ezel sat in a hut, faces covered in dirt, wearing torn up clothes, but covered up in blankets with M4's hiding underneath. Other people huddled around each other inside it. Some of them were also trained operatives in this Sting Operation. The rest were villagers that volunteered to be a part of the operation. The room smelled from the lack of showers and cleanliness. Cloukora would have to make sure the general did something about this village. It wasn't just hygiene there was a lack of; people were starving as well. He couldn't just leave them like this, it wouldn't be right. He couldn't live with himself if he did.

Night had finally come. "Are you sure this gonna work?" Ezel asked Cloukora.

"This is the place he frequents the most, and according to the pattern, where he will abduct nex-" Ezel quickly shushed him.

"Shh. Someone's outside." Sure enough, Cloukora heard men speaking and drawing nearer. It was in a language Cloukora couldn't understand though. A man popped inside and shouted in his language something that made everyone else get up. Even in the dim light, Cloukora could see a small, dark spherical cloud within the man's chest, and a pair of shrouded horns on his forehead. *This must be what a demon looks like.* Immediately, Cloukora, Ezel, and the other three soldiers in the room pulled out the M4's from hiding and aimed the barrels at the man. Outside he heard more shouts, and the sounds of helicopters flying above. Bright lights also lit up the ground outside, in the village.

"Get down on the ground now!" Cloukora commanded. The man dropped his AK-47 he had been carrying, got on his knees and put his hands behind his head. Cloukora went outside to see the same, but with about a hundred men instead, with more being pushed out of the other huts.

The general came out of building from the other end of the village. "Now what?"

"We interrogate one of them." Cloukora sounded sure of himself.

"Yeah, right. They're not gonna tell us where he is."

"That man will." Cloukora pointed to a man that seemed fidgety and nervous. Scared. "He will do *anything* to get away from here." Two soldiers quickly grabbed the man and took him inside an empty building. Not even a minute later, they came back out.

"He's in another village about fifty miles from here, sir." A soldier informed.

"Let's move out!" They all packed up as quickly as they could, and mobilized to the location where Forks was hiding out. Some of the caravan split up to take the enemy soldiers to a prison nearby.

Cloukora burst through the door, with Ezel and the soldiers following close behind, all with M4's resting in their hands; Cloukora didn't think a single shot would need to be fired. Forks was sitting at

An Ally Discovered

his desk and put his hands up in the air as soon as he saw them. Cloukora saw the man as he had saw the one in the other village. Except, Fork's horns were bigger, and so was the sphere of darkness inside him. It almost took up his entire chest. So these *were* demons then, and the horn size is most likely part of their rank. The general walked in shortly.

"Brandon Forks, you are under arrest for the abduction of children, treason, murder- should I continue?" Cloukora whispered something into the general's ear. "You're also being arrested for the murders in Germany."

"Germany?! What the hell are you talking about?" They didn't give him any more time to defend himself. He was taken outside and thrown into a helicopter with armed men, while Cloukora went to get on Wolfstorm's.

But before he could, Ezel shouted at him. "Cloukora!" Cloukora turned around to see Ezel getting on his own chopper. "Why…Why did you tell him that?"

Cloukora was confused. How could he not know? "Because you're my friend, Ezel. If someone wasn't arrested for it, they would have kept looking for you. The world needs more people like you. You make it safe to sleep at night." Ezel grinned.

"Good luck, Cloukora! May we meet again!" The helicopter Ezel had got on took off, and flew north.

"So, does this make us even?" The general asked walking towards him. Apparently he can't do something because it's right and not ask for anything in return.

"We will *never* be even. Not ever." Cloukora assured him and started walking away when he remembered something. "Oh, and I want you to start helping these villages. They need your help whether you want to give it or not."

"And what if we don't?" Did he *like* pissing Cloukora off?

"If I don't see any progress within…I'll give you two weeks. If I don't see any progress within two weeks, I will tell everyone that you didn't kill Oushu, and that he's still out there."

The general was silent for a moment. "You know that's not true."

"Yeah, but the people don't know that." Cloukora had leverage against him if he ever needed it, now.

Cloukora got onto the Wolfstorm helicopter, and shut the door as it took off westward, towards the United States.

Angel's Gaiden

No Rest for the Weary

July 27, 2010
Middle of the Atlantic Ocean

    The Blackhawk helicopter flew over the Atlantic Ocean on its way back to Oregon. Cloukora had his head leaned back on the seat, his disguise lying on the one next to his. The recent mission was exhausting for him. Not physically, in fact he barely did anything that required some kind of combat; he was just sleep-deprived. Bowe was flying the helicopter while Brev was on the phone in the passenger seat of the cockpit. Cloukora looked down below at the ocean, but it wasn't much to look at. For the water was pretty still, and calm.

    "Alright, we'll take it. Thank you, Nole." She hung up the cellphone. "We've got another mission."

    "Another? I guess there *is* no rest for the weary."

    "A governor's daughter was kidnapped by a drug lord down in Miami."

    "Miami huh? Heh, maybe I will get some rest after all." He tried to joke. He was *way* too tired. "Why was she kidnapped?"

    "As usual: for money. The governor didn't pay for his last drug buy like he was supposed to."

    "Figures."

    "He wants to keep it out of the media, and *way* down low. I guess he says he's a changed man, and that he doesn't want to touch any kind of drug ever again. He promises a reward, and that he'll pay for any damages caused in the city if they should occur. He just wants his daughter back."

    Cloukora sighed. "Alright, so how do we find this drug lord?"

Birth

"We're rendezvousing with a contact once we get there. His name's Detective Jonathan Black. He's the head of the DEA section in Miami, and has been trying to track down our guy for three years."

"Cool, wake me when we get there. I'm gonna shut my eyes for a bit." And he did just that.

Miami, Florida

The helicopter rested on the landing pad that was next to the police building, rather than being on the top. Cloukora woke up when he felt the *thump* of the helicopter land. *They should call it helicopter bump. That didn't feel padded at all.* Bowe and Brev got out of the helicopter. When he stepped outside of the helicopter, the rising sun shone brightly in the sky. So bright that he had to rub his eyes just to get them to adjust to the sudden light. As he was doing so, a detective walked up to them from out of the police building, and asked if they were the people they had called. Cloukora abruptly realized his mask was off, hurriedly grabbed it out of the helicopter, and put it on. He was still half asleep and tired.

"Hey, your mask is upside down." The detective pointed out when Cloukora turned to face them.

"Agh." Cloukora quickly turned around, fixed it, and turned back with the mask on right this time.

"He's a little tired." Brev said, supportively. Bowe chuckled.

"I can see that. Anyways, the governor is inside the police station. Follow me." Cloukora grabbed his hoodie, but didn't put it on, and they followed the detective quietly through the building's entrance, and towards the top floor. Cloukora didn't pay any attention to his surroundings; he didn't really care either. He would make sure to take in the scenery later when he was more awake. When they reached the police chief's office, they went inside and sat down in front of the desk with the governor in the chief's chair. Except for the detective, who showed them in and then walked off somewhere.

"Thank you guys for coming. Again, I just want to say I will give you anything you need to get her, and anything as a reward. Just please help me get my daughter back." The governor said before they even had a chance to sit down.

"Of course. We will do everything we can to find this drug dealer, and save your daughter. Now what does she look like?" Brev assured.

"Well, she's sixteen, has blonde hair, blue eyes-is he alright?" He pointed to Cloukora who had started falling asleep. Bowe slapped the back of Cloukora's head with his hand, waking him up. Cloukora rubbed his head and focused as best as he could. "Anyways, she's normal height and she wears really expensive designer clothing. I don't know what it is about women and expensive clothes but, can't say no to my baby girl."

"That helps. I'm sure she's the only blonde, rich sixteen year old in Miami." Cloukora said, who received yet another slap on the back of the head from Bowe. "Sorry. A little irritable at the moment." He said rubbing the back of his head. "Is there anything else you can tell us?"

"She...she has a birthmark. On her right arm. She always wears a locket around her neck that contains a picture of her mother inside. Let's see..."

"I think that's good enough to work with, Mr. Melheim. Thank you." Brev and Bowe got up, followed by Cloukora, and walked outside the office, into the waiting room. "So what do you think?"

"Well the file says this drug lord...Anthony Legardo...has his own street racing gang. He sets up races all over Miami every night. We can start there. We just need someone to do a little street racing." Bowe said and then turned to Cloukora, hinting at who he was referring to.

"Hell yeah, I'll do it." Cloukora eagerly accepted.

"He's not so tired anymore." Bowe joked.

"Alright. Cloukora...go take a nap or whatever on a chair. I'll set it up with the governor." Brev said, and then walked back into the chief's room with Bowe. Cloukora went over to the armless chairs,

bundled his hoodie so that it acted as a pillow and lay down facing the wall. Before Cloukora could fall asleep, a young woman in handcuffs came over and sat down on a nearby chair.

"What're you in for?" She asked.

"Drugs." Cloukora didn't open his eyes.

"Ah. I'm in here for shoplifting."

"I was making a joke."

"Oh. I don't get it."

"It's a reference from Ferris Bueller's Day Off." He sighed with defeat. "Though, I suppose being in an actual police station, it would be taken seriously. My bad."

"Oh yeah. I *loved* that movie."

"It's an awesome movie."

"It is. Well, I can see you're trying to sleep. I'll let you get back to it."

"I've got a question."

"Hm?"

Cloukora lifted his head, finally opening his eyes. "You're actually a pretty nice person."

"Thank you?"

"So, why did you shoplift? You don't seem like the kind of person that would."

"What? You think all criminals are poor, ragged people?" Cloukora didn't reply, and she gave a sigh. "My friends dared me to. They thought it would be funny if we stole something. It was a small thing of course; a keychain. But when the guards caught me, I couldn't see them anywhere as I was dragged out of the mall."

"Kinda shows who your friends are."

"Yeah, I know. I don't even know why I hung out with them in the first place, now that I think about it."

"I would suggest finding new ones, and not messing up your life. You want a future right? Kids, husband, nice job?"

"Yeah…"

"You won't have any of that with a criminal record. Well, I suppose you *could* find a husband, but it would most likely end up being an asshole."

"You're right. I'll do whatever I have to for my crime, and then I'm turning a new leaf. Does that include drugs like weed?"

"Duh, you won't be able to get a good job if you can't pass the drug test. Plus kids shouldn't be around that stuff."

"Wait, what's with the mask?" Brev and Bowe walked out before Cloukora could answer.

"Come on Cloukora. Got a surprise for ya." She said tauntingly as Cloukora shot up out of the chair, almost forgetting his hoodie, and followed them out the door.

"Nice meeting you!" The woman shouted on his way out. Cloukora gave a nod back.

Outside the police building, lining the streets were palm trees that rose high above, providing a little protection from the burning sun. Buildings towered over, reaching a cloudless, blue sky. To his left, there was a beach not far off with people sunbathing all along it, and surfers riding the decent sized waves. The water looked a lot nicer than the water he had seen on Oregon's beaches; these were a teal, light blue where you could see the sand underneath. He still preferred its beaches over this one, though. The smell was wonderful too: there were restaurants up and down the streets with tables and chairs placed outside of them, and whatever they were cooking he could smell the combination of all the food, with the smells blending surprisingly well together. He then took notice of the second scenery of the city: two tanned, young women walking by in colorful two-piece bikinis. Staring, he looked them up and down, admittedly enjoying the sight a little, until he had seen them for who they really were. Inside their chests, as if he had x-ray vision, there resided a small, black, spherical cloud, no bigger than a fist; unlike Brandon Fork's whose was the size of at least three. They had horns, shrouded in black too, that stuck out of their forehead just a little less than an inch out. When he took another

look around, he saw the sidewalks almost filled with demons, with no two pairs of horns matching in size. The battle coming up wasn't going to be easy. He knew that for sure. Remembering why Brev brought him out here, he cleared his throat and turned to her.

"So uh, what is it you wanted to show me?" Cloukora asked. Right then, a dark blue 2010 Dodge Challenger SRT8 pulled up. It had stock decals on it, no fin on the rear like the stock cars usually have though, and a hood scoop on the hood that wasn't stock either. A man got out of the driver side and tossed the keys to Cloukora, who caught them with disbelief. "Seriously? Oh Brev I love you." That produced a chuckle out of her and Bowe as he practically ran over to the driver side. Before he could get open the car door, the detective, Jonathan Black, came outside to join them. He took notice of Cloukora about to get in the car.

"Leaving already for the mission before even knowing what it is? I like your enthusiasm, but you gotta work on that brain, kid." The detective remarked. Cloukora had been too focused on the car that he forgot all about the case. *He didn't have to call me 'kid.'*

Cloukora rubbed his forehead embarrassingly. "Sorry, I was just, um, yeah. Sorry." He walked back to the three standing there.

The detective opened a copy of the file Brev held. "Anthony Legardo is a ghost. This man has dealt drugs, trafficked people, murdered people, his gangs attacked our cops, plus many more violations to go along with those to give him *lifetimes* worth of prison. But we just can't get anything on him. His crates come up with nothing in the records that lead up to him. The drugs can't be traced, and the people we arrest don't even know what he looks like. All we know is what he does, his name, and that he's in Miami. He funds the races that his underlings like to host. So you," He looked at Cloukora; "are going to enter the audition race today, win, enter tonight's race, win, and get your foot in the door. In short, you're joining a gang."

"Joining a- Dammit." He pressed his fingers against the bridge of his nose before sighing. "The things I do for people. Where's this race?"

The detective pulled out a small device with a display screen. "This is a GPS. It will tell you where to go and the shortest routes in the races to help you get there." Cloukora took the GPS and fiddled with it until it suddenly said "Go two point three miles and turn left."

The detective coughed at the interruption. "The audition race is in an hour about 30 miles from here. You might want to get going if you want to make it on time." Cloukora quickly got into the driver side, threw his hoodie on the back seat, put his belt on, took it out of park, and stepped on the gas. After a few blocks he realized his mask was still on, and took it off before sticking it under the seat. The city was just like he had expected and seen in the movies: sunny and full of people and towering buildings. He was enjoying just sitting at the stop light, listening to the sound of the car. That was a big reason he loved muscle cars: because of the roar of the engine. Aside from the *power* of the engine itself, of course. A customized orange 2009 Honda Civic zoomed past all the cars at the light and headed in the same direction Cloukora was going. Cloukora wasn't in a hurry though; he would make it on time to the meeting place. The light turned green and Cloukora lifted his foot off the brake pedal, and put it onto the gas, and the car moved forward. For some reason, this mission and its importance hit him. He wasn't sure why, but he knew he *needed* to find her, and to get her back. At all costs. No matter what it took. Not because he knew it was right, but because somehow, it felt personal.

King Relyt's castle, Scotland, 897

Relyt sat in his chamber room, upon his bed in a linen shirt and loose linen breeches, going over proposals from the people on a squared device similar to an electronic tablet. Which it in fact was. They just weren't meant to be invented until a thousand years later. Just as in the Book of Atlantis, he was the spitting image of Cloukora: He had deep-set brown eyes, long brown hair that was actually longer than Cloukora's, and had a slender body. Though he *did* have some muscle on him, unlike his reincarnation. His room was a little more modern

Birth

than what castle rooms should have been like during that century. Most of the furniture was of that time, but there were also technological things such as a television screen on the wall, and lamps instead of candles. Minor things, but he was always in his study drawing up designs for new technological advances.

His wife, Aurora, walked in from the also modernized bathroom towards the bed. She wore her silky white night gown that was cut down to her knees. She was tall and thin, had long blonde hair, and had the most, soft and elegantly beautiful face Relyt had ever seen. A face Relyt felt lucky to kiss. What he felt even luckier for, was the bump on her stomach. A product of the two rulers of Atlantis, who would one day take over its parents' place on the throne, and watch over the kingdom. Relyt hoped it would be a boy, since it would even it out with the daughter they already had. Of course, he would love the child no matter what gender it came to be.

"Check on Alessa yet?" Aurora reminded before she covered up under the blanket.

"I put her in her room about an hour ago. I will now, though." He sat the tablet device on the wooden nightstand, and walked out the chamber door and down the stone hallways with electrical lamps lining the walls. His daughter's room was right next door to theirs, and when he cracked it open, he called out her name. Her room was more elegant than his, and had more pink to it as well. The furniture, however, was about the same. When he asked "Alessa?" again, there was no answer. He pushed the door wide open, and looked around the room for any sign of her. There was none. The blankets were tossed aside, and the window was open with the pink curtains fluttering with the wind. The room, oddly, was untouched and completely fine. "Alessandra? ALESSANDRA?!" He ran out of the room back to his. "Alessa's gone."

Aurora sat straight up. "What?! Where is she?"

"I have no idea. I mean it's not like she's a teenager yet to wander off. She has no reason to sneak out." Out of a surge of anger, he punched the wall nearest to him, causing his knuckles to bleed.

"Do you think… she was kidnapped?"

Rubbing his knuckles he turned away from his wife. "I know we both don't like the idea, but… it's most likely." He started out the door.

"Where are you going?"

"To find my daughter." He grabbed his sheathed katana that lay next to the bedroom door, walked out, and shut the door behind him.

After a bit of a drive, Cloukora had finally made it to the meeting place: On the third floor of a five-story garage. He parked his car with the other five, which were all customized with varying spoilers and decals: The same Honda he had seen earlier, a black 1999 Mitsubishi Eclipse, a silver 2010 Audi R8, a black 2004 Volkswagen GTI, and a blue 2007 Mazda RX-8. All the other drivers were gathered around each other talking until Cloukora's Challenger came up the ramp and parked in the open space next to the Eclipse.

When he stepped out, they all turned to face him. One of them was a man: tall, dark, and bald. Another man was white, average height, and had curly hair. The third was a woman, who Cloukora admitted had a pretty attractive body and face. *I would totally date her.* She had long, brown hair, tanned skin, and was short compared to the guys around her, except for one. The fourth driver was a bit short, had slick black hair and wore a suit, which Cloukora thought was odd for a racer. The last one was average height as well, and had short, blonde hair. He looked like a surfer, Cloukora thought.

"Hah, you really think that thing will beat my baby?" The surfer rubbed the hood of his car. His was the Eclipse. "Those cars are just for show, man. They aren't good for races these days. Know what I'm saying bra?"

"Well I'd rather roar like a lion, than buzz like a bee." Cloukora remarked.

"Yeah, well, the bee can like, sting the lion. So then the bee wins."

"I'm not going to even dignify that with a response."

Birth

"Idiota!" The woman motioned her hand, expressing how much of an 'Idiota' he was. "Bees die when they sting something!"

A black limousine appeared coming up the ramp to the level they were on, and parked in front of the six racers. Out stepped a tall man in a suit, with short black hair, and looked as though he were in a rush. His name was Diego Barza, one of Legardo's higher-up men.

"Alright people, let's hurry up and do this. I got somewhere to be before tonight. You're racing to Pompano Beach where you will meet up with another associate. Those who make it there will be considered to be in tonight's race. That's all you need to know. No time limit. Go!"

No one wasted any time getting to their cars, including Cloukora, who was actually the first to reach his, and pull out of the parking space. It didn't take long for him to get out of the garage, and start following the GPS. As soon as he got on the main road, the song 'Kickstart My Heart' by Mötley Crüe came on the radio, and on instinct, he stepped on the gas and the car zoomed off down the street, eastward. He was hitting around 55 miles per hour on the city streets; any faster and he'd end up missing the turn coming up. Or worse, crash into another car. He weaved around traffic, which was a difficult task being in Miami, since cars were everywhere despite the time of day when everyone should be at work. The other cars caught up surprisingly quickly, and were right behind him. Before he hit the next light, the GPS told him to make a left, and when he reached the intersection, he quickly pulled up on the e-brake, as he turned the steering wheel to the right, and the car drifted smoothly around the corner. He then put the e-brake back down, and straightened his steering wheel. The Civic and Eclipse were right on his tail now. The GPS said for a right at this next intersection, which was only a three-way intersection, and he drifted again, but this time turned his steering wheel left. Suddenly he heard sirens, and saw cop cars behind him in his rear view mirror. "Hopefully they'll help keep the others at bay." Then he remembered he was undercover and that they would be coming after him too. "Shit." He noticed he had two options: One was a long, dirt road going left, that was a beginning of a construction site for a new building that had not

yet been started on, with construction equipment all along the road. The other was a ramp that was supposed to take them onto a highway that looped around to the other side of the dirt road. Looking at the GPS, he saw that he would be parallel to the other cars on the highway, if they followed the GPS, so he took the dirt road. The rest of the cars went straight as he had expected, but a couple cop cars still followed him. Cloukora avoided the obstacles on the road: cones, long iron bars that would be used to support the building, and construction vehicles. Then, not meaning for it to, a cop car crashed into a steam shovel and started a chain reaction of crashes. The cars piled up until the road was too blocked for anymore to get through. The car phone rang, and he pressed a button near the radio.

"Cloukora, what the hell are you doing?" It was Brev. "Why aren't you following the GPS?"

"Something came up, so I had to take a detour." He swerved around a pile of pipes.

"You should have been fine on the road."

"I know what I'm doing."

"Clouk-"

"Shuddup." He ended the call. He glanced over at the four-lane highway and saw the other cars were straight across from him, heading north as he was. Adrenaline started pumping rapidly through him, and everything slowed down except his eyes, and he saw that at the speed he and they were going, even calculating the turn they had to make, he was going to crash into them. Cloukora pushed on the gas pedal more, and the car hit up to around 95 miles per hour, but the other cars were still coming closer. Any faster though, or any slower, and he'd miss his shot and risk a crash. In fact, he was sure he would. He had to keep his speed just right. Not a mile over or under.

When Cloukora reached the end of the dirt road meeting with the highway, he drifted in with the other cars perfectly, barely missing the front bumper of the Eclipse behind him that quickly took the lane next to him, and the rear bumpers of the cars in front, but still perfect. His car was now surrounded: the Civic and the R8 were in front of him, the Eclipse and RX-8 to his sides, and the GTI behind him. They were

going west now. He put his foot on the brakes a little, forcing the GTI do the same, and then Cloukora turned into the far right lane as the GTI took his place. All the cars rounded the corner to the right, and as he was going down the street, he took notice of an alleyway he passed by.

He slammed on the brakes and turned the car around with a sudden U-turn, and started down the alleyway. Dodging the giant dumpsters and hitting littering garbage bags, he sped as fast as he could down the narrow "road" parallel to the other cars on the actual street. Cloukora didn't think they noticed him, but *he* noticed *them*, and the fact that he was now neck and neck with first place. He needed to go faster, but there were just too many obstacles that were difficult to avoid as it was. He finally reached the end of the alley and drifted right. Not far behind him were the other racers, and as he drifted around the next corner going left, the Eclipse was right on him. But he didn't let up; he kept control of his car, and his speed, and did the same when he rounded the final corner to the left, revealing a long, sandy coast on his right. They were almost there, but the other cars, especially the eclipse were right on his tail. Up ahead, he saw a black limousine parked on the beach. He couldn't lose now. Shifting gears, he accelerated until the car got above 105 miles per hour, and he knew the other racers thought he was crazy, for they were now way behind. Except for the Eclipse, who warily tried speeding up to catch up with Cloukora. The other racers knew going this fast with their destination just ahead would be suicide; there wouldn't be enough stopping distance. As they got closer to the limousine, as Cloukora had figured, the Eclipse backed off and slowed down. But Cloukora didn't let up right away. In fact, he didn't stop until he was only a short distance from the limo. As soon as he hit the sand, he slammed on his brakes, and his car slid along past the limo, making the guy standing next to it throw his hands up to protect himself and his face. Most likely protecting the fancy suit he had on as well.

Once the car fully stopped, Cloukora's breathing had turned heavy. He had never before in his life raced a car. He had never been this daring before, this dangerous, this crazy! All the adrenaline had flooded in from the intensity of the race. And the best part about it was that he won. His first street race and he won.

After a moment of catching his breath, he finally stepped out of the car and towards the limo. "What the hell was that?" The bald-headed man in the suit said angrily, walking towards Cloukora and pointing at the blue-now-covered-in-sand-Challenger.

"I don't like to lose."

"And where the hell is the other driver?" Cloukora just noticed that the GTI wasn't there with the others.

"He crashed." The surfer said with a smirk as he and the other drivers walked towards them both. Looking at the group, he figured that it had to be the curly-haired man that drove the GTI, because he wasn't there.

"You, what's your name?" The bald man turned to Cloukora.

He forgot to come up with a new name, so he went with what first came to his mind: "Chris Newman." He didn't know why that popped into his head first, it just did.

"Chris, you'll take part in the street race tonight. I'll call you and tell you where it's taking place once we decide on the location. The rest of you, go home. If you try to contact us at all, you won't be waking up the next morning." The man threatened before he got into the limo and drove off. Everyone else, reluctantly of course, got into their cars to drive off as well, with Cloukora heading to find something to eat.

Relyt walked through the pouring rain along the cobblestone road, and in between stone buildings with their lights off to either side of him. Rain pelted his wet cloak as he paced through the city, until he came to an inn called "The Wolf's Howl." The lamp outside the door flickered. He would have to fix that. For now though, he had a bigger issue on his hands. He opened the door, leading into a room full of drunks, music, and dancing. Relyt walked over to the bar, and spoke in a soft whisper, making sure to keep a low profile.

"Mac." That was towards the innkeeper.

"Tyler! Oh how good to see you again! How long now? Two months?" The innkeeper knew it was Relyt; Tyler was just a cover

name. It was simple, and it was good enough for drunks that couldn't even get a decent sentence out.

"About a month or so."

"Ah, my memory isn't all what it used to be." The man gave a hearty chuckle.

"Hey, I'm freelancing a kidnapping case. Have you heard anything?"

"As a matter of fact…Yes, I think I have. I was serving a table earlier, and I heard something about a girl they had that they were going to sell. Her name was…Alessandra. The kidnapped girl I mean. They left the inn though."

He was so close, but now he was so far. No way of telling where they had went. "Thanks Mac, I'll keep looking then." He turned to face three men staring him down, one of them taller than he was. "May I help you?"

"It's him. King Relyt." One of them said.

"Look, I'll give you whatever you wa-"

"Heh. Boys, he wants to bribe us. What do you say? Should we take it?"

"I say we kill him." Another said. The three drew swords.

"I don't want any trouble. Let's just walk away." Relyt warned.

"You got it when you asked about your daughter." The third said.

"What did you say?" Relyt readied himself.

"Your daughter is missing?!" The innkeeper asked, shocked.

"Yeah she's probably in Ayr already." The first one said.

"Idiot! Now he knows. Oh well, we'll just kill everyone in here." The second said cockily.

"I don't think you understand who I am, and what I'm capable of." Relyt threatened.

"Yeah, rumors! All that crap about you is, well, crap!" The second said.

The three rushed him, and swung their swords. Relyt grabbed the wrist of the first man, who came at his left, with his left hand, and twisted it, kicked the third man who came at the right into a table a

Birth

group of drunks had been sitting at, and drew his sword from his back to block the sword of the second man who came straight at him. When Relyt drew his sword, it wasn't there originally, but when the place of the handle was grasped, it appeared. Relyt pushed the second's sword down and hit him in the face with the end of the hilt. He turned to face the first man, who was now holding his wrist in pain.

"Now tell me where she is." Relyt commanded.

"Th-th-they left for Ayr. But they're probably camping out in that abandoned house out in the woods." Relyt kneed him right in the crotch, and the man fell down while holding the injured area. The other two were lying on the ground, holding their stomach and face.

"Sorry Mac. I'll compensate you for the table, and fix the light outside tomorrow." Relyt said as he began out of the inn, the sword in his hand seeming to magically disappear.

"No need for that, Relyt. Just find your daughter." The innkeeper replied.

Relyt pushed the door open and walked back out onto the street.

The sun had already set in the west, creating night within the city. The city lights were too bright to be able to see the stars in the sky, which Cloukora had always thought were the best part of the night. It made him wish he was back home where he could see them light up the heavens. His focus went back to the other racers next to him. All four racers, including him, were in their cars, lined up at the starting line. His competition was a red 2005 Ford Mustang GT, a blue 2001 Nissan Skyline GTR R34, and a black 1970 Chevrolet Chevelle Malibu SS. This race was a simple one. No traffic. Just two laps around the "circuit." The circuit was about twenty blocks long and one block wide, and resided next to a tall building where Anthony Legardo will supposedly watch the race from. Cloukora could easily take out all the security and make his way to Anthony, but he had to do this right. He couldn't risk the girl's life.

All the roads were blocked and cleared off so there would be no interference; Anthony must have paid off the city or something of the

sort. Finally, a girl walked in front of the cars, and stood in between the two middle cars so she wouldn't get hit when they took off. She removed her shirt, revealing a pink bikini top underneath that produced whistles from both guys and girls. Cloukora wasn't affected by it, though. He just wanted to meet face to face with Anthony, and get the girl back. He still didn't know why he felt so strongly about this case, but he wouldn't stop until she was found. He would win this race, meet Anthony, take him down, and bring her home. The uneasy thing about all of this though, was that he was alone: He had not told Brev about this race. He had figured it would waste more time than necessary. Plus, he's a superhero: what can be thrown at him that he can't handle? *I can do this. I need to start acting for myself. Brev won't always be there to get my back.* The girl standing in front of them started waving her shirt around, making the other racers rev their engines. She threw it up in the air. *I can do this.* The shirt touched ground. All four racers stomped their foot on the gas, and took off, smoke trailing behind the tires.

    The Chevelle was in first place at the get-go, with Cloukora right behind it, followed by the Mustang, and then the Skyline; Muscle cars were better on long stretch roads. Within a few seconds though, the Skyline had passed the Mustang was right next to Cloukora. As the Chevelle and Cloukora drifted around the corner, the Skyline flawlessly overtook them both and got first. The Skyline suddenly shot forward as if given a sudden boost of speed; they used NoS. Cloukora tried to speed up and take second, but the Chevelle had a lot more power than his own car, and wouldn't let him pass until they drifted around the next corner when his car drifted past the other muscle car. Now it was just him, and the Skyline that was still, thankfully, in view when he crossed the starting line, signaling the next lap. His speed almost caught up with the Skyline, but ended up losing it when they drifted around the first corner again, then caught back up on the second stretch of road. They were now almost neck and neck. Around the second corner, Cloukora didn't make the same mistake: He kept on the Skyline and stayed with it. The finish line was just up ahead, but he still couldn't pass the other racer, no matter how fast he went. They must have ran out of nitrous oxide, though, or else they would have used it and won

already. Then something strange happened, it was barely noticeable but Cloukora managed to catch it: The other driver slowed down. Not much, though; it was only a hair. Anything else would have been too obvious. *Why do they want me to win?* Taking the advantage before the other racer changed their mind, and sped up until he crossed the finish line, winning the race. He slowed his car down and pulled it to the side, before stepping out and meeting the cheering crowd of spectators. He looked at the Skyline that was now parked, but the driver didn't get out. In fact, he couldn't even see who it was through the black-tinted windows. *Who was that guy?* Turning his head towards the building entrance he saw the surfer guy from earlier, near his Eclipse, talking to a suit-wearing security guard, both looking at Cloukora. Something was wrong. Ignoring the crowd, he walked towards the two, plus another two security guards who just joined them.

"Hey! I won the race. I want my prize now!" He shouted once he was in hearing distance. Two of them nodded and each grabbed Cloukora by the arms and took him inside. They led him up to the top floor, opened a door to a room, and shoved him in, but didn't leave. The room looked like a study room: bookshelves, a lit fireplace that was most likely fake, a chair facing the fireplace, and a couple desks with books and other items lying on top of them. Behind the main desk was a large glass window that overlooked the city.

"Boss, this is the guy who won." One of them said.

The man that was already in the room had been walking around, sipping whiskey out of a short glass. He was tall, had long, fine black hair swept back, and a scar on his left cheek. It was Anthony, Cloukora was sure. Cloukora did all he could to keep himself from lunging at the man right then and there. "Ah, the winner. Congratulations my man." He put his hand forward, which Cloukora shook reluctantly, and then walked over to the giant window behind him. "Us winners, you and me, we *make* ourselves winners. We do that by taking it from the other…players, if you will. Things aren't just handed to you in life. You have to take them, by any means necessary. That's why I don't mind cheaters…but deceivers…well that's a whole nother story.

Deceivers make me sick. With their lying and just…you know what I mean right?" He turned and pointed at Cloukora for agreement.

"Yeah, I do. I hate 'em too." Cloukora agreed, but it was meant towards Anthony.

"Sir, this man is an undercover cop. A racer from earlier followed him after the meet-up and caught him talking to a detective." The other man in the suit revealed.

"Is this true?" Anthony asked, walking towards Cloukora.

"Of course not. I hate cops. That douche is just trying to ruin me because I beat him in the race." That was partly true. Obviously he was working with the cops, but he never met up with anyone else after the race. It was pure coincidence that the surfer guy made that accusation.

One of the men took out Cloukora's wallet and read off his I.D. "Cloukora Skyrell. I thought you said your name was Chris Newman."

He needed to try and save his skin. "That's uh, not mine. It's a friend's?" *Why am I such a bad liar?*

"I'll ask you once more. Are. You. A cop?" Anthony was losing patience.

"I told you, I'm not a c-" Cloukora heard a loud bang, and immediately felt a sharp, shooting pain in the back of his right leg, and its force sent him crashing to the floor. The pain felt unbearable, he couldn't move his leg at all, and the force of the bullet had him gasping for air. All he could do was just lie there. He had failed the mission, he couldn't find the girl, and now he was going to die. Die by the hands of this despicable man. Anthony pulled out a gun from his waistband, and pointed it at Cloukora's forehead. The feeling returned. The feeling he had back in Iraq. Where he brutally killed that man. The feeling he had on his cousin's birthday. That strong feeling of anger. He tried to suppress it as much as he could, but it just wouldn't stay down.

"I told you I don't like liars!"

"Where is she? Where's my daughter?!" *Daughter…where did that come from?*

"This guy must be nuts." He told the other two men, and then went back to Cloukora. "I don't *have* your daughter. I have the governor's daughter, but not yours."

"Where is she?!"

"It's a secret." He clicked back the gun's hammer. "Any last words?"

This was it; he couldn't hold it back any longer. All the anger inside him released itself. "Yeah, say hi to Lucifer for me." Cloukora's body started protruding purple spikes, just as he did in Iraq. And as before, his eyes changed too: He now had the inverted Skyrell crest in his eyes, bearing a magenta, sky blue, and gray color. His leg felt stronger, he could stand on it again. After easing up on his leg, he grabbed the necks of the two men next to him, and threw them into the bookshelves on either side. Cloukora's body was now covered in a thin, hard purple armor that had replaced his entire skin, except for his face. He started towards Anthony. "You want to know who I *really* hate? I hate people like you. People that sell young girls for money. Kill people for drugs. Not give a damn about those that they harm. They are the scum, and the filth that corrupts this world. You turn a beautiful world ugly."

Anthony was scared out of his mind. He was backing towards the window, eyes widened and on Cloukora who just kept stepping towards him. "P-please. Don't kill me! I'll change! I promise!" Anthony begged.

"People like you don't deserve a second chance." Cloukora grabbed Anthony by the neck, staring him in the eyes. "They deserve a painful death." His arm heaved and sent Anthony through the window, breaking the glass as the horrible man fell to his horrible death. Cloukora turned around without remorse, and began walking out the room, until he began to feel weak, and collapsed to his knees. The armor that covered him slowly disappeared, and the pain from the bullet wound returned. With a greater intensity than before. He fell completely to the ground and blacked out. But before blacking out, his eyes saw a pair of pink Converse sneakers walk in through the door.

Relyt walked through the dark woods towards the abandoned cabin deep within them. The rain had finally slowed down, and the sun would

Birth

be up in an hour or so. In fact, he could already see the sun coming up behind the mountains. The cabin lay in a large clearing. A campfire was being put out by a couple men, two others were talking with each other, while another man sat next to a girl tied up, talking to her. The girl was Alessa.

Relyt drew his sword, and strode faster towards them. "Give me my daughter back!"

The men stood up and drew their swords. "No way. This girl will sell for a lot of gold. We're selling her to a troll!" The apparent leader stated.

When he was close enough to them, he stopped, but still had his body ready to fight. "Trolls aren't real." Relyt assured.

"Oh, but they are. They're just hidden very deep within the world. Because they had been hunted down and killed so many times. I mean, how do you think fairy tales and myths came about? What do you think *inspired* those stories?"

"What does a troll want with a human girl?"

"To mate with her."

"*Mate*?!" Relyt was furious.

"Trolls are a rare and special species. They don't need to mate with their own to reproduce. The troll will mate with the girl, and the girl will bear a troll child. Of course, the child inside her will be small enough for her to carry. Once the troll is outside the womb, it will grow to its normal size." He said matter-of-factly.

Relyt didn't want to hear any more of this. "I will not tell you again. Give me. My daughter. Back!" All five men charged at Relyt. Relyt quickly slashed the first man's legs in half, blocked the second man's attack and then sliced his chest. Then he stepped around the third, kicked him in the lower back of his leg, stabbed him through the chest, and kicked him off his sword. Relyt spun his sword around, and without looking stabbed the fourth in the chest, who had his sword high up, ready to come down. He turned to face the last man. Relyt raised his hand towards the man, clenched his fist, and pulled in his arm. The man was pulled through the air and brought nose to nose with Relyt, who drove his blade into the kidnapper's chest. He let the man fall to

the ground as he ran over to his daughter. Any other child would have been horrified by the sight of what Relyt had done; having a father that could kill five men without a moment's thought. But, Alessa was not any other. She had been around war since she was born: she knew the way of the blade, and she knew that there are times when one must kill. "Are you alright sweetie?" He asked as he neared her, but abruptly she pointed at something behind him and he spun to face a giant troll. This troll was as ugly as the stories had told. It was fat, green, and tall as a tree, it stunk, and it held a giant wooden club thick as a tree trunk. Its club immediately came down on Relyt, giving him only a second to barely roll out of the way. Relyt hopped onto the club, ran up the trolls arm, and got onto its shoulders, and sent his sword into the creature's neck, but it didn't go through enough; its skin was just too thick. It knocked Relyt off its back, and onto the ground. He quickly rolled back onto his feet and slashed at its ankle, but the sword still didn't go through all the way, and to make it worse, this time it had gotten stuck. The troll kicked Relyt into a nearby tree before he even had a chance to get it out. Relyt put out his hand, reaching for the sword, and as if it could fly, his sword came back to him and straight into his hand. He then summoned Fyron in his other hand, and rushed the beast. Using Fyron, he sliced through one of its ankles and the creature fell to the ground. He jumped onto its jiggling belly, ran up to its head, and stuck both swords into its eyes, producing screams of pain for a few moments. Then, it was silent, and it lay motionless and defeated. It was finally dead.

Relyt walked back over to his daughter and untied her. She wrapped her arms around him. "I knew you would come, daddy."

"Of course. I would never let anything happen to you." He held his daughter in his arms as she let out tears. "Shh, everything's fine now. No one's going to hurt you." The sun had come up above the mountains, shining on both of them. "No one's going to hurt you."

Cloukora sat up in the hospital bed playing with the hospital band around his wrist when Ashley, Brev, and Winter strode in. "Hey, did

you bring what I asked for?" Cloukora asked. Ashley and Winter had apparently been in Miami working on a mission together. Something Brev had not mentioned to him. When he found out that they *were* there, he had asked Ashley to bring him a few items. Apparently the bullet hit a tendon and the doctors needed him to stay for a couple weeks or so to make sure it heals properly from the surgery. So he figured he might as well have something to pass the time. What made it worse was that he found out Brev had called his mom to come down here, so now Bowe was on his way to pick her up. He also found out Winter was the driver behind the wheel of the Skyline, and that she didn't let him win so easily only because she wanted to mess with him. How she got into the race, he didn't know, nor did he care all that much to find out. It was the Ashley part that bothered him. *I'll have to have a word with Brev later about pulling this kind of shit without telling me. In fact, how did this even happen? They only met once!*

"Yeah." She took off the laptop bag around her shoulders, and brought it over to Cloukora. "What do you need it for?"

"Oh, just research."

Winter walked over to Cloukora and her hand went across his face hard enough that his face jerked sideways. "Don't you ever do that again! When you go somewhere on a mission, you tell Brev or whoever else is working with you!" Without another word, she stalked out of the room.

Cloukora gave a grin. "She cares about me." His face became solemn when he remembered the moments before he blacked out. "We didn't find her did we?"

"Yeah, we did." His face lit up. "She was hidden in a secret room in the room you were in. Winter heard crying and yelling coming from inside the wall when she found you. She messed around with a few objects, a secret door opened and there she was." Brev said. "She actually wanted to speak with you."

Cloukora nodded. "Send her in." Ashley walked back out. "Cloukora shouted a "thank you" to her before she went out the door. A few seconds later a girl came in with Detective Black. She looked exactly how the governor described her: blonde hair, birthmark on her

Birth

cheek, and a locket around her neck. Brev decided to leave the room, too.

"Hey there, you're awake. Now you can help me with all the paperwork you put on me by killing Anthony and his two men. Cause I honestly have no idea how you even did it." The detective said jokingly. Or at least, Cloukora hoped he was joking.

"Yeah I'll get right on that." Cloukora joked back.

"Good. Alright, well I'll be out in the waiting room if you two need me." The detective patted the governor's daughter on the shoulder and walked out.

"Thank you for finding me." She said, turning to Cloukora with a smile.

"I wasn't the one that found you. Winter was."

"You had a big part in it."

There was no point in trying to argue. "Ah, well, you're welcome." Cloukora put out his hand "Cloukora."

She put out hers. "Alessa."

"Alessa? Pretty name."

She looked at him funny. "No, my name's Brittany." How did he hear her name wrong? "Well, I gotta get back to my dad. He was hesitant on even letting me come in here to see you. He's afraid if he lets me out of his sight, I'll go missing again." She started out. "Bye, it was nice meeting you." She waved to him as she left the room to himself.

Cloukora pulled out the laptop and flipped it open before going to the Google homepage. After a moment of thinking how to ask the question, he typed it in: *Traits of being reincarnated.* He clicked on the first site he saw and read the qualities of reincarnation quietly out loud. "Depending whether or not they are blood related, the connection between the two persons may be stronger. As well as their looks, and features. Every reincarnation inherits some of the personality from the person in their past life. They also may inherit their emotions. That is why certain subjects affect people's reaction towards them, without even realizing *why* they had reacted." Cloukora pondered for a moment, put the laptop away and pulled out the book of the Book of Atlantis that

Birth

he also had Ashley bring from the helicopter, and opened it up to Relyt's biography before skimming down to the part he was looking for: "One night, King Relyt had went to check on his eleven year old daughter, Alessandra, and found that she was missing from her chambers. After hours of searching, he found her about to be sold to a troll. He had slain the foul creature and the men that were selling her, and brought her safely back home. After that, he had invented a type of security system that would alert you when an intruder is in your room or your home." That's why he had felt so strongly about this case. In his past life, his daughter was kidnapped. That's why he heard Alessa instead of Brittany. He placed the laptop to the side, and hid the book in the laptop bag, which he also put to the side. He laid his head back down to fall asleep.

"Cloukora, we need to talk." Cloukora shot up, trying to reach for a gun that wasn't there, and his eyes darted towards the window. The morning light had shone through the blinds onto an Angel, creating a golden silhouette around it. "Dusk is coming."

Birth

Angel's Gaiden

Nightmare

July 28, 2010
Miami, Florida

    A nurse in teal scrubs walked down the hall of the hospital, towards the room Cloukora had been staying in. She carried food and medicine on a silver tray meant for him: it consisted of a bowl of chicken noodle soup, a plastic container of salad, a bottle of water, and a plastic gelatin cup. All of it chosen by the doctors; those would be the last things Cloukora would *ever* order. She knocked on the door before going in, and as soon as she did, she just about dropped the tray in her hands: Cloukora wasn't in his bed. She set the tray down on the nearby counter and checked the bathroom to find no sign of him. "I have a patient missing!" She yelled as she dashed back out in the hallway. Suddenly another nurse screamed from further down the hall, next to the medical supply closet. Cloukora's nurse jogged over to the closet to find a patient lying down on the floor, out cold with medicine spilled out of its orange bottle and onto the tiles. It was Cloukora.

    The doctors took him off the gurney and put him back into his bed. The lead doctor began checking Cloukora's vitals to see how stable, if at all, he was. "I got breathing. It's very low and faint, but it's there." He tried pumping Cloukora's chest with his hands, but to no luck. "I need a crash cart, stat." A nurse hurried out to the hallway to retrieve one. At that same moment Brev walked into the room. "Ma'am you can't be here."

    "What's going on?" She asked.

"Ma'am."

"I won't ask again." Brev stood her ground.

The doctor sighed as he placed the square ends of the device on Cloukora's chest. "He took a high dosage of Lythezin. A deadly drug if taken in high amounts." Before the doctor could press the triggers on the defibrillator, Cloukora's machine flat-lined. "No, I won't let you die."

"Wait!" Brev stopped him. "Don't do that. I can't explain why, but don't revive him. Just monitor him, and make sure he can't completely die."

"Ma'am, I can't do that. Even if that was possible, you're not his legal guardian. Without their permission, I can't stand by and let this happen."

"Then I give you permission." Cloukora's mom had walked in. Bowe had finally brought her down from Oregon to be with her son while he was hospitalized. "I don't know why he would do this, but I know he has his reason. He wouldn't kill himself, he's not like that. And I trust Brev's judgment on this. Go ahead, leave him be." It was hard for her to say those words, and it even produced a tear on her face. It was her *son* she was talking about after all, and she was just going to put his life in the hands of fate.

As the doctors walked out, except for one to monitor him and to make sure he wasn't dead for too long, she walked over to the side of his bed and sat next to him. Brev joined her, as well as Ashley, Bowe, and Winter, who all had just walked into the room. They all waited around him, waited for him to come back as his heart rate continued to flat-line.

Cloukora walked in total darkness. Where he was, he had no clue. Heaven? Hell? Purgatory? Strangely, he could somehow see. The darkness was around him, but it didn't interfere with his sight. It was as if there were a dim light radiating off his body, except there was no source to be seen. It did, however, annoy him a little, because he felt like he should be able to see further, but couldn't. Then a man in a black

suit appeared in the middle of a dim circle of light that surrounded the figure's feet. The man held himself up on a cane, though he didn't look old enough to need one. If anything, it was probably just for looks. "Cloukora. I didn't think I would see you this early." The man spoke as he walked closer, the circle of light following him with every step.

"Death. I think you know why I'm here." Cloukora stated plainly.

Death sighed. "I do. And, I'm willing to help you, but you know I can't just give my sword out to anyone. You have to prove yourself first."

"Alright then, so how about a deal?" Death nodded, and Cloukora stood up straight and drew Relyt's sword, ready in hand. "Death, if I can beat a challenge of yours, you will give me your sword, and you will heal my leg."

"And if you lose?"

If I lose…If I lose, you can keep my soul." Cloukora put out his hand.

"Cloukora, I accept your bet." Death shook his hand. "Good luck." The man grinned, and in the blink of an eye, Cloukora woke up inside a classroom, with his sword no longer in his hand. Then he remembered where he was: his classroom from elementary school. The school he had transferred to after the move from Tomi and Ashley. He looked down at himself to find that he was a younger age. The same age he had been when he was in this class. He wore a blue flannel shirt with a black t-shirt underneath with a grey graphic of a dragon on it, cargo shorts, and skate shoes. Cloukora touched his hair to see that it was now short; it didn't even reach his ears. That made him a little sad. All of his hair was gone. His focus shifted though, when he started to wonder how he was there. Was he in a parallel universe? An imagined world created by Death? In the past? He needed to know the answer so he could keep himself from screwing something up.

"Hey man, you alright?" Cloukora recognized who the voice came from; it was a friend he had during this time: John. The boy was shorter than Cloukora by a couple inches or so, had ruffled blonde hair, and wore a simple t-shirt and jeans. "You seem a little out of it."

"Yeah, I'm fine." Cloukora replied, unsure if he actually was.

Cloukora glanced around the classroom, feeling all the nostalgia from his past rush into him. The sink where they'd wash their hands after creating homemade clay to his right, and the door leading outside right next to it. The cubbyholes crowded with backpacks and coats behind him. To his left were the large windows that let in a significant amount of light into the classroom. A couch underneath the windows for the few who were fast enough to sit on it and read a book from the large bookshelf adjacent to it. Then there was the large, green chalkboard in front of the class that caused stammering and stage fright for several kids who had been called up there to do questions on the board. Finally, the teacher that stood in front of it, reading off from a math textbook. Ms. Endersten: a young, vibrant, blonde woman with a heart of gold. No matter how crazy the class got, she was able to keep her cool and handle the situation. Seeing her now, with his present, or rather future, mentality, he admitted she was actually pretty attractive. She glanced at the clock before saying "Alright class, recess time!" and closing the math text book. She walked over to the classroom door that led outside and let the class pour out of it, who all ran to the red-themed playground. Except Cloukora, who had decided he was better off leaning against the building, looking all around him, trying to figure out what he was supposed to do. He saw the girl he used to have a crush on back in the day run his direction, but he didn't pay her any mind since he had never got together with her; he never could get up the guts to even talk to her. But to his surprise she *did* run up to him, hugged him, gave him a peck on the cheek, and held his hand. Cloukora taken aback by this sudden gesture, and realizing he was staring dumbfounded at her, he tried to recover by making conversation.

He gently took his hand away. It felt too weird. "Uh, um…I…" Cloukora tried to come up with the words.

"Are you alright? You don't seem yourself today." She raised her eyebrow.

"That's what I asked." John agreed, just hearing the conversation and walking up to them.

"I'm alright. Rachel, when did we ever...start dating? I don't remember us ever..." Cloukora tried comprehending. Since they're together, that ruled out the past.

"Ever since last year?" She laughed. "I always liked your sense of humor, Cloukora." She gave him another peck on the cheek. This was getting way too weird now. "So, my dad says he'll give us a ride to Olive Garden tonight."

"That's, cool." Cloukora said reluctantly. *Did I just accidentally make a date with an eleven year old?* He shuddered at the thought. *I have to get out of this.* "But, I don't think I'll be able to make it."

"Why not?" That had upset and disappointed her a little.

"I have a barbecue I have to go to tonight. It's my...cousin's birthday. Those kinds of things usually go on throughout the whole night."

"Oh, alright. Then tomorrow we'll go."

"Yeah, sure, we'll do that." Cloukora lied. *If this is a parallel universe I can't screw it up for the dude. I know how hard getting a girlfriend can be.* "I'm gonna go think for a bit. I got some issues I gotta deal with." He said before strolling out past the playground, and sitting on the day-fresh cut grass. He didn't want to be here. Not in this time, not now. Something happened during his time in elementary school. Something he wanted to forget, to run away from. Perhaps it *had* made him the person he was today, the hero he strove to become, but it was a heavy burden. One that he wanted lifted off his shoulders, and his heart. *Death, why did you have to make me* this *age? Why couldn't you have made me a little older? Can you please just give me the challenge already so I can go back home?* As if Death heard his thoughts, which he probably did, the sky above had suddenly started forming dark, black clouds. Thunder roared, and lightning flashed across the heavens. "The hell?"

"Something of the sort."

He looked down to see Death standing in the middle of the field. "What is this?"

"Your worst fear." Death said with a grin. Cloukora recognized these clouds.

"Oh no." Cloukora drew his sword from his back and readied it, surprisingly with a bit of an effort. The sword was heavier than it usually was. His strength was affected here, too. "Oh no, no, no, no."

"Oh yes." Death disappeared.

Cloukora knew exactly what was going to come out of those clouds, and he was scared to death of it. A beam of darkness shot out of the clouds and hit the ground a few yards in front of him, causing an explosion in the earth, shaking the terrain beneath him. A tall, muscular man in a suit of armor stepped out of the beam before it closed up and vanished. The armor he wore was bulky, red, and it had been forged out of plate metal. He had long, flowing blonde hair that reached down mid-back, and he wore a red, cloth band around his forehead. On his waist rested a sheathed sword. It was a character from a video game Cloukora used to play, called Fire Blade. In fact, it was the main villain from the game, Delyn. A character feared by all who had played it, because of how deadly he was and how easily he could kill your character. If Cloukora made the wrong move, or let him move first, he was as good as dead. Cloukora charged at Delyn, sword ready, and still hard to wield. When he tried to swing the sword at him, Delyn simply pulled his sword out of his sheath at just the right moment, and blocked Cloukora's attack. His boot went up, and in one swift movement, kicked Cloukora far to the fence on the other side of the field. In an instant, Delyn was right in front of Cloukora, swinging the sword at him. Cloukora barely managed to duck before rolling out of the way of the blow. Cloukora's sword went for Delyn's leg, which had quickly jerked out of the way, as a sword swung down at Cloukora's head. Cloukora rolled out of the way again, and jumped back a few feet.

"Dammit, I can't even touch him." Cloukora's adrenaline began pumping, and able to see Delyn's movements better, saw a blade go right at his chest and stepped to the side to dodge it, along with a couple more swings that were thrown at him. Cloukora managed to block the next swing at him, pushed the sword towards Delyn, and followed with a flurry of non-stop attacks, now putting Delyn on the defense. Cloukora's sword began to feel lighter and lighter with each swing, making his attacks move faster and faster, until they were on par with

Delyn's own. Both were attacking beyond normal human skill; what would take thousands and thousands of years of sword training, they had already achieved it.

Delyn blocked one of Cloukora's attacks and kicked him backwards, with Cloukora barely blocking another strike. Cloukora quickly summoned Fyron in his other hand, and began swinging with both swords, increasing the tempo of the fight even more. The swords were almost a blur of steel and fire, until Delyn had created a shield around himself, keeping the hero from getting too close.

"Son of a bitch." Cloukora rushed at the shield and was immediately pushed back by a burst of force, sending him to the ground. Cloukora looked up to see a transformed Delyn. This new Delyn was even more intimidating and scarier, Cloukora would admit. He had become some kind of demonic creature: Red, muscled skin, his legs became goat-like, horns grew out of his head, yellow eyes, a long tail with a point on the end, and giant dragon-like wings on his back. This was Delyn's final form, and following the transformation would come his final and most powerful attack. Cloukora didn't waste any more time getting back up and rushing him again, but this time, Vesi in place of Fyron. Using the water from Vesi, Cloukora sent a blast of water directly at Delyn, and then moved behind him within an instant and slashed at his back. But instead of the sword hitting him, Delyn's tail had deflected Cloukora's attack, and at the same time Delyn had used some kind of fireball on Cloukora's water blast, causing it to evaporate into the air. Delyn then spun to face Cloukora and brought his sword downwards on Cloukora, who barely kept it from falling on his head with Relyt's sword and Vesi.

Taking the risk of the blade above him coming down, Cloukora swung Vesi at Delyn's side, forcing the creature to jump back out of the way. Cloukora immediately took this opportunity to swing his sword at him again, then swing Vesi, then Relyt's sword, and continued alternating, pushing him further back with each swing. "Eventually I will hit you!" After a few back and forths between the two fighters, Delyn abruptly summoned some kind of ball of dark energy in his palm, and shot it straight at Cloukora. The ball was luckily blocked by Relyt's

sword and Vesi, but it continued to force him backwards until there was no more energy left in the ball. Delyn teleported in front of Cloukora within an instant, and swung his sword at him. Cloukora blocked it again. This time on instinct and with ease.

Snow white Angel wings appeared, sprouting out of Cloukora's back, and Relyt's sword now had a golden aura around it. He didn't know it, but the pupils in his eyes had also transformed from the usual Skyrell crest, and into the Holy Trinity symbol, consisting of three yellow circles connecting at the middle, like a three circle Venn diagram.

Cloukora pulled his sword away from Delyn's, and struck at him again and again. The two fought so quickly, that their swords had become a blur even more, if that was possible, with Cloukora on the offense more than Delyn. Now it was Delyn who could barely keep with Cloukora's attacks. Cloukora finally managed a cut into Delyn's chest; a deep one too. He then dashed around Delyn, slicing the creature's side and back open, and Delyn roared in pain. Cloukora had appeared back on the other side of Delyn, as if he had somehow magically teleported, sword in a horizontal position. Though when he saw Delyn holding a bleeding chest, he knew that wasn't the case: he only moved at an impossible speed. Finally, Cloukora held his hand up horizontally and shot a blast of pure light from a sudden aura around his hand, right at Delyn, creating a huge explosion at the moment of impact. When the smoke faded, nothing was left where Delyn had stood. Only a crater.

The new power Cloukora had gained slowly disappeared: the glow around the sword, the eyes, and the wings, all of it. *That power...where the hell did it come from?*

"It came from within you." Cloukora turned around to see Death standing there. "You may be wondering why this time, why face your greatest fear, and why I made you in the image of a kid. Well, first off, yes, this was an imagined world. You didn't mess with any timelines, so don't worry. Secondly, I'll answer two of your questions at once, I chose this time and to have you that age again, because I wanted to test your inner strength. I wanted to see if you would fight even if you didn't

have the right physical strength to do so. I wanted to see if it is your *heart* you channel your strength from. Lastly, I chose your greatest fear because now you won't be scared to fight Lucifer."

"That hasn't changed. I'm still scared to death-no offense...I think? Anyways, I believe I can do it, but...will I? That's what I'm worried about. All my life I had never stood my ground, or had the guts to do something. I always ran. I always like to think I could, but honestly, I don't know. If I can't even ask a girl on a date, how am I expected to fight the *Devil*?"

"Talking to girls and fighting the Devil are two different things."

"Says you. Women can get pretty devious."

Death frowned disappointedly at him. "Anywho, when you ask a girl out on a date, you're not saving the world and billions of people, your life isn't on the line, and you're not fighting for freedom for both you and those you love."

"How does telling me this help? It only adds even more pressure."

"Because it's in your nature. Fighting, is in your nature. Even though consciously you want to run, you won't. As long as you have a reason to fight, and something to fight for, you will keep on fighting. You won't stop until there is peace in the world. Love, honor, and faith. Those are the things you fight for, are they not?" Cloukora nodded. "Then if you ever begin to doubt yourself, remember those three things. Think about what would happen if you backed down. It would mean you don't love the world, your family, or Ashley enough, you would dishonor your name, and it will mean you have lost faith in yourself, faith in fighting. Because, Cloukora, this apocalypse is happening with or without you. Standing by will not stop it. It won't just go away because you try to ignore it. It doesn't work like that. While your friends die fighting for the world, and while Lucifer enslaves your entire family, you will be cowering in a dark corner waiting for him to find you-and oh he will. So you can either watch the world burn to ash, or fight and extinguish the flames of hell."

Cloukora nodded again. "You're right. I can't give up. I won't. Everyone is depending on me, and I can't let them down. Not ever. I am a hero, and a hero never stops fighting, no matter how he feels or

what the situation is. That's what I told Brev, and that's what I'm going to stick to. No more being whiny and scared and acting like a child. It's time for me to start acting liking a true hero."

Death gave a slight grin. "Good, I know you will. Before you leave, anything you'd like to know?"

"Yeah, why do what you did with the friends and Rachel though? It seemed kinda pointless. And quite frankly, really weird."

"Eh, it was just to screw with you."

Cloukora shook his head in disbelief. "So did I pass your test?"

Death grinned. "Yes. You have proven yourself worthy of my blade yada yada yada. I know that you are in fact, the only one that can beat Lucifer."

"How so?"

"That power you gained against…Delyn, was it? Wasn't just from you, it was the work of God as well."

"Wait, what? From God himself?"

Death nodded. "The prophecy says that a man born of the wolf's blood will sever the Goat's head with the help from the Lord. You are King Relyt's reincarnation and descendant, who fought alongside wolves, God gave you help in this battle, and you're fighting Lucifer, who is in relation with the goat. If he helped you in this battle, he will help you when you go against Lucifer, and possibly future battles to come."

"So what happens now?" Death walked over to Cloukora and put his hand on Cloukora's face. A strange power flowed into him, a dark power. Part of him didn't like it; his heart and body felt cold. But another part wanted the darkness to consume his being, to take him over. That part scared him. But fortunately, within a moment he had felt normal again. The dark and cold feeling was gone. "What was that?"

"You can use Death's Blade now. It is my own sword, passed onto you. But I warn you, do not try to summon it yet, not with that…darkness…already inside you."

"Darkness?"

"Have you not noticed it? Whenever you get anger built up inside of you?"

"Oh, that…Yeah, I get it a lot lately. Ever since…"

"Tomi's death?"

"Yeah. And I transform into some kind of monster. I try to hold the anger back, but sometimes it becomes too much for me."

"That is the tainted side of the Fountain of Youth."

"I thought Relyt only got the good part of it?"

"Yes and no. The tainted part of it still went inside him, but somehow Relyt was able to keep it dormant within himself, never having to use it. Perhaps he just had that good of a heart. Maybe, the rest of the bloodline just built up anger throughout their lives, and it finally came down to you and you have generations of hate boiling deep within you. Your 'Tainted form' could be a way of letting all that hate and anger out." Death waved a hand, "I don't know. I'm not a therapist." He let out a sigh. "In any case, you should wait until you meet with God before you try summoning the Blade."

Cloukora nodded. "When will I meet with him? God I mean."

"That is up to him. I'm sure he'll call you when the time comes."

"Call? I don't-"

"That's enough questions. Time to go." Cloukora and the world around him vanished, and he opened his eyes to find himself back in his hospital bed.

Brev, Ashley, Winter, Bowe, and his mom all sat around him. Ashley quickly went to hug him as soon as she noticed he was awake. Cloukora felt warm tears touch his face, and wrapped his arms around her to assure her he was fine.

"I was scared. I-I thought you were…" She couldn't bring herself to say it.

She let go of him as Brev started. "Cloukora, why the hell would you do something like that?" Brev asked with fury.

Birth

"Um, an Angel told me to do it." He scratched his head and gave a grin. "Oh and I can move my leg now. See?" He shook his leg from under his blanket, to show that he wasn't lying.

None of them really cared, though. "An Angel? *Really*?" Brev gave a look like she wasn't going to fall for it.

"Hey mom, Ashley, I know you're worried and everything, and want to make sure I'm okay, but I need to talk to them. Ashley, it's up to you if you want to stay." His mom opened her mouth to say something, but in the end decided it best to leave the room. Cloukora felt bad, she was his mom after all, and he had probably almost given her a heart attack, but he didn't want her to have to know about this. Ashley looked at the door, hesitating, and then look backed at Cloukora and shook her head. "Are you *sure* you want to hear about this, Ashley?"

Ashley nodded. "Yes. If we're going to be friends, then yes. I want to help you if I can, and I can't help if I don't know what it is you're doing."

Cloukora sat up in his bed. "Alright, well you know about the Nyx incident, Brev, and the mention of the Blade of Michael. Well an Angel appeared to me yesterday, and he explained to me what it is, and that I need it to beat Lucifer when he rises out of hell. Then he told me that in order to get the Blade of Michael, I needed Death's Blade as well, and to get *that*, I needed to die and meet with Death. Which I did. I had to face my greatest fear though, as a kid too. In the end, I got it, but Death said I shouldn't use it until I met with God."

"When are you supposed to meet with God?" Bowe asked.

"Wait, you're going to meet God? What fear did you have to face? What was Death like?" Ashley asked curiously, who received a frown from Brev.

"Ashley, calm down." Winter said. "You can talk to him about it later. This is more important."

"Sorry. I'm just excited to hear about this stuff." She said innocently.

"It's alright. Death...he was a pretty cool guy. I mean he ticked me off, but he was also cool. And as for meeting God, I have no idea.

Birth

Death said I'll be called when I'm called. How he will call me, or when, or where, I don't know." He ignored the fear question; he was too embarrassed by the answer.

"Well, just be prepared for whenever he does. I don't know how much time we have left." Brev reminded. "And why on Earth did you trust an Angel? What if he was working for Nyx?!"

"Well he's not; he put me on the right path. I don't think Death wants the apocalypse to happen."

"But what if he does! Cloukora, you need to think before you do something like this! If you ended up dead, then who would stop Lucifer?"

"And what if I didn't go under? I wouldn't have Death's Blade, and I wouldn't be closer to being able to defeat Lucifer. He told me we had about a week left. Two, tops. There was no time to consult you, I had to risk it. I told you that day, that no matter what the situation was, or no matter how I felt, that I wasn't going to stop being a hero. And a hero takes risks, Brev." Brev ran a hand down her face in frustration, stood up, kicked the chair she was in over, and stormed out, slamming the door behind her. Bowe and Winter followed her out to most likely calm her down, giving Cloukora looks of disapproval on the way out.

Ashley saw them go out, and turned back to Cloukora. "Cloukora, look, I know you were trying to do the right thing, and I understand you have to take risks sometimes. But she's right, you need to be more careful. What if Death *does* want the apocalypse to happen, and getting that sword is going to help bring it about? What if you just single-handedly started the apocalypse? You wouldn't be able to stop it then, because you don't have the Blade of Michael."

"I know how you guys feel about this, and I'm sorry." He let out a sigh. "I would trust an Angel before I ever considered it an enemy."

"That kind of thinking almost got you killed with Nyx, remember? You trusted him, and he almost killed you. Brev told me all about it." She said before he had a chance to ask how she knew.

"But he didn't."

Ashley got up and walked to the door before letting out a sigh. "What's done is done, and you can't do anything about it. But from now on, please be careful. If anything, for me." She turned the handle and walked out the door, letting it shut behind her.

New York City, New York

Ava sat cross-legged on her motel bed, in a black t-shirt, jeans, and heeled boots, studying Venn's sword in her lap. To her surprise, Tomi had given it to her for her to keep as a memory. She sometimes wondered if Tomi had another side to him, one he didn't like showing. "He's always slipping up and doing something nice. Plus this whole not-killing-Cloukora thing is really weird. It's not very villain-like." She didn't know who Cloukora was, or what he meant to Tomi. She just knew that he was a part of Wolfstorm and thus was a target. Pulling the sword out of the sheath, she ran her palm along the blade, the metal smooth to the touch. A tear drop fell onto the sword, and dripped off into her lap. *Venn, I miss you so much...* A knock came at the door, prompting her to quickly wipe the tears away with her hands, sheath the sword and open the door to find Cairne, Path, and Tayge standing on the doorstep. Cairne in his usual preppy-themed clothing, Path in her country, outdoor style, and Tayge in a normal t-shirt and jeans. The sunlight was extremely bright outside, and warm too; the air conditioner had made her forget how hot it was outside of the motel room.

"So, what's the problem?" Path reluctantly asked. She obviously didn't want to be here, and if Ava could choose, she wouldn't be, but Lore was off on another mission, so it had to be Path.

"I've been working at this mission for the past three days, and I can't track down their hideout." She let them in and showed them the wall of papers along the wall, filled with information on the case, and red circles and x's over certain people, places, and times. "I followed some of the demons all over the city, and wherever they went. Not one spot did two of them meet at the same place again."

"You do realize they can just teleport to their hideout right?" Path stated condescendingly, trying to make Ava look dumb.

"Yes, I am aware of that. But I still wanted to try to find their hideout. Except I haven't had any luck with it. So today I was going to interrogate one of them, and when I went to the place they should have been, they weren't there. I went to any other places he could have been at, and he wasn't in any of those locations either. I tried with the other targets as well, but I couldn't find a single demon. That's why I brought you three: Path to track them down, Cairne for some strength power, and Tayge because he can use guns better than we can."

"You don't think you were compromised do you? Cause that would make a whole lot more sense why you can't find them."

Ava was getting tired of her already. "No. I know how to follow a tail, Path." She said with a hint of irritability.

"Alright, fine. Take us to one of the places they've been. I'll see what I can do." Ava nodded before grabbing her sword as well as Venn's, and the four walked out to her car: A white 2005 Ford Focus.

Ava pulled the car in front of a bar called Rattle and Roll. "This is where one of them would hang out every night." Ava said after they all exited out of the car. Ava had both hers and Venn's swords on her back, but they couldn't be seen, for Tomi had a device implemented into the swords to make them appear invisible. He made it so that it would not draw attention to them, and they could go on about their work unnoticed.

"Let's hurry up and get this over with." Path said as she hurriedly walked in, with Cairne following, then Tayge, and lastly Ava who shook her head and sighed. Tayge and Cairne sat in a booth, sitting across from each other, while Ava and Path went up to the bartender.

"So how are things between you and Tor?" Cairne asked Tayge, trying to make conversation.

"Not so great. She's pissed at me for accidentally blowing up her fish." Tayge replied, playing with the salt shaker.

"How'd you manage to do *that*?"

"I was testing out a new water-resistant explosive."

"Let me guess. Your own creation?"

"Yup."

Cairne shook his head. "You and your damn explosives. Or rather your 'babies' as you like to call them."

"Hey, it worked didn't it?"

Cairne just kept shaking his head.

"Hi, we're looking for this man." Path presented the stocky bartender a picture of their target. "Can you tell us anything that might help?"

"He's a short guy." Ava added.

"Oh yes, I know him. A quiet fella. He comes in every day and sits in that chair right there." He pointed to a chair a couple down from where they stood. "The whole time he's in here, he just sits and reads the paper. Doesn't talk to anyone. Doesn't play pool. Hell he hardly gets up to go the bathroom."

Path walked over to the chair and looked around the area. "You said he reads the paper, do you know what section he reads?"

"Um, sports I believe." He looked confused.

Path went into thought for a second. "What date is it today?"

"July 28th." The bartender replied.

"Ava, what other places did you say the people went to?"

"One of them was Fantasy Nights, another was Lights, and-"

"Do you know why someone would go to those places? Besides dancing." Path asked the bartender, adding to Ava's irritation by cutting her off, most likely on purpose.

"People that I hear about going to either of those places go to place bets on football games."

"Thank you. I know where he is." Path walked out the door, and the other three watched in confusion for a moment, before following her out. After the three walked to the car she turned to explain: "Today is the New York Giants game against the New Orleans Saints."

"You think he'll be there? But that doesn't sound like a hideout for demons to be at." Ava questioned.

"It's not. It's a helluva lot worse than that."

Birth

"Why's that?"

"A couple weeks ago the Saints creamed the Giants in a football game, and this is the game where they get revenge and retribution."

"What does that have to do with anything?"

"It's the fifth seal, from the Book of Revelations. 'Under the altar, appeared the souls of martyrs for the word of God, who cry out for vengeance. They are given white robes and told to rest until the martyrdom of their brothers is completed.' I've memorized the whole damn thing. Tomi already said the first three have been broken, this means Cloukora must have gotten the sword from Death, and broken the fourth seal."

"I read it too, and it says Death gets the sword. Plus that passage doesn't relate to the football game in any way."

"That's because it's not straight-forward. Nothing is straight forward. It's all mixed and related with each other, and has hidden meanings. Death did get the sword, but…I don't know. Okay, look, most people today consider football as more than a sport, it's sacred to them. The football stadium is like the altar, which the people are under. They cry out the 'word of God,' which is the chant to cheer on a team. The Giants' home colors are white. Everyone there cheering for them is going to be wearing white."

"So how are the demons involved in breaking the seal?"

"They're not. They probably just want to watch their plan progress even more."

"Can we stop it?"

"So many damn questions woman! No, we can't. Now, get in the car and let's go!" Tayge said, irritated, opening the car door for Ava. "We can at least kill a few of the bastards."

Ava got in the driver's seat without a word, and shut the door. The rest got in as well, and Ava drove towards the Giants' football stadium. Before they knew it, they were parking the car in the stadium parking lot. As soon as the car was parked, they all got out, shutting the car doors behind them. Tayge pulled out a Walther P99 pistol, cocked it, and put it in between his waistband and put his shirt over it to conceal the weapon. Ava laid out her strategy: "Alright, I'll take the main

Birth

entrance, Tayge and Cairne you take the side entrances, and Path will take the other front entrance. And be careful, no innocent deaths. I can't have that kind of blood on my hands." She added. All three walked off from her without a word. She could only hope that they were going to follow her plan; she would be surprised if Path actually did. She turned and walked to the main entrance. When she entered into the stadium, and into the stands, the roaring crowd filled the entire arena. Path was right too: there were a large number of people wearing white.

A mascot walked out into the field with a microphone. "I know you all can't wait to see our Giants squash these Saints, but do not worry, our time is coming. So just be patient and wait until the martyrdom of your brothers is completed!" The mascot turned and stared directly at Ava for a moment, and let out a laugh that made her skin crawl. "Go Giants!" The mascot walked off the field as the crowd began cheering for the Giants again. A man in a seat not far from her got up and walked past her, giving her a wink and a grin. It was the man she had always seen hanging out at the bar whenever she would follow him. Ava quickly pulled out her sword from the sheath on her back, and put it through the man's back. When she pulled it out, the man fell to the ground, clutching his chest while blood began to ooze out from the wound and his mouth.

"Why are you here?"

The man turned his head to look at her with a smile. "You're too late." He collapsed, no longer breathing. She turned to see what was happening all around, then heard a gunshot and some screaming. Next thing she knew, a red glow came from the seat where the man sat, originating from what looked like a crystal. At different areas of the stands surrounding the field, more red crystals glowed. Ava tried picking up the gemstone, but all it did was send a searing pain into her hand. The glow of the crystals all connected with each other at certain points in the stadium, as if they were lasers. Ava knew if she were above the stadium, she would be able to see that they made the shape of a pentagram.

"What the hell did you do?" People from the stands got up and began walking down to the field. It wasn't that many people though,

Birth

compared to how many people were still in the stands. Ava would probably have to guess it was about a hundred, and that they were demons, not people. No sane person would walk down there after seeing what was occurring. Ava saw, to the left side, Tayge with his pistol picking off the ones on his side that headed into the field. On the right side she saw Cairne fighting some of them with hand-to-hand combat and sending them flying through the air. Path was a section over, slashing them with her knife. Ava readied her sword, drew Venn's, and ran down to the field and began slashing the demons populating the grass in half. After the first few though, they began to pull out swords of their own. The swords didn't look like any normal sword she had seen: they were twisted, spiked, or curved weirdly, and they all had a hint of darkness to them all. Despite some effort, she was able to deflect the attacks and take down most of her opponents with ease. After several minutes of sword clashing, blood spilling, screaming, and gunshots, there were finally no more demons to be seen anywhere, and the other three Darkstar members stumbled tiredly up to her. The screams of the people began to get louder. Ava began to wonder why they hadn't left yet, and she saw that they couldn't; all the doors had been shut and locked, preventing anyone from getting out. To make matters worse, the earth below their feet began to shake, crack, and create large holes and crevices in the soil. "It's going to collapse under us." All four of them quickly ran to the nearest stands for safety, and when they got high enough, they saw the whole field fall into a hole of darkness that had replaced the green turf. There was no ground from side to side. Swiftly, demons had begun to climb out of the hole, but these weren't the human-looking ones, these were the demons you had read about in the bible; the demons that looked beastly.

"Welp, I'm out of here." Tayge quickly spread his red wings, and flew out of the stadium.

"Sorry, I don't want to die just yet." Path spread her yellow wings and flew off with Tayge.

Cairne just looked at Ava with worry, and with question to leave, too. "Go, I'll be fine." As soon as those words came out, Cairne spread his orange wings and flew out. Ava couldn't leave just yet

though, she felt like she needed to give these people at least a chance to survive. She ran up to the door people were shoving to get through, which had been difficult with all of the panic from the crowd. Ava stuck her sword into the small crack in between the double doors, pushed and pulled a little, and as the doors finally budged, everyone swarmed out as the demons began chasing them. After getting outside, she spread her brown wings and flew off into the sky to head back to base, where the others had most likely headed.

Birth

Angel's Gaiden

Hell Rises

August 3, 2010
Forest Grove, Oregon

    Cloukora stood outside the church building with both its doors and its bell tower rising above and before him. The band t-shirt he wore today represented the band Airbourne, in red letters over the black shirt. He took a deep breath and stepped inside the church to sit down in a wooden pew in the third row, and looked up at the tall, wooden cross centered in the front of the hall. The room had lit candles that were placed all along tables that lined the walls, and on the altar before the cross. Flowers had also dotted the room in random spots, but most of them were around the cross and altar. There were two other doors in addition to the entrance: one that went to the bell tower, Cloukora assumed, and the other was probably for the priest. No one else was in the room with him; it was just him and silence.

    He folded his hands on the back of the pew in front of him, and lowered his head. "God, I know you're real and I know you can hear me, and I'm sure you're busy with more important things, but I need your help. I can't do this; I just don't think I'm ready for this fight. It's too much and too soon. Why do *I* have to do this, why couldn't someone else take my place? I don't know what I'm saying, I love being a hero, it's just Lucifer is just too strong. I thought I believed I could do this, but I really don't, I'm scared and I'm about ready to just lock myself in my room until it's all over, but I can't. I know I have to do this, I have to fight and *win*, otherwise there would be no point in living for *anyone*. I just need a pick-me-upper, some confidence in myself, maybe a reason why I should go through with this fight besides

the obvious one. I can't do this without you." He waited a minute for some kind of sign, anything to show God had heard him, and when there was none, he sighed. "Well I'm sorry for bothering you, but when you get this, just please help me." He let out another sigh. "Amen." Cloukora got up and walked towards the door.

As he opened the door, he heard someone speak: "Do not worry, God will answer your prayer in time. He is just busy with other things at the moment. He is always beside you though, Cloukora. Do not ever think otherwise." Cloukora quickly spun to see a priest standing next to the altar, making a motion of a cross down his head and across his chest. The man turned to look at Cloukora and give him a nod, before turning back to whatever it was he was doing. Cloukora stood for a moment, trying to comprehend what just happened, and continued out of the church towards his car.

Brev had called earlier about another mission; a *mission* of all things when the apocalypse could happen at any moment! Cloukora thought she must be insane. Especially after that event in New York a few days ago, that even *Darkstar* was involved in. He thought they should be over there helping, clearing out the demons, but Brev only said "We could clear out them all, but they'll only appear in other places around the world. There's not much we can really do, but what we *can* do, is save the people we can right now." As he was getting into his car, he thought he heard the sound of a trumpet, but when he looked around, there was no one to be seen, and nowhere could it have come from. He shook his head and got in the car, then drove off. Apparently he was dealing with a ghost. Again. "I freaking hate ghosts…"

Hillsboro, Oregon

Cloukora pulled into the driveway of a blue two story house. Brev was already there: her Toyota Corolla was parked in the street. Cloukora got out, and knocked on the door to be greeted by Brev, who led him inside. When he walked in, the first room he came into was the living room. What you would find in any average living room, you

would have found there: couches, a coffee table, television, plants, and tall bookshelves. On the far couch sat a woman who must have been in her thirties, in a long yellow summer dress, looking a little frightened. Cloukora sat on the couch across from her, next to Brev.

"So, what's the problem?" Cloukora asked, getting straight to the point.

Brev rolled her eyes. "Cloukora, this is my friend Julia." She gestured to the woman sitting across from them. "Her and her son have been having some…ghost issues."

"Like what exactly?"

"The usual. Noises, misplaced things, stuff falling off of shelves, and cold spots."

"We didn't mind it at all, actually." Cloukora turned his focus to Julia, who had just spoken. "It hadn't hurt us, so we just let it be to do its own thing. That is until…"

"Until what?" Cloukora asked.

She hesitated for a moment before getting up and grabbing a video camera from a bookshelf, and then putting it on the coffee table. Cloukora picked it up, flipped open the screen, and pressed the play button: The camera had been placed in Julia's bedroom, but Cloukora could tell by the darkness outside of the room that all the lights in the house had been shut off, and Julia lay in her bed sound asleep. Suddenly, a light flicked on in the hallway, but he didn't see anyone. Though, he *heard* footsteps as if someone should be there. Cloukora's hairs started to rise on the back of his neck just by watching the video. This was starting to make him tense. He almost thought something was going to pop right in front of the camera. Then a few seconds later, her bed sheets moved to uncover her. Her body rocked a little back and forth as if someone was trying to wake her up to get her to move, but she wouldn't wake. Her body was suddenly dragged off the bed and thrown onto the floor, shocking Julia awake. Frightened, she let out a scream. Cloukora saw a light silhouette of a person staring at the bed; it was hard to see, but it was there. The mattress suddenly flipped over to its side, knocking everything down on the side of the room it landed on. Then a small boy ran into the room right as the silhouette walked

out. Cloukora quickly turned it off and put it back on the table as if it were about to bite him. He wanted to just drop this case and leave until Julia slowly overturned her hands to show her wrists: there were huge claw marks on both arms that went down her entire wrist.

"We...thought it was just a friendly ghost. I don't know why it would up and do something like this."

Cloukora pulled himself together to keep the fear out of his voice. "Sorry to break it to you, but no ghost is friendly. People believe this, and it's not smart. And *because* people think they are friendly, they begin trying to talk to it, to become friends with it, whether it's through an Ougi board, or any other means. All that does, is just let the spirit even more into your house, and lets more inside, because it pries open the gate that separates the spirit world from our world. You, never talked to it before, have you? In any way?"

"I haven't. I mean, I of course asked 'who's there' when I heard noises, but never have I tried communicating with it. Although..."

"Although what?"

"Damien might have. I've seen him playing with someone who wasn't there, but it felt like someone *was*."

"Perhaps it wasn't your ghost that did that to you."

"You think it was a different one?"

"It's possible."

"So what do we do?"

"Go to a relative's house. Stay with them, and we'll stay here and take care of it, or them, or whatever."

Julia nodded, and shouted to the back room as she got up to wait by the hallway: "Damien! Come on, we're leaving!" After a second, a young boy, about eight, walked out into the living room holding someone's hand. That 'someone' was Ashley. Cloukora's eyes widened and he was about to lash out on both her and Brev. She did it again! But, he managed to keep himself calm and relaxed. It wouldn't be professional to do this in front of Julia and her kid. It's not that he didn't want her helping, well he didn't but there was no way of stopping her, but it was the fact they keep hiding it from him. "We're going to grandma's house, is that okay?" Damien nodded, and Julia led him out

Birth

the front door to her car as Cloukora and Brev went over to Ashley. After a moment, they could hear the car zoom off down the street.

"What the hell is going on?" Cloukora demanded.

"I told you, she's having ghost problems."

"You know what I mean." He pointed at Ashley.

She sighed. "Everyone else was busy doing other things, so I was going to end up doing this alone, but Ashley called and I told her I was going on a mission, and she suggested coming along." Brev replied.

"And you just *let* her?"

"I didn't think it was going to be this bad. I thought it was just a bat in the attic or something!"

"What about Miami? Winter couldn't do that alone? Ashley had to go with her on that too? I don't want her in danger!"

"Cloukora, I know you want to protect me because you don't think I can handle myself, but I can." Ashley cut in. "When you and Tomi left, I was alone to defend myself against some bullying girls, and you know what? I kicked their asses into the ground, and they never messed with me again. So please stop treating me like a child!"

"I just don't want to see you hurt. This isn't a bully in high school, this is a lot worse. You can…" He took a moment to get himself to say it. "You could die."

"Don't you think I know that? Has it ever occurred to you that maybe I would love to be heroic and save people too? I know the risks Cloukora, and I'm willing to take them. I am *not* walking out that door, and you won't make me."

Cloukora stood there for a moment then nodded. "Alright, if that's what you want." Cloukora started angrily down the hallway to check the rooms for signs of any ghosts, or, if Heaven forbid, demons. "Just keep your eyes open."

Brev turned to Ashley. "I know you're upset with him, but he just cares about you. How do you think he'll feel if he has to go to your mother's doorstep and tell her you were killed?"

"So you want me to leave, too?"

"No, Wolfstorm could always use help, and I am confident in your abilities. I'm just saying, cut him some slack."

"You're right. I just…I don't like being treated like a child. But I'll try to ease up on him."

"I mean, he *is* a hero now. What would you expect? He wants to save and protect everyone from danger."

Ashley gave a smile. "He just needs to learn that not everyone needs saving."

Brev grinned as well. "Now, we need to set up everything for the night." Ashley and Brev started getting blankets, lamps, and weapons set up in a small area in the living room. They were going to have to shut off the lights and any other power source for the night.

"So, I don't see anything for now." Cloukora said walking down the staircase; while they were still setting up he had went upstairs to check those rooms as well. He heard the trumpet again, and rubbed his ear. He heard it as loud as day. "You guys heard that, right?"

"Heard what?" Brev asked.

"A trumpet sound."

"No, I didn't." Brev said raising her eyebrow and Ashley shook her head.

Portland, Oregon

Kaora and Nole were sitting in front of the monitors at Wolfstorm headquarters. They had been investigating the Iraqi incident all day and ever since Brev had asked them to. It had been tiring work for them both. That is until Nole thought up an algorithm to search through the massive amount of government files and find anything wrong or out of the ordinary with them. Nole claimed that it would allow for them to do more productive activities instead of sit at a computer all day. His idea of productive though was catching up on a racing game on his phone. Kaora, however, was still working on the piece of the titanium cloak that came off of Victor. Nole tried telling her that it was pointless and to face the fact there's someone out there

who was just smarter than both of them. She wouldn't have it though; any chance she got she was analyzing and running tests on it. She was set on replicating it and saving lives.

"Dammit." Nole had ended up losing the race on his game.

"I told you, go easy on the corners. Too fast and you'll go off the track." Kaora said, not looking up from the microscope.

"Oh, like you know how to play a video game." He retorted. "You just like working all the time. You act like fun could kill you."

"Yeah but I know how physics and inertia works. And yes fun can kill. Do you know many people die from roller coasters?"

"Pretty much none?"

She turned around to face him. "Exactly. Because scientists made it safe for people to ride on. Imagine how many more people would die if they designed it for 'fun?' A lot." She turned back to her microscope. "I'd rather not risk my life to ride a cart on some kind of track. Besides, roller coasters turn my stomach."

"Are you gonna pad our kid-" A flashing red warning flashed on the screen. "Hold up we got something." Nole started to push a few keyboard buttons and suddenly stopped. "Who did Cloukora say his friend was again?"

"To...mi." She began until she saw the computer screen. Plastered on the screen was Tomi's face with his name, birthdate, and even his social security number, along with the rest of his information that stretched to the moment he was born. What triggered the alert was his time in boot camp: There was no record of it at all. Even being under Black Ops there would be something to show for it. After a couple more keystrokes he traced a transaction between Chris, Tomi's foster father, and a military official. "Using money to buy your son into the army. And you wonder why I hate politicians, Nole."

"Son of a bitch, we have to tell Brev." Nole dialed her number on his phone.

"Nole?" She said. "They're in the blue bag. Yeah, that one." He heard her tell someone in the background.

"We have a problem."

"What are you talking about?"

"Cloukora's friend that died, his name was Tomi Pendra, right?"

"Yeah, why? Did you find something?"

"Oh yeah. His foster father paid a military official to let him join the Black Ops. No questions asked."

She lowered her voice to a whisper. "That's not surprising. Politicians are weasels: they'll get what they want any way they can. But the question is, is Darkstar connected at all?"

While Nole had been on the phone with Brev, Kaora was putting Tomi's face through face-recognition. "You're about to find out, I'm sending you the photo now. That was taken yesterday. And Brev, it's worse than Darkstar just being connected: I looked at the autopsy reports and the bullet went through the side of the head in both soldiers. Tomi was the only person standing between them both." Brev heard a beep on her phone signaling a message and watched as her phone loaded the picture taken by a security camera: Tomi was walking side by side with Tayge past a diner in Portland. She almost gasped before she stopped herself. He also wore the same leather coat as the man that killed Venn in St. Paul.

Putting the phone back up to her ear, and without letting Ashley hear she said "He's alive, and he's not just working with Darkstar; he's *leading* them. Listen to me right now, no one speaks of this to Cloukora, or Ashley. Got it?"

"Got it." Nole hung up and Brev went to put her phone in her pocket as Ashley walked up to her.

"What'd Nole want?"

"Oh just to, uh, let me know that they were still working on the Iraqi thing for Cloukora. They think they got a lead but they're not sure yet."

"Ah, alright. Hopefully they find something. Cloukora needs some closure."

"Yeah…I hope so too." As she went back to helping Ashley set up the living room, she began to wonder how she would tell them both. To tell them that their best friend was not only alive, but was trying to take over the world.

After they had set up everything in the living room, and everything was shut off, they were about to sit down when the doorbell rang. "I forgot to tell you, when I found out we were staying over, I called for take-out. If I recall, Cloukora, you love Chinese. Right?" Ashley stated as if she could simply do whatever she wanted.

Cloukora was about to say something about it, but couldn't come up with a good reason why it wasn't smart as she opened the door to find the delivery guy standing there. *Maybe I am getting too overprotective.* "You know it. I'm gonna go get a couple things out of my car." He said as he headed out the door. "She's payin'." He pointed to Ashley when he walked past the delivery guy.

"It'll be $21.75." Ashley went to dig cash out of her purse. "Oh nice, a camp-out? I loved those as a kid. Good to know youth still love that kind of stuff." Brev joined Ashley at the door and was handed the bags of food by the man, as Ashley handed him twenty-five dollars.

"Yeah, it's something like that. Thanks for the food." Brev closed the door but not before Ashley assured him they weren't kids.

The delivery guy walked past Cloukora, who was going through his front seats. "Geez, touchy pair aren't they?"

Cloukora grinned. "You have no idea." After the guy drove off, Cloukora looked around and before he could take the gun out of his glove box, he noticed a black Suburban across the street with two men sitting in the front seats. Cloukora almost dismissed it until he remembered that the *same* car drove by his house multiple times before. He checked to make sure he had his throwing knives in his pocket, and walked over to the SUV. He noticed them get a bit nervous when they saw him approaching. "Alright, why are you following me?" Cloukora asked when he came to the passenger's side.

"Excuse me? We're just waiting for a-"

"Don't give me that bullshit. I've seen you drive around my house."

"Look, kid, I don't know what you're talking about, or on, but you should keep your crackpot theories to yourself."

Cloukora flashed a knife and put it to the man's throat. "Whatever the reason, if you hurt anyone I know, you might as well put a bullet in your head because I'll be coming after you." Without another word he turned and walked back to his car. While walking back, he heard the trumpet again, and looked around to find the source. To no avail, he asked the guys in the SUV if they heard it too, but they only shook their heads, mouthed the word crazy, and drove off.

The three sat around the candle-lit coffee table, eating the Asian delicacy they had ordered. Cloukora tried bringing a piece of sweet and sour chicken to his mouth using chopsticks, but it slipped and fell onto his shirt. "Seriously, why couldn't they give us forks?" Cloukora picked up the chicken with his hand and tossed it into his mouth.

"Because you're supposed to use chopsticks with Chinese food, you know, cause that's how you eat food in China. Or rather any Asian country." Ashley explained as if he were an idiot.

"This is America. Not China. They need to at least give you a fork along with them."

"Then get one from the kitchen."

"Tried. They're all dirty. It's amazing how only two people can dirty all the forks."

"Just eat your damn chicken." Ashley said, creating a moment of silence until she broke it again. "So, Cloukora, since you're a hero and all now, have you thought of an alias?"

"I haven't decided on one yet. I had thought about Dr. Feelgood, but I don't want Mötley Crüe to sue me or whatever. Plus it wouldn't be original." Cloukora added.

Ashley laughed. "They might do the opposite. I mean, a superhero using the title of one of their songs, they'd probably think it's awesome! Why did you pick that name anyways?"

"Well, first off the mask is a bit like a doctor's. Second, I'm gonna make the world feel good by saving it. They'll be able to sleep comfortably in their beds. Plus a superhero with the title doctor? I think that'd be badass...Perhaps I'll just let the public decide."

"That's…different, I suppose. But Iron Man has the same name as the Ozzy Osbourne song."

"First off, it's by Black Sabbath, not just Ozzy. Gotta give the band credit, too. Second, the song came out *after* the comic. At least I think it did. I doubt there's any actual connection between the two, anyway."

"Also, the public deciding the name isn't new. I don't know much about comics, but I believe the people picked out Superman's name. I don't know, but I'm sure it's not a new thing. Do you know, Cloukora?" Brev asked.

"Nope. I love superhero stuff, but I never actually got around to reading a comic." He took a bite of his chicken and with his mouthful said "Why are you asking me, anyway? You should know, you're a vam-" He stopped himself. He had forgotten Ashley was there for a moment.

"It's okay, she knows. And like you, I never picked up a comic. But I do know you're right on the Black Sabbath part. People were raging about the comics before the song even came out. I remember hearing that song on my old radio as if it were yesterday…" Brev seemed to be lost in her reminiscing of her past.

Brev started paying attention again when Ashley continued. "Another question, since you're not doing the whole secret routine with friends and family, do you…do you think you might still have girlfriends and stuff?" Ashley asked, stroking her hair back before quickly going back to her food. Cloukora could tell by her awkward actions, she must be referring to herself.

Cloukora gave a grin before saying: "I don't know, maybe. Hell, I can't be lonely my whole life. So you know what, yeah, I'm still gonna try and get a girlfriend. Try being the keyword…"

"I'm sure you'll find someone willing to put up with your new life. Maybe even help you out. You know, someone that will always have your back and stand with you by your side, no matter the storm that comes your way." Ashley smiled, and Brev finally noticed what was going on between the two and smiled to herself. Another trumpet sounded and Cloukora rubbed his ear.

"Another one?" Brev asked, and Cloukora nodded. "This is really strange. Perhaps you *are* just going crazy."

"Ha ha. Very funny." Cloukora said sarcastically. A thump came from upstairs. "You heard *that* right?" The other two nodded and Brev picked up her shotgun, and tossed one to Cloukora.

"Ashley, come with me. Cloukora, you stay on the bottom floor and head towards the back."

"Don't you think I shoul-"

"Go!"

"Fine." Cloukora rolled his eyes and followed her orders. When he was below where Brev and Ashley should be, he patrolled the hallway and the rooms. There was a chance the ghost knew it was noticed and had fled down there. Abruptly, for some reason, it had started to get really warm around him. Then he smelled something burning, and saw the walls of the house get brighter. "Oh no." He spun to see a room on fire, but before he could do anything about it, the whole house immediately burst into flames. Next thing he knew, the floor above him collapsed and fell not even two feet from where he stood. He quickly jumped over the pile of burning wood and ran to the stairs where he met with Brev, who was coughing up smoke. "Where's Ashley?"

"She was just behind me." She said wheezily.

"I'll find her, you get out!" Cloukora ran up the stairs and down the fiery hallway, dodging the falling ceiling and walls, and of course, jumping over the hole that was once a floor. The smoke was now starting to get to *him*. He ran past a room with a woman standing in the middle of it, and realized it was Ashley and turned back to run inside. She was standing in front of a shadowy figure.

"Ashley!" Cloukora shouted as he quickly pumped the shotgun and gently pushed her out of the way, aimed the weapon at the figure, and pulled the trigger. A fan of purple streaks pierced the figure's body and flew into the wall behind it, while the ghost collapsed next to the wall with black blood oozing from its wounds. Not wasting any time, he scooped Ashley up into his arms as another trumpet sounded, and

took her back downstairs to a soot-covered Brev, who was standing just outside the front door. "Get her out of here!"

"Where are you going?" Brev asked as Cloukora ran back inside.

"I saw something!" Without another word, he headed back upstairs and turned into a room. A man stood inside, looking out the window, unaware of the fire. Or maybe he was and just didn't care.

"Hello, Cloukora." The figure turned and Cloukora recognized it: It was the other demon he met; the one that was with Zela. "What have you been up to? Oh wait, I remember. Killing off my partner!"

"Oh, I'm sorry, did I ruin a relationship? There's plenty of other fish out there in the sea. Don't worry, you'll find another." Cloukora was suddenly flung towards the wall, just centimeters from touching the flames.

"Nah, I won't kill you. I'll let Lucifer do it. He's been itching to get his hands on your throat." The flames died out, and the house went dark; the only light came from the moonlight pouring in through the window. Cloukora was released from the invisible grip.

"So what the hell are you doing here?"

"Just keeping an eye on you. Boss's orders."

"And what damage could I possibly do? I don't even know *how* you're making the apocalypse happen."

"And you never will. But we can't be too careful, now can we?"

"No, you can't. I just don't understand why all of you demons don't kill every single human *then* release Lucifer. That would seem a bit more logical."

"Yes, but if we're focused on you humans, God is open to attack us. We take out God though then it's just you humans. And once they see their precious God fall, then no one will retaliate. They'll be like fish in a barrel!"

"Fear. A good tactic. You're still going to lose though."

"Let me guess? Cause you're the strongest? I don't think so."

"Why's that?"

"Because you're even dumber than I thought. You just broke your own rule."

"My rule? What are you- son of a bitch." A red portal appeared behind the demon, and other demons, the beastly-looking ones not in human form, poured out of it. Another trumpet sounded and the demon looked upwards.

"He's almost ready."

"Wait, you heard that too?"

"Well, I *am* a demon. A creature spawned from Lucifer, who was an Angel himself. So it's not much of a surprise."

"What does it mean?"

The demon gave a sly grin. "Goodbye."

"Wait!" The demon disappeared. "Dammit!" Cloukora turned his focus towards the demons coming from the portal, and fired shells into them. Surprisingly, it actually killed them. He quickly ran out of rounds before switching over to his sword he had just drawn out. He got a couple more demons, but it was too late. Too many poured out too fast, too many to fight, so he decided to just retreat and head back outside to Brev. When he reached her and Ashley, he saw that Ashley had snapped out of the trance and was focused again.

"What happened?" Ashley asked. A Cloukora, covered in more soot than Brev, turned to look at the house that demons were now crawling out of and spreading all over the neighborhood.

"It's started." Cloukora replied. A trumpet sounded once again, this time louder, as if it were right by his ears. Brev and Ashley looked around trying to find the trumpet. "Tell me you heard it that time."

"Yeah. How many times did you hear it before?" Brev asked.

Cloukora tried to remember. "Six."

"Then it's definitely started. We need to go. Now." All three rushed into Cloukora's car, with Cloukora in the driver seat. He backed out of the driveway, and sped off down the street towards who knows where.

Birth

Angel's Gaiden

Hell's Bells

August 3, 2010
Hillsboro, Oregon

    The Cuda zoomed down the city streets towards Cloukora's house. They had decided that they needed to make sure his family was alright and unharmed. Black clouds rolled in above them, covering the whole sky. The clouds were so dark that neither the moon nor the stars could be seen; it was just blackness. Dark red lightning flashed in the sky with the roaring thunder following only seconds after. Cloukora could see the city of Hillsboro being overrun by demons whenever he would glance outside his windows. The apocalypse had truly begun.

    "Dammit!" Cloukora finally said after a time of silence sitting behind several cars at a red light. "This is too soon and happening way too fast! We still don't know *where* Lucifer is going to come out of the ground. He could be popping up over in Russia right now for all we know! On top of that, I can't even fight Lucifer yet because I don't have the Blade of Michael because God hasn't summoned me yet!" He punched the horn on his steering wheel signaling the other cars in front of him to move, since it was a green light. It didn't make them move any faster.

    "Calm down, Cloukora. Things may be a little ahead of schedule, but we can still do this. When we get to your house, we'll check on your family, and if they're alright, tell them to go hide somewhere. Then we'll go to HQ and put our brains together to figure this out." Brev assured, trying to calm him down.

    "Alright, fine. We'll do it your way."

Birth

"It's the *best* way, and the *only* way." Cloukora didn't respond, only sat in silence. He honked the horn again when the people *still* wouldn't move. Finally, they began moving to the other side of the intersection. When Cloukora's car began to follow suit, a large semi-truck connected to a cab rammed into the side of the truck in front of him, forcing Cloukora to slam on the brakes.

"What the hell?" Cloukora stepped out of the vehicle as the man in the semi-truck got out, unharmed. Cloukora then saw his true form: a transparent, black spherical cloud in his chest; it was a demon. He drew Relyt's sword from his back, and readied himself for the attack. Before he knew it, more demons had showed up to help their comrade. It didn't matter to Cloukora; he could take them all.
The demon summoned a sword in his hand surrounded by a black shroud. "Oh it's *Hell* alright." The demon swung the sword at Cloukora, and surprisingly, it moved too quickly for him to easily block, but Cloukora ducked, then countered with his own strike, and had managed to follow up with a couple more swings before the demon had used enough force to knock Cloukora's sword out of his hand, and him towards the truck that had been crashed into. On the ground, he quickly scrambled to his feet and looked for a nearby weapon to use to block the charging demon's sword. Luckily for Cloukora, the truck's bed was filled with metal pipes. *This will do.* Cloukora grabbed one of the pipes, held it like a staff, spun, pushed the demon's sword downwards with the one end, and hit it in the back of the neck with the other, knocking it down and unconscious. The other demons had surrounded him within seconds, and Cloukora readied the pipe once again as if it were a staff. There were roughly ten of them all around him. The first one he jabbed in the face with the bottom of the pipe, and noticing another right behind him, pulled the pipe straight back, and hit the other demon in the face as well. He then swung the pipe to his left to smack another in the face, but with the side of the pipe this time. As a group of about four surrounded him, he spun the pipe around in circles, knocking each one out of the way with the long piece of metal. After a while, trying to keep the demons at bay was starting to put a toll on him, and it had begun to make him tired and weary. The pipe was

starting to get heavier on him. Wondering why Brev and Ashley weren't backing him up, he then noticed they already had their hands full shooting purple streaks at waves of demons that wouldn't stop coming at them. There seemed to be no end to the creatures! Realizing that he was using a pipe instead of one of his elemental swords, he dropped it onto the ground, and had Fyron appear in his fist.

"Now this is better." Before he could attack, a man appeared next to him out of thin air. Cloukora recognized the man as the same Angel that had told him to meet Death to get Death's Blade. The Angel put out a hand and all the demons that were around them, suddenly had a bright glow covering their entire bodies, and then they just disappeared, leaving nothing behind. Not even ashes.

"It's time, Cloukora." Not a word could be said before he had vanished into thin air, taking Cloukora with him. Brev and Ashley just looked at each other, both knowing what to do next. Ashley walked over to pick up Cloukora's sword lying on the ground while Brev went to get in the driver seat of the 'Cuda. The sword was a bit heavy for her to hold, since she had never before held a single sword in her hand. She put the blade in the back seat, buckled up on the passenger side, shut the car door, and then they were off towards Cloukora's house.

Tomi stood in a large, almost empty room before screens that hung in midair by themselves. On the screens were different places all over Oregon, mainly Portland. He had instructed Path and Lore to search through the library to try to find anything that will point them to the place Lucifer will be rising from; everyone else was gearing up for the fight. Besides Tor, who stood over a keyboard set on a stand high enough so that she wouldn't have to bend over. Tor was a few inches shorter than Tomi, she was thin, had unnatural red hair just as Tayge did, and reddish-brown eyes. She wore a simple black t-shirt, jeans, sneakers, and a necklace with a skull pendant hanging from it. Tomi then remembered something Lucifer himself had said. "His name gives him more power where it is said…Tor! Look up places in Portland with the words Devil, Lucifer, or Satan in them." He instructed the woman.

Astrea was the only one that wasn't going to be involved in the fight: she just wasn't quite ready yet. *Such a shame. I would have loved to see her dance in battle.*

"I found two places, my lord. One is a gentleman's club, and the other is a catering company." She said as she brought up a map on one of the floating big screens with both locations pinpointed.

"Connect them together." Tomi said, and she did; a red line connected the two dots on the map. He looked at the map for a moment, trying to see if there were any special locations between the two points, but he couldn't find anything. "Can you look up any locations along that line and tell me if there's anything special about them?" Tor nodded, and after a few moments, she looked like she had found something. "Got anything?"

"No, not exactly. Nothing is special about any of those places. Except, that convention center, I remember hearing about a group meeting there sometime tonight while I was hanging around downtown."

"Did they say anything else about it?"

"Yeah, they said they were going to change the world. I didn't think much of it at the time, but this can't be a coincidence. Do you think they're some kind of cult?"

"Possibly. That or demons. We're going to head there."

"There's another problem." She hesitated before saying it. "There's no way into Portland through the roads. They're all blocked off."

"Demons." Tomi said with disgust. "The hills will give us a way in. There'll be fewer lookouts in there." He turned to walk out, grabbing his coat on his way and pulling it on. "Get everyone ready to go." His father, Chris, had just walked through the doors.

"Where are you going?" Tor asked.

"I'm going to let Wolfstorm know." Tomi said as he exited the room, being followed by Chris.

"Working with the enemy huh? That sounds splendid! Let's let them know you actually have a kind heart!" Chris said mockingly.

He abruptly spun around to face the other man. "I am not doing this out of kindness! I am doing this for our survival. We cannot defeat an army of demons alone, we need help. Now, if you want to help us, be my guest. Then we won't need them!"

"Yeah, what am I gonna do? Use the power of politics to defeat demons? I know, I'll pass a law banning all the demons from entering any city! I bet that'll keep em out. Ooh! I can also stab em with my fancy cane!" He held up his cane for emphasis. "I'm a politician. Not a soldier."

"Exactly. So why does it matter?"

"I just wanted to make sure you weren't turning soft or anything, Tomi. What're you going to do when Cloukora finds out?"

Tomi turned back around and continued for the mansion's doors. "He won't."

"So, you're just going to walk onto the battlefield with Wolfstorm and expect them not to tell Cloukora that you're alive and you helped them?"

"Yup. Besides, if you're right and he's with God, he's going to find out anyway."

"Tomi, I swear if you screw this up…"

"I won't." Tomi walked out of the building and into the night, leaving Chris inside. Looking upwards he saw the black clouds had begun to turn red and orange from the fires off in the distance. "I won't." He spread his dragon-like wings and took flight.

Forest Grove, Oregon

Brev arrived at Cloukora's house to find that someone else had already parked in the driveway, so she parked the 'Cuda next to the curb in front of the yard. Both she and Ashley got out of the car to find Cloukora's family hurrying out the door towards both their car, and the visitor's car. The visitor happened to be Cloukora's uncle who had come out of the house right behind the family. "What's going on?" Brev asked.

"I'm taking them to my house where they'll be safe." Daniel replied. "I got them taken care of; you go do what you have to do." Daniel knew exactly who she was. Not just because she hung out with his sister, but he knew about his father's secret life and all about Wolfstorm.

"Are you sure?" Brev asked who received a nod from Daniel. "Ashley, you go with them."

"No. I'm going with you."

"Ashley, going with me today was one thing, but this is too dangerous for you." Daniel stood by the driver side of his vehicle, watching them both.

"I said no! I'm not just going to stand by and do nothing when I know what's going out there!"

"Ashley-"

"I'm going with you and that's final. If Cloukora bitches at you for this, then he can come to me about it! Got it?"

Brev knew she wasn't going to stay no matter how many times she told Ashley, or how hard. "Fine. But if things get really bad, you stay by me. Understand?" Ashley nodded. "I got her." She told Daniel who started getting in his car.

Daniel had his head almost in the door when Ashley remembered Cloukora's sword. "Oh, hey, Cloukora's uncle!" Daniel pulled himself up above the roof, with one leg still in the car, and looked at Ashley. "Does Cloukora have any other sword up in his room?"

"Yeah, I actually got him a katana for his thirteenth birthday. But it's a replica of a sword from some video game or T.V. show. Why?"

"Cloukora left his sword behind." She darted into the house as Daniel shook his head and got back into his car before driving off. The rest of Cloukora's family right behind him.

Ashley ran up the stairs and into Cloukora's room to find a sheathed katana hanging on the wall. It was a pretty plain sword for the most part: its sheath was black, the cloth around the handle and the back strap were a light green, and the handle and square hand guard were a

simple bronze. No marks or any significant carvings appeared to be on the sword. Ashley thought it was ugly compared to Cloukora's-or rather Relyt's-sword that he used now. However it wasn't the sword she was after, it was the sheath. She took the sword off the wall, drew the blade from the scabbard, and threw it on Cloukora's bed before running back down to the 'Cuda. She grabbed Cloukora's sword from the backseat and slid it into the casing, and to her gratefulness, it fit.

"You done?" Brev asked as Ashley tossed the sword back onto the backseat.

"Yup." They both got into the car and sped off towards Portland. But as they turned down the next road they saw a man in a long coat standing in the middle of the street, just looking at them. As Brev brought the car to a stop she saw that he bore a sword on his back. Who this man was, Brev had no idea. She decided to slowly get out of the car and find out who he was. The man walked closer towards the car, the street lamp shedding a little light on him and his face.

"Brev. The showrunner of Wolfstorm." The man knew who she was. She had to have known this guy from somewhere; but the shadows distorted his face too much to recognize him.

"I'm sorry, do I know you?"

"I would hope so; I'm your organization's enemy."

Brev decided to play dumb. "You're with Darkstar?!" She readied her hand near her backside, where her gun rested in her waistband.

"Heh, I run it." Brev immediately drew the pistol and aimed it the man standing before her. Even if it was Ashley and Cloukora's friend, he was still evil. And she wasn't about to risk hers or Ashley's life on trust. But he didn't even flinch at the sight of the gun. "I'm not here to kill. In fact, I'm here to do the opposite. I'm here to help."

She didn't lower her weapon. "Help? Why would *you* want to help *us*?"

"I don't want to, but I have to. Darkstar can't do this alone."

"You don't know how much that made me laugh." She said with a slight grin.

"It sounds crazy, and makes us seem a bit pathetic, I know, but can *Wolfstorm* do it on their own?"

Brev hesitated before answering. "No." She finally lowered the gun. "We can't. We don't even know where Lucifer is supposed to show up." She admitted.

"Well, we do."

"How did you find out? Where is he?"

"I actually had a little chat with Lucifer myself, and he told me, well he told his lackey but I could overhear them, that places with his name give him power and influence in that area. He could project himself in any of those places if he wanted to."

"That totally narrows it down." Ashley said sarcastically as she stepped out of the car, joining the conversation.

The man noticed Ashley and stared at her for a moment with a smile on his face. At least to her it looked like a smile; it was dark so it might have been her imagination. "Oh, but it does." He turned his focus back to Brev. "I've been monitoring demon activity all around the world, and the place with the most activity is right here in Portland."

"Our own backyard."

"Yes, and we think we know where exactly he'll be summoned. It's at a convention center. One of my…agents…overheard people talking about changing the world tonight, and we believe them to be some kind of cult."

"They're going to summon Lucifer." Brev cut in.

"Thanks for interrupting me, but yes."

"Thank you, we'll meet you there."

She started for the car but was stopped by the man. "Wait, there's a problem."

"And what problem would that be?"

"All the roads leading into Portland are blocked off. We think they're demons keeping anyone from interfering with their plan."

"Don't you guys have a helicopter to get past them?"

"No. Unlike you guys, we like to use the wings on our backs. So there's no need for one." Tomi said mockingly.

"Then how are we supposed to get in?"

"Through the hills that surround the city. There will be fewer lookouts in them, and it'll be easier to get through."

"Alright, I'll contact the rest of the group and we'll meet you there once you tell us exactly where. But I swear, if you're pulling any kind of stunt…"

"Again, why would I harm any of you right now?"

"I can think of a few reasons." She hesitated before continuing. "But we'll be there." Brev got back into the car and when she sat down in the seat, the man had disappeared. She glanced all about outside, searching for him through the windshield, but he was nowhere to be seen. After Ashley had got in, they drove off once again. She dialed a number on her cell phone as she was driving. "Nole. I need you to look up a couple things for me." She began after Nole had answered the phone, but it took a few seconds for him to say anything; most likely he had been sleeping.

"Brev, today's a day off."

"Not anymore. Have you looked outside yet?"

"No, why? Kaora, look out the window for me please." He told the other woman next to him, who had probably been woken up the phone ringing. Brev heard a curse word in the background coming from Kaora and 'Demons are running all over the place.' Nole continued on with Brev. "What the hell is going on?"

"Hell. That's what's going on. It's the apocalypse and Lucifer is coming back."

"Son of a bitch. What do you want me to look up?"

"First, places in Portland with the word 'devil' in their names."

She could hear a rapid clicking sound from the other end of the phone, from a keyboard. "Alright, there's a strip club and a catering business with that word. Now what?"

"Is there a convention center somewhere around either of them?"

"Yeah, it's actually right about in the middle."

"So he was right about that then…Now are there reports of Portland being blocked off?"

"Yes. Construction crews have been sighted at every entrance into the city. They won't let anyone through, not even on foot. They claim they're working on a huge project."

"I'll bet. Nole, you and Kaora get dressed. Wolfstorm is heading into battle."

"Battle? Dammit…Where at?"

"We're going to be entering through the hills around Portland. I'll call you and tell you exactly where in a few."

"We'll be there as soon as we can." Nole hung up the phone and Brev dialed another number. She was going to call the rest of Wolfstorm and have them ready.

As Daniel drove along the dark roads, he kept an eye peeled for any ambushes that might come from the trees surrounding the winding road. Some of Cloukora's family rode in his car while the rest were in their own car behind his. After some minutes or so, they finally had reached his house. Still watching the area for enemies, he told them to hurry inside. He noticed his dad, Cloukora's grandfather, was there, as well the rest of the family. Daniel was the last one in and motioned his father, who had been sitting on the living room couch, to follow him into a private room. "Do you think they'll be safe?"

"With us here, they'll be more than fine. Plus we have the shield around the house, so they won't be able to get inside."

"I know, but still. We've never actually known if the shield works or not."

"We just have to be optimistic about this right now. If the family sees either of us starting to worry, they will all panic."

"You're right. We have to be the stro-" They heard a thump on the roof and heard scratching as if something with claws was scuttling across it. They went out of the room towards the front of the house. "No one move or look out the windows." He commanded the family as the two walked to a nearby window. Outside, they saw demons running all over the neighborhood. All of them different sizes and shapes. Only the red bodies and their horns stayed common between them all. They

Birth

also noticed some of them were circling the house, waiting for their prey. The creatures knew there was a shield surrounding the structure and a threat that resided inside of it. "Think we should have some fun?"

"Why not. Let's see if I still got it." He turned to the family. "Everyone, stay inside. Even if we don't come back in, and you hear yelling or screaming, do *not* go out there. Understand?" The family nodded and the two Skyrells quickly opened the door and went outside to face their enemies, the door shutting behind them of course. As soon as they stepped off the porch, demons immediately jumped at them. A large, flaming sword appeared in Daniel's hand and was swung at the demon's side, slicing the creature in half. This sword was quite an unusual one: the blade was large and the tip curved backwards, like a crescent. The hand guard wasn't a regular one either; it stuck out past the front of the blade and then curved upwards sharply with a point, almost looking like a sharp tooth. The handle and the round pommel were the only parts of the sword that were normal.

Daniel's father had a sword appear in his hand as well and sliced the demon that charged at him in two. His sword was far from ordinary. The blade looked like two double-edged swords had been smelted together side-by-side to create a kind of double-blade, and the handle, which was more reminiscent of a katana's, slightly curved towards him. The hand guard was like any other standard broadsword's, but electricity sparked and flashed around it, along with the rest of the rest of the sword. After he struck down another, they noticed more and more were still coming, and an exact replica of the sword he already held appeared in his other hand; he now held two of these lightning swords. Another demon ran up to him, about to strike him with its own sword, but he casually knocked the sword out of its hands with one of his own, and then took its head clean off. More demons poured in surrounding them, but he still wouldn't break a sweat. All of this was too easy for him. He stabbed a demon in the face here, sliced one in half there, and sometimes even took two out at once. When the demons just wouldn't stop coming and seemed endless, he connected the ends of his swords, forming a kind of sword-staff and making the handles, when together, look like an 's.' This made it even easier for him to kill the creatures

since he only needed to use one hand, and because it also gave him more reach and a wider area of attack. He began to spin the "staff" in a circle, creating a blur of electricity, and started lobbing off heads, slashing chests, and stabbing guts. No matter how many they took out, the amount just seemed to double. How could there be so many demons coming after them? He realized this needed to end soon, so he stuck an end of the staff into the ground, and an electric shockwave blasted through all the demons, turning every single one into ash. Of course he redirected part of the blast away from Daniel, as well as the house, so it wouldn't end up hitting him. Now the numbers were a lot less, and they could see that the demons weren't coming towards them anymore, but going towards the direction Portland was in. He and Daniel had finished up the last few straggling demons and readied themselves for more to show up. When none had, they lowered their swords and relaxed.

"Man it's been a long time since I've held Rayos." His father commented, holding the sword up.

"I know what you mean. I forgot how heavy Flaym was." Daniel lifted his sword in suggestion and then had it disappear in a swirl of flame. His dad did the same, but his disappeared in a spark of lightning. "You have to admit it was fun though."

"Yeah, it was…Things are going to change because of Cloukora, aren't they?" His father said, looking towards the swarms of demons running through the streets and yards.

"What do you think? Cloukora discovers his powers and now we're fighting in a huge battle. Things had been calm before we told him who he was. Now, it's life or death. I don't think *anything* will be the same ever again. I just hope he kills Lucifer. I don't want to imagine what life would be like if he doesn't."

"Oh he will. He is Relyt after all."

"Got a point there." They turned to head back inside. "Do you think it was a bad move for us to tell him? I mean, he's never going to experience a normal teenage life -or any kind of life for that matter- and look at what's been happening. I feel like we caused all of this. Like we're to blame for it all."

"No, I don't. The apocalypse would have most likely happened whether or not Cloukora knew. Telling him gave the Earth a fighting chance. And Cloukora was never good as 'normal.' I knew the moment he was born that he was extraordinary. And he knew it too, that's why he's enjoying this life. I'm sure he's struggling with coping and everything and having a hard time accepting what he must do, but deep down, he loves it. He loves saving people and being the hero. What worries me, though, is when word gets out superpowers exist, people go out and try to be the hero, or even the villain. I don't mean the regular people that dress up and play as one. They aren't dangerous. I mean the people that get serious about it, and start experimenting to *create* superpowers. To the point where they actually become a superhero, or a supervillain. The ones that *are* dangerous. As it is, Wolfstorm and Cloukora have their hands full with Darkstar. A third party could be too much for them, and could bring about their downfall. Then who would be left to protect us?"

"Like you said though, he's Relyt's reincarnation. Relyt whose technology in the ninth and tenth centuries was way more advanced than ours! Relyt who defeated King Arthur, the second most powerful man on the Earth at that time. If Cloukora really does have the same amount of power as Relyt did, no one will be able to kill him."

"That's a big if though…Anyway, we should get back in before they get worried."

As they walked up the porch steps, Daniel said "You never did tell me how you're able to control electricity."

His father grinned as he opened the door. "And I never will."

Mt. Cavalry Cemetery: Portland, Oregon

All of Wolfstorm waited on a small clearing of grass that rested on the rise of a hill, with trees around and beyond them. Parked on the road were Kaora and Nole's minivan and Cloukora's 'Cuda; Nole and Kaora didn't have any kids, but the two had been planning on creating a family soon. They were technically in a cemetery, and a section of

graves lay across the street from them. Despite the amount of trees, there was a narrow view where they could see most of Portland, as well as the great Mount Saint Helens. They still had a few more hills to traverse before they reached the city; however, Brev thought it was a wonderful view to look at. If it weren't for the tint from the red clouds above them, it would have been pitch black where they stood. Not far off though were lit-up houses in the distance in the direction they came from, and occasionally a car would drive by, unaware of the event occurring, and even more so of the event *about* to occur. There had also been quite a bit of gunshots, too, most likely from the civilians that tried defending themselves that *were* aware of what was going on. Although the demons were focused on getting to Portland for their master, they still tried to kill anybody that stood in their way.

Though everyone else held some type of a gun, in fact she herself held a SPAS-12 shotgun, she was more concerned with Ashley holding an M4 assault rifle in her hand, shaking, and staring off into the distance towards the city. This wasn't right, putting a military weapon in a young girl's hand to fight a battle. She saw Cloukora's sword sheathed in a plain black scabbard, hanging from Ashley's shoulders by a light green strap, and began to worry about where he was. They really needed him right now. The whole world did.

"Where are they?" Winter asked impatiently, stalking back and forth.

"It's Darkstar, they're most likely never going to come. I bet you all of this is their bloody doing and they're just distracting us while they're out there accomplishing their bloody goals." Of course Bowe would say that; he always over thought things. "We're just sitting ducks for them to drop a bomb on us."

"I say we just screw 'em and head into the city by ourselves." Erro suggested.

"They'll be here." Brev assured, keeping her finger ready in case any demon ran by.

"If they're not here in five minutes, I'm going in." Winter warned, still going back and forth.

"You guys and your doubts." It came from a man strolling up the street, leading a group right behind him. It was the leader that she had encountered earlier: Tomi Pendra. Cloukora and Ashley's childhood friend. A poor young boy turned evil by his foster parent. She recognized some of the other people that followed him, from both reports of other members of Wolfstorm, and seeing them for herself: Ava, Tayge, and Cairne. "Before we get started, shall we introduce each other?" Brev didn't answer; she didn't know if it would be wise to say their names. "Oh fine, I'll go first. My name…you won't know." But she did. All of Wolfstorm, except the two people that loved him, knew who he was. None of them were about to say a word, though. In fact, she still hadn't come up with a way to at least tell Cloukora. She knew it would hurt him so much. "But this is Tayge." He pointed to the man they had encountered at the club before. "Tor." A woman standing next to Tayge with short, unnatural red hair just like his. "Ava." The woman Cloukora and Winter had encountered. Who, Cloukora had informed her, was actually on Wolfstorm's side. "I'd introduce Venn, but, well, he's not here." He got a glare from Ava for mentioning him, but he just ignored it. "Cairne." The muscular preppy guy Winter and Cloukora had also encountered. "Eve." Although this woman wore the same kind of clothing as Cairne, body-wise she was the total opposite: She was thin, somewhat short, had bright, blonde hair, and had no visible muscle at all on her. The next two that were introduced looked like the types of people that loved the outdoors; At least Brev assumed by the clothing they wore. They were what you would usually wear out in the woods or camping: jacket, shirt, jeans, and boots. "Path." He pointed to the woman who had long, wavy, red hair, and a pair of emerald green eyes. She also stood only an inch shorter than the man next to her. "And Lore." He pointed to the man next to Path, who had short brown hair, light brown eyes, and probably stood almost six feet tall. "Your turn."

Brev looked back at Wolfstorm, and Winter said "Go for it." Everyone else hesitated, and then nodded in agreement.

"My name's Brev, I'm the leader. This is Cal, Bowe, Erro, Winter, Avenorra, Kaora, and Nole." She pointed to each of them respectively. "Now can we please go?"

"My name's Ashley. I'm Wolfstorm's newest recruit." Brev shot a look of disbelief at her. She had *not* recruited her! Cloukora was going to kill her. Both of them. Tomi looked at Ashley and Brev had caught a glimmer in his eyes, but as soon as she saw it, it was gone. *He knows who she is. Maybe he* can *be saved...*

"Now, we can go." Tomi said and the rest of Darkstar started off past the rows of graves, and Wolfstorm followed right behind. Brev eyed the leather-coated man curiously. *There's still hope for Cloukora.*

Ashley lay on the slope of a forested hill while some demons passed by on the road just above her. Everyone else had done the same as her; they didn't want to draw attention if they could help it. Darkstar's leader actually protested the idea, and stated that he could easily kill any they came across, but with some persistence from both Wolfstorm *and* Darkstar, which was a wonder to her, he had finally agreed to use as much stealth as possible.

The demons had passed completely by them, and after a few moments, they slowly got up to make sure the coast was clear. None were there. Ashley readied her gun and started up the slope. As she passed by a tree, an arm appeared from behind it, pushing her gun downwards, and then pushing her down the pine needle-filled dirt slope. She rolled a few times before she was able get back up onto her feet, and when her vision cleared, she saw a demon striding towards her. The creature leaped at her, knocking her onto her back again, but she managed to hold the frenzying creature up enough so that it couldn't harm her. The pressure of her back on the sword started to send a pain down her spine as the creature struggled to grab at her throat. She had to kill it somehow. Glancing to her side, she saw the M4 laying in reach, but the problem was letting go of the demon on top of her. If she did, it could kill her. She decided to take the risk: either go out trying, or wait until her arms give out for it to kill her. Letting

Birth

go with her right hand, still barely holding it up with her other hand, she grabbed the M4, and pointed the barrel at the creatures face. "Go to hell." She pulled the trigger and purple bullets flew through its head and out the back, before it fell to her side dead.

She got up and looked around. Everyone around her had some kind of weapon out, fighting off swarms of demons that had apparently came out of nowhere. She felt intimidated that they were all fighting with ease, while it took her an effort to kill just one. *I need to stop this. I need to be strong and fight. They need me! I need to put what Brev has been teaching me to good use.* A demon ran up to attack her, but she grabbed its arm, pulled it past her, stomped its bottom half of its leg, bringing it down to its knees, and then put a bullet in the back of its head. She spun around and began to kill any demon she could aim her gun at, the purple streaks from the barrel hardly missing any shots. She wasn't sure how these bullets were able to kill them, but they did the job so she wasn't complaining. After a while she ended up running out of bullets, and unfortunately, there were no more extra magazines. She decided instead of carrying the extra weight, to throw the gun on the ground and pull out the pistol she had in a holster with one hand, as she held a knife in the other, using the knife hand to rest the gun arm to steady her shots. She continued shooting the demons that were out of her reach, but if they did get too close, she would use her knife to do the job. The knife, also given by Brev, had a purplish glow to it. It was a faint glow, but still there.

Soon she ran out of bullets in the pistol too, and all she was able to use was hand to hand combat, but she didn't think that would last long. She took another look around and saw some of her comrades' attacks were slowing down. This was not looking good for them, especially with the non-stop swarm of demons. Suddenly she heard howling coming from behind her, and when she looked back, there were packs of wolves running through the trees lunging at the demons. One of them ran at her and when she readied herself in case it was going to attack her, it leaped over and landed on the other side of her. She turned to see the wolf growling at a demon that would have killed her

while she wasn't paying attention. She realized why *that* wolf protected her; it was Rhain, Cloukora's wolf. "Rhain…"

"Hey there little doggy. Want a doggy bone?" The demon's growling voice taunted the animal. "You're so cute I could just eat you up. Heh. Maybe I will." In a split-second there was a growl and the wolf was on the demon, chewing its neck out.

    Ashley was glad she was on the right side, but she still couldn't believe Rhain could be that brutal. It honestly scared her a little. She looked to her right to see another demon running at her with some kind of axe, but stopped short, when someone behind it stuck two knives in both sides of its neck. The cloaked man who took the kill, she did not know. She managed to get out a "Th-thank you." but the man only nodded and ran off to kill more. After once again looking around, she saw that not only more people had joined in on the fight against the demons, but also that they had advanced further ahead. Not by far, but it was still a progress. They just needed to keep pushing and they would be in Portland in no time, especially with the help of these wolves and new warriors. She didn't care who they were, just as long as they were helping out. As she began to advance forward as well, she saw a stoned-winged creature swoop down and snatch a demon up, and then drop it back on the ground, killing it. If she didn't know any better, she would say it was a gargoyle, until one swept right past her, and she got a good look at it. It *was* a gargoyle. Ashley didn't know it, but Reapers were fighting alongside them.

    Cloukora stood, surrounded by a bright light. It was like the darkness that was around him when he had met with Death, only it wasn't darkness. Fortunately, it didn't last long, because in a moment he had appeared in a golden city. The Angel that had brought him here was nowhere to be seen. Everything around him was coated in gold: the streets, the buildings, anything that wasn't organic. Underneath it all, holding everything up, was a large, solid cloud. Kids and animals ran throughout the streets without a care in the world, and Adults lounged in chairs, chatting about random things. One of the adults had

finished their bottle of beer, and as soon as it was set back down, it was full once again. It was like magic. In fact, it probably was. "So this is what Heaven is like." All of a sudden it hit him that the kids were in Heaven, and as much as he wanted to feel sad for them, he couldn't. He didn't know why, he just couldn't. *I guess there is no sadness in Heaven.* Looking upwards he saw that the sky had a golden tint to it, similar to the moments before a sunset, clouds surrounded the city but didn't pass over it, and the sun was shining high above. Then he noticed a golden castle towering over everything else. He walked over to one of the citizens. "Excuse me, but that castle. That wouldn't be where God sits, would it?"

The man easily went from the conversation he was already having to Cloukora's. Without any agitation either. They were truly happy. "Yep, that's his. Can you believe it, though? Our creator is *this* close to us! I hope to one day actually meet him...I think that would be the best day of my life..." The man went into a daydreaming state, and Cloukora thought it best to just leave him be and head towards the castle. Surprisingly, it didn't take as long as he thought, and when he reached the golden gates there were two angels standing guard. They donned golden plate armor that covered every part of their body except their head, and stood about a foot above Cloukora. Both had a golden lance resting on their shoulder.

"God has not made an appointment with you. Please make an appointment and come back later."

"Oh, I'm pretty sure he has. The name's Cloukora Skyrell."

One of the guards looked at a list he held. "Nope, I don't see you."

"Well I have to see him. So I'm going to get in one way or another." Cloukora tried to walk through the gates on his own, but an invisible force knocked him back onto the ground. He stood up, moving the arm he fell on to make sure it wasn't broken. "I need to see him! In case you haven't noticed, the apocalypse is happening down on earth, and I need to see God so I can get back to the fight. My friends need me!"

The guard only shook his head. "We are aware, and I apologize but I cannot help you."

Cloukora made Fyron appear. "I *am* getting in there." Another angel walked up to the gate on the opposite side before Cloukora could do anything else.

"Let him in. He's with me." This angel he did not recognize, but he was glad that he was finally being let in. The gates opened and the angel on the other side began towards the castle. Cloukora made Fyron disappear and followed him up the steps and inside. The halls inside were more detailed and beautiful than the whole place was on the outside. All kinds of things were carved into the walls: people, animals, scenes from history, and other strange objects. Along the walls were arches that lined up next to each other, every other arch leading to another hallway. The other arches lead to nothing but a wall.

"So am I meeting God?" The angel didn't say a word, only continued walking. At the end of the hall he stood before the back of an old, bearded man dressed in a white robe, talking with several angels and giving them commands. There was a noticeable bald spot on the top of his head.

"My Lord. He's here." The old man turned around to see Cloukora.

"Cloukora Skyrell. The world's savior!" The old man had a loud and strong voice despite his looks. Cloukora didn't have to ask to know who this man was. He was the being that had created all of Earth and the rest of the universe, whose existence has been questioned since religion first appeared. This was God, and Cloukora was looking right at him!

This is no time for autographs. There are more important matters to worry about. "I've been told I needed to see you in order for me to defeat Lucifer."

"Good, getting right to the point. Yes, that is correct. Do you have Death's Blade?" Cloukora nodded. "Good. To obtain the Blade of Michael you need to draw forth Death's Blade."

Cloukora immediately tried making it appear. He wasn't scared of Death's warning, and he knew it was because God was there; Cloukora

trusted him. But nothing happened. "How am I supposed to make it appear?"

"Anger."

"Anger..." Cloukora tried to make himself angry, but it wasn't working. The one time he *wanted* to be angry, he couldn't. He closed his eyes as if it'd help him focus more, and began to think about Lucifer winning because he couldn't do this one thing. He thought about Lucifer crushing the world beneath his feet, killing everyone in sight, his friends, his family...Ashley...He could see Lucifer torturing them all in Hell. The anger began to swell up inside him. This time he didn't try to hold it back, he let it flow through him, and could feel the spikes starting to come out of his arms, back, and legs. His eyes changed to the inverted magenta and sky blue Skyrell crest. Just like Iraq, Miami, and the park. Then he felt himself gripping something heavy and opened his eyes to see that he held a fearsome-looking sword. The hilt was pretty normal besides a spike coming out of the pommel and on each side of the hand guard. The blade though, had small spikes coming from the steel near the hand guard, resembling a handsaw that took up a third of the blade. And near the point of the sword, were two horns coming out from each side of the blade. A dark aura had also surrounded the sword. This wasn't a normal sword meant just for slicing and stabbing. This was a blade meant for tearing enemies apart, to rip them to shreds. He looked up at God and heard an angel near him speak.

"My Lord, do you think this is a good idea? He could go nuts and kill us all! After all, he's the one that killed Nyx!" The angel gestured at Cloukora.

"He was a piece of shit traitor. He deserved to die."

"Nyx was a good man! He would never hurt us, or the world! And don't swear in front of the face of the Lord."

He felt a little ashamed that he had. Swearing was one of his bad habits that he now wondered if he should try to get a hold on. "Tell me, do you think I deserve the Blade of Michael?"

"No, it should not be touched!"

"Not even for the one who is to *stop* this apocalypse?"

"It is *not* to be-" The sword in Cloukora's hand pierced through the angel's chest.

"Nyx said he had people working for him that would keep me from getting the sword." The angel disappeared in a blinding light.

"I always knew he was a traitor." God said matter-of-factly. "Now, for the sword." God gently put his hand on Cloukora's forehead, and Cloukora felt a rush of power similar to when Death had done the same, but this time he felt hope and happiness instead of darkness and anger; He felt like he could take on Lucifer now. When he looked back at his arm, the armor and spikes all over him began to recede back into him, and he felt something sticking out of his back, and when looked to his sides, he saw white angel wings spread out. The sword that was in his hand was now a different one: the handle was made of white silk and two sets of thin yellow cloth snaked down it, creating multiple infinity symbols on each side. The hand guard was made of gold and came at a forty-five degree angle pointing downwards on both sides. The blade was quite long and thick, like a claymore, and near the hand guard it looked as if someone had seamlessly smelted the sword with an x-shaped piece of metal, giving off the shape of a star. Surrounding the sword was a bright, golden aura. Cloukora felt that if he were any other average person, he'd probably need two hands to hold it. The boost of power was the only thing allowing him to hold it with ease. "You are ready."

"Before I go, may I ask a few questions?" God nodded. "Well, first off, if you knew he was a traitor, why didn't you just get rid of him? Or any of the other traitors?"

"I wanted them to get close to their goal and fail. To feel like they were winning until at the very last moment, their plans get swept from under them and gets torn to pieces. I wanted them to know that I could tear them down when they're at their strongest. However, I had let them get too close and now you humans are paying for it. I suppose even God can get ahead of himself…"

"Wouldn't it be better if you just wiped out Hell in the first place?"

"I suppose, but if Hell didn't exist, then people would think it's okay to do whatever they wanted. Believe it or not, but the idea of Hell has scared many people and prevented them from committing horrible acts. Of course, Hell doesn't necessarily need to actually exist to still scare them, but demon sightings keep them from believing that there isn't one. So, demons need to exist for that reason. Believe me, I hate that they're around, too, but people need some kind of fear."

"Makes sense, I guess. Now, those trumpets I heard earlier, what was that?"

"They were the seven trumpets. Each trumpet signaled a part of Heaven's army that was ready to fight. You heard them because you're the one that will stop the apocalypse and send Lucifer back to Hell. You had a connection with Heaven that allowed you to hear their sound. The last trumpet was for the whole world to hear. To let them know what is coming."

"That brings me to another question, why don't you just take care of Lucifer yourself?"

"You and Wolfstorm need the practice, and the strength to fight the enemies to come. But the main reason is that I've become more of an observer than an interferer. I've begun to lose some of my power. Millions of years of taking care of the universe will do that to you. Plus, you having to kill Lucifer is probably the only thing keeping Tomi from killing you."

"Tomi? Tomi's *dead*. I saw him die!"

"Right, you don't know. He is alive, and well. In fact, he's the leader of Darkstar, the organization you and Wolfstorm are fighting."

"No...Tomi would never do something like that. He's not like that."

"You're right, he's not. But whatever's inside him is."

"What are you talking about?"

"The Fountain of Youth. When he was younger his father had been dosing him with it every day. It was the reason Tomi was sent to a foster home, because he was tired of the experimenting and he killed his father with Excalibur."

"Excalibur? I thought that was King Arthur's sword." God nodded. "Wait, Tomi is a descendant of King *Arthur*?" God nodded again.

"The Fountain of Youth also changed Tomi. Darkness grew inside him from further doses. His foster father had actually been friends with Tomi's real father, and they discussed a lot about the Fountain of Youth and its powers once Tomi's dad had told Chris, the foster father, about it. Chris wanted power just as Tomi's dad did, despite already being a politician, so he continued his friend's work, injecting Tomi with the Fountain and training him to become who he is today. A powerful and dangerous man with a split personality and an unstable mind."

"What *is* the Fountain of Youth anyway?"

"I don't know."

"But you're *God*. You're omniscient, you know everything!"

God shook his head. "This…This creation, was not of my doing. I do not how it was created, or who or what created it." He rubbed his hand over his bald spot.

"There's actually something God *doesn't* know about?"

"Unfortunately yes, and it's really bugging me. Something was somehow made without my knowledge! Can you imagine how mad that would drive someone? You are the creator of all things and yet something exists that you didn't even create! All I know is after it popped up in the world, I saw a shadowy man. I do not know who this man is or anything about him. Or even if he *is* a man. I have been trying to figure it out for thousands of years, and I still don't have a single clue. It's God's own anomaly."

Cloukora wasn't sure what to say. How was he supposed to comfort *God*? "I'm sorry, but I'm sure you'll figure it out. You *are* God after all!"

"Yeah, maybe. Well it's time you should get going." Cloukora nodded. "One more thing: be careful of Tomi. I can try to hold you two off from fighting each other, I don't want to see two good friends having to kill one another, but it will eventually have to come to it."

"Why? What do you mean?"

Birth

"Tomi is the real antichrist. One day he will attempt to raise Lucifer himself. If he succeeds, then there won't be any stopping him. Lucifer will be at his full power, and *will* crush anything in his path."

"Tomi doesn't bear the mark of the beast though. At least I don't think he does."

"Not physically, but…Tomi was born July sixth, nineteen-ninety-two. March sixth, two-thousand-and-one was the day of his first kill. October sixth, two-thousand-and-nine was when he officially formed Darkstar."

"The biggest three main events of his life landed on the sixth day of those months…I kinda get it. It's a weird way for it to work, and slightly less dramatic, but the point is that it does…So I'm going to have kill Tomi…My best friend…My life just gets better and better, doesn't it?"

"I can take away your powers, if you want, and give them to someone else. That I *do* have enough power for."

"No. No one else deserves this kind of burden. I'd rather carry it than have someone else deal with it just because I don't want to."

"Now that…that is a true hero." God put his hand on Cloukora's shoulder.

Tomi pulled his sword from the chest of a demon and stood in the midst of the chaos. They had managed to push the enemy out of the forest and into a suburban neighborhood. He looked around and saw both organizations fending off groups of the creatures, alongside the wolves and Reapers; he knew the new warriors had to be Reapers by the gargoyles. They were not doing it with ease though; some of them began to slow down and looked like they could collapse at any moment, even the Reapers. He himself was starting to get a little tired from fighting for so long. Behind a group of bushes on the side of a house, he saw Ashley cowering. *She doesn't deserve this. She should be at home right now sleeping in a warm bed!* He noticed several demons approaching her when all she had was a knife and her spirit, which seemed to be wearing down now. Two sides of him were arguing: One

side says to forget about her, and the other reminded himself of who she was, and who *he* was. Casually, he moved through the carnage around him, and every now and then cut a demon down that had crossed his view. The voice kept yelling at him to leave her alone. *Fuck her! You're not a hero, you're a villain and you have other things to worry about! Don't show her your soft side! You are going to screw everything over and do you think Chris is going to be too happy when you do?! Stop Tomi, you don't know what you're doing!* He just ignored it, but how, he did not know. Perhaps his love for Ashley overpowered this voice. *I wish I could hear her voice all the time, if that's the case.* He finally reached where she was and cut down the demons that were about to kill her. He put out his hand to help her onto her feet, handed her an extra pistol he had on him, and then strode off without a word.

"Thank you." Ashley said, but he just kept walking.

A hole appeared in the sky above them and a bright light poured out of it, followed by golden-armored warriors with wings on their backs, rushing at the demons below with swords and shields also made of gold. They were Angels, and thus Tomi knew Darkstar was no longer needed. "Everyone go back to base." He spoke through an ear piece, and Darkstar and himself spread their wings, and flew off into the dark, starless sky. Tomi's wings were dragon-like, while the others' resembled an Angel's wings: Ava's were brown, Tayge and Tor's were red, Cairne and Eve's were orange, and Path and Lore's were yellow.

Brev saw the other organization take off from the battle and saw Ashley standing there, watching them as they flew away. She also noticed Ashley holding a gun in her hand, and strode over to her, shooting any demons that were in her way, which were starting to dwindle down. When she made it to the young woman's side, Ashley took notice of her. "What was that about?" Brev asked. She had seen Tomi save Ashley, and wanted to make sure she was alright.

"I honestly don't know. Their leader just came up to me and helped me out, handed me this gun, and then walked away. Didn't say anything."

"Strange…"

"Yeah. Think he might have another side to him?"

"I'm sure he helped you out just so you would think that. So you'd let your guard down around him, and he could…well you know."

"Maybe. I don't know why, but I feel like I know him. It's weird. His eyes seemed so familiar…"

"I don't know. What I do know is that we have a war we need to finish." Brev needed to change the subject. She wasn't sure how well she'd be able to keep up the lie, or how long. *When the time is right.*

"Yeah, you're right. War." She looked around and saw that the demons were being pushed back, and went back to shooting them one by one, choosing her shots carefully as to not waste any bullets; after all she only had one clip left. She wasn't going to give up until she was dead. Abruptly a bright beam shot down into the ground near them, and where the beam just was, Cloukora stood in its place, still in his Airbourne t-shirt and jeans. Even though he looked the same, Brev could sense more maturity in him, she felt an air of confidence about him, and he *stood* with confidence, too. She noticed he had a white Gibson Flying V guitar on his back: the body was an upside down 'v' and the head was triangle-shaped with three tuning pegs on each side of it. The bridge of the guitar, the strings, pickups, knobs, and the tuning pegs were all golden, and the neck was charcoal black.

"Sorry, was in a meeting with the boss." Cloukora joked. Maybe he didn't mature. "Do you guys have my disguise? I can't go out there like this. People will know who I am, and I can't have that yet."

"Yeah, I brought it along with me. It was in your car anyway. Figured you'd probably need it." Brev dug into a backpack she had brought along to hold ammo and other things in it, just in case they needed it, and pulled out Cloukora's hoodie, gloves, mask, and handed them to him.

"Thanks." Cloukora motioned the guitar for Ashley to hold while he put his costume on. Winter ran up next to them, slit a demon's throat with a knife she held in her hand, and kicked the creature backwards. If it wasn't for her, Cloukora would have been demon food just then.

"What the hell are you doing? We're still fighting!" She took a defensive stance around them as Cloukora was putting on his gloves, and kicked any demon that had tried to get close to them. "Hurry up!" She was becoming agitated. Cloukora finally zipped up his hoodie and put on the mask. Lastly, he put the guitar over his back again.

"Alright. I'm goin' now." Cloukora started off towards the city.

"Cloukora, wait!" Cloukora stopped and looked back to see Ashley come up to him with Relyt's sword in her hand. "You forgot your sword." She handed it to him and he took the sword out of the plain scabbard, and made it disappear in his hand.

"Thanks, Ashley. Here, you keep the case." He handed her back the sheath.

"Hey, don't get yourself killed out there. There are people that want to see you back here. People that really care about you. People like me. I don't know what I would do if you…died. We already lost Tomi…"

Cloukora wrapped his arms around her. "It's alright, Ashley. I'll be back, don't worry." Cloukora started off before he remembered something and turned back around. "Oh, and Winter."

Winter quickly snapped a demon's neck before turning her attention to Cloukora. "What?!" She asked irritably right as Cloukora had spread large, white angelic wings from his back, each the size of a single man.

"I got my wings now!" He stated excitedly as if it should mean something to her. Whirling around once again, he took flight into the starless sky, above the attacked city.

"And he's supposed to be the one to save us." She said hopelessly.

"I have faith he can do it. He may seem immature, but he's a damn good fighter. And a damn good hero. He won't rest until we're all safe and Lucifer's defeated. And even then I'm sure he'll keep on fighting. For us, for the world."

Cloukora felt the rush of the flight as he flew over the burning city below; destruction had now engulfed it. Every time he looked down, his stomach lurched, not just because of the height, which frightened him a bit, but also because of the chaos in the streets. People ran screaming for their lives, running from the demons trying to kill them. Others took advantage of the circumstances by robbing stores, mugging vulnerable victims, and even some just killed for the enjoyment. He knew these were people, and not demons, for there were no black spheres inside their chests. However, there was still some hope, Cloukora thought, for some people with the will and ability, fought back against the evil creatures. They rescued as many people as they could and killed as many demons as they could. His fellow humans weren't going to just roll over and die. Cloukora wanted to so badly swoop down and save them himself, but he knew none of it would matter if Lucifer rose and took over the world. The needs of many outweigh the needs of the few. Another decision he would have to make that he didn't like. He sped on through the sky towards the calm, wide blue Willamette River towards the convention center just on the other side of a bridge. But as he neared it, the river was no longer calm: the waves began to swish around violently, crashing into the waterfronts on either side. High enough to reach land and destroy the trees, décor, and even some people along the river. Looking down at the city, he could see the earth began to crack, utility poles falling over, and buildings starting to sway. It was almost time.

As he neared the other side of the bridge, he heard a crash followed by a loud snap, and when he glanced behind him he saw a support cable flinging wildly and a bridge about to fall apart. One of the waves must have gotten tall enough and crashed into the side of the bridge and broke the support cable. He would have continued on, but people were scrambling all along the bridge. *Dammit, Lucifer can wait.* Swooping downward, and next to the bridge, he had Gaoth in his hand and began to use all of his might to control the wind and air to hold up the bridge and its falling pieces enough for the people to get off of it; it felt as though he was holding it all up by himself. *I can't let up, these people are counting on me.* The pressure was getting worse, he felt like

he was about to give. Next thing he knew he was taken by a wave and dragged under the raging water. *Son of a bitch.* He darted back out of the river against the force of the water, to see the bridge collapsing again as cars, and unfortunately, people were sliding off the slanting slabs of concrete. He wasted no time in holding it back up, and it looked almost as if it wasn't broken at all, despite a few large cracks here and there. *Those people...I...I'll mourn for them later. I have to worry about saving those I can save right now.* As soon as every single person was finally off the bridge, he darted back through the air towards the convention center, allowing for the bridge to collapse into the water along with a large number of cars. Losing their vehicles would no doubt put a dent in their budgets, Cloukora was sure their insurance didn't cover apocalypses, but he didn't have time to save the cars, too. He had wasted enough of it on saving the people.

He landed on the building across from the convention center and gave himself a breather. The wings on his back vanished in a flurry of white feathers, and Fyron appeared in his hand. He formed a shield of fire around him, but only enough to just dry his clothes and his hair; the weight of the water would slow him down. Plus, he admitted, he didn't want to look like a wet mop facing the king of Hell. After he felt dry once again, Fyron disappeared as did the shield of flames around him. Then he remembered the guitar on his back and how it got swept under the water along with him. *Shit, it better still work.* All around the convention center, he could see demons swarming in to join a large mass of other demons; both in human bodies and in their natural form. The city was destroyed: the waves from the river had created water damage on the waterfronts, countless buildings and homes were set ablaze, and vehicles were wrecked along the cracked and uneven roads and were set on fire as well. People were still fleeing the area as straggling demons hunted them down; apparently they didn't care for their master as much as they did killing. Before he could take a step forward the ground shook tremendously and the convention center began falling apart.

Next thing he knew, a giant red fist broke through the collapsing roof of the convention center, and the earth began to crack and break

open all around it. The cracks began to spread deeper into the city, and buildings started to fall into the ones large enough to swallow them. Eyeing past the debris, he could see the edge of a gigantic hole and a swaying light bouncing off its walls. A large flame spurted out from the great fissure, one so big that Cloukora could feel the heat emanating off of it from where he stood. He knew it had to be Hell, and this beast coming out of it, was Lucifer.

The beast's hand grabbed the ledge of the giant hole that had once been the convention center, and pulled itself out from the fiery abyss. The fallen Angel stood upon its enormous goat legs and towered high above Cloukora, above everything. Lucifer's skin was maroon red, he had giant black horns protruding from his forehead, pupil-less yellow eyes, long, black claws, and a red pointed tail that could wipe out an entire skyscraper. The beast caught a glimpse of Cloukora and let out a mockingly laugh. "*You* are the twerp that is supposed to kill me?! What do you plan to do? Play me to death with your guitar?" Lucifer laughed even harder, echoing throughout the entire city. He grinned and swung his claws at Cloukora.

"No, I want to make a deal." The claws stopped short of hitting Cloukora, who stood unmoved, by only an inch.

Lucifer brought himself down onto his hands, both the size of the building Cloukora stood on, and leaned in closer to the hero staring him down. "A deal? Hah! Are you serious? You want to make a deal with the *Devil*?" He let out another laugh. It was starting to get on Cloukora's nerve. "You must be a crazy son of a bitch to ask such a thing."

Can't he just shut up and agree to it? "Yes. I challenge you to a guitar duel. If I win, you go back to Hell quietly. If I lose, you can have my soul."

"Relyt's soul *and* destroying the world? Oh ho, this just might be the best day of my life. And I've lived a pretty long life. I accept your challenge!" A sphere of fire surrounded Lucifer and he had transformed himself from the large beast to a human being in an instant, appearing on the roof Cloukora stood on. The "man" wore a black jumpsuit, like a prisoner or a mechanic would wear. On his face was a

grizzly black moustache and beard that connected to his short, black hair. In his hand he held a guitar: The body looked like the wing of a bat, the fret board was made up of miniature skulls, probably fake, and the head stock of the guitar was a goat head with ruby red eyes with six tuning pegs on each side. This guitar was fit for that monster. "You can go first."

    Cloukora sighed, brought the guitar to the front of him, pulled out a guitar pick and tensed up before he began strumming the strings. He was nervous about it not functioning from water damage, but to his relief, it worked. He first started with simple chords and strumming down fast and heavy. It was almost as if the guitar was plugged into an invisible amp because the sound could be heard throughout the entire city. He began to switch chords more often and faster and would throw in a few notes that went along with the melody he was playing, and then abruptly played some notes near the bottom of the fret board and slid a finger along the bottom string up back to the top. To give a backbeat to Lucifer's playing, Cloukora strummed a simple rhythm.

    Lucifer played a couple quick and heavy strums and then played fast notes along the bottom three strings on the upper part of the fret board. He then worked his way down the fret board, while still playing notes, towards the bottom, where he played even faster. He ended his part with a long high pitched note, and then strummed a heavy rhythm for Cloukora.

    Cloukora went right to playing quick notes at the bottom of the fret board on the bottom two strings, fingers moving rapidly. Then Lucifer did a short solo himself, and then it switched back to Cloukora, then back to Lucifer again. The speed Lucifer was playing was unbelievably fast; no human could play as good as he was now. At the end of his solo, he ended it by playing notes each one lower in sound than the last until he played a note at the top of the fret board on the top string, and then muted his guitar. Next was Cloukora. This was his last chance to prove himself. He played simple chords but played them at the bottom of the fret board as quickly as he could, then he switched to playing notes, letting some ring longer than others, used the whammy bar, bending some notes and clumping others together in a quick burst.

His guitar playing was just angelic, and it was faster and better than what Lucifer had played. He had barely picked up a guitar before, and he beat the *Devil*. Where the playing came from, he wasn't sure. These new powers must have heightened his senses and abilities, allowing him to be more dexterous and know which note to play next by ear. Cloukora let the final note ring for a few seconds, and then muted his.

Lucifer's guitar disappeared in a flame as Cloukora put his behind his back again. "I guess I have to admit defeat. You won. You beat the devil! Congratulations! As I am a man of my word, I will now leave Earth be. Goodbye, Cloukora. It was a nice battle while it lasted." Lucifer bowed and disappeared in an instant, but then re-appeared right before Cloukora, with a blade ready to slice him in half. Cloukora easily pushed down the sword and clocked Lucifer in the face with an elbow. Without giving his opponent a chance to react, he roundhouse-kicked Lucifer in the chest towards the edge of the roof, and followed up with a punch, knocking him off the tall building towards the street. Cloukora made Relyt's sword appear in his hand and then jumped down after him, into a fast free-fall towards the street below, sword pointed downward to stab Lucifer in the chest.

Right before Cloukora hit the ground Lucifer rolled out of the way of the blade, and recovered, sword in hand. Cloukora pulled his sword out of the ground to swing it at Lucifer, who simply parried the attack and then struck back at him, But Cloukora went around the strike, to Lucifer's side, and swung again. It was Lucifer's turn to step out of the way and make Cloukora miss his strike, before grabbing the hero by the hoodie and throwing him into the nearby café on the corner. Cloukora broke through the glass window and flew across the countertop, knocking down the coffee machine and coffee packets that sat on top of it, and skidded across the floor. The alarm went off, making a loud woo-woo-woo sound, alerting authorities of an intruder; the intruder of course being Cloukora. As he slowly stood up, the sound of glass crunched below his feet and he noticed it had cut him all over his body. His back was sore too; he still had the guitar behind his back, so it didn't help with easing the impact. Grabbing it by the guitar strap, he pulled it over his back and saw the dented, scratched, and bent white

guitar before setting it next to a counter. He didn't need it anymore and it would only slow him down.

Lucifer stepped inside the café, still holding his sword. "And here I thought I thought I had to worr-" Nearby, a mix of energy drinks, soda, juice, and water abruptly burst out of their containers, broke through the glass of the several sliding-glass door fridges, and blasted into Lucifer's chest at high pressure, sending him flying back into the street and crashing into the asphalt. Cloukora picked up Relyt's sword and paced towards the king of Hell, who was now just getting to his feet. As he neared, they both heard a loud rumble and looked down the street where the sound came from: A runaway MAX train was heading right for Lucifer. Cloukora saw a grin on Lucifer's face, and right as the train was about to collide, Lucifer jumped through the glass window of the conductor's cockpit. Quickly, before letting it get away, Cloukora ran towards the max and used the wind to force one of the side doors open, and leapt onto the still-moving train. Starting for the cockpit he had to suddenly move to the side as its door flung at him at a deadly speed. If he hadn't dodged it, the fight would have been over right then and there.

Lucifer charged and swung his blade at Cloukora, who blocked it with his own and went for a strike, Relyt's sword slicing through the yellow pole used by passengers to hold on to, and by luck, avoiding Lucifer's block by a centimeter before slicing the beast in the chest. The next swing wasn't as quick or as lucky and was blocked by Lucifer. As were the multiple swings after that. Even though his sword was cutting through anything in its path, Cloukora knew this space was too small to fight in. As if Lucifer read his mind, he sent a quick fist to Cloukora's face and kicked him against a door of the train. "This is where you get off." A large ball of darkness flew from his hand at Cloukora, but at the last moment, Cloukora was able to bring his sword up to keep it from impacting his body. Unfortunately, the pressure of the blast was too strong to force back, and it sent Cloukora and the doors flying off the MAX train and through the air across a city park. His body rolled and skidded along a large brick surface like a ragdoll, landing on a quiet splash fountain; a fountain that shoots water from

the holes in the ground. In addition to the cuts from the glass, he now had scraps and more cuts from the hard landing.

How...How am I losing? I was faster than this with Victor! Or maybe...Lucifer's just that fast... Lucifer casually stepped off the speeding train without any effort and started towards Cloukora. Another ball of darkness appeared in his hand, and as he neared closer and closer, the ball got bigger and bigger. *I should use my new power, but the question is, how much power is* he *using? If he's barely tapping into his, then mine may not do much good.* There was no more time to decide: the ball flung right at him, and midway through the distance, the sphere instantly grew into one the size of a car! The ground rumbled below and before the darkness could hit him, a river of water shot from under the bricks and surrounded Cloukora like a shield, taking the impact of Lucifer's attack. But while it slowed down the sphere, it wasn't enough to stop it completely, and the ball of darkness broke through and hit the ground right in front of Cloukora, the blast sending him back into the wall of a shopping mall across from the park. The impact knocked the breath out of his body and sent crippling pain all throughout his back. He sat up against the wall, but when he tried to stand he couldn't move his legs; he couldn't get up. This was it. Lucifer appeared in front of Cloukora, blade going right for his heart. Then, as if almost miraculously, the Blade of Michael appeared in Cloukora's hand before him, keeping Lucifer's sword from killing him. Though, it didn't completely block the attack, for the blade had pierced through his shoulder. But there was no pain flowing through Cloukora's body now, only power. *Divine* power. Large white Angel-like wings suddenly spread from his back, and Cloukora glared into Lucifer's eyes with his own Holy-Trinity-pupils: three intertwined perfect circles. "You picked the wrong time to come back." A golden aura surrounded Cloukora then exploded into a burst of light, sending Lucifer flying across the park. "Payback's a bitch isn't it?" Lucifer got back on his feet and another ball of darkness shot at Cloukora, but with ease, the Blade of Michael sliced it in half, and the split pieces flew into the mall behind him, creating giant holes in the wall. Golden aura appeared around Cloukora's hand and formed its own sphere. Flinging it at

Lucifer, it knocked the king of hell back several meters. Not letting up, he sent a barrage of Holy spheres as he walked towards his opponent, until he finally stood over a now-weak Lucifer bent over on all fours. "So that was all you had?"

"No." Before Cloukora could stop him, Lucifer had him by the hoodie and in an instant they were both above Earth, floating in outer space. Cloukora wasn't exactly sure how he was breathing, but he figured it must have been from the divine power he now held. And of course Lucifer was still alive, and in anger at Cloukora living. "Why won't you die?"

"Why do you have to be such a whiny bitch?" Cloukora retorted.

"A whiny bitch? Do you even know *why* I was cast out of Heaven?"

"Yes, you thought Angels shouldn't have to bow down to us humans. Which, with the way we are today, I agree with you. We've gotten too full of ourselves and think we're above every other life form. But what you've done since is unforgiveable. Creating Hell, creating demons, and spreading evil and sin among all of us. You've helped kill so many people. Adam and Eve may have eaten the fruit but you were the one that pushed them to do it. You caused the fall of humanity. For that, I hope God never forgives you." Lucifer gritted his teeth and furrowed his brow. "You know, you ask me why you were cast out of Heaven, but let me ask you something. Do you know why God wanted you to bow before humans? It wasn't to be submissive or obedient or to put them up on a pedestal, it was to show humbleness and that no matter how much power you have, that you shouldn't abuse it. That power doesn't make you superior to everyone else. I'd even go as far as to say it was to put others above you, to show selflessness. Something you lack."

"I don't need anyone's forgiveness but my own! And I have forgiven myself long, long ago. I do not regret a single thing I have done, nor should I. Having power and not using it is a waste! One who doesn't exercise it does not deserve to wield it! All I want to do is use that power to control the world and make it a better place. I'm only

giving them what they need. If you're as good of a hero others say you are, you should understand that. You should feel the pain everyone is feeling and how broke the world is."

"You're right, I do. But us humans don't need to be controlled, we just need to be led." The golden aura surrounding his hand grew brighter and larger and formed another sphere of holy energy in his palm. "And I will be the one to lead them." As the ball of light shot at Lucifer, the fallen Angel sent his own blast of darkness that negated Cloukora's and followed up with a much larger sphere that went straight for Cloukora. Using the Blade of Michael, he held it back from hitting him then managed to gather the strength to deflect it into deep space. Right as the swing followed through, Lucifer was right in front of him and grabbed Cloukora by the hoodie, and the next thing he knew he was flying at a high speed towards Mars' surface, and once he passed through the atmosphere, the pull of gravity sent him crashing into a red mountain. He tried using his wings to slow himself down, but the speed of the throw was too much to resist. As soon as he back on his feet though, he pushed himself back into the air and towards Lucifer who was now darting at him from the sky above. The two rushed through the air at extreme speeds, but at the last moment they would have collided, Cloukora swerved to the right by a few inches to dodge Lucifer, and quickly grabbed his opponent with a choke hold and placed his free hand on the other fighter's back. The aura around the hand grew brighter and larger until he finally released the charge of holy energy into Lucifer's back, driving him into the red dirt below. Bringing both auras around his hands together, Cloukora charged up a large amount of holy energy and shot it like a beam at Lucifer, trying to hit his running target but instead only tearing large rifts into the red earth. Lucifer suddenly spread a pair of demon-like wings and flew back up towards Cloukora, evading several quick beams of light, and sword ready to strike. Even though Lucifer was speeding at him, when their swords met, Cloukora had the upper hand with momentum because his sword went with gravity while Lucifer's went against it. Not to say the block wasn't easy, but after some strain he was able to push Lucifer away towards the ground before his opponent flew back

to meet swords once again. This time coming at Cloukora much stronger, and starting a chain of furious brandishes between both swordsmen. Each strike more vital to block than the last and each strike quicker. This fight was the opposite of what any other normal fight would be: Instead of getting tired, they seemed to be getting stronger and faster after each swing. Until Lucifer had cheap shot Cloukora by socking him in the face with his free hand, knocking Cloukora off balance, and before Cloukora could regain himself, Lucifer knocked him back with another from his sword hand, and followed up with a large blast of darkness that sent Cloukora flying out of the atmosphere and back into space. He charged Cloukora for one last stabbing blow, one that would end the fight. Cloukora saw his opponent rushing at him and readied his blade. As Lucifer's sword was in range, Cloukora swung his sword upwards diagonally and took off Lucifer's entire sword arm. As the king of hell was still trying to process what had just happened, Cloukora sent the Blade of Michael into Lucifer's chest. Holy energy transferred from the golden aura and into Cloukora's sword, and began to build up inside of Lucifer's body. The light burning brighter and overflowing from the body. "Go to hell." Finally, Lucifer's body abruptly burst into oblivion as the impact of the blast knocked Cloukora unconscious and sent him flying into deeper space. Drifting through the dark abyss, the wings on his back and the sword in his hand slowly disappeared.

God watched Cloukora through an ornate bowl filled with some kind of clear water. An angel stood next to him. "What're you going to do?" the Angel questioned.

"A hero destined to be there for the people. A person who is to protect and save them throughout his whole life; to keep them from evil. A person who will carry that burden, do you not think they should deserve some kind of happiness? Or should they live their life as some kind of slave with nothing to live for?"

"Well, my lord, I think good deeds should be done without expecting anything in return."

"I'm not asking whether or not he should *expect* it. Should he be happy during the time he serves the people?"

"I suppose so, my lord. *No* one should be unhappy." God touched the bowl of water, creating a ripple. "What was that for?"

"I'm giving him happiness…"

Cloukora's body flickered and then re-appeared near the atmosphere of a giant, blue-green planet. One that was much bigger than Earth, and was in an entirely different solar system far off in another galaxy. Spaceships, satellites, and space stations orbited this planet. A planet way more *advanced* than Earth was. It would take at least a century for his planet to have had that much technology.

A small spacecraft shuttle, that would be fit for only a few passengers, had taken notice of Cloukora's unconscious body, and began to approach him. The ship's thrusters diverted to the side, to spin itself around so that its rear was in line with Cloukora. The hatch door opened and Cloukora drifted into the back of the ship. Once he was fully inside, the door closed shut.

The anchorwoman adjusted her blazer as the cameramen and crew across from her readied themselves and the equipment for the broadcast. Tonight had changed the world, and someone needed to step up and talk about that change. And she was the one who was going to do it. The director counted down. "Five, four, three, two." The 'one' was mouthed in case of it being broadcasted.

"Good evening, America…Tonight…Tonight was a tragic event for the world. A lot of people died this evening, innocent people, by things we don't know. Things we don't understand. Some say they were demons, and that tonight had been the apocalypse. That it was the end of the world. But what we do know, is that whatever it was, one man stood up to end it. One man took up arms and stared into the face of evil." On the television screens of every home, video clips of the fight between Lucifer and Cloukora played back to back. There was a

surprising amount of videos and angles they were recorded from; some of them were recorded just feet from Cloukora! "A man that had fought for a world full of complete strangers. A man that fought to keep us alive, and to keep us free. He is why you're all safe at home right now. Because this man saved us all. Yet no one knows what happened to him, or if he's still alive. A stranger could have possibly died for us, and we wouldn't even know it. Every social network has been blowing up with posts from all over the globe, talking about tonight and the hero that had kept it all from happening. Supporting what he did, saying their thank yous, and calling him a savior. They have even come up with a name for our hero. A name that I also see fit." She took a moment before continuing. "He has been dubbed…The Seraph."

Birth

Angel's Gaiden

Eight Legged Bastards

Bonus Chapter

Gaston, Oregon

The military truck moved along the dirt road with speed towards its destination located somewhere in the deep, dark woods, but it didn't move too fast for the six soldiers in the back gearing up for their mission. These soldiers were different from most, for they didn't have ranks or medals. They were mercenaries for hire and they were hired to secure a facility that had been overrun. By what, they did not know, they were only warned to expect the unexpected. Bruno was the large one of the bunch and cradled a heavy machine gun in his arm. "So what the fuck are we doing again?" He pulled out a cigar from a pocket, put it to his mouth, and lit the end.

"We're fucking your mom." Johnny remarked while loading rounds into a magazine for his M4 assault rifle; they all carried the same gun except Bruno, and that was because he thought bigger was always better. The joke got some laughs out of the rest of the group, but Bruno wasn't impressed.

"Ha ha, very mature."

"Just like your mom?" Johnny gave him a grin. He looked around for more laughs but only found straight faces and shaking heads.

"Alright Johnny, now you're just stretching the joke." Captain warned. He was their leader, un-appointed of course, but no one dared to challenge his place. Plus he had gotten them through every mission they've ever been on, so they couldn't complain.

"Sorry Cap'n." Johnny went back to loading his rifle.

Birth

"Really though, what are we doing?" Ace asked as he loaded his pistol's magazine; only he and a few others had finished getting their guns ready: Bruno, Captain, and Demon. After shoving the magazine into the pistol and cocking it, he placed it into his holster on his right leg.

"No clue. Our only orders are to get into the facility, eliminate the threat, and destroy it leaving no evidence. Don't know what the threat or the evidence is. Not even a map."

"We're going in blind." Johnny stated and Captain nodded.

"Well that's great. We might be walking into a military trap and I'm the only one bothered by it." Ace said as he threw his arms in the air.

"Me and Sparky checked it out. They have no connections with the military; they're clean." Captain assured.

"Like that makes a difference…" Ace put a toothpick in his mouth and sat back, creating a few moments of silence.

"Sparky and I." Bruno stated and everyone looked at him oddly.

"What?"

"Captain said 'Me and Sparky.' It's 'Sparky and I.'"

"Since when did you become a grammar expert?"

"Since I started reading a book on grammar."

"How about you read the book on nobody gives a fuck?" Ace was obviously in a bad mood. Or perhaps he was just on edge.

"Demon, what do you think?" Blaze asked, who was smoking a blunt of weed; he had finished readying his gear. That wasn't why they called him Blaze though, but it did have a part in the reason. Demon was sitting still, staring off somewhere else. He differed from the group by his black clothing he wore- the others wore regular military clothing- and the katana on his back. There was also his attitude: he was calm, quiet, and always kept focus.

Demon looked at him. "I really don't care." He rested his head on the wall of the truck and turned to look out the back of it, watching the dirt road disappear when the light from inside the truck no longer reach it. "That stuff is bad for you."

"Weed? Yeah, and I suppose doctors give it to patients to kill them, right?"

"Remember that mission we went on in the Amazon? To contain that virus?"

"What about it?"

"I was looking at some medical reports and found that for years, decades, weed has been experimented on and that ninety-eight percent of weed in distribution today has some kind of dangerous chemical in it. I think I saw one that would cause a man to lose his genitals. Not slowly or biologically, I mean physically and it would happen instantaneously. Just drop to the ground right then and there. The man would eventually die from blood loss. You wouldn't believe how many cases there were."

"Whatever, you're just making it up." He looked around and saw the rest of the group looking at him. "He's joking right?" The group shook their heads. "Nah, nah. I'm not listening to you guys." He put the joint back in his mouth and breathed in a huge amount, and then let out the smoke. The truck finally stopped and everyone got out to look at the facility.

The darkness of the night made it hard to see perfectly, but from what could be made out, it was a short one-story, steel and concrete, rectangular building. Small fluorescent lights that were spread equally apart around the building walls gave a little light. The group of men walked towards a large steel plated door with a line going down the middle. Captain pressed a few numbers on the keypad next to the door, and the door split in two vertically, allowing an entryway inside.

After they walked in, the doors shut behind them, and the lights turned on. Or rather attempted to; a lot of the lights flickered while only some stabilized. There were three enclosed station areas: One to the left, one in the middle, and one to the right. The walls of each area were steel framed with broken windows all the way around. Blood stained the floor, walls, and even the ceiling, and the office furniture lay strewn all around. But there was no one to be seen. Not even a single body. "Alright, our employer says the main objective is in the medical office, so we need to find that. Wherever the hell it is…" As they slowly

moved into the corridor between the middle and the far right room, they heard glass crunching under their feet.

They continued walking down the hall when they saw a blood-stained sign pointing to the medical office on the wall. They walked by more rooms just like the ones out front, but it wasn't only blood all over, they noticed spider webs scattered, too. Not only small ones, but huge ones as well; they were big enough for a man to be captured in. Above the door of one of the rooms was a sign that read "Medical Office" and the group headed inside of it. Computers, and lab and medical equipment took up the space of the room, along with medical supplies. Captain immediately went to one of the computers and started accessing it with a flash drive, Blaze went to look through a bunch of files, and Johnny went over to a giant white ball sitting on a desk. It looked like a large cotton ball, but the outer material was sticky, as if it were spider web.

"What the hell?" Johnny asked as he scraped off some of the material after touching it.

Blaze suddenly dropped a file he was reading. "Oh shit."

"What? Did you find it?" Captain asked, standing up quickly, giving his full attention to Blaze.

Blaze took the blunt out of his mouth, threw it on the floor and stepped on it, and then backed away from it as if it were about to kill him. "Demon was right. I'm never touching weed again." Captain only shook his head and went back to accessing the computer.

Demon noticed some miniature habitats usually used for bugs, and looked inside one. He saw a ladybug trying to walk with a leg three times bigger than the rest of its legs. He then looked through another one with a scorpion that was larger than it should be, but its tail was smaller than its normal size. "What were they *doing* in here?"

Johnny was still looking at the giant ball. "Hey Ace, come look at this." Ace walked over and stood next to him. "Doesn't it look kinda like a giant spider egg?"

Ace studied it for a moment. "I wouldn't mess with that."

"Why?"

"Just don't." Ace left Johnny's side to ask the Captain how the process was coming along.

Not heeding Ace's words, Johnny poked at the ball with the barrel of his gun. When nothing happened, he pushed it inside. For a second, there was nothing. The silence was the calm before the storm. All of a sudden millions of tiny spiders poured out of the white ball, climbing the wall around them and on Johnny's gun that still had its barrel inside the ball. The spiders moved too fast for him to do anything, because in a split second, his body was covered in them. They were pissed. The rest of the group saw what was happening and fired shots at the arachnids as they tried to flee from the room. "Captain, let's go!" One of them shouted as the group ran out.

"Give me a second, I'm almost in!" There was a loading bar on the computer screen that began to fill up; it was at ninety percent now. He shot a few bullets at the spiders coming at him, and when the bar reached a hundred percent he took the flash drive out of the front of the computer, put two bullets into the tower with his gun and ran out, stopping short at the door. On the ceiling was a spider that was bigger than he was, with its eight, beady eyes staring dead into his own. Captain aimed his gun to shoot, but the spider was faster than the trigger and leaped at him before a shot could be fired.

Forest Grove, Oregon

Cloukora leaned over the edge of the LeMans to get to the bottom of the engine block where the spark plugs should be. The current issue with the car was replacing the old spark plugs with new ones, and that was just what Cloukora was doing, or trying to anyway. Jack was replacing the plugs on the other side one by one, as was Cloukora. Cloukora finally got the fourth and last new spark plug in and got the spark plug wire to snap over the plug's tip. "Alright, start her up." Jack told him as he finished with his own side. Cloukora went around to the driver's side, sat in the seat and put the keys into the ignition and turned it, waiting for the roar of the engine. That magic

moment when something you put hard work into finally comes to life. He closed his eyes. Nothing. Cloukora tried again, nothing. "Come on, it should be at least making *some* noise by now!" Jack went over to the other side to make sure Cloukora did it right, and then stood up with a look of disproval and holding up a spark plug. From here it didn't look like anything was wrong with it. "You broke it."

"Aw f-" Cloukora's head went forward and honked the horn before the word could be finished. He stepped out of the car, trying to decide if he should apologize or not, but not before his phone rang. "Brev." Cloukora went outside to stand away from the garage while Jack continued working. The sky was a clear blue and the sun was hotter than usual today, but it was perfect when a cool breeze blew through Cloukora, blowing his hair in the wind. That was the only annoying thing about long hair: the wind always messed with it and he didn't have to look in the mirror to know it didn't look right. He patted his hair down and told himself the heat was better than the freezing cold. Hitting a hand on a metal piece while pulling on a socket wrench in the middle of winter…He shuddered at the thought. "Yeah?"

"Hope you're not busy right now, cause you got a mission."

"Well, actually I am a bit busy. Can I do it later?"

"No. I'm sorry, but we gotta do it now. This mission is way too important to put off."

Cloukora sighed before reluctantly saying "What's the job?"

"I'm not sure. The details are extremely classified, not even Kaora or Nole can figure out what they are, but it's definitely serious. All we know is there's information in a facility a few miles outside Gaston that was working on something and then something happened and now that evidence of that something needs to be destroyed before someone else finds it and does something with it."

"Why us?"

"They tried sending in a mercenary squad and they didn't make it out. The people who hired us haven't been able to establish contact with them; they assume they're dead. Cloukora, these guys were highly-trained, heavily armed, and they *failed*. Whatever is in that building isn't human, and needs to be killed before it gets out."

"Alright, get the team ready to go and I'll meet you in Gaston." Cloukora was going to hang up the phone when he said "Oh, I'll bring Rhain. He needs a walk; he's starting to get a little chubby. Plus his smelling capabilities could come in handy."

"Are you sure?"

"Yeah, I'm sure. He's a strong wolf, he can handle it." Cloukora said, smiling, as he scratched a tired Rhain's head that had just walked up to him after running around in the backyard. Rhain lolled his tongue, enjoying the petting from his companion, while still looking around and keeping an eye out for anything suspicious or harmful. Or at least that's what Cloukora had thought.

"We'll meet you there, then." Brev hung up and so did Cloukora.

"Sorry, Jack, I got something to take care of." Cloukora gestured with the phone as if it would make it clearer why he was going. "I'll help you work on the car when I get back."

"That's fine, I needed a break anyways." Jack said as he wiped his hands on an oily rag. "I'll clean up here, you go get yourself ready." He went to start putting the wrenches away when he added: "And be careful!"

"I know, I will." Cloukora said as he went inside to grab the bag containing his costume and other emergency needs, and came back outside with Rhain following right behind. They both got in his car then drove off towards their destination.

Gaston, Oregon

The 'Cuda arrived in Gaston and Cloukora pulled it over to a curb on the side of the road, while cars that had been behind him, zoomed past. After the road was clear, he stepped out of the car and waited with Rhain by a closed down grocery store. He wondered who she was bringing along, but then he realized that was a stupid question; she would most likely bring Bowe and Erro. Sure enough, he was right: Brev pulled in front of Cloukora's car with her usual Corolla, and out

Birth

of it came Bowe, Erro, Brev, and Cal. *I forgot about Cal…Must be from not being on enough missions with him. I should ask Brev to change that.* He did feel a little bad about forgetting him, though. "So which car are we taking?"

"We can just take yours." Erro pulled out several duffel bags from Brev's car, "Pop the trunk." And after Cloukora opened it, she threw them in his. While he slammed it shut, everyone was piling into his car and strapping their seat belts on. Rhain ended up having to sit on Erro's and Bowe's laps because there was no room on the floor for him. "Geez your dog is heavy." That got a growl from Rhain. "Um, Cloukora?" She said worriedly as he got into the driver's seat.

"Rhain, calm down." Rhain immediately stopped growling and put his head back down. "He doesn't like being called a dog."

Erro shook her head. "Sorry Rhain. Your *wolf* is heavy." After about a half hour drive, with Brev's directions, they came to a small, one-story steel and concrete building.

"So this is it?" Bowe asked as he stepped out behind Erro, Rhain, and Brev. Cal followed Cloukora out his side. Cloukora opened the trunk again and Brev took out the bags to open them on the ground next to the car. Inside one of the bags were armored tactical vests, another contained M4 assault rifles and pistols, and another had filled magazines for the guns. She handed a vest to each person, and while they were strapping them on around their torsos, she began sorting out the guns and ammo. The vests were black, had three pouches for rifle magazines, three for pistol magazines, one for a walkie-talkie, another for what Cloukora assumed was for miscellaneous items, and a holster for a pistol.

The vest felt a bit heavy on Cloukora. "I think I need to start working out. I don't think I'm supposed to feel the weight of this thing."

"Considering Kevlar isn't that heavy I would think so too." Brev insultingly agreed.

"It's made out of Kevlar? Sweet."

"Yup." Brev stood up above five piles of weapons and ammo. Each one with a M4 assault rifle, USP .45 handgun, four M4

Birth

magazines, and four handgun magazines. The M4s had several attachments on them: a flashlight, red dot sight, and a fore grip. Brev had taken a handgun out of a pile, loaded a magazine into it, cocked it, and then placed it in the holster on her vest. After everyone had done the same, as well as loading the M4s and placing the extra magazines into the pouches, Brev handed them each an earpiece. "This is how we'll communicate with each other if we get split up. We shouldn't have to though; this should be a walk in the park. All we have to do is go in, destroy the evidence, and get back out. Understood?" Everyone nodded their head in agreement. "Let's go." After cocking the assault rifles they walked to the door of the building, took a deep breath, and then opened it by pressing the buttons on the keypad: five zero four nine.

"What the bloody hell happened here?" Bowe said wide-eyed as soon as the opened door revealed flickering lights and blood and shattered glass scattered all across the main room. The odd thing was that there were no bodies to be seen. "These people were slaughtered!"

"I don't think any of them stood a chance." Erro speculated.

Brev was the only one taking all of this in casually; Rhain was even hesitant to go in. Then it hit him. *Wait, how the hell is she taking this so well? She's a* vampire *and it's a blood buffet in here!* After thinking about it, he realized she's probably trying to do all she can to ignore it to keep herself from licking the blood clean off the floor. Before he could stop himself, it came out: "Hey Brev, just out of curiosity, how can you be so cool about all of this? I mean you are a vampire and all."

"Hey, I'm a vampire too!" Cloukora did it again: he forgot about Cal.

"I'm trying not to think too much on it so I don't start stuffing my face with it." Brev replied with a hint of irritability.

So Cloukora was right. "Oh…So, what *does* blood smell like for you guys?"

"Chicken."

"Seriously?"

"No, but it does smell delicious." She gave a look at the blood before shaking her head. "Can we please start looking? We're still standing in the doorway." She started away from the door.

"Sorry, I shouldn't have asked." He said apologetically. The group readied their guns and walked inside, checking the corners of the three rooms making sure no hostiles were hiding in any of them. "Clear."

"These are just offices, let's keep moving." Brev said. Cloukora could sense that she wanted to get out of there as quickly as possible. So did he. They crept down the hallway, ready for anything to pop out at them, until they saw the medical office sign and then picked up the pace and followed it into a room filled with medical equipment and bug habitats. Inside were scattered files, a damaged computer tower with bullet holes through it, and blood scattered everywhere with a trail of it leading from the computer and out the doorway, which Rhain now sat by, keeping watch. "Whatever did this likes to drag its victims away."

"Uh, guys, I think I found something." Erro pointed to a shell that was missing a top.

"It looks like a spider egg." Bowe suggested as he stepped towards it. As he did, he felt his foot step on something and when he lifted it, found a small flash drive with a small amount of blood on it. He picked it up and put it in the unused vest pocket. Kaora and Nole could look over it once they got back.

"Yeah, maybe a cobweb spider egg?" Erro added.

"Whatever kind it is, it's big to lay that size of an egg, and now that there's babies on the loose…"

While Cloukora was listening to this, he was in somewhat of a frozen state. *Spiders. I fucking hate spiders. Why spiders? Why? Why couldn't they be something less scary, like ghosts or werewolves? Hell even demons!* He felt something crawl up his back onto his shoulder, and when he turned his head, saw a larger-than-normal scorpion with a small tail perched upon it. "AHH!" Cloukora jumped and frantically brushed at his shoulder, knocking it off before repeatedly stomping on it with his foot. He felt the rest of his body, still freaking out, until he noticed everyone was staring at him, even Rhain with his tongue

lolling. "There was a scorpion on me." They just continued staring. "It could have killed me!" When they still wouldn't stop looking at him oddly, Cloukora coughed and composed himself. "Anyways, so we're dealing with spiders?"

"Afraid so." Erro said poking at the broken shell.

"We have to destroy the facility anyway, let's just nuke the damn thing."

"Unless you want to go to jail, we can't." Brev reminded.

"I'm fine with that."

Brev shook her head at the amount of seriousness in his voice. "I'm sure there's another way, but we need to-" Rhain suddenly stood up, tail pointed, and growled at something down the hallway. A shot of web stuck to the wolf and dragged it down the hall.

"Rhain!" Cloukora quickly ran out just in time to see a spider pull Rhain around a corner and raised his gun to fire at it, but reluctantly lowered it when he realized it was too late. "Son of a bitch. We have to go get him."

"Didn't need to tell us that." Cal smirked and readied his M4 as he led the group out and down the hallway. As they progressed further through the facility, they noticed web covering the walls more often and in more abundance. The web on the floor stuck to their shoes, forcing them to have to put more lift into their steps.

Cal held up his fist, signaling for the group to stop. "Hear that?" Further down the hall, around a corner was the sound of clatter on metal, as if someone or *something* was running. Everyone gripped their guns tightly, ready to aim, and when the sound got closer, they aimed them down the hallway, fingers on the triggers. A man in a black military-like outfit appeared from around the corner, running towards them, an M4 hanging from his shoulder.

"Run!" The man shouted, gesturing for the direction behind them. Immediately following him was a swarm of thousands upon thousands of spiders, all of different species, running along the hall right for them.

"Oh shiiiiiit!" The group opened fire on the giant bugs that charged at them, but it was futile; more and more just kept coming.

Cloukora noticed a flammable barrel not far off from them, in the midst of the swarm. Aiming at the barrel, he fired a few shots into it, causing it to explode on impact, but he stopped the fire before it could get too close, and redirected it at the spiders, forming the flame into a wall that traveled quickly down the hallway. The wall made an opening for the man then quickly closed behind him, and chased off the creatures, burning those not quick enough, as well as the corpses left behind, into ash. After the fire disappeared around the corner, Cloukora let out an exasperated breath.

"What the hell was that?" The man asked as he looked at each member of the group for some kind of explanation.

"Better question is, who the hell are you?" Cloukora asked right back, still trying to catch his breath. Not summoning Fyron took a bit out of him to control those flames.

"The name's Ace. I'm in-was in- a group of mercenaries hired by the owners of this facility to destroy it along with the evidence. Before we could, we were overrun by those…things! They killed my whole team. And if it wasn't for you guys, I would be dead too, and that's why I'm probably telling you all of this because if I was on any other mission I would be lying out of my ass. I didn't even know the fuckers could exist!"

"Heh, you get used to it. Name's Cloukora by the way."

"Brev."

"Cal."

"Erro."

"Bowe."

"Nice to meet you all, but we should get out of here." Ace suggested.

"That's not an option." Cloukora said stubbornly. "Those bastards took my wolf."

"Your *wolf?*" Ace looked even more confused now.

"Yes." Cloukora answered as if having a wolf was normal.

Despite the confused look on his face, Ace went with it. "Alright…Fine, I'll help you. If it helps me get out of here safely, but

I'm currently empty on ammo." Cloukora tossed two magazines to Ace.

"Now you aren't."

"This is more than enough." Ace said confidently.

"You'll still need 'em more than me."

"I highly doubt that." Cloukora didn't reply back, he figured Ace could find out on his own. "So what *did* happen back there with that fire?"

"Believe me, you're better off not knowing." Cloukora said as he moved quicker to get ahead of him.

Brev walked up next to Cloukora and lowered her voice to a whisper. "Are you alright?"

"Yeah. It took a bit of my energy, but I'm fine now."

"Why didn't you use Fyron then?"

"There wasn't enough time. If I did, they would have got to us before I could blow the barrel. Plus Ace would have saw and that's not something I want right now, or what we need. It has been getting easier though. Slowly, but it's better than it was last time. I've actually been practicing controlling elements, like puddles of water or candle flames. Small things."

"Don't worry, you'll get there. You *are* Relyt's reincarnation after all."

Cloukora shook his head. "But I'm not him. I don't have the amount of power he had, nor will I ever be as great as he was."

Brev stopped Cloukora in his tracks and looked him straight in the eyes. "Power does not mean one is great, Cloukora. A poor weak man who saves someone's life is greater than a powerful rich man who is corrupt with greed. You of all people should know this. Even if you don't come close to Relyt's power, I do know this: you will fight tooth and nail for this world. Therefore I trust you with my life. But if you start talking like this, doubting your abilities, my confidence in you drops. As a hero you can't falter, you can't doubt your strength. That will cost lives. You need to trust, you need to *believe*, in your own power, and keep that belief until the day you die, and never give up on it. You need to be a *hero,* Cloukora." Cloukora looked down

shamefully as he took it all in. She was right; he needed to pull his head out of his ass and get his shit together. They both noticed the rest of the group looking at them. "Sorry, let's keep moving."

As they continued down the web-covered hallway, Bowe showed Ace, who had been walking alongside him, the flash drive he found. "Hey, you wouldn't happen to know what's on here, would you?"

"No, our Captain is the one that extracted the information. And we didn't have time to look when spiders swarmed us because one of our squad members had to be a fucking idiot. But there is one more member left: Sparky. He stayed behind for this mission. He's more of a tech guy anyway, so he could definitely help us out."

"Ah, well we got some people of our own that could help, too."

"Maybe both could work on it together. If we can out of this place that is."

Cloukora walked across a loose, metal floor grate, and felt something pull at his leg, tripping him, and dragging him. He spun onto his back to see a web from a spider pulling him down towards the hole underneath the grate, and tried to fire shots at it from his rifle, but failed as he was pulled into the hole and fell to the dirt ground below. Luckily no bones were broken, but his left arm was dislocated, and he had to stand up slowly, holding his shoulder to face the giant trapdoor spider in front of him, moving its mandibles. The little light from the grate above allowed him to see that much.

Cloukora couldn't move. His body was frozen from pure fear, from the eight-legged-and-eyed creature standing over him. The spider lunged at Cloukora, and before it could reach him, a grey wolf ran from behind the spider, onto the spider's back, and sunk its teeth into its thorax. The spider let out a screeching noise from the pain. Cloukora grinned; it was Rhain. Shaking himself awake and making Fyron appear, he walked up to the arachnid and slashed the blade across its face. "Good boy." Popping his arm back in place, not without pain of course, he walked past Rhain, petting the wolf's head on the way through. After giving one last look at the large spider, Rhain followed his companion down the tunnel made of dirt and web, the only source

of light illuminating from Fyron. "Now to find the others." He tried using the earpiece but all he heard was static. He must be too far down.

The rest of the group looked at the grate Cloukora had been taken down. The bottom was barely noticeable, and they could only see a Cloukora frozen by fear. "We gotta go down there and get him." Ace said. "I lost my team, I can't deal with losing any more lives. Do you have any rope? We can throw some rope and climb down there and-" Ace noticed they were just staring at him.

Erro shook her head. "We want to save him too, more than you do, but trapdoor spider holes are deep, the fall would kill us. Cloukora would want us to keep moving and find another way to get to him." She started walking further down the corridor. "Besides, we have evidence to destroy. We cannot let this get out."

The group followed Erro deeper into the facility, making their way down several floors. Finally, they came down a hallway that led through a doorway into a giant empty metallic room that had another door at the far end. The room was about the size of a high school gymnasium with so little light that the ceiling was covered in shadow. "Uh, guys." Ace whispered. "Look up there." He pointed to the corner of the ceiling, where a large, black spider with a spherical abdomen was resting. "I think that's a Black Widow." They slowly walked towards the door but before Cal could step out with everyone else, the door abruptly slid shut. Brev banged on the small bulletproof glass window on the other side of the door, trying to break it open, somehow thinking it could help.

"NOO! Cal!" She screamed, on the verge of tears. Something Brev had never even come close to doing.

But Cal seemed calm, as if unaware of the elephant-or rather giant spider- in the room. "Go, I'll be fine. I promise." He put his hand on the window as a few tears fell out of his eyes. "Go."

"I'm gonna get you out of there." Next to the group, a light flashed on in a room they hadn't noticed next to them, and standing inside was none other than Tomi, leader of Darkstar, looking right at

them through the glass window that separated both parties. "You son of a bitch! I'll kill you!" Brev punched the glass, only managing a small crack; the glass must have also been bulletproof. Tomi flipped a switch and the lights in the room Cal was in flicked on, waking the spider from its slumber. The Black Widow gracefully crawled down to the floor, and towered above Cal.

    Cal turned to face the giant arachnid. Without a moment of hesitation, he drew his pistol and aimed it at the spider, but only to have it knocked out of his hands by a spider leg, and he knocked against the wall by another. "So growth isn't just physical then," he said wiping blood from his lip as he stood back on his feet. "It's mental too." A leg darted at him, and after an easy dodge, he grabbed it and snapped the limb in half, following up with his fist flying towards the creature's face only to be blocked by its leg. Feeling a large jab through his chest, he looked down to see the limp spider leg pierced through the vest, his shirt, and into his body. Grinning, he grabbed the leg and pulled it further towards him until it tore off from the spider's body. The creature screeched and staggered around until it turned its focus back onto its prey. "That hurt..." Cal said looking into the Widow's eyes with his own pitch black eyes and fangs, hoping it would strike fear into the spider. And for a moment he felt like it had.

    Still staring into its eyes, he pulled out the limb from his chest, leaving a gaping hole in his body that didn't take long to heal and regenerate back to normal. "You're going down, bitch!" Cal swatted away a leg with the one from his chest and struck it through one of its eyes, provoking it to chomp at him. Grabbing the mandibles before they touched him, he pushed them outward in opposite directions all the way until they snapped, and could no longer be used. Quickly hopping onto the spider's head, he took the leg from the eye and sent it into the spider's skull, making it waver and stagger until it finally collapsed and lay motionless on the hard, metal floor. "Heh, that was easy." He jumped off its back and started towards the door until he heard a cracking sound, and looked back. There had been an egg sac underneath the abdomen and now there were baby spiders swarming out of it. They were small, though bigger than even a tarantula, but too

many to effectively counter; after all, he wasn't Cloukora. He couldn't summon a fireball to throw at them. He backed himself against the wall and heard a clank. After putting his palm to his face and muttering a "Forgot I had this thing." he pulled the M4 from behind his back, aimed, and fired at the pests skittering across the floor to exact their vengeance on him. There were probably hundreds of them, maybe even more.

Running out of a magazine, he went to switch it out and saw a frightening sight: The spiders joined together to create a figure of a featureless man with the exception of being made up of black and red. "The hell? Is this some kind of crappy science fiction movie made by some pothead! Fucking spiders..." A stream of them shot out of the figure's hand at Cal, who managed to roll out of the way, but was followed by another quick stream and knocked it away by using the gun as a bat. Feeling a pain in his neck he went to brush it off and ended up whacking a spider off that held a piece of his flesh in its mandibles. "Now I understand Cloukora's hatred for you." He stomped on the creature as the wound healed itself. "Gonna have to do better than that." He taunted. Still holding the gun as a bat, he ran towards the figure and swung at its body, breaking the chain of spiders and sent them flying, but in an instant it had formed back together. A hand of spiders grabbed a hold of his throat and held him up in the air. As he tried to grasp for oxygen, spiders crawled off the hand on his neck and onto the rest of him. The feeling of spider legs holding him was weird, but he forgot all about them when he began to feel sharp pains occur throughout his body. The spiders were eating him alive. Managing to gather the strength, he swung the gun awkwardly at the arm as if it were an axe and severed the spider arm, leaving the spider hand still there. After standing upward and hastily brushing them all off, he saw dozens of bite marks, flesh torn from his body, and felt bites on his neck. *I'm safe from being poisoned, my vampire blood takes care of curing that, but if enough were on me, they would be able to eat me whole.* As if jinxing himself, the spiders assembled together to make the figure larger, erect high above him, and then they dispersed all over the room like a giant wave, engulfing him within. He swung and swung at the creatures,

trying to keep them off, but he was neck deep in a pool of the arachnids. His arms began to tire, and his swings became less frequent while the flesh tearing became more. Eventually, he couldn't hold them off any longer, and he was swallowed by the sea of carnivorous spiders. But before they could eat the last of him, a sound of a pin being pulled was heard where he was dragged down to, and in seconds the room was filled with a massive blaze of fire and explosion. The fire and smoke died down and the room was now empty besides parts of the charred, giant Black Widow scattered all over.

"Well hello to you too." Tomi said haughtily through the speaker in the wall. "Don't worry, I won't be long, I just came here to pick up a couple things then I'll be on my way."

"What are you doing here?" Brev asked, teeth bared.

"Didn't I just say?"

"It's the secret to the spiders, isn't it? What the hell do you plan to do with it? Create giant ones?"

"Obviously." Tomi said derisively as he pressed a couple keys on a keyboard while Brev took a moment to think.

"Wait, were *you* the one that founded the research?"

"Oh ho, no. No. If I had, spiders as tall as houses would be roaming around Earth by now. It's a shame they left these beautiful creatures trapped in their cages. No, my research will improve them and make them indestructible. And of course, they will help me take over the world." He gave them a sinister grin until a large creature interrupted by bursting through the floor several feet behind him and continuing up to the ground above. Tomi walked casually to the tunnel the creature made and looked up to see a giant spider leg disappear over the burrow exit, which now let the remaining light from the sunset emanate through.

"Tomi!" He turned his attention downward to see Cloukora and Rhain at the bottom of the tunnel, staring up at him. "Answer me!"

Tomi turned his head to look over his shoulder. "Best I get going. I guess you guys win this time." He said admittedly. Dragon

wings appeared on his back, and he glanced back down at Cloukora. "Goodbye Cloukora." He then took flight out of the tunnel and to the outside world.

Cloukora and Rhain walked through the dirt tunnel until they approached a small set of steps that led back up to a white-tiled floor of the facility. "Finally, a step closer." They stepped through a white tiled hall, past glass panes with a horrifying mixture of blood and spider webs covering them. He gulped and held down some vomit when he saw a trail of blood on the floor and a handprint on the wall becoming another trail parallel to the one on the floor. Someone's body was dragged off to someplace. Where, Cloukora didn't know. Nor did he really want to find out. He did his best to fix his view forward and ignore the horror around him.

"…No, my research will improve them." Cloukora heard Tomi's faint voice echoing from a location off in the distance. He needed to hurry now. Turning his walk into a sprint, he finally did manage to forget about the blood all about him. His new focus made sure of that.

Running out of breath, he stopped near a window pane that separated the corridor from pitch black darkness. Leaning up against the wall, he heard a click of a switch that turned on the light on the other side of the window, and when he looked through it, he nearly screamed in terror. On the other side of the glass was a Tarantula spider taller than a two-story house, and about as wide as two, with eyes half the size of Cloukora. It had been slumbering in a hanger-like room until he had turned on the lights inside. Its eight beady eyes shot open and stared at him. He felt like it was staring into his soul. He couldn't move his legs, he felt frozen. *This is just pathetic. My phobia is going to get me killed!* One of its legs crashed through the glass, grasping at air for Cloukora. Dropping quickly to the floor, to take cover from the glass and dodge the spider, he saw the leg twitching just above him, almost in reach. Cloukora saw Rhain a few feet away, lying on the floor as well, away from the spider's grasp. *Thank goodness. I don't know what*

I'd do if I lost Rhain. After a few moments, the leg withdrew, and when Cloukora stood up he saw the giant spider pull itself back as if it were about to leap, and it in fact did. Right at Cloukora! He barely got his legs to move enough to dive out of the way towards the ground as the spider tore through the facility above him, its strength tearing apart everything in its path, creating a large tunnel in the direction of the surface. After regaining his foothold, he looked up to see Tomi several floors above him. "Tomi!" All the other man did was just gaze down at him, as if he were nothing but an ant. "Answer me!" Tomi turned towards something else for a moment, muttered something he couldn't hear, and then soared off with dragon-like wings, away from the facility. "Son of a bitch." He needed to get to the surface to kill this thing before it destroyed the nearest town and cause panic.

Cloukora scrambled up the tunnel as quickly and as easily as he could; grabbing onto pipes and ledges was not as easy as it seemed. Water burst out of some pipes, making things harder to hold on to and stay balanced, and ledges would give out as he tried to grasp a hold of them. Making it over an edge of the floor Tomi had stood on, he saw through a window Brev and the rest of the group, with Brev crying, and everyone except Ace comforting her. Then he noticed it. Cal wasn't there. He ran up to the glass as Rhain hopped up onto the same floor as the others took notice of them.

"Cloukora! You're okay!" Erro said with relief, walking up on the other side.

"What happened? Did Cal…" She only nodded. "Oh…Shit man…I'm sorry Brev, he was a good man." He gave a moment before continuing. "I know this isn't the right time right now, but there is a giant-ass tarantula on the loose above the surface and we gotta take care of it."

Erro nodded again. "Alright, we'll meet you back up on the surface."

Cloukora turned around to start climbing again and realized he could just use wind to get him to the top. *I can't believe I always forget I have powers.* He shook his head to himself, created Gaoth in his hands and had a giant, continuous gust of wind to go upward to the outside of

the tunnel, as if the facility was letting out a large exhale of breath. "Alright Rhain, let's go." They both ran towards the wind and jumped into it, taken away to the surface and landed softly on their feet on the lush green grass. As he expected, the giant tarantula was heading towards Gaston. But what he *didn't* predict, was the spider leg piercing through the red, metal roof of the Hemi Cuda, smashing and flattening the car like a pancake. "N-no. Noo! My baby!" The others had finally made it up and out of the facility. "It killed Ruby." He gestured his hand towards the crumpled car.

"Who?" Bowe asked. Brev was still silent and staring at the ground.

"My car. The damn spider killed my car." He got too caught up with his car that he forgot about what had happened to Cal, and when he saw Brev, sadness washed over him. *I've never seen her like this before. I just wish there was something I could do to help. I hate feeling helpless...*

"You can get a new one." Erro said leading Brev to the military truck that was used by the mercenaries Ace was with. She just didn't understand. "We're heading back to HQ to grab the chopper."

"Where's Ace?"

"Inside setting the charges." With that, Ace ran out holding a detonator and he must have pushed the button because the structure abruptly exploded in every single direction and sent pieces of it flying everywhere, as well as caved in the entire tunnel the tarantula had made. Though some spiders, some even taller than a normal person, had made it out beforehand. "You comin?" She asked after everyone was in the truck.

"No, I'm gonna get a start on tracking the stupid thing down." He really was pissed about his car.

"Your choice. Good luck." The truck quickly turned around and drove down the dirt road, gone within a few seconds.

Not wasting another moment, he and Rhain were dashing through the woods as fast they could. Well, how fast Cloukora could go; Rhain would have run faster but he had decided to hang back with his companion. Hearing a small rustle in the trees behind them,

Birth

Cloukora spun while taking his pistol out of his holster, aiming it at a large, yellow-spotted spider lunging at him, and pulled the trigger, sending a bullet through an eye and into its skull. Before it even fell to the ground they took off again towards Gaston. Several more times they came across spiders, each one bigger than the last. Though it didn't matter, because he had bullets to shoot them down, and if needed, Fyron to cut them all down to size.

At the edge of the forest he could see the giant spider towering above the buildings, leveling them to the ground and shooting web all over the town, covering cars, buildings, and even people. Seeing where the web came out of made him squirm, and almost throw up. "That's just nasty." Running to the back of a building under the spider, he jumped onto a garbage dumpster and then onto the roof, while Rhain stayed below. A corner of it was missing from where a spider leg had crushed it. As a leg swung by him, Cloukora jumped at it, stabbing it with a throwing knife, holding on while the leg swayed him, and when he got another chance, he stabbed it again with another knife, but slightly above him, giving himself more stability to climb up it. He continued upwards as if the leg was a moving rock wall. At one point he almost lost his balance and fell off and it was only by luck he was able to regain it. After reaching the top, he unsheathed Relyt's sword from his back and began towards the head until a sudden barrage of bullets flew all about him and rained upon the tarantula, piercing its flesh, causing the creature to stagger and screech and throw Cloukora off its back. Luckily, he managed to send his sword into the side of the spider and use it to swing back up onto its back. Then he saw the shooter: the Wolfstorm helicopter with Gatling guns mounted on the sides. "Well that was pretty fast." While dodging the shower of metal, he mustered up his strength and dragged the sword through its entire body, slicing it open all the way to the head, where he made Fyron appear and struck it into its skull. Shrieking and thrashing around, the spider crashed into the surrounding buildings, causing even more damage, until fire channeled into Fyron and spread throughout the entire body, burning every last bit of the creature in a ball of flame until it was just a pile of ash and burnt spider chunks.

Cloukora stood up from the pile of ash, that he was now covered in, and somehow let out a cough and sneeze at the same time. "Damn ash. Damn spiders. Damn experiments. Damn everything." He mumbled to himself. While brushing some of the grey powder off, he saw the Wolfstorm helicopter land in the middle of the street in front of him, the force of the rotors blowing ash all around, which would have flew into his eyes if he had not covered them in time with his arm. Still shielding his eyes, he made Fyron disappear and picked up Relyt's sword from the pile of grey before making it disappear as well. Stalking his way out of the mass, he walked to the helicopter cabin, got in, and shut the door after Rhain hopped in. Brev, Bowe, and Erro were sitting down in the seats of the cabin, while Winter and Avenorra sat in the cockpit. "Heh, think you can fly this, Winter?"

"Think you can fly my foot up your ass?" She snapped back as she flicked a couple of switches and brought the helicopter back into the air.

"No thanks, I'm good." He let out a sigh of relief. "Anyways, I'm glad this is all over. Now I can go home, relax and work on my car- wait. Shit, I forgot it got smashed!"

"Sorry bro, we're not quite done yet." He hadn't seen Ace by the window loading a M4 with a magazine.

"So what's next then?"

"Nole dug into the records of the facility and found there were others involved in the experiments. Some have even gone beyond spiders." Brev said. She seemed to be getting her head back in the game.

Good for her, it must take a lot of strength to already be focused. "I'm guessing there are other facilities?"

"Yup, but unfortunately they're spread out all over the country."

"All over-How the hell are we supposed to get them all before they disappear? They would know we're coming by now, they're not going to just sit and wait for us to put a bullet in them."

"We already contacted the military and gave them the locations of the other facilities. They're working on it too."

Birth

"So where to?"

"There's a CEO pulling the strings all over in Oregon right in Portland. We're going to take him down."

"Shouldn't we take him alive? Get more information out of him?"

She stared flatly at him. "We have all the information we need." She tossed a loaded M4 to him.

Cocking the gun with a grin he said "Payback's a bitch, ain't it?" The cabin door opened above a skyscraper a few feet down. One by one they hopped down onto it, guns ready and headed towards the roof access door. As far as Cloukora could see around him, there was gunfire, explosions, and giant spiders destroying everything as far as the eye could see.

Tall, thin, and blonde Charlotte was tossing the salad vegetables in a large, plastic bowl when Rick strolled into the kitchen. He was tall as well and muscle-built with short, black hair. He placed his hands firmly on the grey, marble counter island and leaned forward, eyeing the food she was preparing. "Dinner smells delicious."

"It's just pre-cooked lasagna, Rick. Not like I made it myself." She smiled.

Grabbing the plates from another counter, he walked over to where Charlotte was standing and wrapped his free arm around her and kissed her neck, producing an even bigger smile on her face. "True, but I know what *will* be yours." He placed the plates on the island and wrapped his other arm around her.

"And what's that?"

"Dessert."

She let out a giggle which brought a laugh from him as well. "Should we skip dinner?" She teased.

Rick pondered for a minute and looked at the lasagna in the tinfoil pan. "Nah, I can wait. It looks too delicious to pass up."

"*This* is why I love you." She placed the bowl down, turned around, wrapped her arms around him and kissed him on the lips. "You're not a horn dog." He returned a kiss that would have lasted

longer if they had not heard a thump above them. "Ugh, mice again?" On the roof, unknown to them was a spider a slight bigger than a dog, skittering along on the surface.

"I'll take care of them tomorrow. We should be fine for the night." He rubbed the sides of her arms and gave her another kiss. A loud boom was heard outside.

"Come on people it's not the Fourth!"

"Eh, leave them be. I like fireworks. Besides, we got our…gourmet dinner!" They laughed again before grabbing the food and plates and taking it to the dining room to set it on the wooden table. Not a second later after sitting down, Charlotte got back up and headed towards the kitchen. "Damn, I forgot the salad dressing."

"Tsk tsk. Come on Charlotte, focus woman. I need my damn dressing!" He said jokingly.

She walked back into the kitchen to the fridge, opened it and grabbed the salad dressing before closing it again. She turned to see the back door wide open. "Rick, come here." She tried saying as low as possible, but loud enough only for him to hear. She crept slowly to the back door, careful not to make any sudden noise. Poking her head outside into the night she looked around for anyone lurking in their backyard. Hearing patter on the floor behind her, she turned around and the last thing she would ever see was a large, hissing spider lunging at her.

Glossary

Aaron Skyrell (E-ren SKY-rehl): Cloukora's grandfather and Daniel's father. Only one to ever control lightning and wields Rayos. Was the real leader of Wolfstorm until leadership was passed to Cloukora. *See also Skyrell.*

Alessandra Skyrell (A-li-SAHN-druh SKY-rehl): Relyt and Aurora's daughter. *See also Skyrell.*

Angel's Gaiden (AYN-jelz GY-den): Gaiden means Chronicles in Japanese, so it's actually called Angel's Chronicles. Gaiden is used as symbolism to bring the two cultures together: English and Japanese. It's also the title of the series you dingus.

Arthur Pendragon (ARR-ther PEN-drag-en): The king of Avalon. Tomi's ancestor. Also Relyt's best friend before being consumed by the power of the F.O.Y. Wielded Excalibur and fought alongside a dragon companion. Used to be a good man, then became greedy and obsessed with power when the F.O.Y. was discovered. He's a good example not to do drugs.

Ashley (ASH-lee): Cloukora and Tomi's childhood best friend. Not afraid to speak her mind and say what needs to be said. After discovering Cloukora's secret and Wolfstorm, began training under Brev. Stubborn little turd.

Astrea Brennis (A-stre-uh BRE-nis): Victor Brennis' daughter. After her father's death, she was recruited by Tomi into Darkstar where she has begun her training to control her powers: manipulating anti-matter. Doesn't care for the other side of the story.

Aurora Skyrell (AH-RAW-ruh SKY-rehl): Relyt's wife, and Atlantis' queen. A strong woman of her time. She helped inspire the females in her city to become more than they were. To become stronger themselves and do what they were told they couldn't do. After Relyt passed away, she disbanded Atlantis altogether. Could make you shut up with just a glance. *See also Skyrell*

Ava (AY-vuh): Venn's lover. F.O.Y. gave her skills with a blade, just like Venn. Though she's not as strong as Venn, she never gives in. Wields a sword and a shield.

Avenorra (A-vuh-NAW-ruh): The other hand-to-hand expert on Wolfstorm. Like Avenorra, gained an increase in agility and fighting skills. Owns a lambo.

Bowe (BOH): Erro's lover. Due to the Fountain of Youth (F.O.Y.), his focus, dexterity, and sight increased greatly, allowing him to become a superb marksman. Hails from the land of crumpets.

Brev Hart (BREV Hart): Despite Aaron being the real leader, she did most of the actual leading. Strong, mainly uses a shotgun for a weapon, and is Cal's lover. She's also a bit of a biter.

Cairne (KAIRN): Eva's lover. Due to F.O.Y. he gained immense strength, superb combat skills, and a slight healing factor. Not very bright and little to no morality for anyone else but his teammates. Cocky and thinks he's the strongest.

Cal (KAL): Brev's lover and the only other vampire in Wolfstorm. He's calm but strong, and even acts like a father figure sometimes. Wait…who are we talking about again?

Chris (KRIS): Tomi's foster father. He was Tomi's real father's friend, so he had known about what was being done to Tomi. After taking Tomi in, he continued the work, only in a better manner. Is a politician that likes to work from the shadows. In other words, every politician ever.

Cloukora Skyrell (KLOW-kor-uh SKY-rehl): A seventeen year old who, due to his family's past, develops superpowers. Can control elements and his adrenaline. Hates people that are willing to harm others. Also likes long walks on the beach. *See also Seraph. See also Skyrell*

Daniel Skyrell (DAN-yel SKY-rehl): Cloukora's uncle and Aaron's son. Controls fire and wields Flaym. *See also Skyrell*

Erro (E-roh): Bowe's lover. As with Bowe, she gained powers that allowed her to be a master marksman. Bowe would never admit it, but she's a better shot than he.

Eva (EE-vuh): Cairne's lover. As with Carine, gained a large amount of strength, combat skills, and a slight healing factor. Personality is also similar as well.

Ezel (ET-sel): A Reaper Cloukora met in Germany. He was enlisted in the Pope's army to assassinate those that are evil, especially demons. Hasn't had much interaction so is hard to talk to.

Flaym (FLAYM): Daniel's sword used to control fire. Variation of the word "Flame."

Fyron (FY-rahn): Cloukora's scimitar made of fire. Word is made by combining "Fire" and "Pyro."

Gaoth (GWAY): Katana that lets Cloukora control wind. Irish/Scottish Gaelic for "Wind."

Kaora (KA-or-uh): Nole's wife. She's an expert at computers and science, and even more so after being exposed to the F.O.Y. Slightly uptight, non-religious, and uses reasoning for everything. Has a cat and two dogs.

Kayla Nedly (KAY-luh NED-lee): Transwoman that Cloukora meets at the Winchester House. Has a sweet personality but can be vulnerable due to the trauma she faced as a kid. Has an odd ability to keep ghosts from touching her. She ain't afraid of no ghosts.

Lore (LOR): Path's lover. Abilities are the same as Lore's. More empathetic than Path.

Lucifer (LOO-suh-fer): Satan. The Devil. The king of Hell. Whatever you want to call him, he's a powerful being that is hell-bent on controlling the world. Wears a jumpsuit for some reason.

Neró (NE-roh): Other hook sword of water. Greek for "Water."

Nole (NOAL): Kaora's husband. Like Kaora, excels at science and computers. Unlike, Kaora, he's mellow and relaxed, religious, and not afraid to make emotion-based decisions. Goes to bed by 10pm like a lame person.

Nyx (NIKS): An angel who works for Hell and is trying to help bring about the apocalypse and Lucifer's rise. Should be called Joe, for being too slow.

Oregon (OR-e-gen): The beautiful, green state located in the Pacific Northwest. Don't ever call it "OR-eh-gahn". "OR-uh-gun" is also acceptable.

Path (PATH): Lore's lover. Senses and deductive reasoning enhanced by F.O.Y., making her a great tracker. Level-headed and loyal.

Rayos (RAY-oas): Aaron's double-bladed lightning sword. Spanish word for "Lightning."

Relyt Skyrell (REH-lit SKY-rehl): The king of Atlantis. Ancestor of Cloukora. The most intelligent man of his time, of our time. Before F.O.Y., his only powers were his high intelligence, elemental swords, and running with wolves. After F.O.Y., his brain power, reflexes, sight, and intelligence became superhuman. Has a wife and two daughters. Was the type of man that could win the Nobel Peace Prize and not even accept it. *See also Skyrell.*

Rhain (RAYN): Cloukora's wolf companion. Befriended Cloukora on the Skyrell camping trip, and left his family to be by his human companion's side ever since. Favorite foods consist of bacon and bacon.

Rulx (ROOLKS): Lucifer's right hand demon. Was partners with Zela for a while. Also can't get over the past.

Seraph (SER-ef): Cloukora's alter ego. The angel that watches over all. *See also Cloukora*

Skyrell (SKY-rehl): The royal family of Atlantis. Every member has powers to control elemental swords, have a special connection with wolves and dogs, and control their adrenaline. Although, in many family members, the powers are dormant and can only be surfaced by wearing the necklace created by Relyt. Few have accessed them without the help of the necklace.

Tayge (TAYJ): Tor's lover. Is an expert in bombs, guns, and explosives. Even more so from the F.O.Y. Is a self-serving person and has no remorse for his actions. Cold-hearted bitch.

Terra (TE-ruh): Cloukora's broadsword that lets him control earth. Italian word for "Earth."

Tomi Pendra (TOH-mee PEN-druh): Cloukora and Ashley's childhood best friend. Pushed by both fathers as a kid to inject the F.O.Y., he developed dark superpowers and formed a split personality. His mind is unstable and wields Excalibur. Also has major daddy issues.

Tor (TOR): Tayge's lover. Is also an expert in bombs and explosives, but instead of guns, is an expert in computers. More human than Tayge and reasonable. Is the "T" in T n' T.

Venn (VIN): Ava's lover. F.O.Y. increased his sword skills. Wields a sword passed down in his family that can allow him to shapeshift into a ghost. Though not as crazy as Tomi and Tayge, he's still not a good-hearted person. Fellow metalhead.

Vesi (VE-see): One of the two hook swords that lets Cloukora control water. Finnish word for "Water."

Winter (WIN-ter): The hand-to-hand combat expert of Wolfstorm. Speed, agility, and fighting skills were increased by F.O.Y. Temperamental. Needs anger management.

Zela (ZAY-luh): Rulx' partner and middle (wo)man between Hell and Nyx. Probably got a 0 on her S.A.T.s